BIRTH OF A REVOLUTION

DEFENDER SERIES

BIRTH OF THE DEFENDER
Prequel

THE MISSION
Book 1

DEFENDED
Book 2

TREASONOUS ACTS
Book 3

IN EVIL'S GRASP
Book 4

MISSION ABANDONED
Book 5

BIRTH OF A REVOLUTION
Book 6

QUESTIONS OF TRUST
Book 7

REVELATIONS
Book 8

BIRTH OF A REVOLUTION

DEFENDER SERIES

Book 6

REGGI BROACH

Defender Christian Publications
Harrison, Tennessee, USA

Published by Defender Christian Publications, Harrison, TN, USA

First edition printed 2022
ISBN: 978-1-950038-10-7 (paperback)
ISBN: 978-1-950038-11-4 (eBook: ePUB)
ISBN: 978-1-950038-12-1 (hardback)
Library of Congress Control Number: 2021953449

PUBLISHERS NOTE:

This is a work of fiction. Names, characters, places, and incidents either are a product of the author's imagination or are used fictitiously, and any resemblance to actual persons, living or dead, business establishments, events, or locales is entirely coincidental. The publisher does not have any control over and does not assume any responsibility for author or third-party web sites or their content.

The scanning, uploading, and distribution of this book via the Internet or via any other means without the permission of the publisher is illegal and punishable by law. Please purchase only authorized electronic editions, and do not participate in or encourage electronic piracy of copyrighted materials. Your support of the author's rights is appreciated.

Defender Publications books are available at special discounts for bulk purchases, for sales promotions, or corporate use. Special editions, including personalized covers, excerpts of existing books, or books with corporate logos, can be created for some titles. For more information, contact Defender Publications at: SpecialSales@RBEnterprises.info

TABLE OF CONTENTS

Captain's Roster

SS *Evangeline* Crew Manifest

Captain (Capt.) David Alexander – assigned to command, adjunct training as a pilot, security officer, a field medic and basic engineering

Commander (Cmdr.) Brynna Alexander – assigned to command and diplomacy, adjunct training as a pilot, basic security, a field medic, and basic engineering

Lieutenant Commander (Lt. Cmdr.) Braxton Flint – assigned to engineering specializing in mechanical, structural and architectural engineering, adjunct training in command, qualified as a pilot and field medic, and basic security training

Lieutenant Commander (Lt. Cmdr.) Lazaro Dominick – assigned to engineering specializing in mechanical and astrophysics, a qualified pilot, adjunct training in command, field medicine and security

Lieutenant Commander (Lt. Cmdr.) Jason Adams – assigned as physician/surgeon, qualified pilot, and navigator, adjunct training in psychology and sociology.

Lieutenant (Lt.) Thane Ryder – primary pilot, adjunct training in security, navigation, field medicine, and basic engineering

Lieutenant (Lt.) Alexia (Lexi) Flint – ship's psychologist, morale officer, sociologist, an adviser to command staff, adjunct training in mechanical engineering

Lieutenant (Lt.) JG Laurel (Laura) Adams – nurse, botanist, secondary navigator

Ensign Aulani Ryder – primary communications, computer technician, adjunct training in security, field medicine

Ensign Cheyenne Dominick – primary linguistics, secondary communications officer, adjunct training in computer technology and security

Chief Petty Officer (CPO) Jacob (Jake) Holden – primary security officer, adjunct training in command, piloting, field medicine, basic engineering

*In all thy ways acknowledge him,
and he shall direct thy paths.*
Proverbs 3:6 KJV

ACKNOWLEDGMENTS

I've struggled for several years wondering if writing Christian Sci-Fi is what God really wanted me to do. I searched the scriptures for answers and writing Sci-Fi isn't in the list of spiritual gifts, nor is it named as a fruit of the Spirit. Here's what I *have* found. God has called us to be witnesses to his message of salvation. He called us to glorify him in all that we do whether it is secular or sanctified. Every aspect of our lives is to be sanctified. I took one of my few talents and dedicated it to spreading the gospel in a way that may reach someone not otherwise reached. Every book I write is prayed over before I start, while I write, and when I am done. My most heartfelt prayer is that if he doesn't want me to do this, then stop me. This is my sixth book, and he hasn't stopped me. I'm hoping, praying, and researching opportunities to expand to other forms of media.

God has given me many wonderful people around me contributing to my success. Although I am not rich or famous, I consider this endeavor to be a success. My husband, Ron, has ever been there for me. He encourages and inspires me. He works tirelessly learning software as the publishing requirements change. I am thankful for my editor, Janelle, who puts up with my lack of commas and encourages me with her enthusiasm.

Many members of my family contribute to my books in so many ways including technical specs, choreography, cover art, proofing, and the list goes on.

A very special thank you goes to Jake Wallin for agreeing to be the face of Capt. David Alexander.

You can thank a number of my coworkers, friends, and family for certain names in the books. Several people have said they wanted a character named after them. A few names were pure coincidence.

I also want to acknowledge you, the reader. I love nothing more than providing you with spiritual uplifting and a time of enjoyment. I pray that this book touches your heart.

x

XI

M.I.A.

"Captain to the bridge! Captain to the bridge!" A desperate voice called out on the ship-wide comms.

Capt. Alexander was reclined on his bed watching an entertainment audio-visual presentation. Hearing the urgency in the voice coming through the speakers, he rolled out of his bunk and raced toward the bridge. It only took thirty seconds for the Captain to make it, and it was the longest thirty seconds of the panicked bridge officer's life.

"Status report!" Capt. Alexander belted before his foot landed on the bridge deck plate.

"Sir, we're surrounded by three Commonwealth Pacification Fleet ships. They're demanding to board us," the First Officer reported.

The Captain took his place in the command chair, "Open a channel."

The face of an admiral appeared on the screen.

Capt. Alexander got to the point, "This is Capt. Alexander. Identify yourself and your intentions!"

Adm. Garcia responded equally as bluntly, "Capt. Alexander, I've been looking for you."

"Why? We're just honest, hardworking traders, doing our jobs. We're not hauling contraband of any kind. We aren't even loaded. Move aside and let us pass."

Adm. Garcia smirked, "I think I know just how honest you and your crew are. Let me ask you this, Captain. If I pulled up your crew manifest, would I find any outstanding warrants?"

Capt. Alexander scowled, "Who are you and what do you want?"

"I'm Adm. Edgardo Garcia of the Commonwealth Interstellar Force SS *Stalwart*, and I want you, Capt. Alexander. I have a warrant for your arrest signed by Supreme Executor Luciano Hale himself."

Capt. Alexander's crew cast shocked glances at their Captain. Capt. Alexander returned a concerned look around the bridge, "Supreme Executor Hale? There must be some mistake, Admiral. I'm an honest businessman and certainly not one important enough to get the attention of the most powerful man in the galaxy."

Adm. Garcia leaned forward slightly, "This isn't an argument you're going to win, Captain. Now, we can do this the easy way or the hard way. The easy way is I send a shuttle over, and you surrender yourself to my troops. The hard way is I disable you, send several shuttles over, arrest your entire crew, and impound what's left of your ship. Take your pick."

The look on the Captain's face was one of anger instead of resolution. He glared at Adm. Garcia for a moment before answering.

"You win. Send your shuttle. I'll meet your men in the shuttle bay."

The Captain angrily slapped the button to close the comm channel. Glancing around at his bridge crew he vowed, "If anyone of you is responsible for this, I will find out, and you'll pay dearly for it. There's no place in this galaxy you can hide from me."

The men looked at each other blankly. None of them had anything to do with getting their Captain arrested, nor knew why the ruler of the entire galaxy would be involved. The ship's First Officer stood to take his Captain's place in command, "Any orders, Capt.?"

"I'm hoping to get this obvious misunderstanding cleared up quickly. I suggest you take the ship and lay low on Dursa for three or four days. I'll try to meet up with you there. If I don't make it, let our contact know… discreetly, what happened. If he thinks this is too hot, he may not want us anywhere near them. If that happens, pick up a couple of legitimate loads of cargo. Keep a low profile until this blows-over then try again."

"Yes Capt.."

Capt. Alexander turned to head to the shuttle bay. His First Officer added one last admonition, "Captain, I hope this works out for you."

Capt. Alexander nodded, "Me too."

****

The irate Captain headed to his quarters to square a couple of things away before heading to the shuttle bay. The bay was nearly repressurized when he reached the airlock. The safety disengaged allowing him to step through the airlock. Securing the hatch behind him, he was careful to keep his hands in plain sight. He approached the shuttle slowly. He watched the movements of the troops as they used equal caution leaving their shuttle and approaching their target. Capt. Alexander raised his hands in surrender as the gap between himself and the encroaching troops closed. The men quickly surrounded him and placed him in binders. He was scanned for contraband and hastily loaded onto the shuttle. Inside of sixty seconds, the bay was depressurized, and the shuttle was on its way back to the *SS Stalwart*.

The troops deposited their captive into a detention cell. Capt. Alexander's binders remained in place which he thought was rather odd. He paced anxiously in his cell wondering what was wrong. He thought about inquiring from the troops who brought him in, but decided a foot soldier wouldn't have the answers he wanted and needed.

****

An hour later, he was pulled from his cell and escorted to Adm. Garcia's office. The Admiral waved him to a chair in front of his desk. The two guards dropped him roughly into it and retreated to the outer office.

As soon as they were alone, Capt. Alexander leaned forward. "Adm. Garcia, may I ask what this is about? Why am I being detained?"

Adm. Garcia folded his arms across his chest and leaned back in his chair. "I told you. I have a warrant for your arrest."

"What are the charges?"

"Treason. High treason to be more specific," the Admiral responded confidently.

"You've got to be kidding me. Against who? The Commonwealth has no enemies. Who could I possibly be subversive with? You and I met some years ago, but do you have any idea who I am? I mean, who I *really* am?"

Adm. Garcia smiled smugly, "I know exactly who you are. You are Capt. Tristan Liam Alexander of the Commonwealth Interstellar Force's Infantry Division. You are an Intelligence officer assigned to the Covert Operations Department."

"I'm no double agent, Admiral. Why am I *really* being detained? Why did you risk my op? I've been undercover on this job for nearly two years. I was about to get in deep enough to take down our targets. Do you know what kind of damage you've caused?" Capt. Alexander spat angrily.

"I doubt this will be your concern for much longer. We've got bigger problems. You said the Commonwealth doesn't have any enemies. I guess you didn't catch Supreme Executor Hale's last public address."

"I've been working with a bunch of lowlife criminals. No, I didn't catch the latest news report. I don't have a clue what you're talking about. Any enemies I've come into contact with were nothing but common criminals, not the types who were capable of treason."

Adm. Garcia studied him carefully, "When was the last time you talked to your son, Captain?"

"Davie? I haven't seen him since he graduated from the Academy. He was headed down a good road. We've chatted on comms a few times over the years, but that's it. What's he got to do with… whatever this is?"

Before Adm. Garcia could answer, his office door chimed. Edgar pressed a button to admit Adm. Robert Deacons. Adm. Deacons sat at the end of the desk so that he could see both men.

Capt. Alexander nodded to Adm. Deacons, "Robert, it's been awhile."

"Tristan, it's good to see you again. I'm sorry it's under such difficult circumstances," Adm. Deacons responded tersely.

"Robert, what's going on, and what does David have to do with this?" Tristan demanded.

"Edgar, with your permission?" Robert glanced at his superior.

Edgar nodded. He preferred to watch and listen to the exchange and draw his own conclusions.

"Tristan, have you seen or heard from any of your family over the last few months?"

"No, absolutely not. You don't do that in my line of work. It could get me killed, or it could get *them* killed. Are you going to tell me what's going on?" Tristan demanded.

Robert leaned forward. This wasn't an easy thing to share with his former brother-in-law.

"David is wanted for treason against the Commonwealth. He was in command of an Exploration Class vessel. This information is highly classified. He and his crew were sent out to undeveloped worlds to locate followers of a *being* known as Pateras El Liontari."

"Being? What do you mean by being?" Tristan questioned.

Adm. Garcia leaned forward as well, "So, you've never heard of him?"

Tristan was puzzled, "No, why did you use the term, being?"

Adm. Garcia watched Tristan's behavior closely as he explained, "Pateras El Liontari is a non-corporeal superior alien being."

Tristan sat back in his chair. He grinned and laughed outright, "You're joking. There's no such thing. I've been a lot of places and seen a lot of strange things, but they were all explainable by science."

He laughed until he realized the two Admirals were deadly serious, "You're not joking?"

Adm. Deacons took up the explanation, "David and his crew found this being. The Liontari have infected his mind. We think we can get him back, but we have to find him first. He and his crew took Jessica, Abby, my mother, all of the family, and disappeared. He destroyed the military base on Romajin during their escape."

Adm. Garcia clasped his hands together and leaned forward propping on his desk. "This is why we pulled you out of your assignment, Capt. Alexander. We need you to help us capture your son and his crew."

Tristan stared at the two Admirals. Both men were deadly serious.

"I—I'm having a little trouble swallowing this. My son… destroyed an entire military base? And he's guilty of treason against the Commonwealth? Robert, how did this happen?"

Robert lowered his head, "This is all my fault. I trusted him to be strong enough to resist the enemy. I'm sorry, Tristan. There's uh… something else you should know."

"What?" Tristan responded gruffly.

"If we can't free him from the Liontari influence… we will have no choice, but to execute him."

Robert swallowed hard. It was difficult enough thinking of his nephew being executed, but to have to inform his father made it even worse.

Tristan flexed against his binders. His jaw tensed. Although he had not been involved in David's life since he and David's mother, Jessica, went their separate ways; he still felt a small amount of responsibility for the boy. He had fond memories of the young man. Resolve crept in and forced him to accept this absurd set of circumstances. Tristan relaxed his tight muscles and looked at the two Admirals.

"What do you need me to do?"

SURROUNDED

The *Evangeline*, a now renegade ship heavily sought by the Commonwealth, cautiously approached the third planet of the Pillan star system.

The Commonwealth was searching for this ship and eleven other Explorer ships in the fleet. Some were obviously guilty of treason like the crew of the *Evangeline,* while others were merely suspected of it. Supreme Executor Luciano Hale, the head of the Commonwealth and essentially the most powerful man in the galaxy, was no longer taking chances with the Explorer Fleet of ships. He ordered them to return home when problems began to arise. As the risks of their traitorous ways increased, he sent out a new fleet of ships, manned by super-soldiers, to seek out the Explorer ships and destroy them with one exception. He wanted the Captain and First Officer of the *Evangeline* captured alive.

The Commonwealth was seeking to stamp out an enemy known as Pateras El Liontari and his son Arni Sotaeras Liontari. Supreme Executor Hale had done everything in his power to stamp out primitive beliefs and practices, the beliefs in extra-terrestrials, superior beings, and to teach humanity about total equality. The Commonwealth was founded on principles of a shared economy, knowledge, and resources.

The mission of the twelve Explorer Class ships was to make alliances with new worlds and ferret out the footholds of the Liontari forces. They weren't equipped to fight a war and only barely equipped to defend themselves. The crews were ordered to evacuate and report the location of any enemies they found. They were advised that the enemy was capable of mind control and to avoid them at all costs.

The crew of the *Evangeline* was among the first to succumb to their powerful enemy. It wasn't by coercion as the Commonwealth Intelligence Reports suggested. It was by choice. The Commonwealth had lied about many things. Capt. David Alexander turned his back on the Commonwealth and joined his enemy's cause. His crew followed almost as quickly and easily.

The *Evangeline* knew it was considered public enemy number one and was doing its best to keep a low profile. The *Evangeline* and the *Emissary* met up two months ago on Ela Prime. The two Captains were at odds until the fleet of super-soldiers, known as the Nefil, tried to wipe out both crews. Capt. Nathaniel Weiseman and his wife had been friends with Capt. Alexander since they were teenagers. Despite their friendship, they weren't inclined to trust Capt. Alexander or his traitorous crew initially. The presence of the Nefil changed things. Since leaving Ela Prime, the two Captains went their separate ways searching for the remaining Explorer Class ships. If the Supreme Executor and his Nefil Super soldiers located the other ships first, they were each slated for destruction.

Pillan II was the last known location of the SS *Malachi*. The *Evangeline* approached Pillan II on full alert.

Capt. David Alexander was one of the youngest Commonwealth Captains in the fleet. Although he was young and inexperienced, he had learned a lot the past year commanding the *Evangeline*.

****

"Lt. Holden, I want you to plot three possible routes out of this system. Lay in each course and put them on standby. Ensign Ryder try hailing the *Malachi* and keep monitoring the area for any transmissions. Commander, I want you watching long-range sensors, and Chief, watch the short-range sensors for changes in heat, light, or energy signatures."

Capt. Alexander punched a control on his comm unit and hailed the chief engineer.

"Lt. Cmdr. Dominick, keep this link open and be prepared to flood the net with tachyons if we need to get out of here quickly."

"Yes, Captain," his voice acknowledged through the speakers. Lt. Cmdr. Lazaro Dominick pulled the scanning displays up on his engineering computers. He wanted to see what the bridge crew was seeing as quickly as they saw it.

The serious navigator, Lt. Marissa Holden, focused on her star charts and plotted two quick, easy routes out of the star system. She and the helmsman, Lt. Thane Ryder, had come to respect each other's abilities. The third route was fraught with more course changes and obstacles. If the easy routes were unavailable, she knew Thane would excel at getting them through a more difficult path. The more difficult the course, the better he performed as a pilot. A year ago, she would never have considered this path as a viable escape route. A year ago, she wouldn't have dreamed they would *need* an escape route.

"Courses are laid in, Captain, and copied to your display."

David gave a cursory glance at the first two flight plans. Marissa heard a short laugh escape the Captain's lips as he reviewed the third one. She glanced up at him. He gave her an appreciative nod before turning his attention elsewhere.

A heavy silence settled over the bridge as Ensign Aulani Ryder sent out short-range hails intended for the *Malachi*. The attractive young ensign glanced at the Captain.

"Sir, I'm not getting any response, just lots of static. And sir, the static seems a little off."

Thane glanced over his right shoulder at his wife, "I thought static was what you were supposed to get when things are off."

Capt. Alexander turned his attention to Aulani, "Put it on the main speakers."

Ensign Ryder complied.

David listened for a moment, "I agree, something sounds off. Let me try transmitting a personal message and see if they're out there somewhere but refusing to answer the standard hail. If I were afraid this was a Commonwealth trap, I might refuse to answer a standard hail too."

Capt. Alexander touched another control on his console, "Capt. Logan, this is Capt. Alexander of the *Evangeline*, come in please."

David paused. He glanced at Aulani who shook her head. David continued to broadcast his message, "Capt. Logan, I know what you've been told about me, but we aren't here to harm you or your crew. Captain, we just wanted to warn you about the Nefil. Executor Hale is sending out super-soldiers to destroy the Explorer ships. Captain, you and your crew are in danger. We can help if you'll let us."

The heavy silence settled on the bridge as they waited for a response. Aulani's eyes grew wide suddenly. She swiftly put her input on the main speakers.

"Captain, I think this is a problem."

The static came through again—only it was louder and had a distinct pattern. Several crewmen recognized the pattern simultaneously.

"We're being jammed. Everybody strap in. Lazaro, get the net charged! Commander, what's on the scanners?"

Cmdr. Brynna Alexander watched her screen intently. She looked up as she pulled the safety bar across her lap to keep her secured in her seat.

"There's nothing on the scanners, but if I were a large ship and going to hide I would come from the direction of the sun. If it's a Nefil ship, I would hide on the moon and camouflage."

Security Chief Jake Holden glanced up from his station, "I've got nothing—Wait, the Commander's right, there's a Nefil ship coming in behind us from the northern pole of the nearest moon."

Brynna chimed in with an update from her scans, "There's a Pacification Fleet Ship coming in from dead ahead. It just popped out from behind the first planet. Captain, her net is saturated. She can reach full speed before we can."

Chief Holden jumped in again, "We have a second Nefil fleet ship coming out of the atmosphere on Pillan II. She's coming from the Southern Hemisphere."

David pulled his safety restraint across his lap and secured it in place. The inertial dampeners handled the worst of any maneuvers, but they were still subject to some bouncing around.

"How long until our nets are full, Lt. Cmdr.?"

Lazaro's voice came through the speaker, "If we keep on our current speed, about fifteen seconds. If you start pushing the engines, it could take up to thirty seconds."

"How long until those ships are in firing range?" David snapped.

Jake responded first, "The one coming from Pillan will be in range in six seconds."

David didn't wait for any other information. He knew Jake had given him the biggest threat first.

"Take us over the Northern Pole of Pillan and down the far side!"

He hoped there weren't any other ships waiting on him on the far side of the planet.

As the *Evangeline* crossed over the Northern Pole, Jake called out, "We have another incoming ship headed for us. A second Pacification ship dead ahead. I estimate its firing range to be about thirty seconds."

Before David could issue another order, Brynna interjected, "Captain, there's a hurricane on the planetary surface. It's a deep-sea storm. No land masses on the scanners. Sending coordinates to all stations."

Brynna sent the information as a warning to David and Thane in the event they wanted to lose their pursuers in the atmosphere.

David grinned, "Lazaro, how long until net saturation?"

"Ten more seconds barring excessive energy demands," Lazaro's voice belted.

"Are the nets of the Nefil ships loaded with tachyons?"

Both Brynna and Jake quickly informed him the approaching ships were near seventy-five percent saturation.

"Thane, you're gonna love this. Head for that storm. Keep us above it. Lazaro, get ready to dump some tachyons from the net," David continued to grin.

Although Lazaro was in engineering where no one could see his face, it would have been highly amusing as it betrayed his thoughts.

Dump some tachyons? He just asked me to fill the net with tachyons. Why would he want to dump them?

Thane glanced back. He wasn't sure what the Captain was planning but seeing his grin, he knew it was going to be fun.

Brynna trusted her husband's judgment but she wasn't sure being surrounded by four enemy ships was a good reason to be grinning. His grin was making her nervous. Her eye caught Aulani's. The two shrugged at each other.

The *Evangeline* dove into the atmosphere and raced for the storm. The two Nefil ships chased after her closing the gap.

"Put our forward trajectory on the main display screen and the tactical grid on the holographic projection," David ordered.

The image of the storm appeared in front of the crew. None of them had ever been near such a storm. They had learned about hurricanes in school as children and seen news reports about them. This one was worse than any they had ever heard reports about.

Brynna decided to throw more pertinent information at him, "Captain, that hurricane is one of the worst on record according to the historical archives. Its winds are hitting nearly two hundred miles per hour."

David glanced at her, "How deep is the ocean here?"

David heard Marissa gasp, "Oh no."

Brynna swallowed, "Land masses are well below crush depth."

David slapped his comm unit, "All hands, secure all stations and personnel. Prepare for impacts and loss of gravity. Lt. Cmdr. Dominick, prepare to adjust the artificial gravity to compensate for the G-forces."

"Captain, what are you about to do? I need to be prepared," Lazaro asked cautiously. Questioning a Captain's orders was never the wisest course of action, but he *really* needed to know.

"Captain, the closest Nefil ship is entering firing range!" Jake bellowed.

Aulani added, "They're hailing us with an order to surrender."

"Thane head for the eye of that storm! Put us in a tight circular pattern inside the eye matching the speed and direction of the storm."

Thane grinned and shoved the controls forward starting a steep dive. The *Evangeline* dove harshly toward the surface of the planet. They just missed being grazed by a laser blast from the Nefil ship. The ship rattled and groaned as they approached the storm.

Brynna volunteered one more pertinent piece of information, "Captain, if that lightning hits us while the net is this heavily saturated…" She left her sentence and the implication hanging. She knew he understood the consequences. She wasn't entirely sure why she felt compelled to remind him of the possibilities.

David's eyes cut toward Brynna briefly, acknowledging he heard and understood her. He continued to stay focused, "Lt. Ryder, don't lose our friends. Slow us down a little and let them catch up. As soon as we reach the bottom layer of the cloud cover, head into the storm matching speed and direction. Lt. Cmdr. dump those tachyons as fast as you can, the second we leave the eye of the storm."

Marissa was scared to death but kept updating her flight plans for leaving the star system based on their current location and the last known locations of the two other ships in space. The young lieutenant was having second thoughts about staying with the ship with the upcoming birth of their first baby. She and Jake had argued at length about her choice to stay aboard ship. At this particular moment she was having doubts about her decision.

With her flight plans as current as she could make them, there wasn't anything she could do except watch the situation unfold in front of her.

Marissa never expected to have children and just carrying this child was a gift beyond measure for her. She wondered if putting her baby at risk like this was the wrong thing to do.

David saw Marissa gently rubbing her belly as though she were offering comfort to her unborn child. He expected there would be a discussion about it before long if they survived the next hour.

The rattling and groaning subsided as the ship settled into its trajectory and no longer bucked against the atmosphere. A high-pitched whine remained. Thane kept the ship in a wide circular pattern inside the eye of the hurricane. He went as close to the inner storm wall as he dared. Their initial descent began at speeds of 500 to 600 miles per hour. If the ship was going to pull out of the dive before hitting the water, they needed to slow down. The *Evangeline*, and presumably the Nefil ships, were capable of underwater maneuvering, but if they hit the water at that speed, they would be smashed by the impact. Thane gave the appearance to anyone watching, of a cautious pilot. In reality, he was following the Captain's orders to let the Nefil close the gap between them.

The first Nefil ship entered behind them taking on a far more aggressive approach posture. Her pilot rapidly closed the gap between the two ships and attempted to fire at the *Evangeline* again. The rapid maneuvers made targeting difficult even for the advanced Nefil fleet.

The Nefil ship was armed with the most advanced equipment available to the Commonwealth. The ships were designed for the simple tasks of housing twelve genetically enhanced soldiers, and chasing enemies of the Commonwealth. Although the ships were slightly larger than the Explorer Class ships, they contained only what was necessary for the survival of the soldiers housed onboard. The rest of the ship was devoted to speed and weaponry.

Thane fired his reverse thrusters and adjusted the pitch to slow the craft. He made the adjustments at random moments to throw off the Nefil's targeting computers.

David watched the second ship come into firing range and gave Thane a heads-up. Thane adjusted his strategy to keep the two ships vying for the targeting solution.

The time from orbit to reaching the bottom of the hurricane only took about eight minutes. It was the longest eight minutes of the crew's lives. As they neared the bottom of the hurricane's eye, David leaned forward in his seat again.

"Lazaro, start dumping tachyons! Thane, head into the inner wall of the hurricane and hug the surface of the water. On my mark, climb into the clouds."

No one dared breathe. David watched the tactical display until he saw both ships follow them in side by side. The ships were attempting to flank them on both sides. David wanted to ask if the two ships were emptying their tachyons because if they had, this wouldn't work. There wasn't time to find out at this point. He leaned forward a hair further as though his posture could direct the ship.

"MARK! RAISE SHIELDS!" He shouted.

The ship lurched upward. The lightning struck the shields. Jake re-configured the shields to deflect the lightning. The lightning was drawn to the tachyons. The charges amassed along the *Evangeline's* wake of tachyon particles and caught the two Nefil ships off-guard. They hadn't raised their shields in time. A second later the massive electrical charge overloaded their net and flooded their matter/antimatter chambers. The two ships lost control and collided into a massive explosion.

David leaned forward until his body was pressed firmly against his restraint, "Thane, dive into the ocean, NOW!"

As soon as the ship broke the surface of the water and submerged David issued one more hasty order.

"Shut down all external power. Let the ship drift. Lazaro, shut down all power except minimal life support. Commander, get me random short bursts on the scanners."

The crew waited quietly. In a moment, Brynna reported, "I show large pieces of debris settling behind us. Both Nefil ships were destroyed."

Everyone breathed a sigh of relief except Jake.

"Captain, we still have two Pacification ships in orbit. We're no match for those, and we can't stay here. If they even suspect we survived that explosion, they'll just stand guard until they can get a couple more ships in here with atmospheric capabilities. They could also wait until we have to surface, then fire that energy cannon and destroy us from space like they did on Galat."

Thane gave Jake an annoyed look, "You sure know how to snatch defeat from the jaws of victory. Can't you just enjoy the moment?"

David gave Thane a wry smile, "It's okay, Lieutenant. Jake is right. We haven't won this one yet. Let's play dead for few minutes, catch our breath then tackle the next problem."

Brynna added more enthusiasm to the conversation, "Captain, this storm is moving away from us. If we stay here, we'll be out from under it in about forty minutes. Also, at our speed of descent, we'll reach crush depth in half that time."

David shook his head, "Anybody else want to brighten my day?"

Marissa glanced up with a deadpan look, "I think my water just broke."

David and Jake both responded in shock, "What? Are you sure?"

Marissa couldn't hold her expression in place any longer. She smiled shyly, "Just kidding," She wasn't typically a jokester, but she couldn't resist this one time.

David wiped the frustration off his face, "Thank goodness. Let's get moving. Damage report?"

Each crew member checked their assigned areas and reported no damage. The nets were devoid of tachyons, so they would have to build their tachyons from nothing.

"Lt. Cmdr. Dominick, can we build our tachyon levels while we're under the surface of the water?

There was silence for a moment before he responded, "We can. I suggest reconfiguring the shields to collect energy from the surrounding area to speed the build-up."

David scowled, "You aren't suggesting we collect tachyon particles from the water and atmosphere, are you?"

"No sir. I'm suggesting we use the energy collected from the storm and the water to power the ship's engines and life support while we use the matter/antimatter engines to build-up tachyons. We should be able to speed the process if we aren't using the energy from the engines to achieve escape velocity. Give me a couple of minutes to make the adjustments then we can collect energy from the waves, wind, and lightning."

David continued to scowl, "I thought we needed to dump the tachyons, so the lightning didn't blow us up."

"I can build them up inside the engines for a short period before releasing them into the net. I can hold them until we're clear of the storm. We should reach saturation about the time we reach orbit. Be sure and choose your route carefully. I'd hate to get us ready to get out of here only to get shot down by the Pacification ships."

David took a deep breath, "Understood, Lt. Cmdr.. Is everybody ready to go again?"

Most of the responses were less than enthusiastic, except Thane who was quite eager.

As soon as the shield configuration was complete, David ordered Thane to move the ship toward the surface of the water matching the direction of the swirling winds. He stayed along the more virulent inner wall to avoid detection from space. As they neared the upper edge of the hurricane, David gave a last warning.

"When we leave this hurricane, we'll be visible from space and those ships can shoot us down. We can't see them until we get clear of the storm either. Watch those scanners and get the location of those two ships as fast as you can. Lt. Holden, be ready to update our course. Here we go, people. Thane, put us on the outer wall and be prepared to head straight for space when I tell you."

Thane grinned but focused on holding the ship steady. He kept his eyes on his display and gave a brief acknowledgment of his orders. His hands carefully manipulated the controls and edged the ship toward the outer wall of the storm.

Brynna and Jake searched the skies for indications of the two ships in space. The ships were orbiting the planet strategically. One ship traveled around the northern hemisphere while the other stayed 180 degrees behind it in the southern hemisphere.

Having the data they needed, the ship ducked back into the storm. The storm was in the northern hemisphere. As soon as the northern ship passed across the horizon, David ordered the ship out of the storm and the atmosphere. Marissa laid the course in. The course change included two brief dips into the upper atmosphere, long enough to heat the outer hull of the ship with a reentry burn. The net reached saturation as they departed the atmosphere the last time as Lazaro predicted. The two ships detected them and altered course to intercept. The ship furthest from them hailed them with a warning to stand down. The ship closest to them powered its energy cannon and fired as Thane activated the tachyon drive. Everything went black.

GRAMMA?

The crew sat in the dark, trying to make sense of their situation. It took Capt. Alexander two seconds to process and react. He felt the artificial gravity release his body causing him to bounce against his restraints. Knowing his console was probably inert, he punched two buttons on his bracelet. The first button activated a portable light source. The second activated his comm unit, which didn't require the ship's power to operate.

"Lt. Cmdr. Dominick, I need power and fast."

There was an eerie silence followed by the sound of clicks, snaps, and rustling movements. The lights and displays came back on. David took a deep breath as the artificial gravity caused him to settle back into his seat. It had only taken a few seconds without the air recycling system to make the air stale.

"Commander, Chief, what's the status of those two ships? Lt. Ryder, Lt. Holden, what's our course and speed?" David barked, thinking they were seconds away from being boarded and arrested.

Brynna and Jake glanced at each other. Neither one could make sense of their scanner readouts.

Thane and Marissa were giving each other similar looks.

When no one answered, the Captain tensed, "Somebody give me some information and fast before we get blown out of the sky."

Thane finally answered, "Uh, Captain, the best I can give you is… we're going that way, very fast."

Thane pointed toward the front of the ship.

Marissa knew his description of their current status was too vague. "Captain, we're traveling on inertia and bradyon power. The tachyons have degraded in the net. It's going to take a minute to figure out where we are, but we are not in the Pillan system, we're not in any system at the moment."

David looked back and forth at the two. Thane shrugged and nodded in agreement with Marissa.

David turned his attention to Brynna and Jake, "What do you two have for me?"

Brynna looked as befuddled as the others. Those two ships are not in scanning range, and we are no longer near the Pillan sun."

David glanced at the blank faces around him. He slapped his comm unit again. "Lt. Cmdr. Flint, report to engineering. Lt. Cmdr. Dominick, report to the bridge as soon as you are relieved."

David turned to Aulani. "Any traffic on comms?"

Aulani shook her head, "No sir. Do you want me to try and tap into a relay station to see what I can pick up?"

David wanted to say yes, but knew better. "Not until we know what happened."

David turned to Brynna, "Did that energy cannon hit us?"

Brynna was already studying the logs. Scowling, she looked at the Captain, "The logs indicate a power spike just before everything went dead."

"Everyone conduct a full system check and find out where we are."

David released his restraint. He got out of his seat and paced for a moment while waiting for the engineer to join them on the bridge.

Remembering Marissa's tension earlier, he moved in front of her station. Leaning in he quietly asked, "Lieutenant, are you and the baby alright?"

Marissa nodded, "Yes, Captain, we're fine."

Something in her face was unconvincing. David followed up. "Marissa, if you need to start your maternity leave, I need to know. You're the best navigator I've got, but you're getting to a point where you're going to have to step away for a while."

"I know, Captain. I can't sit in my quarters and do nothing though, sir. I want to stay on duty as long as I can."

David stared at her for a moment. She was holding something back. "Talk to Jake and Lexi if you need to. Let me know if there's something I need to know. You know you've got my full support, right?"

"Yes sir, thank you, sir. I'm just a little rattled… and tense," Marissa rubbed her belly again.

David scowled at her. "That's the second time you've been tense in ten minutes. Head down to the infirmary, and let Jason check you out."

"I'm fine, sir. It's nothing… really," Marissa insisted.

David straightened, "Alright, I'll take your word for it, for the moment. Don't wait until we're in a crisis then decide it's something."

David was beginning to have second thoughts about allowing the lieutenant to remain with the mission. He understood her reasons for wanting to stay. He had given her his word that he would protect her and her baby. Keeping her close made him feel like he was keeping his promise, until now.

David saw Jake giving them curious glances. He decided to put the conversation back on track.

"Have the computer compare the stars around us to the course you laid in. Maybe something just spurred us along our intended course."

"Yes, Captain," Marissa smiled gratefully. She wanted to keep working.

David moved to Thane's station. Thane confirmed that the ship was still traveling at a high rate of speed.

Thane glanced casually at Marissa. "Is everything okay, sir?"

David didn't want everyone distracted by Marissa, so he quickly put them back on task.

"No, everything's not okay. We're lost in space with the entire galaxy hunting us down. We're going nowhere at a high rate of speed. Find out where we are before we find ourselves in the middle of a Commonwealth convoy of Nefil ships."

Thane nodded and refocused his attention. "Yes sir."

Jake was focused on Marissa. Hearing the Captain rant put him back on track.

David moved toward Jake and Brynna's stations. Lazaro stepped onto the bridge. Locating the Captain, he moved to report to him formally. David waved him off and asked, "What happened to this ship? Why did we lose power, and is anything broken?" His question was slightly pedantic, but it was to the point.

Lazaro was consumed with the same questions. His words were slow to come.

"Let me tackle the easy questions first. Diagnostics are still running, but as far as I can tell, everything is working. We lost power because there was an energy surge that overloaded the ship's primary power coupling. I reset it, and it's got everything running again."

David scowled. There were systems in place to prevent this sort of thing. There were secondary and tertiary power routings to keep things running if the primaries failed.

"Why didn't the backups prevent us from losing power?"

Lazaro inhaled sharply. "This wasn't in any of the lower level systems. This was the primary power coupling coming directly off the main engines. What I think happened is we got hit by the energy cannon, and our shields were still configured to collect energy. It overloaded the main engines."

David realized what happened. The shields had collected the energy from the energy pulse and fed it straight into the engines creating an overload in a place where redundant systems weren't yet available. The backups and redundant systems occurred after that point.

"Captain, I've got our location," Marissa piped up.

David whipped around. "Where are we?"

"We're seventeen light years from Pillan. We're on course for our next destination. We're only about eight hours away from the mining colony on Zulimar at tachyon speeds."

Capt. Alexander turned back to Lazaro. "How did we get here?"

Lazaro grimaced, "I have an idea, but I'd like to get a consult before I answer that question."

Brynna twisted in her seat to face the Engineer.

"A consult? From who? We're a little short on people we can call right now."

"Robin Alberto or Hugh Kelly."

Robin and Hugh were engineers the crew encountered on the planet Drea. Their specialty included the harnessing of tachyon energy and wormhole technology.

David stared at Lazaro for a moment to process his request. Deciding it was a reasonable course of action he returned to his seat, "Ensign Ryder, hail Drea III. Commander, compile the files of what just happened and send them to Aulani, so she can forward them if needed."

****

A few minutes later, the face of Moderator Tarmon appeared on the main screen. Her smile was warmer and friendlier every time she spoke to them as their alliance grew.

"Greetings Capt. Alexander, what can I do for you?"

David smiled warmly in return. "It's good to see you, Moderator. Let me get to the point, and we can get back to the pleasantries later. My Chief Engineer needs to consult with a couple of your engineers. We've had something happen to us that we can't explain. He thought perhaps Robin Alberto or Hugh Kelly could help us. I'm sending you the file now."

David nodded at Aulani, who initiated the data transfer.

Moderator Tarmon watched her display and forwarded the information to the appropriate parties.

"Alright Captain, the information is on its way to the department chair. I'll let you know as soon as I hear back from them. Is everything okay?"

"Aside from being seventeen light years from where we were fifteen minutes ago and no explanation, we're fine," David replied wryly.

"Is the Inter—er—Lord Liontari, is he with you? Perhaps he intervened?"

Moderator Tarmon had known Arni as their highest religious leader and referred to him as the "Intercessor." Arni tried to convince her to call him by his name. Calling him "Lord Liontari" was as close as she could get.

"No, I'm afraid he's no longer with us," David lamented.

"What? I don't understand. You were so important to him. Why would he leave you?" Moderator Tarmon looked alarmed.

David forced himself to relax. "He's traveling with some friends of mine. He didn't abandon us. We still talk to him, just not physically. I suppose he could be the reason we're out of danger. If we can't come up with a plausible understanding of these events, then that's what we'll go with."

Moderator Tarmon was relieved, "Are there any messages you would like me to pass along to your family?"

David smiled warmly as he thought of the family he had been unable to talk to for several months. "Please give them my love and tell them I asked about them. Give my regards to your father. I hope he's sleeping well."

David grinned. The man had lost quite a bit of sleep trying to educate David in the knowledge of Pateras. The Captain went on to add, "Ensign Ryder is forwarding another file to you containing personal messages from the crew to their families. Did you manage to get all of them to safety?"

Moderator Tarmon's face changed. Her body tensed.

"I will pass the messages on. Let me get an update on that and get back to you. The last report I had, said there were a couple more rendezvous pending."

David saw the Moderator glance at Aulani. He abruptly changed the subject.

"Moderator, because of our recent unexplained incident, we're going to reach our next destination sooner than expected. Do you think that's going to cause any problems?"

"No. Mr. Rune knows who you are and what you're up against. He's prepared to help you whenever you get there. He did have one question. He asked me if your ship has submersible capabilities. I didn't know. He did say it was alright if it didn't, but it would be easier to hide your ship if it was amphibious."

Thane scoffed at the question.

David gave Thane an annoyed look before answering.

"Yes ma'am, we're capable of maneuvering in water, even during a severe hurricane."

Moderator Tarmon glanced at the young man but kept her comments addressed to the Captain.

"That's good. Captain, I will get the information you requested as quickly as I can. It's good to see you again. May the Timeless One be always at your side."

David nodded respectfully, "Same to you, ma'am. I look forward to hearing from you."

Capt. Alexander closed the link and ordered, "Lt. Holden lay in a course for Zulimar. Lt. Ryder, load the net again, and activate the tachyon drive to get us going a little faster. Ensign Ryder, change our I.D. beacon to match the signature of the SS *Talon*."

"The *Talon*, sir? We destroyed that ship. Won't that raise some red flags?" Aulani objected.

"It's possible. If we use our own, it will certainly raise red flags. I doubt anyone is looking for a decommissioned ship. If they look it up in the database, it will draw attention. Not many people have seen the Nefil ships or our Explorer ships. It's never safe to question a Commonwealth ship."

Aulani smiled. Capt. Alexander wasn't that much older than her, but he managed to instill her with a great deal of confidence. She fully realized his statements were laced with doubts, but she relaxed knowing he was in command. Her father used to give her the same feelings of security. She wasn't about to let the Captain know she just compared him to her father, but the similarities were clear in her mind.

David saw Marissa rubbing her belly again. He stood and issued another round of orders.

"Cmdr. Alexander, you have the bridge. Chief Holden, Lt. Holden, we have some down time for a little while, get some sleep. Everyone will need to be on their best game when we reach Zulimar. Ensign, notify me as soon as you hear from Drea."

****

David stepped off the bridge and waited in the corridor for Marissa and Jake. When the two stepped off the bridge and the door slid shut, David approached them. As soon as Marissa saw his face, she knew what he was about to say.

"Jake, I would like you to escort your wife to the infirmary, and let the Doc check her out, please. Have the Doc report back to me, and the two of you get some rest."

Marissa stepped forward nervously, "It's just a few contractions. They're normal. Please don't take me off active duty. We're too close to uniting the other ships."

David reached out and took her hand. He spoke as gently to her as he could, knowing her hormones could erupt at the slightest provocation.

"Marissa, I promised I would protect you and the baby. I intend to keep that promise even if it means protecting you from yourself. I also have the rest of the crew to protect, and I can't do my best for everyone if I'm worried about you. If the Doc says you are fit for duty, then I'll keep you on duty. It may be modified, but it will be duty. Are you good with that?"

Slow, quiet tears rolled down her cheeks. She nodded. The lump in her throat made it too hard to speak.

David squeezed her hand. He nodded to Jake to escort his wife away. Jake gave a weak smile, "Thanks, Captain."

Trying to lighten the mood a little, David turned to face the couple as they walked away. "Did you decide on a name yet?"

The two stopped and looked at him.

Jake shook his head, "No sir, still working on it."

The Captain grinned mischievously, "David is a good name for a boy."

Jake grinned, "We'll add it to the list, sir."

****

An hour later, Dr. Jason Adams called to report Marissa's condition to the Captain. Marissa's contractions had subsided and were the result of slight dehydration. The dehydration was the result of an embarrassed young lieutenant's fear of needing to leave the bridge to use the restroom frequently. Hearing the last part of the explanation, David decided he needed to make sure the young woman had adequate accommodations for her situation. He wasn't sure how to go about it, but maybe Brynna, or the ship's psychologist, Lt. Lexi Flint could help him out with that one. There was a lot to this female stuff.

David wanted to return to the bridge to relieve Brynna or catch a nap himself, but he sensed he needed to be alone in his office when Moderator Tarmon hailed him. He didn't have much longer to wait.

"Moderator Tarmon, hello again. I'm alone in my office. I sensed you didn't want to talk publicly earlier. What do you have for me?" David got to the point.

Moderator Tarmon was an attractive older woman. David didn't know her exact age, but guessed she was in her mid-fifties. Her hair was pulled into a neat, tight bun at the back of her head. The color was a mixture of gray and dark brown. Her features reflected kindness and composure. On their first trip to Drea, she treated the crew with the utmost respect and professionalism, even though she despised everything they stood for. She treated them fairly and civilly, even while she was arresting them and charging them with heinous crimes. David had nothing but respect for the woman.

"Captain, there's been a problem with Ensign Ryder's family. Her parents and sister didn't heed the warning your Chief sent out. I sent people to their home. We got them out before the Commonwealth got to them, but they are currently unaccounted for. We lost one man in the process. I talked to our operative a few days ago and gave them two places to go. One of the places I sent them was Zulimar. I just thought you should know. If the Ensign runs into her family unexpectedly, it could be cause for concern, especially if they were being pursued. They've been careful. They have changed methods of travel and destinations frequently. I'm afraid the Commonwealth could be trailing them to get to you. Please be careful, Captain."

David stared at her face on the screen as he considered her disclosure. "I appreciate the information and the warning. I promise we'll stay on our toes."

Moderator Tarmon prepared to transfer the call to her team of engineers to discuss the *Evangeline's* unexpected travel boost.

David had one more request before moving on. "Moderator Tarmon, may I ask one more thing?"

"Of course, Captain. Whatever it is, I will do my best to help you."

David smiled, "I hope this request will be the easiest thing I have ever asked."

"Captain, I know our relationship started rather… precariously, but I have come to care about you and your crew. You are part of our family. What is it you need?"

"I am a soldier, and I fully understand the need for titles, but would you mind calling me David? Particularly in less formal settings?" David was fond of the woman and her family. She had saved his family's lives by transporting them to Drea. Her father's part in altering David's loyalties to the Commonwealth created a close bond. Finding out his family was conscripted from Drea to serve the Commonwealth made the Moderator more like family, although they weren't technically related.

The woman smiled at him. "I will do my best to honor your request. You saw the difficulty I had with the Intercessor. I respect you, young man, in ways you can't possibly imagine. Calling you by your earned title conveys that respect, at least in my eyes."

"I appreciate that ma'am, but you said we were part of your family. Families don't stand on title or ceremony," David argued gently.

Saundra smiled warmly, "You are a wise young man. I will defer to your name where appropriate if you will do me the same courtesy. Do we have a deal, David?"

"Yes, Saundra, I believe we do," David returned the warm smile, "I will inform the Ensign and the crew about Aulani's family and the potential for a trap. Thank you for all your help."

"David, if her family is found, let Mr. Rune know, and steer clear of them if you can. He can get them to safety without exposing you and the others," Saundra advised.

"Good to know. I'll pass that along. Anything else?" David prodded. He needed to get more work done and needed those answers about what happened to his ship.

"No, that's it. I have my engineering team on standby. Did you want your Chief Engineer to join you in this discussion?" Saundra's hand was poised on a button to hand the *Evangeline* off to her staff.

David nodded and quickly summoned Lazaro to his office. The two sat in front of the larger screen at the table.

Moderator Tarmon smiled slyly before she handed the call off, "Captain, I think you will thoroughly enjoy meeting with my new Engineering Department Chair."

"Engineering isn't my forte', but I'll do my best," David smiled. He sensed she was up to something when the picture changed and the face of Kay Deacons, known to the Dreans as Tyra Paulson, appeared on the screen.

"Gramma?" David stared at his grandmother in surprise.

"Davie! It's so good to see you. How's Brynna?"

"Uh—she's fine. Gram, you retired, quite a while ago. How is it you are an Engineering Department Chair?"

"I think I have a few good years left in me. Watching you fight to spread the knowledge of Pateras and coming here gave me a new-found drive and energy I thought I had lost when your grandfather died. It's mostly a desk job and an advisory position, so it isn't too strenuous for an eighty-year-old woman," The spry woman's eyes twinkled as she spoke.

David was glad she chose her words carefully. They didn't think the Commonwealth could track their transmissions, but it was best to be careful.

Her eyes grew serious for a moment. "Have—Have you talked with your Uncle Rob? Is he alright? Is he still loyal to the Commonwealth?"

David's uncle, Adm. Robert Deacons, was no longer loyal to the Commonwealth, and his grandmother knew that. He answered with equal furtiveness.

"The last I knew, he was fine and his loyalties have not wavered. He also hasn't caught us, for which I am very thankful. I didn't care for the way he treated us the last time he caught us."

Kay wiped a silent tear from her cheek. She knew her son and grandson were in difficult positions. She had seen

David after he was captured and tortured, partially she presumed by her son, David's Uncle Rob. She knew the situation was unavoidable to prevent them from both being destroyed. It was a hard memory to erase from her mind.

Kay decided it was time to change the subject.

"I understand you have a problem you need a consult on."

David waved at his companion. "You remember Lt. Cmdr. Dominick? He can probably explain the situation better than I can."

"Yes, I remember Mr. Dominick. I reviewed your files. I have one question that wasn't clear in the data you sent. Were your shields still configured to collect energy?"

Lazaro searched his memory for a moment. "Yes ma'am, they were."

"I'd like to review the files in greater detail with my staff. I'm told you know Robin and Hugh."

David nodded. "Yes, we know them. Do you have at least an idea what happened?"

"I can't say for certain, but when you travel using tachyon energy, you essentially are creating a rolling wormhole. It's like the wormhole doesn't quite form. A wormhole pocket forms directly in front of you, and it pulls the ship along like a constant rolling downhill. With your shields configured to continue drawing energy in, it took the energy cannon blast and overpowered the tachyon drive, creating a full-blown wormhole. I'm anxious to review this data in depth and any more information you can get me. Under normal circumstances, that energy pulse should have pulverized your ship. I'm glad it didn't, by the way, but this could add a weapon of sorts to your arsenal if I can work out the details."

The three discussed the situation. After a few moments, Lazaro excused himself to give the Captain time alone with his grandmother. David asked about his family members who were hidden away on Drea with her. His grandmother proudly reported the family was getting settled into their new lives. David's sister was pursuing her career at the Astrophysics Engineering Academy. His half-brother was enrolled in a local school, and the rest of his family were getting settled into jobs.

As much as David would love to continue visiting with his grandmother, he knew they needed to keep the conversation short. He asked her to give his love to the rest of the family.

"Davie, I'm proud of you, son. Be careful. The Dark Lord is not one to be trifled with. Pateras can carry you through anything, but don't get cocky. I look forward to the day we can celebrate our victory together."

ELABORATE PREPARATIONS

Six hours later the *Evangeline* was approaching Zulimar. The bridge was fully staffed.

Zulimar was a very warm and wet world. The world was ninety percent water. The land masses were small, mountainous and in clusters. The land was rich in mineral deposits of tetrabradium and other highly sought after minerals.

David's hail was greeted by a man a little older than himself, with a businesslike demeanor. He paid little attention to the ship.

"SS *Talon*, welcome to Zulimar Mining Colony. I am Neal Rune, the facility's Materials Coordinator. I wasn't expecting you for several days, Capt. Doherty."

"I hope we haven't inconvenienced you, Mr. Rune. Our schedule got an unexpected boost," David spoke calmly.

"No, it's fine. I just need to be certain your ship has aquatic maneuvering capabilities so that I can assign you a docking slip," Mr. Rune droned.

"Yes, we have aquatic maneuvering capabilities. We are capable of maneuvering to 3000 feet below sea level with full shielding for a limited time. We can only handle about 2400 feet without shielding," David kept his tone just as businesslike.

"That depth is well beyond what you'll need to dock. Land is a premium commodity on Zulimar, so we have limited aerial approach docking slips available. I am uploading docking instructions for your helmsman, now. I can meet with you at your convenience to discuss your needs during your visit. Welcome to Zulimar, Capt. Doherty."

"Thank you, Mr. Rune. *Talon* out."

Aulani forwarded the docking information to Thane and Marissa's stations. David simply ordered, "Take us in, Lieutenant."

As the ship descended to its docking station, Aulani cocked her head curiously. "Captain, why was he calling you Capt. Doherty? He's supposed to know who we are, isn't he?"

David turned to answer the question but spoke so the entire bridge crew could hear his answer.

"He was calling me by the name that matches the crew manifest for the *Talon*. It keeps our identities off the books. I plan to address this at the staff meeting. It might be best if the crew refers to me as Capt. Doherty or just Captain anytime we're in public."

Aulani shivered, "Captain, I don't even like to think about that monster. He was evil. You aren't evil."

David's mood was pleasant but businesslike. His face changed to reflect his sorrow and regret.

"Thank you, Ensign, but I'm probably responsible for far more deaths than he was. I don't know his history, but I do know mine, and I can claim responsibility for an entire planet plus a few others."

Aulani didn't want to leave the Captain in a pool of regrets.

"Captain, you were unwittingly, partially responsible for the deaths on Galat. You never wanted it to happen, and you never believed it would happen. That monster was sadistic. He enjoyed killing and torture. Whether it was six or six million, he was far more evil than you."

The other crewmen on the bridge quietly agreed with the Ensign's assessment.

"Point taken. I still did wrong by the Galatans. They're dead, and I was the one who betrayed them. I can't fix the past, but I'm going to do my best to protect the future from further atrocities," David sighed.

"I don't mean to change gears, Ensign, but I need you to call Lt. Cmdr. Adams and Lt. Adams to the bridge."

Dr. Jason Adams was a Lt. Cmdr. by rank. His primary responsibility was ship's physician. Every member of the crew had primary and secondary functions. Jason served as the relief pilot as his secondary position. His wife, Laura Adams, was a Lieutenant Junior Grade. Her primary duties included botany and assistant medical officer. Her secondary position was relief navigator. The ship's original mission was to go to undeveloped worlds and offer services and technological advances in exchange for their loyalty to the Commonwealth. Jason and Laura had been integral parts of that mission. Now that Laura had acquired hydroponics equipment, she was attempting to supplement the ship's food supplies. Being hunted by every major ship in the galaxy as public enemy number one meant restocking their food stores would become more difficult.

David saved the couple the trouble of reporting officially when they stepped onto the bridge.

"Oh good, you're just in time. Jason, how much experience have you had at aquatic maneuvering?"

The ship was entering the atmosphere and moving into the prescribed approach pattern.

Jason shook his head. "Not much. I've done simulated maneuvers, and I had to do a couple when I first qualified as a pilot, but that was ten to fifteen years ago. I haven't had cause to do one since."

Laura's experience was more recent, but just as negligible. Navigators had to qualify as pilots first before specializing in astro-navigation. Her skills as a pilot were less prominent.

David instructed them to observe Thane and Marissa in the water landing. The Captain hailed ship's psychologist, Lt. Lexi Flint, to bring two extra chairs to the bridge for the couple to use while observing the landing and underwater maneuvering.

Lexi brought the chairs as ordered. Seeing Lexi's face, David knew there was a problem. Her annoyance at her assignment to carry chairs to the bridge was clearly displayed. This problem surfaced at a good time as he was in need of Lexi's professional skills. Perhaps he could kill two birds with one stone.

When the ship launched, their first assignment was a three-week journey. Lexi's primary responsibility as the ship's psychologist was the ship's morale officer. Three weeks in a cramped ship with people who were barely more than strangers and each couple newly married, except for Jason and Laura, could be enough to spark homicidal rages.

Upon reaching each targeted planet, Lexi's job was to advise the Captain and commander about cultural issues and potential emotional reactions by indigenous populations. First contact situations could be highly volatile. It was also Lexi's responsibility to evaluate the crew for signs of stress.

Although her primary duties were quite extensive, she chose to pursue engineering as her secondary responsibility. She chose it because, barring the unexpected crisis, relief engineers were secluded in the engineering department with menial rote tasks that required little thought. It gave her the mental break she needed. If anything went severely wrong in engineering, her duty would be to contact the primary engineer and perform the emergency protocols she was trained to do until he arrived. She was by no means an engineering expert, just a glorified maintenance person. It worked for her and the ship. Lexi was extremely intelligent, and her brain could function well in areas that were polar opposites. The other thing she enjoyed about engineering is that it gave her and her husband common ground.

Lt. Cmdr. Braxton Flint was an architectural and structural engineer. Braxton was third in command of the ship and served as a relief engineer.

The Captain watched Lexi quietly and efficiently perform the menial task. She was careful to avoid eye contact, especially with David. She never balked or objected in any way, but her mind was clearly elsewhere.

Before leaving the bridge, she meekly asked, "Will there be anything else, sir?"

David raised his hand to hold her off for a second.

"Cmdr. Alexander, can you take over? I need to address a couple of issues with the Lieutenant in my office. Once we're docked, I would like you to join us."

Brynna moved to David's station as he escorted Lexi from the bridge.

****

The Captain presumed Lexi was concerned about her job status. It could seem like her job was no longer relevant since they abandoned their original mission of first contact situations.

David kindly offered her a seat at the table. Sitting across from her he began, "Lt. Flint, I need to discuss some things with you. Obviously, our mission parameters have changed, and our jobs are changing with it. This is bound to bring an added element of tension among the crew. Sending competency reports to Commonwealth HQ is one of those areas that has changed. I prefer HQ not know the mental status of the crew."

David smiled slightly, trying to insert a small amount of humor into the conversation.

Lexi gave him a brief smile in return, "You're right, that probably isn't the best idea."

David continued, "I do want you to do quarterly evaluations of the entire crew, at least for the next six months. Send a copy to me, Cmdr. Alexander, and Dr. Adams. Get Dr. Adams to do a similar evaluation of you."

Lexi looked ill. "Captain, is this a mercy assignment to make me feel needed? I can assure you, I'm not feeling useless. I'm quite capable of—"

"Lieutenant, are you refusing to obey a direct order?"

"Uh… No sir. I just meant—"

"Lieutenant, we've undergone a serious upheaval in all aspects of our lives. I've been distracted by running this ship, leading our new mission, and trying to learn all that I can about Pateras. I'm afraid I have neglected the mental health of the crew. I apologize for that. This crew has gone from being highly desired soldiers of the Commonwealth to highly desired criminals. We were the cream of the crop, and now we're fugitives. We've lost our friends, families, and careers in a very short amount of time. Jake and Marissa are about to have a baby they never expected to have. Having a baby on board is going to affect the entire crew. I know the crew trusts and depends on Pateras, but we don't need to drop our guard in any area."

Lexi's face sobered. "Yes sir, I understand."

"This brings me to the main reason I needed to talk to you. Ensign Ryder's family didn't take Jake's warning seriously."

Lexi scooted forward in her seat. "Have they been arrested?"

David shook his head. "Not to my knowledge. They managed to escape with the help of Drean operatives. One of the operatives didn't make it. I was told they might be headed here. Here's the hard part; if we locate them, we have to stay as far away from them as possible.

"Stay away from them? Why? Shouldn't we try to get to them to offer them our protection?" Lexi was well versed in human behavior. Her war tactics and battle strategies were less informed.

"The Commonwealth may have allowed them to escape hoping they would lead them to us. Moderator Tarmon said Mr. Rune could get them to safety. We just need to keep our distance and point them out to him. There's no guarantee they're headed this direction, but we need to be prepared."

David paced in the tiny office. He was not involved in the circumstances leading up to this situation, but he still felt responsible.

"Captain, do you want me to explain the situation to them?"

"Them?" David stopped pacing.

"I was including Thane. This is his family too."

David shook his head and resumed casually pacing.

"No, this is my responsibility. I wanted you here in case Aulani needed some grief counseling."

Lexi's demeanor shifted. Her earlier sullen appearance gave way to more energetic professionalism.

"Captain, you aren't interchanging the words 'fault,' and 'responsibility' are you?"

"What do you mean?" He calmly asked.

Knowing what she did about the Captain, she expected him to react defensively, especially if he was guilty. Lexi pushed further to test him.

"Are you afraid Aulani will hold you responsible or blame you for this?"

David's face remained calm but concerned.

"Blame me? What is that supposed to mean? Do you believe this is my fault?"

David was gently pushing back with equal voracity.

Lexi passively redirected him to her original question.

"I haven't given any suggestion of my opinion. I asked if you thought Aulani would blame you."

David knew this was the result of some of his actions, but not his fault. In previous months he had acted erratically and blamed himself for things that were clearly out of his control. This time he did not react rashly.

"Lexi, it's true I'm responsible for this crew, and I honestly hope Aulani doesn't blame me for this. I suppose anyone can react unreasonably. I would like to know why you're trying to blame me."

"Me? I'm not blaming you for this. You have a habit of accepting blame where you shouldn't. I'm just testing the waters," Lexi explained hastily. She didn't want the Captain to misunderstand her intentions.

David planted his feet firmly shoulder-width apart. Folding his arms across his chest, he scowled, "And this brings me to the last thing I wanted to talk to you about."

Sensing his displeasure was with her, Lexi felt the color in her face drain away with the confidence she was feeling seconds ago. "Yes sir?"

She wondered why she was afraid of him. She remained aboard the ship voluntarily. He couldn't put her on report or ruin her career. That had already been done. He couldn't dock her pay because the crew were no longer getting paid. He could throw her off the ship or confine her to quarters. She decided she was more afraid of disappointing him than anything else.

"Lt. Flint, even though our mission has changed, your skills are vital to our new mission. I need you to stay on top of things. Your responsibilities are to maintain the morale of this crew and provide advice to the Commander and me. Are you having trouble fulfilling those duties?"

Lexi studied him intently, "No, Captain, why would you ask that?"

Before he could respond, his office door chimed alerting him to a visitor, "Enter," He called out.

David's wife and First Officer, Cmdr. Brynna Alexander, joined the two officers. David motioned her to a chair. Brynna sat down and waited for David to speak.

"Lieutenant, over the last few hours, I have pushed most of this crew to their limits. You were annoyed that I asked you to carry a couple of chairs onto the bridge. I can only surmise that a) I was keeping you from something you deemed more important, b) you deemed the task to be beneath you, or c) you were ticked off at me for some reason. Which one was it? Or was it something else?"

Lexi blinked in shock. She carried the chairs in promptly as ordered. How did he know she was annoyed by it? "I—I—I'm sorry, sir. Forgive me."

David was nonplussed by her apology.

"I accept your apology, but I need the answer to my question. What bothered you so much about carrying two chairs onto the bridge? Were they too heavy?"

Lexi blinked nervously again. She looked down at her hands and picked at the cuticles. David waited patiently for her to respond. After a prolonged silence she finally spoke, her voice wavering dangerously as she neared tears.

"I'm sorry, sir. I think I just felt lost."

David's tone and posture softened. "Lost? How so? Your job hasn't changed," David protested.

"I'm sorry, sir. I disagree. With everyone depending on Pateras, they've changed. Not that this crew was remotely unstable, but they are steadier than ever before. Considering the things we've experienced, this crew should be a wreck. They aren't, not even close to it. They don't need my skills as a psychologist. Even Jake doesn't need me. No one is holding grudges against him anymore. I enjoy the therapeutic release of working in engineering, but it's not my primary desire and spending too much time there could cause me to resent it. Pateras has replaced me."

Brynna decided to jump in. "Lexi, we can't live in a crisis, just to give you something to do. It's a good thing that we aren't constantly in need. Our missions have always had highs and lows. There will always be times when we need your skill-set and times when we don't. Personally, I expect the next couple of weeks to need your skills quite a bit."

David needed to inform Aulani about her family, and soon. He decided to put the matter to rest as quickly as possible.

"The Commander is exactly right. You have provided an invaluable service to this crew. The things that occurred before we committed to Pateras were minor. The things you handled afterward were major. Your actions kept this crew together and functioning. You helped my family come to terms with what was happening to them. You helped the crew forgive and accept Jake. You know how much I internalize things. You were right that the crew needed to know what I faced at the hands of Supreme Executor Hale. Brynna needed to know and needed me to talk about it. I would never have said anything about it if you hadn't pushed me."

David sat down in his chair. Looking her in the eye, he gently spoke, "Lexi, the next few days we will be meeting with the other Explorer Ships. Their worlds have been turned upside-down as well. Tempers are going to flare. I need you to be at your best; no more silent pity parties. If you ever feel like this again, you need to talk to me or the Commander about it. I can NOT take on Luciano Hale and the entire galaxy if I don't have your support."

Lexi's eyes widened and her mouth fell open. "Captain, you don't really think you can take on the entire galaxy by yourself, do you?"

David leaned back in his chair and soberly answered. "No, of course not. I figured it would take three or four of us to do that," He held his face as straight as he could until Brynna's lip twitched. His face gave way to a broad smile.

Lexi scowled at him. "That wasn't funny."

"Your face was pretty funny when you thought I was having delusions of grandeur," David argued.

David could see Lexi's face soften, indicating it was safe to move on.

"Anything else before I call Aulani and Thane in?"

Lexi wiped away a final tear. "I'm sorry again, sir. I promise I won't let my feelings run away with me anymore."

"Lieutenant, you are not allowed to internalize either. Okay?" David clarified, "If I'm not allowed, neither are you."

Lexi nodded and acknowledged the order. Seeing her comfort level had improved, David tapped his comm unit and summoned Thane and Aulani to his office as soon as their stations were secure. He ordered Cheyenne to the bridge to cover comms and Jason to remain as the Officer in Command.

****

Jake wasn't comfortable leaving his station yet. He voluntarily stayed put, despite Marissa's urging him to return with her to their cabin. Security Chief Holden wanted to be sure the crew hadn't walked into a trap. He preferred to continue to monitor the scanners for approaching ships or troops greeting them at the airlocks. Marissa finally gave up on her dedicated, but suspicious and paranoid husband. She followed Thane and Aulani off the bridge. When the two stopped outside the Captain's office door, she jokingly asked, "So what did you two do to get into trouble?"

Aulani shrugged. Grinning, she added, "I'm not usually the one in trouble. It's normally him," She playfully shoved her husband.

Thane shrugged innocently. "I didn't do anything… this time. Maybe it has something to do with our next mission."

Marissa grinned again, "Maybe he's anticipating you causing trouble."

"What about me? I'm not likely to cause problems," Aulani was a stabilizing force for Thane.

Marissa shrugged, "He may need all hands-on-deck to keep him in line this time."

Thane mockingly took offense. "Wait, are we talking about me, or Jake? I don't get into trouble like Jake does."

Marissa laughed. "Sometimes I think you've been taking lessons from him. You two better get in there before you get into more trouble," Marissa rubbed her belly and waddled toward the elevator to return to her quarters.

****

Thane punched the button at the door to the Captain's office to alert him to their presence. When the door opened to reveal the Captain, commander, and ship's psychologist waiting on them, Thane looked at Aulani and said the only thing he could, "Uh-oh."

"Come in. Have a seat," David invited.

Thane wanted to make a joke to lighten the seriousness in the room. He wisely chose to say nothing. The somber looks were making him too nervous.

"Captain, has something happened?"

David sat down closest to Aulani.

"Yes, but the first thing you need to know is, to my knowledge, no one's been harmed. Ensign Ryder, I do have to report that a concerning situation has developed regarding your family."

Thane grasped Aulani's hand tightly. Aulani glanced appreciatively at her husband.

She turned her attention back to the Captain. "They didn't make it to Drea, did they?"

"No, they haven't, yet. They didn't run when Jake told them to. A Drean party got to them in time to get them out before the Commonwealth could arrest them. One of the Dreans died in the rescue. They couldn't make it to the rendezvous point. The remaining Drean agent is with them and trying to get them to safety. They've been traveling under the radar. According to Moderator Tarmon, one of the possible locations they could be traveling to is here on Zulimar."

"Somehow I knew it. I know the Dreans were holding the personal messages until each family was brought back to Drea. When I never got any responses from my messages, I knew they hadn't made it back there. Why am I just now hearing this? Why didn't she say something sooner?" Aulani asked somberly.

"She didn't say, and I didn't get into that with her. Perhaps she kept expecting the situation to resolve and didn't want to worry you prematurely. I can only speculate on that. Aulani, there's something else you need to understand. When we head into the colony, we will need to keep our eyes open for them. The thing we can't do is make contact with them. It's possible they were allowed to escape in the hopes they would lead the Commonwealth to us."

Aulani stared at the Captain as she tried to make sense of what he was telling her. Fear for her family's safety welled up within her. "We can't help them?"

David reached forward and took her free hand in his own. "No, that isn't what I'm saying at all. Mr. Rune can get them to safety. We have to point them out to him."

"So, what's the plan?" Aulani was tense.

"I'm going to give the crew this information in the briefing in an hour. I need whatever pictures you have on file to give to the crew. They need to be on the lookout for them. This isn't our primary mission. It cannot take precedence, but we also can't ignore it. We will do whatever we can to get your family to safety. You have my word on that. The one thing that worries me is, if the Commonwealth is following them, they could lead them to every Explorer crew and knock all of us out in one swift blow. Do you understand what's at stake?" David watched her closely.

Aulani's eyes darted around, looking at nothing in particular. She knew what was at stake. It wasn't an easy thing to accept. The Captain's plan could mean sacrificing her family to save their crew and the crews of the other eleven ships.

She finally gathered her strength and brought her gaze back to the Captain. "I understand, and I will do whatever you need."

David squeezed her hand warmly. "Aulani, you let me know what you need. I don't want to make this any harder on you than it already is. Lexi is here if you need her."

Aulani focused on Lexi's face for a moment.

"If this goes badly, I will certainly need her and everyone else."

Thane and Aulani left the Captain's office to pull together the pictures the Captain requested. Thankfully, they had some time to process the situation and recover before the briefing.

****

An hour later, Capt. Alexander was repeating the information to the rest of the crew along with the warning to keep their distance.

"Our primary mission on Zulimar is not to locate Ensign Ryder's family. We will do whatever we can to find them, but not at the expense of our primary mission. This mission could prove to be extremely dangerous. I will be meeting with Mr. Rune to find out what arrangements he has made for us."

Braxton shifted in his seat, "Captain, you haven't told us what our mission here actually is."

"I've kept that information quiet for the last couple of months because there was too much at stake."

"Couple months? You've had this plan in the works since we left Ela Prime? Why keep it from us?" Braxton was concerned the Captain was afraid of being betrayed.

"We're meeting with representatives from all the Explorer ships. I didn't want you to know, in case we were captured," David explained.

Jake was sitting in his usual spot in the corner, rocking his chair back on two legs. Being careful not to lose his balance, he raised one hand to ask a question.

"Captain, you kept this information from us to protect everyone, not because you don't trust us?"

His relaxed posture eased the concern of the rest of the crew. If their paranoid and formerly traitorous Security Chief wasn't concerned, perhaps no one else needed to be concerned either.

David casually answered, "This was for your protection, as well as the other crews. The only ones aboard any of the ships who knew were the Captain and First Officer. Herein lies the problem; any one of the others could turn us in if they don't believe Executor Hale intends to destroy them."

The Captain imagined the crew had a million questions, but the gravity of the situation weighed heavily on them. He quickly moved on, hopefully answering some of those questions.

"According to Moderator Tarmon, Neal Rune is an ally and can be trusted. He's doing everything in his power to keep us safe."

Thane leaned forward, intending to ask one of those million questions. David raised his hand to stop him.

"Please, hold your questions until I finish. If I haven't answered them by the time I'm done, then you can ask. Make yourself a note on your datapad so you don't forget what it was."

Thane sat back in his seat, looking annoyed. He made a notation as ordered and resumed listening to the Captain's briefing.

"Our goals for this stop are to 1) form an alliance with the other ships, 2) restock our fuel reserves, 3) plan our next moves and 4) locate Ensign Ryder's family and get them to safety. Those are not in any particular order, nor are they at the expense of maintaining our safety."

Jake sat his chair down abruptly getting the entire crew's attention. They were accustomed to his impetuous objections and prepared to listen to his overly cautious banter with the Captain.

"Chief, wait until I'm done, please," David repeated.

"Negative, Capt. Alexander, I don't have a question. Mr. Rune is outside the airlock signaling to get in."

"Escort him in. I'll record my briefing, so you don't miss anything."

Jake trotted out of the Dining Hall and headed to the airlock. Brynna activated the computer and began recording the briefing.

David continued, "Since we arrived a couple of days early, we're going to go into the mines and mine the ore we need to restock our fuel reserves. We have the time to mine what we need and additional fuel for the other ships. These mines are far richer than the ones we encountered on Medoris. Perhaps having the gift of fuel will pacify any ill will the others may have toward us."

Laura raised her hand, frustrating the Captain, "Alright Lieutenant Adams, what's your question.

"Captain, why would the others bear us any ill will? We aren't the ones trying to kill them," Laura asked.

David looked at Lexi, "Lt. Flint, would you care to field that one?"

Lexi flinched slightly. She wondered if this was another mercy assignment. Remembering the Captain's orders not to second-guess him or throw pity parties for herself, she quickly dismissed the thoughts and answered.

"Yes, Capt. Alexander. It's possible that the others believe our treason is why they are now considered traitors. They might consider turning us in to get back into the Supreme Executor's good graces."

Cheyenne frowned. "But isn't that exactly what happened? They're being hunted because of us, aren't they?"

Jake and Neal Rune walked into the room as David answered.

"Yes, that is exactly what happened, but we are not the ones trying to destroy them. Supreme Executor Hale is the one doing that, but they may not see it that way."

David turned his attention to his visitor. "Mr. Rune, welcome aboard."

David stepped forward and offered his hand.

Neal Rune was approximately forty years old with short, dark, wavy hair. A few stray gray streaks added personality to his subdued, businesslike appearance.

Neal met him in the middle of the room and shook his hand. "Thank you, Capt. Alexander."

"I thought we were supposed to meet in your office a little later today," David folded his arms across his chest. He was hoping the change in plans didn't indicate a problem.

"I thought perhaps due to the sensitive nature of your situation, it might be best if I came to you. I have no reason to believe anyone is watching me or monitoring my activities, but why take chances? The more you and your crew are seen, the greater the chances are you'll be recognized. Would you like me to go over what I have prepared?"

"Sure, go ahead," David stepped aside and leaned against a table to give the man the floor.

"This data crystal contains the complete layout of the mining colony. The Dreans have private entrances and exits so their movements can remain obscured from the general population. The Dreans provided significant funding for the development of this colony, and as part of that arrangement, they secured a portion of the mine for their private use along with facilities for housing, management, and operations.

"The Dreans lease on the area is run through a dummy corporation. There won't be any financial trail to follow for the ore or use of the facilities. The berth you are docked at belongs to the Dreans. They rarely use it, and it is one of the deepest berths we have, which should make it difficult for the Commonwealth to scan the area and find you. They can probably determine there's a ship here, but I doubt they can figure out whose ship it is. I've flagged the areas dedicated for the Dreans. You'll be guaranteed privacy and full access to those areas. I put access codes to those areas on the data crystal. Please let me know what you need when the others arrive, particularly where security is concerned."

Before Jake could react to Neal's reference to security measures, David asked, "What sort of security measures are already in place, and what do we have available to us?"

"I've given you access to the entire colony's audio-visual surveillance feed, as well as long and short-range sensors. I would advise you to use ours and not your own. If approaching ships detect your scans, they could trace it back to your ship. Tapping into ours keeps you hidden, but able to keep watch."

"Won't the external access to the sensors raise red flags with your security staff?" Jake questioned.

Mr. Rune shook his head and smiled a telling smile, "You aren't the first clients to request discretion. We maintain several guest access user profiles. Our security people ignore the accesses unless you use it to cause problems for our people."

Jake scowled, "You referring to smugglers, aren't you?"

Neal smiled even bigger. "It's illegal to aid a smuggling operation, Mr. Holden."

Brynna shifted uncomfortably in her seat, the concern on her face was clear to all. "Mr. Rune, I have a question pertinent to the safety of our people."

Mr. Rune refocused his attention on Brynna, "Yes, Commander?"

It struck Brynna as odd that he called her by her rank since introductions had not been made. She amended her impending question to reflect her curiosity.

"You seem to know quite a bit about us, and since Moderator Tarmon vouched for you, I can only assume she trusts you. For my benefit though, could you please tell me why you are so willing to help us, knowing the entire galaxy is out for our blood?"

Neal glanced at the anxious faces in the room. "Moderator Tarmon didn't tell you?"

David stood up from leaning against the table. "Tell us what?" He was slightly tense at not having an important piece of information.

"Captain, Commander, I'm a Drean citizen. They sent me out here to get this job for the sole purpose of being a liaison to the outside world. The mining company doesn't know where I'm from and I have no loyalty to the Commonwealth."

The tension in the room dropped dramatically. David went on to explain, "I guess she forgot to mention that. Did she alert you to the issue of some missing family members?"

Neal glanced at Aulani, "Yes, Captain, she did warn me about that a couple of days ago. I've had a computer facial recognition program running from the moment she contacted me, to alert me if they show up."

Aulani's face relaxed thinking her family would be found quickly. Neal knew their system wasn't foolproof.

"Captain, not every place on the colony is monitored, and the operative who's bringing them here knows how to avoid them if he needs to. He will head for the Drean sector and contact me from there."

Lexi studied the man intently, "Mr. Rune, did you lose anyone to the Commonwealth fifty years ago?"

Neal cocked his head quizzically, "No, not that I'm aware of. It was before my time, but I remember studying about it in school and my parents were bitter when they discussed it. I think they may have known someone who died or was taken, but they didn't talk much about it. Why do you ask?"

Lexi locked her eyes on his, "We're putting our lives on the line by coming here. The Commonwealth rewarded Dreans fifty years ago who agreed to work for them. I just wanted to understand your motivation for working for both sides."

Neal bristled visibly, "Let's get one thing straight. I do NOT work for the Commonwealth. I work for the Drean Government. I was assigned here to work within the Commonwealth territory. Essentially, I would be considered a Drean Spy. If the Commonwealth catches me, I will die before betraying my people—or you. Are we clear on that?"

David stepped forward to smooth the obviously ruffled feathers.

"Forgive us, Mr. Rune. Lexi is our ship's psychologist, and she likes to know what we're dealing with. Any Drean who wanted to work for the Commonwealth as a double agent could earn a position of high esteem with Supreme Executor Hale. She meant no disrespect. She's a student of human behavior, and she's seen what the Commonwealth has done to and for Dreans, my family in particular."

Neal tried to push his feelings aside and move on.

"Captain, Moderator Tarmon gave me rather extensive files on your entire crew. You have my word. I will protect you with my very life. She's told me you have the Intercessor's blessing and you serve Pateras. You are under my protection as long as you are here."

David decided it was time to move on, "Thank you, Mr. Rune, for everything. Where do you plan to put the other ships when they arrive?"

"If you would care to pull up the schematics from that data crystal, I can show you more precisely," Neal was just as ready to put the conversation behind him.

Brynna plugged the data crystal into the computer terminal and displayed the images on the large screen in the room.

Neal touched the screen and manipulated the image until a side view of the entire colony was visible.

"I have reserved the bottom two levels of docking stations for the other ships. There are six levels above that. I've closed the sixth level for scheduled maintenance. I will space our regular traffic out, so they hide the bottom levels as much as possible."

"Why close the sixth level?" Cheyenne questioned abruptly.

Neal was surprised by her question. His files on the crew indicated her specialty was linguistics, not security or logistics.

"The—uh—closing of the sixth level prevents other ships from getting close enough to spy on you, and it forces my staff to keep the traffic heavier higher up. It keeps your presence hidden."

Neal touched the screen and placed several ships on the diagram. He placed some representative ships on the lower docking rings and several on the upper rings. Turning the image to a top view, only the ships on the top levels were visible.

Pointing to the image, he explained, "Normally we don't get a lot of activity, and we try to space out the ships as much as possible. By limiting what's available, the upper docking slips are more densely populated which means if a ship tried scanning to the bottom of the docking platform, they can't scan past the first few levels. The ships in the upper docking rings block those scans. Just as a word of warning, the thing we can't do is stop another ship from permeating the water outside the docking approach pattern and scanning."

Neal resized the image and turned it upright again. Pointing to an area outside of the typical landing zone. He pulled another image of a representative ship from the map legend and guided it into a pattern circling the docking platform. The image continued to circle as he spoke.

"If a ship really wants to see what's down here, they can stay outside the area designated for docking approaches and scan whatever they want. If it's civilian, our security forces can chase it away, but if it's a Commonwealth ship, we can't touch it. We can distract it a little, but that's it. My hands are tied where that's concerned."

"I hope we've covered our tracks enough to keep that from happening. If something of that nature were to happen, do your best to cooperate and don't give yourself away. If we get arrested, our fate is in the hands of Pateras, not Luciano Hale. Don't risk blowing your cover. We don't want the Commonwealth to find out about the Drean's extended reach," David strongly advised.

"I need to make assignments for my crew. If you have the time, I would appreciate it if you could hang around. More questions could come to light. It might also be helpful for you to have some idea what my people are doing."

"Of course," Neal nodded and took a seat near the back of the room.

David hurried to get their business conducted so Mr. Rune could return to his post.

"I want one person on duty on the ship at all times. I want the bulk of our personnel working the mines. Mr. Dominick, you are in charge of that project. Get us restocked as fast as possible then we can continue mining for the other ships. As I understand it, these mines are rich in both tetrabradium and tetratachium?"

Mr. Rune nodded, "Something else you need to be aware of Captain, the ore deposits will block the signals to and from your bracelets while you're in the mines. There are relay points every fifty yards in the tunnels. You'll need to log into the station relays using the access codes I gave you to get your signals through."

"Understood. I'm putting three of you in the general population to watch for Ensign Ryder's family and crew members from the other ships. I want everyone in civilian attire. Our faces have been plastered all over the news channels, but they used pictures of us in our uniforms. I want us to keep a very low profile. We'll trade out every few hours so no one gets too tired in any capacity. We'll keep to the colony's regular daytime hours. I'll post a schedule on the specifics in a couple of hours. In three days we'll meet with the other crews in the Drean meeting room. I would prefer to have as many of the crew present as possible. I want the others to see we're in this together. It will also help to be able to watch each other's backs.

Any questions?" David scanned the room. Jason was scowling and debating about asking something.

"Doc, is there a problem?"

"I do have an issue to discuss with you, but I'm not sure this is the appropriate time or place," Jason continued to scowl. He glanced at Marissa catching her eye.

Marissa grimaced. She knew he was referring to her.

"Oh, just spill it, Doc. It affects everyone."

David motioned for Jason to state his problem. Jason shifted uncomfortably in his seat.

"Captain, I would prefer Marissa to take shifts here on the ship or short shifts in the general public areas. She does NOT need to be in those mines for any reason, and she doesn't need to be walking for hours. I'm okay with her taking a couple hours at a time but no more than that."

David glanced at Marissa. Her look was more reflective of guilt than objection. David discerned she knew her delivery date was too close for more than that. He also knew she felt like she was letting her shipmates down.

"Well, I hate to tie you down Lieutenant, but somebody's got to do it. I'll work out the rotation and let you get out as much as I dare. Don't overdo anything because when you go down, it takes four of my crew out and keeps the rest distracted. Got it?"

Marissa looked lost for a moment, "Four?"

David folded his arms across his chest again.

"Yes, four, unless you intended on delivering this baby by yourself. I assumed you would need Jason and Laura and I also assumed you would want Jake there."

Marissa blushed for a moment. She squeezed Jake's hand.

"I'm sorry, sir. I forgot about it taking the others out of circulation."

"You were right when you said this affects us all. It's going to take all of us to get through this and get this baby raised," David smiled gently to give her some reassurance.

Neal looked at the young woman. He had not noticed her large belly earlier. His eyes grew wide as he realized what was going on.

Without thinking he blurted out, "You're traveling with a pregnant woman on a Commonwealth military ship?"

Jake's chair landed on all four legs with a loud thud.

"That's what I said! He let her stay on board," his voice announcing his angst over his wife's choice.

Before the conversation went any further, David raised his hand to silence them, "Whether I was right or wrong, what's done is done. Let's just move on. If there are no further questions, check the duty logs in an hour and see where you are to report. Dismissed."

The crew dispersed and prepared to go to work.

ZULIMAR

Aulani stood on the mezzanine overlooking a major plaza of the Zulimar mining colony. She was technically off-duty, but she continued to observe the dwindling occupants below her. It was late, and the shops and restaurants were closing. She had been there several hours watching the citizens and guests move through the area. She tried to focus on each face, searching for a familiar one. It was the end of the second full day of looking. Her assignments varied between working in the mines, manning the comm station aboard their ship, searching for members of the other Explorer Class ships and searching for her missing family. She spent more hours than assigned watching the plaza. Some of the other crews were located, but her family as yet weren't. There was no guarantee they were even headed here.

The sight of the remaining stragglers strangely burdened her heart. Each person she saw was going about their business, unaware of the developing war. Her dependence on Pateras was growing exponentially. She wondered how she ever survived without him. Their relationship was like nothing she had ever experienced before. He knew her better than Thane. She never had to worry about hiding things from Pateras. There were things about herself she despised and didn't even share with Thane, some of those ugly little things no one likes to admit about themselves. Pateras knew them all and cared about her in spite of them. He knew when she needed love and understanding. He also knew when she needed a swift kick in the pants. He always gave her whichever she needed whether she liked it or not. She had to admit, she thrived even with the swift kick. How did these people survive without him? She had been without him most of her life, but that time seemed so far away now.

Aulani's eyes continued to search the faces below her. Her eyes contacted a man walking toward her in the plaza. The man stopped when their eyes connected. It was Thane, looking for his missing wife. The look in his eyes conveyed multiple messages. His heart was heavy for the pain he knew his wife was feeling as she worried about her missing family. He knew she worried about them getting caught and wondered what they would suffer at the hands of Luciano Hale. His eyes told her how much he loved her and wished he could make her pain go away. The last message they imparted was that it was time to return to the ship for the evening.

Aulani sighed and motioned toward the nearest set of stairs. Thane headed the direction she indicated, to meet her. Aulani moved toward the stairs until she heard a noise behind her. She stopped and turned around for a moment. The mezzanine was populated with winding corridors of offices. Most everyone had left the area at the end of the business day, several hours ago. Aulani couldn't make out any further noises or movement. Deciding it was an echo from the plaza below she moved on.

Aulani reached the landing on the stairs the same time Thane did.

"You didn't have to come up the stairs, Thane. You could have waited for me at the bottom," she smiled at her handsome husband.

Thane wrapped his arms around her and pulled her close, "I couldn't stand to wait that long to see you."

Aulani's smile grew larger, "Thanks for caring. I needed that."

"I know," Thane gently released her from his hug. With one arm around her, he guided her down the stairs, "Besides, you're easy to love. You've got the hard job."

Aulani twisted to look him in the eye, "What do you mean by that?"

"You have to admit loving me isn't the easiest job you've ever had. I'm a little hard to put up with," Thane grinned at her, "I admire you for trying though."

Aulani gave him an odd look until they reached the bottom of the stairs. The second they came off the last step, she stepped in front of him, staring hard into his eyes.

She firmly stated, "Thane, you're no harder to love than I am. Don't ever say such a thing again. I chose to love you because you're worth it. Don't insult my choices."

Thane looked off to one side for a moment as he considered her admonition. Seeing the seriousness in her face, he decided to explain his comment honestly.

"I'm sorry, I didn't mean to insult you at all. I was trying to lighten the mood. I can honestly say that I'm amazed that you chose me, despite my childish flaws, but I am SO glad you did. I love you more than anything. I knew you were worried about your family and I wanted to offer a small distraction and bring a smile to your face. You forgive me?"

Aulani smiled kindly, "Yes, I forgive you."

Thane leaned forward to kiss her. His even-tempered wife pulled back and turned her head.

Thane grimaced, "Oh, very funny."

Aulani moved around him so she could see up the stairs.

"I'm sorry, Thane. I keep hearing noises. I thought I heard somebody whispering."

Thane turned abruptly to see if he could hear or see anything. The only noises he could hear were distant conversations of cleaning crews and restaurant staff as they closed up and headed home. Nothing got his attention, but the potential for trouble worried him.

"Let's get back to the ship."

Aulani was wearing a scarf to avoid being recognized. She pulled the scarf tighter around her head. The two hastened across the plaza toward the elevator. They kept their heads down and glanced behind them frequently.

Thane glanced behind them again, "Aulani, I think we're being followed. I'm not sure we should go to the ship. Let's head to the surface."

The two ducked into an elevator and sent the vehicle upward. While the elevator climbed, Thane took a moment to notify the Captain of their situation.

****

David wanted nothing more than to grab a weapon and take off after his distressed crewmen. He knew they were right to avoid leading whoever was after them to the ship. Their task on Zulimar was more important than two individuals.

David acknowledged the information, "Keep your comms on. I will consult with the others and feed you information as quickly as I can get it."

"Understood, Captain," Thane replied rapidly.

"C'mon Aulani, let's get moving before the next elevator reaches us."

The two headed through a corridor toward the outside.

****

David summoned Brynna, Braxton, and Jake into his office and contacted Neal Rune. The group reached the office as Mr. Rune's face appeared on the large office screen.

"Mr. Rune, two of my people may be in trouble. They think they're being followed. They didn't want to lead anybody here, so they're headed for the surface. Do you have any place they could lay low for a while?"

Neal squinted his eyes for a second. He was already in bed asleep and wasn't thinking clearly, "Uh… give me… uh… just a sec… okay, got it! There's a hangar that's closed for repair on the surface. The caretaker has a bunk in there. It's nothing fancy, but it's empty and fairly secure. Their access codes can get them in, and it can't be traced back to you, me, or the Dreans. It's hanger bay three."

"Thanks, Neal. I'll pass that information on. I guess we owe you another one," David answered quickly.

"No problem. It doesn't really compare to what we owe you. Call me if you need anything else."

Neal knew the Captain wanted to move on and tend to his people. He was hoping he would get a chance to talk to the Captain in greater detail about his experiences with Pateras and the Intercessor. Right now wasn't the time to express his exuberance over meeting someone who had been in the actual presence of Pateras.

****

Capt. David Alexander hailed Thane and told him where to go but advised him to lose whoever was tailing him first. Thane acknowledged and headed in a new direction.

The Captain discussed the matter with his staff. Despite their desire to go to Thane and Aulani's aid, they agreed to monitor them for now. Even Jake agreed.

****

The Ryders headed toward the beachfront through a dense section of tropical flora. Thane pulled his weapon and nodded quietly for Aulani to do the same. The two of them split up. Thane moved off to the side and took cover while Aulani took a wider more obvious path to draw out their pursuer.

Using herself as bait, Aulani stepped into the bright moonlight. A familiar voice cried out, "Lani!" The woman screamed when Thane grabbed her. He shoved her against a tree and aimed his weapon at her. Aulani recognized the voice and the scream. She bolted back to Thane's position. Thane was already slamming the young woman with a barrage of questions.

"Who are you? Why are you following us? Who's with you?" He demanded.

Aulani peered over Thane's shoulder, "Kina?"

Thane backed off when he heard the name, "Kina? As in, your sister, Kina?"

Aulani's family had been too far away to come to their wedding. The two had a brief and businesslike ceremony. Thane told his family after they were married. His mother was not amused. The couple were only married for a couple of months before their mission began. Aulani had met Thane's family briefly, but Thane had never met Aulani's.

Thane lowered his weapon and released his grip on the young woman. Kina fell into Aulani's arms and cried. She had

59

spent the last two months running for her life, fearing for her sister's life and not understanding why. Aulani comforted her sister for a moment while Thane made a quick circle to be sure no one else was following them. By the time he returned, Kina was calm again.

Aulani turned to introduce the two, "Thane, this is my sister Iokina Malo. Kina, this is my husband, Thane Ryder."

Thane slid his weapon into his holster and offered his hand to Kina.

"I'm glad to finally meet you. I'm sorry it was under such difficult circumstances."

Kina hesitated before agreeing to shake his hand. Her parents were convinced that whatever they were suffering had to be Thane's fault even though they scarcely knew what sort of trouble had befallen them. Kina shook his hand but stared at him coldly.

Sensing her discomfort, Thane tried to smooth things over quickly.

"I'm sorry if I was rough on you. I didn't know who was following us. We've been on the run and watching our backs for months. Please, forgive me."

Kina nodded a small semblance of forgiveness.

"Lani, what's going on? Why are there people after us and after you?"

Before Aulani could answer, Thane interrupted, "We need to get out of sight."

Aulani grabbed her sister's hand and followed Thane at a brisk pace toward hangar bay three. Once inside the bay, Thane gave the sisters a few minutes alone while he scanned the perimeter for anyone following them.

"Kina, where are Papa and Mama?" Aulani asked.

"I left them on the mezzanine. Mama saw me go after you. She was afraid to follow you. I have to get back to her. She'll be scared to death."

Kina wiped a stray tear from her eye, "Aulani, what is happening to us? Who are the people chasing us?"

Aulani sighed and took her sister's hands in her own, "Kina, what did the man who brought you here tell you?"

"Not much. He said it was best if he told us very little until he could get us to safety. He said his people owed you and your crew a great debt, and saving us from the people trying to harm us was a small payment for what they owed you. He told us because of that debt, you and your crew were now being hunted down," Kina stopped and waited for whatever Aulani was about to share.

"Our mission was to search out the strongholds of a new Commonwealth enemy known as Pateras. This next part is going to be hard to accept," Aulani explained.

"I've never heard of Pateras," Kina denied.

"Just keep in mind Supreme Executor Luciano Hale sent us on this mission," Aulani knew the truth would be hard to swallow.

Kina did little more than scowl.

"Pateras is a… supreme alien being. He –"

"Wait, what? There's no such thing. Do you mean he's genetically engineered?" Iokina's education was in human microbiological tech. She was no expert in human genetics because her specialty was nanites.

"No, that isn't what I mean at all. Pateras… isn't… human," Aulani proceeded cautiously.

Kina laughed outright, "Lani, what is wrong with you? You outgrew fairy tales a long time ago. Have you lost your mind completely? You've gone space happy."

Aulani squeezed Kina's hands more tightly to impress the importance of her words.

"No, Kina, I have not lost my mind. I've met his son, Arni. I haven't seen his father myself, but I've seen what Arni and his father are capable of. They can manipulate matter on a cellular level. I've seen them bring the dead back to life. I've seen them heal both minor and major injuries with nothing more than a thought or a gentle touch. I've only known Arni a few months, but the things I've seen him do are amazing."

Thane approached the two women cautiously, not wanting to disturb their conversation.

"I don't get it. If you discovered a sentient alien life form, it would be the find of the century. Why would anyone be after you for discovering an alien life form?" Kina pulled away from Aulani, pacing restlessly.

Aulani wasn't quite sure how to explain their situation.

Thane stepped in to try and help, "Kina, Supreme Executor Hale already knew they existed. He sent us to find human populations who were loyal to Pateras so he could wipe them out. Luciano Hale is the self-declared enemy of Pateras."

Kina scowled at Thane, "My parents were right. This is your fault they're after Lani and my family. None of this would ever have happened if you hadn't married my sister."

Thane was taken aback by her brutal honesty. He stared at her with his mouth hanging open.

Aulani jumped up, "Kina! This is my fault, not Thane's. I committed treason! I chose to do it myself! He didn't talk me into it. You want to blame somebody, blame me or blame Executor Hale, not Thane!"

Kina glared at both of them.

Thane finally stepped forward and spoke softly, "Kina, the first world we went to on this mission was populated with good, peaceful people. I made friends with a little boy there. He was bright and eager to learn. I taught him how to make gliders and kites. A couple of months later we discovered he and his little sister, his parents, his neighbors, and every single man, woman, and child on that planet were destroyed by the Commonwealth."

Thane turned away as the thought of the children he and Aulani befriended weighed him down.

Knowing his pain, Aulani went to him and placed her hand gently on his back. Thane turned and wrapped his arms around her. The two said nothing.

Kina continued to scowl, "But if they were enemies of the Commonwealth…"

Aulani whipped around angrily, "We offered them membership in the Commonwealth. They agreed. We established an alliance with them. The alliance was contingent on them giving us whatever information they had about Pateras. They did everything we asked of them and more. Do you *really* think a ten-year-old boy or his four-year-old sister were enemies of the Commonwealth and deserving of a death sentence?"

Kina looked at the ground, "I don't understand."

Thane and Aulani looked at each other wondering how much more to tell Kina.

Kina saw their nonverbal debate, "What? What aren't you saying?"

Thane stepped closer to her.

"Supreme Executor Hale has a history with Pateras. He wants to do whatever he can to hurt him. He knows he doesn't have the power to destroy him, so he's hurting him the only way he can. Pateras El Liontari cares very much for humanity. Executor Hale is trying to destroy any human being loyal to him. We are loyal to Pateras. Executor Hale is using you to try to get to us."

"So, change your loyalty back to the Commonwealth. We can get back to normal," Kina pleaded.

Aulani shook her head at Kina's pedantic suggestion, "It's not that simple. Who's going to accept a traitor so easily? Even if we wanted to, it's too late. Executor Hale will execute us regardless, and probably any of our family members to be certain knowledge of Pateras doesn't spread. If he catches you, he'll interrogate you, torture you, and finally, he will execute you, and Papa, and Mama."

Kina looked as though she were about to be sick.

"Why did you abandon the Commonwealth for a stranger?"

Aulani knew she was unraveling everything her sister believed. It was clear Kina was having trouble processing it all.

"Because Pateras cares about me, and all of humanity. Executor Hale doesn't. He was the one who authorized the destruction of the world we mentioned earlier."

Kina wrinkled her brow, "Why haven't we heard anything on the news about the destruction of this world?"

Thane looked at her sorrowfully, "It was a Level Two on the developmental scale. No one knew anything about it, and no one will miss it."

The young woman was shaken.

"I—I don't understand. This doesn't make sense. These things just don't happen."

Her knees suddenly feeling weak, Kina sank into an office chair. Her posture denoted one who sought to protect herself from the assault on her sense of justice. As her head cleared, she looked up.

"I need to get back to Mama and Papa. They're bound to be terrified by now. I've been gone too long."

Aulani glanced nervously at Thane, "Kina, we can't go with you. You have to go back alone."

"Lani, you have to come with me. Papa and Mama have been worried sick about you. Mr. Bennett, the man who brought us here, said he was taking us someplace safe. You can come with us. You'd be safe there," Kina pleaded.

"Kina, if the wrong people see us together, it would put a lot of people in danger. I know where Mr. Bennett is taking you. It's only safe as long as we stay away. If they find out so many of us are there, they'll send ships to destroy the whole planet just to get to us," Aulani explained gently yet firmly.

"How do you know where we're going? Mr. Bennett hasn't even told us. He says it's safer if we don't know," Kina was still shaky. She took a deep cleansing breath to try and pull herself together sensing she was going to be moving again soon.

"Kina, I can't tell you that either. Go back to Mama and Papa. Tell them it was a mistake, that it wasn't me you saw. When you get to safety, then you can tell them. Tell them… tell them I am a willing follower of Pateras. Let them know I love and miss them. I'm doing the right thing, and I don't regret it. I hope they aren't disappointed in me, but this is the way I want it. Don't say anything until you're safe. The less they know, the better. They can *not* come looking for me. They have to get to safety."

Kina watched Aulani's face as she spoke. The urgency faded into a strange calm and even some form of pleasure. Kina knew Aulani had said everything she intended. She stood to go. Kina hugged her sister tightly whispering admonitions to keep herself safe and affirmed her love for her sister.

Thane held Iokina back from leaving until he checked in with the ship. Jake was tapped into the mining colony's security feed as promised by Mr. Rune. He was watching the feed for any unusual activity throughout the colony.

Nothing stood out, so Capt. Alexander gave Thane the go-ahead to send Iokina back to her family. He gave Thane one more message to pass on.

"Lt. Ryder, have Miss Malo let Mr. Bennett know, Neal Rune's been informed of their presence on the colony, and he's expecting them."

Thane and Aulani sent Kina out alone and followed her from a discreet distance. The couple waited before entering to avoid being associated with her. Thane's short-range scans revealed no unusual movement. He kept his comm link to the ship open so that the Captain could warn him of anything further out.

As they waited for Kina to get clear of the entrance, Jake sang out in Thane and Aulani's earpiece, "There's six bogeys moving with a purpose toward your location on the opposite side of the upper-level mezzanine."

Thane jerked his sidearm out of its holster.

"Are they headed for Kina or us?"

"I can't tell yet. Split up, and we can see who they follow," Jake spat quickly.

Without waiting for orders, Aulani grabbed her weapon and bolted toward her sister's location.

Thane yelled after her, "AULANI! NO!"

Thane updated Jake as he took off after his wife, "Chief, Aulani's gone after Kina. I'm heading in too."

The Captain was monitoring the situation with Chief Holden. His voice took Jake's place in Thane's ear.

"Acknowledged, Lieutenant. The Chief and I are in route. The Chief is right. Split up and head for the center of the Plaza's upper level."

****

Brynna and Braxton took over monitoring the internal security feed. David worried as he and Jake ran toward their fellow crew members. They were too far away to affect the outcome.

Aulani caught Kina and pulled her roughly down a side hallway. The three changed directions.

Brynna quickly updated everyone involved, "Lieutenant Ryder, I believe they are tracking one of you. They just altered their course to match your new route."

David tapped his bracelet and reinforced his previous command to split up and head for the center of the plaza. His instructions reached Thane and Aulani as they neared an elevator. Thane stopped short. He ordered Aulani to backtrack to the previous elevator and Kina to take the one right in front of them. He informed the two women he would proceed to the next one a couple hundred yards down the mezzanine.

Aulani stubbornly refused, "I'm not leaving Kina unprotected."

Thane quickly got frustrated, "Aulani, we aren't leaving her unprotected. If we stay together, we could be leading them straight to her. We don't know if they're tracking her or us."

"But we can't…" She protested again.

"Ensign! You have your orders," Thane returned sternly.

The hurt look on Aulani's face said more than Thane cared to think about. Softening his tone, he added, "Aulani, Pateras is in control and greater than us. Leave it in his hands."

Aulani glanced at Kina. Before she could react, Jake's voice came through her earpiece, "Aulani, he got you out of prison, he can take care of her. Trust him to handle it."

Security Chief Jake Holden, a staunch believer in following every regulation to a fault, the same man who had betrayed them to the Commonwealth, was now advising her to trust the one he had adamantly opposed.

Kina saw something change in Aulani's face. The fear and worry melted away leaving that same calm look she witnessed a few minutes ago in the empty hangar.

Aulani nodded, "Do as he says. You'll be fine. We have more help on the way, but we need to get closer to them."

Kina grabbed onto Aulani's arm, "Lani, I'm scared."

Aulani glanced at Thane. She smiled weakly at him, "Trust me."

Aulani stepped onto the elevator with Kina and spoke to the elevator's voice-activated terminal, "Upper-level plaza."

The elevator repeated the destination back to her, and a light on the display panel illuminated indicating their intended destination. Aulani blurted out, "Do not come back up. You'll be fine."

Before Kina could comprehend what was happening Aulani jumped off the elevator as the doors closed trapping Kina inside. Kina slammed the softer bottom side of her fist against the elevator door.

"Lani! No!"

The elevator descended to its destination.

Aulani raced to her assigned elevator and Thane ran for his own. The men converged from two directions on the elevator Kina was using. One stayed behind in case their target returned to the upper levels via the same elevator. The others ran for another elevator.

Kina's elevator opened to the plaza. Kina instructed the elevator to take her back up. The elevator politely declined her request stating her request as being an invalid destination. She made several other varied attempts, but the computer refused to comply.

A new voice came through the speaker, "Iokina Malo, I am Lt. Cmdr. Braxton Flint. I am a friend of your sister. You need to head to the center of the plaza and wait for our rescue team in the garden area. They'll help you, but you need to close the gap between yourself and them. Go. Thane and Aulani are headed there too."

Kina finally gathered enough nerve to head into the plaza. She kept watching behind her for whoever might be after her. She spent so much time watching behind she plowed straight into someone and screamed.

****

The man she ran into grabbed her forcefully and quickly covered her mouth with his hand. Instinctively Kina tried to break free of his grip to no avail. The man gripped her more tightly and pulled her into a secluded area. When Kina continued fighting, the man whispered to her, "Kina, stop fighting me. It's Samuel."

Samuel felt her relax. He slowly pulled his hand from her mouth and turned her to face him.

"What's going on out there? Where have you been, and who's after you?"

The young woman was too frightened and breathless to answer. Samuel kept glancing behind her for signs of anyone following her. Samuel shook her gently, "Kina, who are you running from? I have to know. Tell me what's going on."

Samuel heard footsteps and voices. He grabbed Kina, pulled her into the shadows, and covered her mouth again.

A man and woman came from opposite directions. The two carried weapons. The woman looked frustrated.

"Where did she go?"

The man shook his head.

"I don't know. You go left, and I'll go right and head further in. Maybe one of the others has found her."

Samuel raised his weapon to fire at the couple. Kina fought to stop him, pushing his arm away so that he couldn't get a clear shot. The man lowered his weapon and relaxed his grip, "What was that about?"

Kina's eyes teared up, "That's my sister and her husband."

Samuel's eyes widened, "They're part of the crew of the *Evangeline*? Thank you, Intercessor," Samuel looked upward and spoke into the empty air.

Kina gave him a puzzled look. Samuel opened his hand slightly to reveal the lethal setting on his weapon.

He quietly whispered, "If you hadn't stopped me, I might have killed the Intercessor's messengers. Are they looking for you? Do they know you're here?"

Kina nodded, "They gave me a message for you. They said Mr. Rune knows you're here and he's expecting you. They also said someone was tracking us. They don't know who or which one of us is being tracked."

****

Thane stopped and took cover in the arboretum in the center of the plaza. He quietly asked Brynna for an update.

"Commander, we've lost Kina. Do you have her location?"

"She's about a hundred yards behind you between two small structures, but she's not alone. I'm tracking via infrared scans. Those bogeys are converging on her location. She must be the one they're tracking. Sending the layout to your display now," Brynna quickly advised, "Lt. Ryder, the Captain is closing on your location. Don't move in until he can back you up."

Aulani looked like she was ready to tear through every structure in the plaza with her bare hands. Thane prudently sent her to circle behind the men pursuing her sister. He reasoned she wouldn't move in until she got into an appropriate attack position. The position he assigned her was the furthest away and would take the longest time to reach. Thane moved cautiously into a similar opposing position behind the men. The Captain and Security Chief watched their bracelets to monitor the progress of Thane and Aulani.

The men moved stealthily into positions around the narrow service pathway Kina and Samuel were hiding in. Samuel switched his weapon to a lower setting. He grabbed Kina's arm with one hand and held his weapon in a defensive position with the other. He edged forward watching and listening for movement.

A great deal of the lighting in the plaza was from a glass dome at the top of the structure. The only light gleaned from the dome at present was from two small moons. Footpath lights illuminated the walkways, and dim lights from the corridors along the upper floors shed small amounts of light. A couple of hours earlier there were lights from shops and restaurants flooding the area, but those were now extinguished.

Seeing and hearing nothing, Samuel pulled Kina behind him and headed toward the arboretum. They covered only about ten feet when the five men surrounded them brandishing weapons.

The ringleader of the group was a mere arms-length from Samuel. Each man aimed their weapon at the other.

Neither one flinched. The leader firmly ordered, "Drop your weapon, and nobody will get hurt."

Samuel didn't budge. He kept Kina directly behind him.

"Do you really think I'm going to give up my advantage?"

The man blinked. Samuel smiled. He had planted a seed of doubt and suspicion. His smile only served to plant the seed a little deeper. Knowing what he did about Commonwealth soldiers or soldiers of any kind, Samuel knew he only needed to stall for a few minutes until reinforcements came. Even though he had never met Capt. Alexander, the man had a reputation for survival. It was a reputation made possible only by the Intercessor, Arni Liontari, but a well-deserved one.

Samuel took advantage of his adversary's doubt, "What do you want?"

The man's eyes narrowed, "I want the girl and her parents. You are free to walk away if you give me those three."

"Why?" Samuel demanded. A movement in the background caught his attention. Being a properly trained soldier, he didn't shift his focus despite his urge to look.

The man was quickly growing impatient, "That's not your concern. Look, you're outnumbered five to one. I'll even let you keep your weapon, just put it away and give me the woman. Tell my men where to find the other two, and you can walk away unharmed. If you don't, I'll take my chances and have one of my men shoot you. The choice is yours."

Samuel kept the weapon trained on the leader but pulled his arm slowly down.

"Her parents are two levels up in an empty office. It's office number B224."

Samuel pulled Kina in front of him and wrapped his arm around her waist.

"I'm sorry, Kina."

"Samuel, what are you doing? Please don't do this," Kina trembled.

The leader nodded at two of his men who headed toward an elevator. The leader held out his free hand.

"Hand her over to me then you're free to leave."

In a flash, Samuel shoved Kina under a nearby table and threw his body on top of her to protect her. David and his crew fired at the remaining three men.

The ringleader managed to avoid the first barrage of Tri-EMP pellets but dropped his weapon in the process. His anger at being played flared. Grabbing a knife from his belt, he rolled toward Samuel and Kina. The man had been paid to capture Kina and her parents alive and well. He knew he didn't dare harm Kina, but his instructions were unclear about anyone else involved. He wasn't about to leave any witnesses. Samuel checked to see if the coast was clear yet. He raised his head in time to see the knife coming at him. He blocked the blade's original trajectory, but the knife still sliced into his side. He fell away from Kina. As he rolled to the ground, he raised the weapon in his other hand and fired. The ringleader convulsed and collapsed onto the ground.

Hearing the commotion, the other two men returned to find themselves surrounded and promptly captured. The last man to join the party was the one left up top making certain Kina's elevator didn't return. Seeing his comrade's predicament, he chose not to resist.

David informed Brynna of their situation, "Commander notify Mr. Rune we have six prisoners that need attending to and one medical emergency."

Jake, Thane, and Aulani guarded the prisoners while David and Kina moved to help Samuel. None of them were carrying emergency medkits. Aulani yanked her scarf off and tossed it to Kina to help stop Samuel from bleeding.

Samuel was going into shock but forced himself to focus on Capt. Alexander. His hands were shaking. He broke out in a cold sweat and became nauseated. He knew he needed to make sure the Captain knew where Kina's parents were hiding, just in case.

"C-Captain Alex-xander… Kina's p—parents… level A… 224. They're terrified. You—You have to g-get to them. G—Get them to Drea."

Several security guards raced into the area and arrested the prisoners. The officer in charge identified himself to David as Constable Hinson.

"Constable, we need to get this man to an infirmary, right away."

The Constable scowled, "Our infirmary isn't meant to handle injuries of this nature. We'll have to airlift him out to a facility, several hundred miles from here. I have a portable medkit with me, but our infirmary does little more than patch small abrasions, and it isn't even open right now. It would take a few minutes to get the doc in there, and the clinic open."

Aulani started to ask the Captain if they could take Samuel back to their ship. She was prepared with several arguments. She needn't have bothered.

"Chief, Ensign, take the young woman to retrieve her family and bring them to the ship. Lieutenant help me get this gentleman to our med bay," David was careful not to call names or establish clear relationships. He wasn't sure how safe they were in the hands of these security officers.

Constable Hinson pulled out the medkit and a portable stretcher. David quickly treated the man's injuries long enough to stabilize him for transport and placed a warming blanket on him.

Constable Hinson leaned closer to David and softly whispered, "These two men can help you back to your ship. They've come a long way to be here and know the Intercessor well."

David thanked the Constable. The four men rushed the injured man to the ship.

Jason and Laura were standing by when they arrived. The two quickly got to work repairing the man's injury.

David stopped by his quarters to clean himself up before returning to the bridge.

"What's the status of Ensign Ryder and her family?"

Brynna frowned, "They are finally on their way here, but it took some convincing to get the Ensign's parents to come. They were not happy about this situation."

David nodded his understanding, "Escort them to the guest quarters when they arrive. Send Thane down as soon as he's available," He left his command chair and went to the guest quarters to prepare for their arrival.

Entering the quarters, David started a pot of coffee and pulled out a pitcher of ice water. Thane joined him momentarily. Knowing he didn't have much time, the Captain blasted Thane with questions.

"Lieutenant, when your wife's family gets here, I need to know what I'm dealing with. What do they know about this situation? How well are they taking it and what am I walking into?"

Thane stood in an "at ease" posture and reported off to the Captain even though he hadn't been formally addressed.

"Captain, Ensign Ryder's family is aware of very little. They know they were in danger. They don't know where Mr. Bennett was taking them. They are blaming me for leading Aulani astray, and Kina was having trouble believing Executor Hale destroyed Galat. They will not be receptive to anything you tell them. Oh, and Captain, I've never met Aulani's parents."

David stared at Thane a moment, "I see."

David tapped his comm unit, "Lt. Flint, report to guest quarters immediately."

Lexi was already in bed asleep when Capt. Alexander called. It took her a minute to understand what he was saying. She washed her face to clear the cobwebs in her mind and dressed. It was a silly thing to wonder, but she wasn't sure what to wear. The Captain had ordered them to dress in civilian attire in public, but this didn't sound public. She decided to wear her casual uniform. She entered the guest quarters behind Ensign Ryder's family and Jake.

CH 5 - ZULIMAR

PAPA AND MAMA MALO

The living room area of the guest quarters was crowded with hateful glares and nervous tics. Jake assumed an overbearing stance, blocking the exit. Aulani's mother was clinging to Aulani. Kina stood at her father's elbow, afraid he would react badly. Thane moved nervously from one place to another. This was not the way he wanted to meet his in-laws for the first time. He grabbed a cup of coffee for himself, wandered over to Lexi and offered to get her a cup, trying to look busy.

David was the only one who seemed relaxed. He was leaning against the wall near the coffee pot. He sipped on his cup of coffee and waited for an awkward silence before standing upright and approaching the huddled family.

"Chief Holden, you're dismissed."

Jake hesitated, then smartly replied, "Yes Captain."

He didn't always think the Captain was right in his approach, but his actions proved to be the correct ones, more times than not. Jake thought his presence would impart a sense of control onto their guests through a minor amount of intimidation, given they were belligerent upon meeting him and Aulani earlier. Jake promptly turned and left as Capt. Alexander moved his freshly prepared refreshments onto the coffee table.

"Would anyone care for some coffee or water?" David offered and set the tray of liquids down.

Aulani's father moved directly into David's face and ranted in his native language.

David glanced at Aulani. "Ensign, perhaps you would care to make some introductions."

David and the crew normally spoke in Intergalactic Standard. It was taught in all schools under Commonwealth jurisdiction. David knew Aulani's father was familiar with I.S. even if he wasn't overly comfortable with it.

"Yes Captain. Papa, this is Capt. Alexander. Captain, this is my father, Inoke Malo. This is my mother, Maleah Malo and my sister, Iokina."

Inoke Malo didn't back down, nor acknowledge the introduction. David continued to sip his coffee casually, but didn't back away. He glanced at Thane and Lexi. Aulani recognized her cue to introduce the others as well.

"Papa, Mama, this is Lt. Lexi Flint, our ship's psychologist, and this is my husband, Thane."

David waved the two forward. Lexi moved more comfortably than Thane. She didn't attempt to come between Inoke and David, but greeted the man warmly.

"Mr. Malo, it's a pleasure to meet you. Aulani speaks highly of you, your wife, and daughter. She is a strong woman and a fine officer. Does she get those traits from you?"

The stare was broken for at least a second as Inoke glanced at Lexi. His gaze vacillated between David and Lexi. As soon as his gaze turned away from David, the Captain sat in a chair. He invited the others to sit down as well.

Kina and Maleah took their cues from Inoke. Inoke stubbornly refused, "I will not sit down until I get some answers."

David leaned forward. "I will gladly answer your questions, Mr. Malo, but this conversation may take a little while to finish. You are quite welcome to continue standing if that's what you want. I would think a man on the run would rest when he got the chance. Do you need something to eat? Our food isn't the greatest, but it fills the belly and meets nutritional guidelines. Perhaps your wife and daughter would like to sit down?"

Inoke looked into the tired, frightened faces of his wife and youngest daughter. They looked so weary. Glancing at Aulani's pleading face, he decided to give in on this one point. If they were going to argue every point, it was going to be a really long night. Inoke nodded to his wife and daughter. The three sat on the sofa. Inoke's posture remained belligerent, despite his seated position.

Lexi sat in the chair at the opposite end of the couch. Thane pulled two smaller chairs from the opposite side of the room over for himself and Aulani.

David leaned forward. "What would you like to know first, Mr. Malo?"

"What have you done to my daughter, and why have you endangered my family? Why are we running for our lives, and how can we return to normal?" He fired his questions in rapid and demanding succession.

David got right to the point.

"I've done nothing to your daughter. She chose this path of her own free will. After we're done here, Lexi and I will leave, and you can discuss it with her if you wish, but I have not even remotely pushed her into this. I volunteered to leave the ship when I made this decision. I offered the crew the opportunity to leave at any time. She's free to go if she wishes. I won't stop her."

David paused before moving on to the second question.

"I apologize for placing your family in danger, although that wasn't entirely my fault. One of my crew betrayed us to the Commonwealth. Our escape is what put your family in danger. The messages my Security Chief and Ensign Ryder sent were intended to warn you and get you to safety. I'm told by Mr. Bennett's superiors you didn't take that warning to heart and get yourselves to safety."

David let the implication that Inoke was guilty of placing his family in danger sink in. He wasn't prepared to say it outright.

"This leads me to your next question. Your lives are in danger because Supreme Executor Luciano Hale is willing to use whoever he can to stop us. He tried to use my family against me, and he won't hesitate to use you against Aulani and ultimately me."

Inoke blinked heavily. "We are loyal Commonwealth citizens. We've done nothing wrong. You're the one who should be held accountable. I should contact the nearest military base and tell them where you are."

David remained casual in his posture. He couldn't allow Inoke to do that, but didn't want to appear threatening at all.

"You could do that, but you should know the consequences of your actions before you do."

Kina glanced at Aulani who evaded her look. "Capt. Alexander, are you threatening us?"

David set his cup of coffee forcefully on the coffee table.

"I am not the one you need to be worried about. I have business to conduct here on Zulimar, and I can't allow you to interfere with that, but after it's concluded you're free to do whatever you like. If we're captured, they will attempt to get us to betray Pateras. They will interrogate us, and they will torture us again."

"Again?" Maleah spoke for the first time and glanced at Aulani.

Aulani twisted in her chair as she tried to escape the memories running through her mind. Catching her mother's eye, her look told Maleah more than she wanted to know.

David watched Maleah to see if she had further questions. He decided she wasn't ready to ask whatever was on her mind. "Our mission, assigned by the Commonwealth, was to find the strongholds of Pateras and report them. The worlds we were looking at were non-spacefaring worlds. We did our jobs. We found a peaceful planet called Galat. The people were friendly and welcomed us warmly. They provided for what few needs we had. We helped them make some technological improvements in areas of farming, architecture, education, and self-defense. They agreed to be loyal to the Commonwealth and told us everything they knew about Pateras, which was plenty. As soon as we realized it was a major colony of Pateras, we left and reported it. A few months later, we discovered the entire population was destroyed by the Pacification Fleet, on the direct orders of Luciano Hale. Not one single person was left alive except the one person capable of leaving the planet at will."

Aulani scooted forward in her chair.

"Papa, I can't support such actions. It happened to other planets too. Children we taught and played with were killed for no reason other than they loved Pateras and his son Arni."

Inoke blustered, "Surely there was a way to handle this through legal channels."

David shook his head. "I tried that. I took it to Adm. Deacons, who told me the Admiral's board sanctioned the action."

"What about the Commonwealth Advisory Council? You could have taken your case to them," Inoke argued.

"Please tell me which world you think would stand alone against the Supreme Executor and the entire Commonwealth galaxy? If word got out that planets were destroyed for being Commonwealth enemies, who would want to risk their own planet?" David countered the man's argument.

"One other point on your third question, I told you Executor Hale wouldn't hesitate to use you against us. What I said is true. I had an aunt many years ago. I never met her. Her name was Abigail. She and my grandfather's family were taken from a planet that was not a part of the Commonwealth. The Commonwealth wanted my grandparents to work on highly sensitive propulsion projects. My family served Pateras and refused at first. My aunt was twelve years old. She was murdered in front of her parents and her siblings to force my grandparent's cooperation."

Maleah turned pale and gasped, "Pakelo!"

Inoke glared angrily at his wife. There was a reason they spoke their native language more easily than Intergalactic Standard.

"I told you never to speak of him!" Inoke angrily addressed his wife in their native language.

Aulani looked confused, "Who's Pakelo?"

Maleah refused to submit to her husband's demand.

"Pakelo was your older brother."

Aulani scowled, "My brother was Palani. He died in the line of duty serving the Commonwealth three years ago."

"Pakelo was older than Palani. Your father was a very influential young politician. When the Commonwealth approached us to join them, they encouraged your father to support the proposition. He opposed it. Pakelo was five years old," Maleah continued sorrowfully.

Inoke again ordered her to stop speaking, only this time his order sounded more like a desperate plea. "Maleah, you must stop this!"

Tears ran down her face. "No, I'm tired of not being able to say his name and remember my firstborn son. He deserves to be remembered!"

"Pakelo got sick, very sick. It happened suddenly. We were at his bedside when he passed. Two men met us outside his hospital room. They expressed their sympathies to us then suggested such a tragedy could have been prevented if we had been members of the Commonwealth."

The longer Maleah spoke, the angrier Aulani became.

"I remember that day as though it were yesterday. Aulani, your father was carrying Palani, and I was holding you. You were just a baby. One of the men stroked your head and said, 'I would hate for any of your other children to get sick.' I was terrified for you. Your father demanded a comprehensive autopsy for Pakelo. Pakelo had a disease no one had ever seen before."

Inoke bowed his head sorrowfully, "I later learned the disease came from off-world. It was brought by the Commonwealth. It was a genetically engineered virus. You can't contract this disease by casual exposure. It has to be actively introduced into the bloodstream. My son was murdered," he spat angrily.

Maleah looked stricken, "You never told me that Inoke. Why have you never said anything about this?"

"I didn't want to cause you any more pain, and I didn't want you to hate me for what happened to our son," Inoke confessed.

Maleah cried outright. She grabbed onto her husband's hand. Words escaped her, but she needed him to know she didn't blame him for what happened to their firstborn son. Inoke wrapped his arm around her. Kina leaned in to comfort her mother.

Aulani sat out of reach and in shock. She had never known she had another brother. Thane leaned closer to her to offer her comfort.

Lexi spoke softly to Capt. Alexander, "Captain, this is a lot to put on them, but I think they're ready to hear the rest."

Inoke shook off his sorrow and looked at the Captain.

"Hear the rest of what?" His tone was less demanding this time.

David nodded to Lexi to explain. He needed Mr. Malo to understand the entire crew was together in their understanding and beliefs.

Lexi took a sip of her coffee before launching into her unbelievable explanation.

"You need to know who Pateras and Luciano Hale really are. This is going to be hard to believe, but neither one is human. They are superior alien life forms. Before you ask, we know this to be absolutely true. We've seen demonstrations of their power, and the Captain and the Security Chief have seen Luciano Hale change physical forms. We have some proof if you need to see it, but not as much proof as we would like."

Having come from a newly space-faring race, the Malos were more prepared for such a possibility and less conditioned by the Commonwealth.

"We've never seen aliens. Why haven't we heard about this?" Inoke asked calmly.

David picked up Lexi's explanation.

"You haven't been told because Executor Hale doesn't want anyone to know who or what he is. Commonwealth worlds are indoctrinated to believe that humans are the only sentient life forms. He doesn't want anyone suspecting or believing anything else is out there."

Kina asked, "But why? What does it matter?"

Aulani answered, "Luciano Hale doesn't want anyone to believe such a being as Pateras exists. Pateras cares about us and what happens to us. Luciano doesn't. Luciano Hale wants to hurt Pateras any way he can. He isn't powerful enough to cause Pateras any actual harm, so he's getting back at him the only way he can, by hurting us."

Inoke was having trouble understanding the struggle.

"Why involve us in any of this? If Executor Hale has a grudge against this Pateras, why involve us?"

Knowing it was time for him to step back and let his crew gain some confidence, David deferred to his subordinates. They looked at each other and to their leader, expecting him to fill in the blanks. David held his hand out, motioning them to go ahead.

Thane had kept quiet, knowing his in-laws didn't care much for him. He chose this point to assert himself.

"Pateras is the creator of everything. He created us. He also created Luciano Hale. Luciano Hale rejected Pateras. Now they are at war with each other. Nothing evil can stand in the presence of Pateras. Luciano Hale is pure evil. He tried to kill us, on more than one occasion. If he finds us, he will kill us. We remind Luciano Hale of what he's lost. He hates the fact that Pateras cares about us."

Inoke looked confused. "You are speaking of a deity. The Commonwealth has forbidden such beliefs. I have never been interested in such things, so it was not a problem for me to give them up. Aulani, you were raised without any knowledge of these ideas. How can you embrace such fantasies?"

Aulani spoke boldly, "I met the son of Pateras. His name is Arni. Arni saved our lives. I've seen him heal the sick and injured. He brought the dead to life. He gave his life to save ours and Pateras restored his life. It's hard to explain, but he means more to me than anything else. I have a purpose now."

"You've grown weak and following a religious cult for the weak-minded. This man has caused you to lose your mind," Inoke bellowed as he gestured at Thane.

"No, Papa," Aulani responded calmly, "I chose to follow Pateras before Thane did. I've seen Arni break the laws of nature. He rescued us from the prison on Romajin. He restored the Captain's life, he restored Marissa's life, and made it possible for her to have a baby. I have seen so many amazing things. This entire crew should be dead several times over, but because of Arni, we're alive, and we're fighting back."

"Fighting back? You are what? Twelve or fourteen people? Your ship is one small ship against the entire galaxy. You have lost your mind!" Inoke was losing patience.

Thane jumped in again. "Mr. Malo, there were twelve of us against ten thousand people on that military base on Romajin, plus the three flagships in space. This one little ship shouldn't have escaped at all. Pateras is more powerful than anything or anyone. He's been waiting for the right time to show himself."

David leaned forward. "Mr. Malo, whether you like it or not, whether you believe any of this or not, your life as you once knew it, is over. You will have to be taken to a safe location to protect your family from Executor Hale. You asked when your life could get back to normal. It won't unless Executor Hale is removed from office and we get pardoned."

"You think you'll get me to believe your story just because you were healed from some nearly fatal injuries? Doctors do that all the time," Inoke argued.

"Papa, the doctor didn't heal his injury. He died. He was definitely dead. He was shot with a bow and arrow. The doctor didn't get to him in time. We can show you evidence to support what we've told you, but ultimately, you're just going to have to choose whether you believe us or not. None of the evidence is totally beyond question."

The Captain's comm unit beeped at him. David answered.

"Captain, I'm sorry to disturb you, but I've got Mr. Bennett patched up, and he's asking to see you. Actually, he's begging."

"Tell him I'm on my way."

David closed the comm channel and addressed the room.

"You'll be safe here for tonight. Please make yourselves comfortable. Ensign, see that they get whatever they need, including access to whatever data files they want to see. No outside comms though. I encourage you to use Lt. Flint's services as needed and get some rest. Tomorrow, we'll see about getting you to your new home. Any questions before I step out?"

Kina looked wide-eyed at the Captain. "You were really dead?"

"Yes, I was," David answered honestly.

"What was it like?" Kina asked.

David smiled. "I was taken to see Pateras two times. The first time, I wasn't dead. The second time was after Arni died and was brought back. The first time... I wasn't permitted to see him directly. He confronted me with the evil within myself. It was painful, frightening, and overwhelming. There was an incredible rift between us even though he was right in front of me. The second time, I was welcomed like a long-lost relative, like I was finally home. When the time came for me to leave, I was disappointed. I wanted to stay with him, badly."

Lexi glanced at Thane and Aulani. The Captain had never shared that information with her before. The look of shock told the others exactly what Lexi was thinking. Why would he share this now? Lexi decided it must be because Kina needed to hear it.

David moved to the door and told the others he would be available in the morning if they had more questions.

Inoke stood quickly, "Capt. Alexander, may I accompany you? We owe this man a great deal for protecting us."

David nodded, "Of course."

****

Captain Alexander led the way into the infirmary where he found Jason arguing with his patient.

"You need to get back into bed. The anesthesia is not out of your system yet," came Jason's exasperated protest.

"I'm weak and slightly woozy, but I'm fine enough for this," Mr. Bennett responded.

"Fine enough for what? If you don't get in that bed, I'll get my Security Chief to put you back in it," Jason retorted.

David approached the two men.

"Gentlemen, what's the problem?"

Samuel had managed to dress himself in nothing more than his pants. His shirt was drenched in blood and lying on a table nearby. His pants were also spattered with drops of blood. Steadying himself with the bed beside him, Samuel dropped to one knee.

"Capt. Alexander, I am honored to be in your presence."

"My presence? Why?" David glanced at the Doc and Mr. Malo curiously.

"You are the Defender and Messenger of Pateras. You are one of the twelve twelves. Because of you, we can survive the coming destruction of the Reckoning," Samuel stared at the Captain in awe.

David was not pleased. "Mr. Bennett, I had nothing to do with that. The Intercessor is responsible for it. I'm just doing the work he asked me to do, which is to tell everyone else what he's done. I'm an ordinary man, and Arni Liontari is my protector and defender. I'm not his defender. I'm one of the ones responsible for the deaths of those on his home planet, remember?"

"You're the Defender of his message, not the Defender of Pateras. You are one of the twelve twelves spoken of in the Ancient Texts," Samuel insisted, "You and your crew were once hated on my planet. Now you are highly revered. We didn't understand what was happening in the beginning, but now we do."

"I see. My doctor is one of the twelve twelves, is he not?" David asked slyly.

"Of course, all of your crew are revered on my planet," Samuel explained, being careful not to mention the name of his home world around Inoke despite his earlier slip-up in front of Kina.

"My doctor's message to you was to stay in bed. Is his message irrelevant or unimportant? I brought you here so he could save your life. Why do you risk causing yourself further injury?" David asked pointedly.

Samuel bowed his head. "I'm sorry. I never meant to be impertinent. I only wanted to tell you how much I appreciate all you've done for me, for the Malos, and for my people. I owe you my life in more ways than one."

David reached out and offered the man his hand. "A handshake would have sufficed. Let's get you back to bed."

Samuel stood slowly and wavered before climbing into his bed.

Inoke stepped forward as soon as the man was settled. "Mr. Bennett, I owe you my life and the lives of my wife and daughter. Thank you for protecting Iokina, even at the risk of your own life. What can I do to repay this great debt?"

Samuel shook his head. "You don't owe me anything. I protected your family because they asked it of me. You owe them, not me."

Inoke glanced at David, "My family and I need to rest tonight. Tomorrow, we should talk again. Perhaps your story has merit."

David smiled, "I would be glad to talk with you more. I will be in the Dining Hall in the morning at 0800 hours. Mr. Bennett, if the Doc releases you, feel free to join us. I think Mr. Malo would benefit from hearing your perspective."

Samuel propped up on his elbows, "I would be honored, sir."

David shook Samuel's hand. He offered his hand to Inoke. This time Inoke shook it. David escorted him to the guest quarters then excused himself to return to the bridge.

****

After speaking to Brynna and Braxton, the three determined the men were tracking them in some way. David decided they needed to be examined to find the tracking device. He discreetly hailed Thane and Aulani to escort their family to the infirmary for a quick scan. Capt. Alexander alerted Jason to expect them.

A few minutes later, David joined the group in the infirmary.

"Captain, I scanned each one for tracking devices and nanites. There were no nanites present in any of them, but I found a tracking device in Iokina. Based on the scarring around the device, I would say it's been there for at least six weeks or longer. I can't tell you definitively, it could be as long as two or three years," Jason updated the Captain.

David glanced at Brynna, "So, they've known where she is all this time. Why not take her before now?"

Brynna scowled, and Kina looked scared. Kina finally asked, "Are—Are you going to take it out of me?"

David smiled kindly. "Of course, we will. I just need to know where to put it once we get it out."

Brynna cocked her head slightly. "Where to put it? Aren't we going to destroy it?"

"I want to know how it got there," Kina added.

"Did you have any periods of being unconscious or feeling drugged in the last few months? It would have been followed by a period where this place in your back was slightly sore," Jason queried.

Maleah and Inoke moved to the foot of Kina's bed. They had been cleared by the doctor to leave whenever they were ready.

Maleah scowled, "The night we were almost taken, Kina was grabbed by two men. By the time Samuel and Lucas got to her, she was lying unconscious on the floor with binders on. Samuel and Lucas managed to free her, but Lucas died as a result. Kina complained of several bruises in the days after that."

David folded his arms across his chest. "How many men did they send to apprehend you?"

Samuel was sitting up in his bed, paying close attention to the discussion.

"Captain, I strongly suspected at that time, they were letting us escape. I thought they might be intending to follow us to determine where we were going, but I didn't have any way to find out for certain. Every time we nearly made contact with one of our operatives, something like what happened tonight would happen."

"They aren't trying to apprehend you. They're trying to apprehend whoever's helping you or else they're trying to find out your final destination so they can get the entire crew's families," Brynna surmised.

"It makes sense," David agreed. Something inside him said there was more to it than this, "Doc, can you tell if that thing will know it's been removed?"

Jake interrupted, "Captain, I took the specs the Doc got from his scans and ran it through our database. It will send out a breach signal if the temperature drops below ninety degrees or gets above one hundred ten degrees. If we take it out under controlled circumstances and keep it at a normal human body temperature, we could… huh… I just thought of something," Jake grinned mischievously.

David planted his feet shoulder width apart and folded his arms across his chest, "So, spill it, Chief."

"Put the chip into one of those guys who attacked us tonight and put him aboard a slow-moving freighter headed halfway across the galaxy," Jake grinned again.

David rocked side to side slowly on his feet. He stared at the floor and pulled at his lower lip. In a moment, he looked up and grinned, "Doc, can you keep it warm enough to transport?"

"Sure, Captain, but you aren't really going to…" Jason hesitated.

"Why not? They did it to us first. I like the idea. Let them chase their own man across the galaxy for a while."

David grinned as enthusiastically as Jake.

Brynna simply shook her head at the two men. The idea had merit, but she doubted its merits were the primary reasons for this decision.

"Go ahead and take it out, but arrange to jam it until it's in an appropriate environment to keep it from accidentally signaling whoever's watching it. Make it look like random signal interference. Aulani can help you with that. Leave it sitting in the controlled environment tonight, and I'll talk to Mr. Rune about it in the morning. If we trigger it and can't reset it, destroy it. Questions?" The Captain calmly ordered. His blatant grin was gone, but he was still amused.

Jason chased the unnecessary personnel out and pulled out the privacy screens while he worked. Jake and Aulani stayed at the computer terminal in the infirmary, programming it to jam the signal from the tracking device. Five minutes later the device was placed into an atmospherically controlled container, and Kina's tiny incision was healed. Jason promptly ordered her to go to bed. It was getting quite late by this point, and no one was getting a full night's sleep.

****

David and Samuel met with the Malos the next morning as promised. They each told their stories about Pateras and his history with the Commonwealth. Inoke finally decided Aulani had chosen the best course possible. He still was not sure about Thane until one particular story came out. Aulani told her father how Thane risked his life to allow her to escape the Nefil troops on Ela Prime. Inoke wasn't sure any man was good enough for his daughter, but now he was willing to give Thane a chance. Maleah and Kina were ready to accept Thane wholeheartedly.

Braxton came down from the bridge, grabbed a cup of coffee, and sat at the already crowded table with the Captain.

"Captain, I have a message from Mr. Rune. He's on his way to meet with you. He said he should be here in about ten minutes."

David stood to go, "Thank you, Mr. Flint. Mr. Bennett, part of this concerns you. Would you care to join me in my office?"

"Yes Captain."

They disposed of their breakfast dishes and headed to the Captain's office. Braxton met Mr. Rune at the airlock and escorted him to the Captain's office. David invited him to sit at the table with him and Mr. Bennett.

Neal offered his hand to Samuel. "Mr. Bennett, it's good to meet you. I've heard good things about you."

Samuel smiled, "I'm sure it was all exaggeration. I'm pleased to meet you too. How long have you been stationed here?"

"Three years, give or take," The man replied. His assignment was initially to survey the area and learn the inner workings of the colony. He was hired by the colony two-and-a-half years ago.

David moved the conversation beyond pleasantries and inquired about the men who attacked the Malos the previous evening.

Neal answered with the update he received from his security personnel early this morning, "Constable Hinson questioned all six men at length through the night. They claim they were hired by a bounty hunter. They don't have a description of the man who hired them. He did his business with them through encrypted messages, data crystals at designated drop points, etc."

"What were they supposed to do with the Malos when they caught them?" David asked.

"They were given an advance on their payment, which included the funds to rent a room. When they had them in custody, they were to leave a data crystal at the drop point telling their benefactor where to retrieve them."

Neal leaned forward and placed his arms to rest on the table as he watched Capt. Alexander scowl. It was clear something wasn't sitting right about this situation.

"Captain, what's bothering you about this?"

David hesitated before answering. "This is a lot of trouble for a bounty hunter to go to. There has to be more to this."

David rubbed his chin thoughtfully. "Arni, what am I missing?" He spoke aloud to the unseen presence.

Neal winced at the sound of Arni's name, and Samuel simply looked shocked. It didn't go unnoticed. David wasted no time in addressing their discomfort.

"Gentlemen, I was introduced to the Intercessor on Galat by his name. He preferred to be called by his name and told Moderator Tarmon as much. He is my friend, as well as my Intercessor. I know he hears me and even knows my thoughts."

Samuel nodded, "You're right, of course. It's just that we were taught to revere him and hold him in the highest regard. I'm not accustomed to such a casual approach to one so powerful. Did he answer you, by the way?"

The Captain's frustration was obvious on his face, and his answer merely confirmed what Samuel already knew, "No, not yet."

Samuel leaned back more relaxed, "At least you've known him long enough and well enough to be confident that he will answer you."

The Captain relaxed a little more when Samuel voiced what David already knew to be true.

"You're right. I do expect him to tell me or show me when it's the right time. His time and mine are not usually in agreement. One of my crew told me one time, just do what you would normally do until Arni tells you something different. It seems like sound advice, so that's my plan."

Neal's brow furrowed. "What would you normally do? This isn't a normal set of circumstances."

David grinned wryly, "Sit here and wonder why a bounty hunter would go to so much trouble."

Neal and Samuel grinned with equal fervor.

"Is it too late to set a trap for our bounty hunter?" David queried more enthusiastically.

Neal nodded, "I'm afraid so. Our guys told us they were supposed to make contact by 0600 this morning if they were successful. If I had known sooner, we could've set something up. They were told if they failed, they were to return the advanced credits to the drop location. They said the bounty hunter issued some rather stern threats if they tried to stiff him on the credits. Maybe we could do something with that?"

David grinned and tapped his finger on his lips thoughtfully, "What did you plan to do with these guys?"

Neal sighed, "Unless someone wants to stick around and press charges, we'll have to let them go. Samuel can't do that, and we don't want the Malos names to come out in any investigations. Their names would get somebody's attention and even if it takes a little time, someone would start watching the colony. Drea is trying to establish more safe havens, so we sure don't want to lose them faster than we get them set up."

Samuel looked intrigued, "You have an idea, don't you, Captain?"

David's grin grew as he leaned in and told the two men about Jake's idea for using the tracking device they removed from Kina.

"Tell your prisoners they are facing some pretty stiff penalties for attempted murder, but the victims would prefer to make this go away quietly to avoid other bounty hunters. Have Constable Hinson offer them a deal. Transportation will be arranged for them to leave the colony permanently. They will have tracking devices placed in them so if they return to the colony, the Constable will know it immediately. One of the chips will be the one we removed from Kina sending that bounty hunter off the planet long enough for us to finish our business here and leave."

Samuel grinned, "I like it."

Neal was not enthused about the idea, "Suppose that bounty hunter decides to eliminate witnesses or take his frustrations out on those men. I can't sanction setting them up to be murdered."

David's conscience was pricked. He was about to deny being responsible for another man's actions when he remembered denying his own responsibilities for the deaths occurring on Galat. He hadn't killed anyone there, but he had unwittingly set them up to die.

"I'm not suggesting that. Put the proper safeguards into place. Have the ship's Captain keep the men in custody and give him ample warning about the situation. Notify him of any ships that appear to be following them. Once our bounty hunter figures out he's been tricked, he'll steer clear of those men to avoid getting himself caught."

Neal mulled it over in his head, "This may mean sending my Constable back to Drea after this. I suppose it won't be too hard to bring in someone new to take his place. If you're sure those men won't be harmed…"

David shook his head, "I can't be certain of that. We can take precautions, but there are no guarantees. Leaving them here could also get them killed."

Samuel joined in support of David's plan, "These men chose to play in a dangerous game. As the Ancient Texts have said, 'Those who take up arms against another should be prepared to lose whatever they were prepared to take.' They are in Pateras' hands."

"One last question for you, Neal. What's the plan for getting the Malos to Drea?" The Captain wasn't trying to hurry them off his ship, but he knew the longer they were around, the greater the risks were for the entire crew and the crews of the other eleven vessels.

"I can send for the pod at any time. I would prefer to only send for it once and take the Malos, Samuel, and Constable Hinson if necessary, at the same time. I would like to keep the Constable here until your fleet is departing if possible.

If anything goes wrong, he can become our missing fall guy," Even though Neal wasn't a soldier, he was a decent strategist.

David nodded, "Makes sense. I would like to remain here until they're safely away. If you need to, you can point to my ship and say you haven't seen them since we left. It's not like they really need another reason to hunt us down. I do have access to a computer virus if you need one to wreak havoc on your systems."

Neal scowled, "I'll… uh… keep that in mind."

David laughed at Neal's hesitation, "I don't have access to that computer virus anymore. The crew took away my access to it and nearly mutinied over it."

Samuel even looked concerned, "What?"

"It was my fault entirely. I hadn't joined Pateras at that time, and my judgment was impaired by exhaustion and extreme stress. My crew had every right to be upset with me for infecting my ship with a virus. I had a good reason, but it was still a bad idea. I was joking when I offered you the virus. You guys need to have a little fun."

Neal shook his head. This Captain was not what he expected at all. This man had the weight of the entire galaxy on his shoulders, and he was sitting here making light of very serious circumstances.

"Captain, how are you so lighthearted in the face of this?"

David smiled, "When I was a boy, my grandmother, Kay Deacons, also known as Tyra Paulson, used to tell me, 'Davie, when times get rough, you can laugh, or you can cry, but laughing's more fun.' My Gramma was an incredibly smart woman."

Samuel smiled, "I've heard of your grandmother. She was a retired Engineer who is now spearheading the tachyon engine development projects. She's an admirable woman."

Neal wasn't familiar with Capt. Alexander or his family. He was less inspired by his story.

"Captain, if I get found out, I'll be treated like a spy. I can't say I'm even remotely prepared for that possibility. I'm an administrator, not a trained operative. This job scares the life out of me. I don't see how you do it. I'm not on the front lines, and I'm scared. You've got the entire Commonwealth breathing down your neck. I'm willing to die to protect your people and Drea, but getting caught is a constant worry for me."

The Captain wasn't trained in anything more than basic psychology, but he had a knack for it. He saw that Neal needed a serious answer.

"I take things one day at a time, one minute at a time. Things have been easier since I turned everything over to Pateras. If I'm alive, I'm following his plan and doing the jobs he asks of me. If I die, I know it isn't the end of me. I will be alive in his realm or alternate reality or whatever the correct term for it is. There are a lot of things I don't know yet. In either case, I will be alive in some form with him. How can I lose?"

"What about torture? What if I can't stand up to it?" Neal didn't want to disappoint Pateras or the Dreans whose secrets and anonymity were dependent on him.

David sighed, "Torture is not fun. That's true. I've been there and have no desire to go through it again. When I was tortured on Romajin, I followed my grandmother's advice as long as I could. I… almost lost it… near the last. Pateras took care of me. He sent Jake in to push me to the point that I regained my ability to fight. I can't sit here and worry about what might happen. I have to focus on what is happening right now. I'll worry about torture when the pain actually starts."

Seeing the somber look on the Captain's face, Neal regretted bringing up the matter, "Forgive me, Captain. I didn't mean to cause you any distress."

David smiled again, "I'm willing to die for Pateras if that's what he requires of me. Arni died in my place. How can I do any less? I would prefer a quick, painless death without torture though."

Neal smiled weakly, "My head understands, but my heart isn't as convinced."

THE CAPTAINS MEET

The crew of the *Evangeline* walked into the large meeting room capable of holding over one hundred people. The room's outer wall was a window to a scenic panorama of undersea life. The planet's small land masses were uniquely sculpted by terraforming technologies to prevent erosion, maximize the availability of farmland, and yet remain aesthetically pleasing. The crew was immediately captivated by the seascape displayed in front of them. The subdued lighting in the room only served to accentuate the effect.

The crew's nerves were on edge. The next few hours were crucial to this phase of their mission. The peaceful seascape alleviated some of their angst. The entire crew was present for the meeting, including a very pregnant Marissa.

Capt. Alexander made assignments for each of the crew. Marissa, Cheyenne, and Aulani were on guard at computer terminals. They watched the scanners for suspicious movements from space, the other side of the planet, and movements within the colony.

The area was completely cleared of mining colony personnel. This section of the colony was the part on lease to Drea and kept devoid of uninvited guests or workers. The *Evangeline's* crew were in uniform except Lt. Holden, who had been unable to fit into her uniforms for several months.

Jake and Braxton manned the entrance to the conference room to provide a familiar face. Not everyone knew each member of the Explorer mission teams, but the uniforms were distinctive. Their uniforms were designed specifically for the Explorer missions and were slightly different than the standard Commonwealth Interstellar Force uniforms. Seeing the uniforms and the rank would hopefully put their visitors at ease, knowing they were in the right place.

Capt. Nathaniel Weiseman, his wife, Dr. Stephanie Weiseman, and Cmdr. Silas Asher, of the CIF SS *Emissary*, were the first to arrive.

Braxton saluted, "Welcome Capt. Weiseman, Dr. Weiseman, Cmdr. Asher. It's good to see you again."

Capt. Weiseman and Capt. Alexander were very much alike in their thinking. Capt. Weiseman's three crew members were in uniform instead of civilian attire. Capt. Weiseman returned the salute and shook hands with Braxton and Jake. "Gentlemen, it's good to see you both as well. Chief, has your wife had her baby?"

Jake grinned nervously, "No, not yet, but any day now."

Stephanie scowled, "Your Captain's a little insensitive to have you out here in the field while your wife is safely tucked away near an infirmary."

Braxton and Jake looked at each other sheepishly. Jake finally responded, "Uh… Marissa's inside on duty."

Nate said nothing. He doubted he would have allowed a pregnant crew member to stay aboard his ship and often wondered why David had. If he said the wrong thing, his wife and Chief Medical Officer could take her frustrations with Capt. Alexander out on him.

Stephanie folded her arms and scowled, "I think I will have a word with him and your Chief Medical Officer about that!"

Jake stepped forward tenuously. "Before you do, ma'am, you might want to know two things. First, he and the doc tried to take her off duty days ago. She went ballistic. She insisted she would go stir crazy if she couldn't work. Second, the Captain wanted the entire crew here for this meeting. He wanted everyone to know we were in this thing together."

Silas shook his head, "Oh, you have got to be kidding. He brought the entire crew out into the open? What is it with your Captain? I—"

The door to the elevator opened at the other end of the hallway, and three people stumbled out. An older man with two younger women, one on each side of him, stumbled down the hallway. The three were laughing and giggling as they zigzagged toward the doorway.

Jake did a hasty threat assessment. The women were in their mid-twenties. They were oblivious to everything around them except the man between them. The man was more of a puzzle. He was in his fifties and old enough to be the father of the young women at his sides. His eyes surveyed each individual and every doorway in the hall. His hands stayed in plain sight. Something was familiar about the man. Jake couldn't put his finger on it, but something wasn't right.

Seeing the five officers standing in the hallway, they stopped uncomfortably close to them. All three smelled of some form of alcoholic beverage. The man's hair was salt and pepper color and unkempt. He looked like he hadn't shaved in days. The man let go of one of the giggling women and searched his pockets while he spoke.

"Is-zis where the party is? I got—uh, my invitat—my invitation is, where's my invitation?" The man weaved and bobbed as he looked for his missing invitation.

One woman's hair was ornately styled on top of her head. The man looked at her hair.

"Wait, I—Here—it iz. I… (hic)… foun' it," The man reached into the giggling woman's hair and removed a data crystal, which he tried handing to Jake.

Jake had his hand on his weapon from the time the doors of the elevator opened. His mind was on high alert. His situational awareness watched the man and the two women for movements toward hidden weapons while his peripheral vision watched the elevator at the end of the hall for the approach of troops, in case the three in front of him were meant to be a distraction. He didn't want to overreact to a harmless drunk, but he didn't want to get caught with his defenses down.

The man, seeing Jake's hand resting on his weapon, leaned in closer. Whispering in an obnoxiously loud drunken voice, he confessed, "I don't really have… (hic)… an invitation. Thas a bri-i-ibe."

The man moved uncomfortably close to Jake's right side. He put his hand on Jake's shoulder and leaned heavily on him, which hindered his weapon arm.

"There's ten—ten credits on the data crystal. Perhaps you could jus' look the other way and let the ladies and me into the party?"

Jake pulled himself out from under the man's weight. He took on a more official "police" stance and spoke firmly.

"Are you attempting to bribe a Commonwealth official? With ten measly credits? Perhaps I need to check and see if there are any outstanding warrants for your arrest here or on any other Commonwealth planet."

The man staggered, "Don't be ridiculous my good man. I am a solid citizen of the Commonwealth. I would never try to bribe an occifer of the Commonwealth," The man scowled at Jake's teal colored shirt. He leaned in and loudly whispered, "Your shirt is the wrong COLOR. No one's going to believe you're a Commonwealth occifer, but if that's how you're going to be, I will take my pretty ladies and find another party."

The man put his arms around the two women who were giggling at nothing in particular. One of the women stroked Jake's cheek. "You should have let us in. I bet we could have had lots of fun together."

The man grabbed the young woman and pulled her back to his side. "Let's you and I go have some of that fun. C'mon ladies. Next round is on me."

The Commonwealth Officers watched the three as they zigzagged through the corridor and re-entered the elevator. The tension in the corridor sky-rocketed when the three approached them. It took a couple of seconds after they were gone before anyone was ready to resume the conversation.

Jake was the first to speak. "Commander, scan me for trackers or bugs."

Braxton was distracted with his own worries. "Do what?"

"Scan me to see if they planted any surveillance devices on me," Jake reiterated.

Braxton activated his scanner and did as requested. He scanned the others as a precaution. When they came up clean, everyone relaxed and joked casually about the three drunks.

Silas even smiled. "I thought he was going to have you in a corner when he told you your shirt was the wrong color. What were you going to do if he had pressed that one?

Jake smiled. "I would have asked him just how much he had to drink. Then I would have told him this was blue," Jake pulled at his teal shirt as he spoke.

Stephanie grinned, "You would have tried to convince him he was too drunk to even see colors correctly?"

"Sure, I would. If that didn't work, I would have given him his ten credits back and told him the next round of drinks was on me. I didn't want to draw on him unless there was no other choice. I had another half-dozen ideas ready," Jake grinned.

Capt. Weiseman stared at the closed elevator door. Silas noticed the Captain's preoccupation. "What's bothering you, sir?"

Nate pulled his eyes off the door and refocused them on Silas. "Something about that guy was familiar. His voice reminds me of someone. I'm not sure who yet."

Jake cocked his head sideways. "You noticed something too?"

Stephanie rethought the events. "You're right, Nate. He did remind me of someone, but I can't quite place him either. Give it a few minutes. It'll come to me."

Nate nodded and decided the three should go on inside. They moved through the doorway and greeted the *Evangeline's* crew as though they were old friends. The *Emissary's* crew had only met the *Evangeline's* crew a few times in relation to their mission, but their last meeting two months ago created a deep bond between them.

****

David eagerly greeted his old friends, Nate and Stephanie. Once past the normal pleasantries, David quickly asked, "How did things go with Arni? Is he coming to this meeting?"

99

Nate grinned and winked at Stephanie. "He didn't really want to see us. He wanted to see Arni. I think my feelings are hurt."

Stephanie smiled at Nate's humor but didn't join in ribbing their friend. "Do you blame him? Arni's unlike anyone else we've ever met."

Silas was far more sober in his response. "If it weren't for Arni, none of us would still have our wives, Capt. Weiseman."

Nate looked lovingly at his wife. "That's true. Okay, I'll forgive you… this time. Arni said he would see us here. He did say one troubling thing."

David grinned. "Only one thing? Somebody's slipping, and I doubt it was Arni."

Nate's face clouded. "He said he was going to be leaving soon but would send another to be with us. I don't think he was referring to another humanoid."

The door opened, derailing the conversation. A tall, dark, sturdy man entered the room, wearing the Explorer class uniform with Captain's insignia. David and Nate immediately greeted the man and assured him he was safe. The newest Captain was several inches taller than either David or Nate.

David stuck his hand out to the man, "Welcome Capt. Silvain. It's good to see you."

Capt. Silvain surveyed the room before accepting David's hand. "Capt. Alexander, is this your entire crew? I thought you only requested a representative contingent from each ship."

"You're right. Yes, my entire crew is here. I didn't want to put your entire crew at risk in case we were found. My crew is working and sending a message of their own. Each one of my people is committed to this path. They're here to indicate that we're all in. They're ready to give their lives if necessary to see this through. We can talk more about this later. You remember Capt. Nate Weiseman?"

Nate offered the man his hand to shake as well, "Capt. Silvain, it's good to see that you're alive and well. I hope your crew is safe as well."

"They are, but until I am satisfied, that is all I will say about them," Capt. Silvain was clearly not as relaxed as Nate or David.

David clasped his hands behind him and rocked on his heels.

"That's completely understandable. I would be the same way if I were in your position. If I inadvertently make further inquiries about your crew, feel free to remind me to back off. The same goes for any of my crew if they get too inquisitive."

Capt. Silvain scowled at David. He wasn't sure if the man was impudent or genuine. David casually oriented Capt. Silvain to the room and introduced him to those already present.

The door opened again, and three others entered. David handed Capt. Silvain off to Nate and moved to greet the newcomers. These three were in civilian attire. David recognized each one as Captains of three more ships. He enthusiastically greeted them. It was still early for the intended meeting time, and already half of the Explorer Fleet was accounted for. Brynna joined him to greet the newest arrivals.

David gave the three a moment to size up the room before approaching them. He reintroduced Brynna. She knew them from the mission training. David introduced them anyway to keep things on a polite and courteous level.

"This is my wife, Cmdr. Brynna Alexander. Brynna, this is Capt. Angela Smith of the *Messenger*, Capt. Patrick James of the *Concord*, and Capt. Alec Roan of the *Deliverance*."

Brynna smiled warmly. "It's good to see you again. I'm sorry it's under such difficult circumstances."

Capt. Smith got off to a brisk start. "Is somebody going to give us an explanation of what's happening to us? My crew and I were nearly killed by... forgive my bluntness... a sadistic bunch of... overgrown... science experiments."

Her inclination was to use less than professional language. Her training as a Captain and a diplomat allowed her to keep her inclinations under control, but only by a slim margin.

Capt. Alec Roan jumped in just as aggressively, "I'd like some answers too. My people and I would be dead if it weren't for Angela. She came to warn us about those new ships after my crew and I were rounded up by whoever those guys were. She saved our backsides out there."

"They're called the Nefil. As soon as the others get here, I will gladly give you as many answers as I can."

Capt. James folded his arms across his chest. "How do we know this isn't some kind of trap? Maybe you're trying to get as many of us as you can in one room to turn us over to the Commonwealth or to see who's loyal and who isn't."

"I have no intention of turning anyone over to the Commonwealth. I can't vouch for the trustworthiness of anyone other than my crew and Capt. Weiseman's crew. Any of the other ten Captains could have alerted the Commonwealth to this meeting, but it wasn't one of us," David assured the man.

He wasn't ready to answer any major questions yet, so he offered the needed distraction of refreshments. The offerings were cookies, crackers, coffee, and water. He did have one curious question, "Why is it each of you came alone? I really expected to see more security officers."

"We brought security officers. We left them in the hallway," Angela was a few years older than David but found herself to be a lone woman in a man's world. She worked hard to get where she was and was aggressive by nature. Her eyes searched David's for weakness or deception.

David allowed her to look into his soul before continuing. He pointed to the women monitoring the computers at the far side of the room.

"You are welcome to place your security personnel wherever you like. I have three people monitoring long and short-range scanners and local traffic for any unusual activity. Your security officers are welcome to remain outside or come and go as necessary. They can oversee my people at the monitors if you wish."

****

In the corridor, Braxton and Jake found themselves in a staring contest with the three security officers from the latest arrivals. Sensing nerves were on edge, and things could only get worse, Braxton sent Jake into one of the adjoining rooms to get chairs for themselves and their guests. Jake placed the chairs down for the three security officers first. The three refused to be seated, even after Jake and Braxton sat down to wait for their remaining guests.

Braxton got frustrated with the three. He leaned over to Jake and softly whispered, "These three are going to spook whoever arrives next if they don't relax a little. You got any ideas?"

Jake squinted at the trio of security officers.

The door to the conference room opened and Capt. James stuck his head out for a moment. "Lewis, with me!"

Security Chief Jenna Lewis hastily followed her Captain inside, leaving the remaining two feeling less at an advantage. Jake and Braxton attempted to make small talk, which failed miserably.

This time, Jake approached the two remaining stalwart brutes. "Gentlemen, my Captain and crew have no intention of trapping anyone. He would like the chance to speak to all the Captains, but if you keep looking like you're about to tackle the next person off that elevator, this meeting is going to be over before it starts. I understand you have orders to protect your Captains. You are welcome to remain here, go inside the conference room, or move to one of the side offices and use the surveillance feeds to do your jobs. If you choose to remain out here, I suggest you sit down."

The two men were assigned to security aboard their respective ships. They had trained with Jake, and both clearly recognized him.

One of the men stepped forward and got into Jake's face. He glanced at Jake's rank, "Chief Petty Officer Holden," his acrid tone reflected his lack of respect for Jake, "We, both outrank you. You've got no business giving us orders. So, why don't you and your buddy sit down and mind your own business."

Braxton wasted no time getting on his feet to back Jake up. Braxton severely outranked the two security officers, and he was preparing to exercise his rank, but Jake didn't give him the opportunity.

Jake folded his arms across his chest. He never took his eyes off the man in front of him. "I see you remember me. I suppose you'll also remember the day Nicholai Duscha was defeated in hand to hand combat?"

The two men glanced at each other. They were each soundly defeated by Nicholai in the training classes. Their thoughts recalled the incident in question. Nicholai was larger than the two of them. He had gone against Jake whose frame was even smaller. Jake had dispatched the large man quickly and decisively.

Jake gave them a moment to remember the scenario. "Gentleman, I am no longer loyal to the Commonwealth, and I am not bound by their regulations. I am strongly advising you to RELAX! Are we clear?"

The second man glanced at Braxton. His posture clearly changed as he sat in one of the chairs. Seeing his backup back down, the man gruffly answered, "Understood, Chief."

Jake relaxed his posturing and turned away from the two men. He and Braxton returned to their chairs. Jake pulled his chair slightly away from the wall.

Braxton leaned in as they sat down. "So, tell me about this 'Nicholai' incident."

Jake pushed his chair back onto two legs. He settled in when the elevator opened to reveal none other than Capt. Talaith Bowen and her security officer, Chief Warrant Officer Nicholai Duscha.

Jake hopped to his feet and greeted the two enthusiastically. "Capt. Bowen, Chief Duscha, welcome. Nicholai, it's great to see you again. We were just talking about you, my friend."

The two belligerent security officers glanced at each other and said nothing. Their bouts with the large man had sent them both to the infirmary. Jake, by comparison, was a pipsqueak. They each wondered how he had bested the man.

Braxton stepped forward and introduced himself. He invited them both to join the others in the conference room. Capt. Bowen glanced at the two men sitting meekly near the door.

Before she could ask, Braxton volunteered the information. "Capt. Smith and Capt. Roan preferred to leave their security officers covering the entrance. Capt. James' security officer is inside."

Capt. Bowen's response was brief and cryptic, "I see," She started to lead her Security Chief through the door. Talaith stopped and quietly asked, "Lt. Cmdr., am I walking into a trap?"

Braxton didn't blink.

"Not one of our making, ma'am. Capt. Alexander wants a straight up meeting with the rest of the Explorer ships to lay everything out in the open. He's not loyal to the Commonwealth any longer, and he has good reasons for it. The crew of the *Evangeline* is behind him, all the way. If there's a security breach, it's not one of us."

Talaith seemed satisfied with Braxton's answer. She knew if she could catch him off-guard, a lie would be easier to detect. She was at least satisfied that no other information, correct or otherwise, could be gleaned from further conversation.

Capt. Bowen entered the amphitheater. Her security officer followed her in and moved to a strategic location.

Braxton looked at Jake and back at the door where Capt. Bowen and Chief Duscha had just gone through, "Wow, Chief, he's a lot bigger than you and those other two," he nodded toward their two more belligerent security companions, "How did you beat him?"

"Things aren't always what they seem," Jake said simply, then sat down again.

****

David greeted Capt. Bowen as eagerly as he had greeted the others, offering his open hand to her.

Talaith looked at his hand, "I'm not sure if I want to shake hands with a traitor and a man capable of destroying an entire military base."

David knew someone was bound to react like this. He was surprised it hadn't happened sooner.

"We'll get into the specifics of this once everyone arrives. Suffice it to say, my crew and I had nothing to do with the deaths on Romajin. My treason, you may or may not agree with, but I refuse to allow the Commonwealth to commit wanton acts of murder against unarmed civilians. Whether you shake my hand or not is your choice, but at least keep an open mind about who's really guilty here."

Talaith clasped her hands behind her. She wasn't ready to be seen shaking his hand as yet. She also wasn't as skeptical as she appeared. Her response was again, "I see."

Capt. Bowen moved past Capt. Alexander to learn what she could from the surrounding activity.

A few minutes later, the four remaining Captains joined the group. Capt. Bryan Wallace of the *Bounty* came with his ship's psychologist. Capt. Christopher Logan of the SS *Malachi* came alone. Capt. Ajani Davu, of the SS *Pioneer*, was introduced to the crew of the *Evangeline* as the brother of Deka Davu, the navigator serving aboard the *Emissary*. Capt. Sarah Clements of the *Ambassador* brought her First Officer, her ship's psychologist, and her security officer. Capt. Tas Gellert of the SS *Explorer* came alone.

David was pleased to see every ship was represented. As the last one entered, David offered Capt. Gellert some refreshments. After getting him settled, David moved to the podium to prepare himself. Although he had rehearsed what he planned to say several times, a case of stage fright sidelined him. He stared out the window at the various sea creatures flitting back and forth in front of him. He was about to address his peers and openly confess his treason. He had accepted his treason, but confessing his transgression to the men and women he had trained with suddenly filled him with doubts and fears.

Brynna joined him.

He glanced sideways at her, "Yes, Commander? Is there a problem?"

She watched the seascape as intently as he did. "I was just about to ask you that. You've hesitated," She spoke softly in tone and attitude.

"I don't know. All of a sudden, I have these doubts and fears. These people are my peers. I worked hard to earn their respect. I'm about to confess my treason to them. I know they already know about it, but I'm afraid of losing their respect."

Brynna smiled at his reflection in the glass. "I have two questions for you, Capt. Alexander. The first one is, have you spoken to your commanding officer about this? The second one is, what did the Ancient Texts say about fear and doubt?"

David turned to face his wife. He stroked her face gently. "There are times when I'm glad I married you, then there are times like these when I'm *really* glad I married you. Thank you."

Brynna kissed the heel of his hand and walked away from him, smiling. She already knew the answer to the two questions. David was trying to do this on his own and hadn't consulted their new benefactor. He had forgotten that fear and doubt were the weapons spoken of in the Ancient Texts as the weapons of Luciano Hale. Executor Hale may not be physically present, but his supernatural capabilities made his presence possible.

David turned for one last look at the seascape and whispered, "Arni, I need you."

A voice whispered quietly, "I'm here."

Strengthened by Brynna and Arni's support, David approached the podium. "If everyone would like to take their seats, we'll get started."

He was one of the youngest Captains among the Explorer ships. Nate was several months older than him, and only one Captain was actually younger. Capt. Talaith Bowen was one year younger than him. All the other Captains were older and more experienced.

Jake and Braxton quietly entered the amphitheater, catching David's eye. David watched as they casually took seats in strategic positions in the back. Their movements indicated all was well, yet they were prepared for the unexpected. David waited another moment until everyone got situated.

"Thank you for coming. I know being here puts you and your crews at great risk. I'm going to be as quick and straight to the point as I can. I have proof for most of the things I'm about to tell you, and we've put everything we can onto a data crystal for you. Listen to what I say and review the evidence. You'll have to make up your minds for yourselves about the things I can't prove. The crew of the *Evangeline* no longer works for the Commonwealth. If you decide to ally with us, come back tomorrow evening, and we can discuss plans for the future. If you don't want to join us, then you're welcome to take your chances on your own. I strongly suggest you park your ships somewhere and disappear until this blows over. If you don't believe anything else I say today, at least believe this: Executor Hale will not rest until he finds and destroys all of us, no matter where your loyalties lie.

"Supreme Executor Luciano Hale has lied to us on several points. The first point is this, Pateras El Liontari does not conscript people against their will. If that were true, Arni Liontari would have taken all of us by force before now. How many of you have crossed paths with the forces of Pateras?"

Every hand in the room went up. David took a deep breath. "It appears you've all run across him. How many of you have been conscripted? How many of you have been forced to serve Pateras?"

No one raised a hand. Several exchanged uncertain glances. David recognized the signs. Several had chosen to join him, but they were not forced. David moved on quickly to avoid losing control of the meeting.

"You know, I'm going to put this even more bluntly than I originally planned. I'm not trying to manipulate you. What you do is up to you. I just want you to have all the facts. Pateras is not a recently discovered superior alien being. He is known as the Timeless One and written about in the Ancient Texts because he is timeless. He's older than the universe. He is the ultimate supreme being. Supreme Executor Hale knows this. He sent us out, not as ambassadors, but as spies. He intended to destroy any world inhabited by followers of Pateras. The Commonwealth destroyed six million people on Galat III. They destroyed the populations on Strabothon and Julley. I haven't seen Strabothon or Julley myself, but Executor Hale admitted in my hearing to giving the order to destroy them like he did Galat. There may have been others.

"The big question you really need to ask is why destroy low-tech planets with no strategic value and are no apparent threat. Galat III worshiped Pateras as a god. There are lots of worlds that worship the sun, moon, stars, statues, etc. Those haven't been destroyed. Why is Pateras different?"

David paused to give them a chance to consider the reasons before offering his proposition.

"He's different because, for one, he's real. He's not the delusion of a primitive society. He's clearly a powerful being. Executor Hale didn't lie about that part."

David sighed. This next part was the hardest. "Most of you have more experience in space than I do. Please trust me. I know this next part is going to sound really insane, but it's true. Luciano Hale is attacking followers of Pateras because he used to be a follower himself. Luciano Hale is a superior alien being. He is inferior to Pateras, and he knows it. His goal is to…"

Before he could go any further, several people were on their feet.

Capt. Silvain was the first to interrupt. "You ARE insane. You've gone space happy. Do you even hear what you are saying? Executor Hale is a man just like you and me."

Several others objected strenuously.

David raised his hands to get everyone's attention again. "I told you I would provide proof wherever I could. I do have a small amount of proof for this one. The proof, such as it is, will be given to you on the data crystals. Before I explain the information on the crystal, let me ask you this, 'If we were sent to find the strongholds of a clearly superior alien being, why would anyone think only one being exists?' Isn't it possible there is an entire race of alien beings? We already know Pateras El Liontari has a son, Arni Sotaeras Liontari."

The grumbling and objections dwindled to low mutterings. The young Captain had a point. If there was one such powerful being, there had to be more.

David moved on to discuss his proof. "Executor Hale is limited by Pateras in what he can accomplish. My crew and I were taken prisoner on Romajin. I saw him change from a human form to… something else. After Pateras freed us, Executor Hale tried to convince my Security Chief to return to his service. When Chief Holden refused, he attacked the man's wife by changing his form again. He manifested himself as her husband and threw her against a wall. She was able to scratch his face and get a DNA sample. The DNA sample was unlike anything we've ever seen before. It proved the Chief didn't attack his wife."

Stephanie decided to play "devil's advocate" to help David out. "A false DNA signature could be manufactured with temporary stability. Whatever DNA you have put on those data crystals could be faked."

David stared at her for half a second before he realized what she was trying to do. "Yes, it's possible, but I didn't fake any of this. I know you have no reason to believe me. Here's the one thing I couldn't do. I know several of you have already run into the Nefil."

Capt. Gellert raised his hand. "I'm sorry, the Nefil?"

David's eyes locked with Capt. Smith and Capt. James. They immediately knew who he was referring to.

"The Nefil are a genetically engineered group of soldiers designed to be stronger, faster, and more intelligent than normal humans. They are educated and trained to be ruthless and unswerving from their mission. They were given state-of-the-art gear and technology. Their mission was to find the twelve Explorer teams and take us out, regardless of who we are loyal to. They were designed and commissioned by Supreme Executor Hale. There is a press release given by Executor Hale about them on the data crystal."

"What does this have to do with the DNA profile?" Having already seen the Nefil, Capt. Smith was fairly certain where Capt. Alexander was going with this information, but she was worried he would soon get side-tracked.

"The DNA signature we found from Luciano Hale was incredibly unique, but the Nefil had similar DNA. I'm no geneticist, but my Doc tells me they are genetically related. The example he gave was comparing a wolf and a dog's DNA. Executor Hale being the wolf and the Nefil being the dog. He said our DNA was closer to the flea on the dog by comparison."

Stephanie scowled at David. His example was positively crude. Her scowl caught his eye.

David jumped in and quickly explained, "I know the example is drastically off, but I'm not a man of science. The Doc had to dumb it down for me. My point is, if you've encountered the Nefil and kept a record of their DNA, I couldn't anticipate the DNA and create a reasonable fake match. I suppose there's still reason for doubt, but that's why I'm giving you what evidence I have and will let you decide what to think."

The room quieted for a moment. Capt. James raised his hand. "Capt. Alexander, exactly what are you proposing? We're twelve people, twelve crews. I don't care for these odds. One Pacification Ship can knock all twelve ships out and never get a scratch on her hull."

David moved from behind the podium and stepped closer to the group. "The first thing you need to remember is that although you have never seen Pateras, he's real and far more powerful than anybody or anything. The odds are in his favor. The second thing you need to know is I'm here to warn you about the dangers if you don't already know. I'm not suggesting anything specific. I'll gladly give you some options. Pateras gave everyone a choice on who to serve. Executor Hale is the one who's trying to take that choice away."

Capt. Davu had taken more than he could stomach. He challenged David openly. "You're telling us you ruined your career, the careers of your crew and got all of us on the galaxy's most wanted criminals list for what? So you can live in a fantasy world?"

Capt. Clements joined him. "Capt. Alexander, surely you did more than that. Your explanations are that of a man who has lost his mind. It's not something to get all of us killed. What aren't you telling us?"

Capt. Bowen kept her seat but added her own question. "What happened to the base on Romajin?"

David raised his hand to stop any further questions. "I'm not trying to hide any information from you. I am cutting a few corners to get the facts to you as succinctly as possible. I'm not living in a fantasy world, Capt. Davu."

Capt. Roan headed for the door. David called out to him. "Capt. Roan… Capt. Roan… Alec, please wait."

Alec turned around angrily. "Why? So you can waste our time with more lies? Sarah's right. Executor Hale wouldn't be chasing us down without a really good reason, and your foolish story may be enough to get you court-martialed or locked up in a hospital, but it's not enough for them to come after us."

Capt. Davu moved down front. "What did you expect to accomplish with this nonsense? Did you think we would blindly follow you? Why did you bring your entire crew down here and invite us to only bring a security detachment? You want us to trust you, but you more than have your back covered. You're telling us Pateras is more powerful than the Commonwealth, yet you depend on your crew for protection. Don't you trust us… Captain?"

Hearing the anger in the Captain's voices, the crew drew closer to their Captain and took on a defensive posture. David's eyes swept through the group making contact with each Captain and their support personnel. As his eyes landed on Nate, his friend gave him a subtle nod. Nate whispered something to Stephanie and Silas. The two left the assembly. Most saw Capt. Weiseman sending his wife to safety. David saw something very different.

"You want to level the playing field? Fine. Let's make it just us Captains. Send your extra personnel out and so will I."

Ajani Davu postured, "You first!"

David stood strong and stalwart. "Crew of the *Evangeline*!" he belted, "Take a walk!" His eyes landed firmly on his First Officer and wife.

She knew this was not the time to argue with him. Dismissing his crew severely altered the odds he faced with the other Captains and their ancillary personnel.

Brynna handed him some data crystals then motioned for the crew to leave the room. Braxton took the lead. Brynna brought up the rear with Jake and Marissa directly in front of her. She hesitated before leaving the room. She glanced over her shoulder fearing this could be the last time she ever saw her husband.

Seeing the look on her face, David's frustration with his peers dissolved momentarily. He smiled lovingly at her from across the room. "All the way to the ship, Commander. If you don't hear from me within three hours, secure our cargo and leave here. Arni's got this."

Brynna smiled back at him with a similar inflection. "Yes, Captain."

David watched her take a deep breath. He saw her lay her fears aside and rest in the realization that Arni was in control. He smiled again. This time it was a smile of comfort in knowing his wife trusted him and she trusted Arni.

****

Over the past year, Arni had gone from being his enemy, to his ally, to someone he was no longer capable of living without. The thought was odd, even to him. David had never depended on anyone other than the Commonwealth.

His parents separated when he was twelve, around the time he joined the Commonwealth Interstellar Force Youth Academy. He remained in his mother's custody, but he only saw her during school breaks. His father was a soldier in the CIF Infantry Division. David's father had little contact with him after his parents went their separate ways. His uncle, Adm. Robert Deacons, the man who spearheaded the Explorer Mission was David's immediate supervisor until Capt. Alexander committed treason.

The CIF was all he depended on for a majority of his life. He had never known Superior Beings existed, and now he depended on them daily. Executor Hale bragged to Capt. Alexander how he cut everyone off from their support systems making them solely dependent on the Commonwealth government. The short-term marriage contracts kept husbands and wives apart, split children from their parents, caused them to move from one location to another, leaving friends behind. The Commonwealth provided basic needs during disasters, prescribed what language was spoken, and removed criminal elements. It put everyone on equal footing. There were no religions save the worship of the Commonwealth if it could be called worship. No one could be condemned for not holding a particular set of beliefs because the only beliefs were the Commonwealth Charters.

****

The other Captains sent their ancillary personnel out of the room. The two security officers in the corridor stayed put.

With the room clear, David jumped in to get control again.

"Here are the crystals I promised you. The bottom line is this, whether you believe me or not, Executor Hale has sent the Nefil to destroy all twelve ships regardless of your allegiance. I brought you here to warn you, to form an alliance and a plan of action, and by now I know your fuel supplies are dwindling. I have fuel for each of you whether you join Pateras or not. You'll need it if the Nefil or the Pacification fleet find you. It's not a bribe or a bargaining chip. The location of the containers is on the data crystals."

Capt. Silvain moved down front on the far side of the seating area, "What if we turned you over to the Commonwealth? Does anyone else think Supreme Executor Hale would be grateful enough to take this kill order off us?"

Capt. Logan stood quickly, "I'll gladly give it a shot."

Capt. Sarah Clements kept her seat, "Capt. Alexander, you're obviously mentally unstable. I'm sorry to have to say that, but you need help. The Commonwealth can treat you."

Capt. James shook his head. "From what I saw of those Nefil, they aren't the type to be reasoned with. If Executor Hale sent them out after us, I'm not sure he would be inclined to bargain."

"I am in agreement with Sarah. You aren't well, Capt. Alexander," Capt. Silvain looked almost sorrowful, "We're placing you under arrest."

David stared at the floor for a moment. He really hoped it wouldn't come to this. A familiar voice whispered to him.

"I've got this."

It was enough to give him the courage to keep fighting.

David raised his hands slowly in surrender, "I do suggest, if you turn me over to the Supreme Executor, you only give him my dead body. He promised to destroy anyone I might influence. Funny how the Romajin Military Base blew up right after we left."

Capt. Gellert met Arni and the followers of Pateras in his own travels. He trusted Arni far more than the Commonwealth at this point. "No one wants you dead," He was hoping his comment would cause cooler heads to prevail.

Capt. Davu's eyes bored holes into David. "Alive or dead makes no difference to me. I just want my life back."

David laughed, "You just don't get it, do you? You aren't going to get your life back—ever."

David dropped his position of surrender as he strode calmly to Ajani Davu.

"If you pretend like nothing has happened and you've never seen me, the Nefil or the Pacification Fleet will hunt you down and kill all of you. If you head to the nearest military base and report this entire thing, he'll gather whatever intel he can, then he'll execute you and your crew. If you run and hide, they'll hunt you down until the rest of us can expose his crimes. If you join us in fighting him, you'll be hunted, and your lives will be in danger until we win this thing. There is NO NORMAL. Your life as you knew it is over."

David turned, walked away from him, and folded his arms across his chest.

Ajani breathed hard. He grew angrier with every breath. If this brash young Captain were right, his life and his career were nothing but dust.

Feeling the anger seething from his co-conspirator, Capt. Logan pulled a set of binders from his utility belt. "Let's get on with this. Capt. Alexander, you're under arrest," Chris took a step toward David.

Capt. Weiseman scooted forward in his seat. "You're making some pretty big assumptions, Capt. Logan."

Chris stopped to address Nate who was sitting only a couple of rows back. "What do you mean?"

"You're assuming we're all in agreement. You're assuming he doesn't have a backup plan, and most of all you're assuming Pateras is going to allow you to arrest him," Nate stayed seated and appeared at ease. He wasn't, but he was doing his best to give that impression.

Christopher Logan smiled sardonically, "You're joking. How could we not be in agreement?"

Nate glanced casually at the seascape and repositioned himself in his chair.

"You're actually going to pick one of the lesser points of my arguments to fault? That's hilarious. There are two powerful beings at war with one another, neither of which you know much about, and you're going to be worried about whether you and I agree on this matter? You've heard from our superiors what Pateras is capable of, and you don't think he's going to take issue with you trying to arrest one of his own."

Capt. Logan froze as he considered Nate's words. Executor Hale sent them to find this superior being, so he clearly wasn't a fairy tale, but exactly how powerful was he?

Capt. Clements shook her head, "He's not a superior being. He just has technology we haven't figured out yet."

David whipped around to Sarah. "Technology you haven't figured out yet? Sarah, did you ever wonder how we escaped Romajin? We were imprisoned in a CIF military prison, for six days. They cut off our food and water after three days. Would you like to know how we got out of there? Pateras sent a—a messenger who led us out. We walked out to our ship and flew away. His technology, as you call it, kept us invisible and unheard by every guard and passerby. We walked unimpeded out of a secure prison facility, out to the tarmac, and into our ship. Are you certain you want to go against that kind of power?"

Sarah pushed back, "Your Security Chief had access to that facility. He got you out of there."

"Captain, I need to say something."

All eyes turned to the back of the room where a very pregnant Lt. Marissa Holden stood with Jake a step behind her.

"Lt. Holden, you were ordered back to the ship," Capt. Alexander scowled at her presence and the presence of his Security Chief. "Chief, get her out of here."

"I'm on maternity leave, Captain. I'm afraid you can't give me orders right now," Marissa's tone was stoic rather than insubordinate.

David looked at Jake, "Chief?"

"I'm only here for her protection, sir," Jake knew his Captain was doing his best to protect the crew, but he also knew his wife wasn't going to back down this time.

David was frustrated, "Fine, make it quick," He glanced at Nate who returned a subtle nod. Capt. Weiseman remained sitting forward in his seat, making it easier for him to jump to Capt. Alexander's aid if necessary.

Marissa moved in front of the room and identified herself. "My name is Lt. JG Marissa Holden. I'm the navigator aboard the *Evangeline*."

"Breaking all the regs, aren't you, Capt. Alexander?" Capt. Logan snidely remarked.

David said nothing to Capt. Logan or to Marissa. He decided anything he said at this point would be useless.

Marissa was undaunted by Capt. Logan. Her eyes scanned the room making contact with each individual. "I need to tell you some things about Pateras and why we chose to follow him," Marissa touched her belly gently before continuing. "This baby should never have happened. I was given temporary sterilization, like all the other women before our mission started."

Capt. Clements coldly retorted, "We all know that technology fails sometimes."

Marissa smiled, "You are quite correct. Technology can fail us."

Sarah meant that the technology preventing Marissa's pregnancy was obviously flawed. Marissa's agreement and her smile were unsettling. Capt. Clements scowled. Where was this young woman going with this?

"Technology failed me. I had an incurable condition. I wasn't supposed to be able to have children."

Jake stepped to one of the computer terminals in the room and pulled the information on Marissa's condition up on the display. He put the data alongside Marissa's personal medical file.

Marissa explained the nature of her condition and pointed to the diagnosis listed on her service record. "The physicians at CIF HQ didn't want to bother with the temporary sterilization on me."

Sarah butted in again. "You see technology was wrong. You weren't sterile after all," she retorted coldly.

"But, I was," Marissa argued. "The Admiral's board insisted I receive the procedure despite my diagnosis."

Capt. Angela Smith scooted forward in her seat. Her interest was piqued. "You were doubly protected from getting pregnant. You believe Pateras is somehow responsible for this?"

Marissa took a deep breath. The next part of her story was going to be hard to swallow. "I—uh, I—"

David jumped in to help her. "Lt. Holden was snatched, quite literally from my hand by a tornado. She… died from a broken neck in the tornado."

Ajani Davu backed off when the two crewmen from the *Evangeline* entered the room. He wasn't sure who, among the other Captains was on his side and who opposed him. With the added crew from the *Evangeline*, he doubted the odds were in his favor. Ajani stepped forward angrily. "I've heard enough. You can't stand there and tell me you were dead beyond what our medical technology can heal."

Jake stepped away from the computer terminal and closer to his wife, "We searched for her all night. She was dead within minutes of being snatched by the tornado. We didn't find her until early the next morning. She was missing for eight hours and dead for nearly that long. I carried her body out of…"

Jake swallowed hard as he remembered the painful events, "I carried her back to the surf-ve. Her body was broken, and her skin was cold. You didn't have to be a trained medic to know she was long gone."

Marissa sensed the struggle Jake was facing and picked up her tale from him. "Arni Liontari took me to see his father, Pateras El Liontari. I was terrified. I stayed with him until Arni said it was time to return to the ship. Arni restored my body to perfect health. I didn't know exactly how perfect until I discovered I was pregnant a month later. Dr. Adams didn't check to see that the sterilization was still intact. He discovered later it wasn't."

Capt. Davu, Capt. Logan, and Capt. Clements looked at each other. Suspicion reared its ugly head. Each one now suspected Marissa carried the offspring of this advanced alien being. They quickly decided she and her child could be extremely dangerous.

Arni gave the gift of discernment to Capt. Alexander, and he found himself using it more frequently. Sensing their fear, he jumped in. "We've seen Arni bring people back from the dead on several occasions. He did it for me as well. I died on Tudoren when I took an arrow to the chest. I've spoken to Pateras personally twice now."

Christopher Logan got in David's face. "You expect us to believe you've been dead twice and came back to life. That's absurd!"

David calmly replied. "No, I was only dead the second time. Our point is this, Pateras is not what Executor Hale told us. He's far more powerful than—than anything. Pateras created this universe, and he could wipe it out with nothing more than a thought. He cares about what happens to it and to us. He doesn't want to destroy us. He does want us to serve him, but he isn't going to force your cooperation like we were told. He's done nothing but help us. This is a war between Luciano Hale and Pateras. We're the prize in this war. The only problem is Luciano Hale wants to see us destroyed. He wants us to side with him, which will result in our destruction. Pateras is trying to save our lives."

"That's enough! Let's take a vote. If you believe Capt. Alexander and stand with him raise your hands," Capt. Logan belted.

David stepped forward. "No! Go back to your ships and review the evidence first. Present it to your crews. If you stand with me, and with Pateras, we can meet again tomorrow evening. There will be no votes taken tonight."

"What are you afraid of Capt. Alexander? Are you afraid you're outnumbered? What's really on these crystals? Is there some kind of virus or tracking device?" Capt. Logan challenged again.

David stepped into Capt. Logan's face. "You want to know what I'm afraid of? I'm afraid of failure and losing. There's nothing but data on those crystals, no tricks, no traps, no viruses. I'm being straight with you. What are you afraid of, Chris? Are you afraid to find out you've been living and believing a lie all this time? Are you afraid I might be right? Put one of the crystals into the computer terminal in here if you're worried about it. Look at it on an isolated system or find another terminal anywhere on the colony. I assure you, it's safe."

Capt. Davu glanced at Capt. Clements. He nodded for her to review her crystal in the meeting room computer console. She walked past Jake to the terminal. She plugged the crystal in and initiated a scan of the contents for viruses or any other unexpected programs. As the scan was running, she watched Ajani closely. The scan revealed only data on the crystal. Sarah nodded at Ajani. "It's clean."

Capt. Logan stepped away from David and wandered aimlessly behind the podium before turning around to speak. "Okay, you were right. The crystal is what you said it is. Let's move on to our next step."

David rotated his position in time to see Sarah reaching for her weapon. He called out to Jake who had his back to her. "Chief!" His warning came too late. David heard a Tri-EMP power-up behind him and fire. A pain ran through his body, his muscles convulsed, and darkness overtook him.

In one swift move, Ajani jumped behind Marissa. He wrapped his left arm around her neck, pushed his Tri-EMP into her side, and twisted to face Chief Holden.

Sarah drew on Jake but didn't fire. "Stand down, Chief. Ajani doesn't want to hurt your wife, but he will stun her if necessary. I don't imagine that will be good for your baby, if that is indeed, your baby."

Jake had his weapon in his hand with lightning speed, but even that wasn't fast enough. He turned to assess Marissa's predicament. Jake fingered his weapon as he weighed his options.

Marissa was trained as a security officer. She waited calmly watching her husband. She wanted to be ready for whatever hint he gave.

Sarah moved closer behind Jake, "Put the weapon down Chief, or I'll put you down. We'd rather do this without casualties."

Jake slowly raised his hands in surrender. Before dropping his weapon, he made one point. "For the record, that is definitely my baby. If you hurt my wife or my son, I will hurt you twice as badly," Jake lowered himself to his knees and placed his weapon carefully on the floor.

Capt. Logan was preoccupied placing binders on the unconscious Capt. Alexander.

Nate stood cautiously, not wanting to spook Ajani. He moved to the end of the row and came toward the front of the room. "Ajani, don't hurt her. She's just confused."

Hearing Nate's voice, Ajani jerked to put Marissa between himself and Nate. "Keep your distance, Capt. Weiseman. I know you are friends with Capt. Alexander. Let's keep this simple. I intend to turn these three over to the Commonwealth. I don't intend to harm them, but I want my life back. I'm confident they will bargain with us. If you want no part of this, then leave. If you want in on this agreement, drop your weapons on the front seats. You can pick them up as soon as the call to the Commonwealth has been made."

Capt. Clements placed binders on Jake and positioned him on the floor next to his unconscious Captain. "I guess we're going to take that vote now."

Sarah searched Marissa for weapons and put a set of binders on her. Ajani continued to hold her in front of him. Keeping his weapon trained on the young lieutenant, he addressed the other eight Captains. "Decide now. If you are with us, put your weapons down and sit on the second row. If you want out, just leave."

Nate glanced at the door. He mentally spoke to his new mentor. "Arni, help them, please."

Nate waited and listened to the silence in his mind.

Capt. Alexander roused. He groaned and worked himself into a sitting position leaning against the base of the podium. His head was far from clear. His eyes landed on Jake. "Did we win yet?"

Jake attempted to emulate his Captain's jovial attitude in the face of adversity. "Not yet, sir. Perhaps if you would quit napping on the job," The words were there, but Jake's tone didn't quite reflect the attitude.

David shook his head to try to clear it. His return quip was lacking as well. "I'll work on that."

Nate, Alec, Patrick, Angela, and Tas moved toward the exit. David, seeing Nate leave, struggled to stand. Chris pushed him back to the ground. David called out to his friend. "Nate, don't do this. Get Marissa to safety, please."

"Sorry, Davie, I've got my own crew to look after. I can't help you now," Nate gave David a purposeful look.

David stared after Nate as he turned and headed for the door. Jake glanced at David. A question burned in his mind, but he kept it to himself.

Marissa watched the five Captains leave. She looked to Jake and David. She was nervous but knew Arni would find a way to get them out.

The remaining Captains sat down and relinquished their weapons with the exception of Capt. Silvain who watched the departure of the other Captains in the corridor. As soon as the elevator door closed, Taye turned to the others. "They're gone. We're clear."

"Make the call," Chris ordered.

David looked at Jake and Marissa. "It's in Arni's hands."

TRUCE

"Ajani! NO!" A voice called out from the doorway.

Capt. Davu was leaning over the computer terminal. His eyes jumped to the speaker. "Deka? Why are you here?"

Lt. Deka Davu, Capt. Weiseman's navigator, took several steps into the conference room. Nate walked in behind him. Ajani was startled by the appearance of his younger brother. He raised up. He knew his brother was aboard the *Emissary*, but no Captain was willing to risk his crew on this meeting.

"I came to stop you from making a mistake. Capt. Alexander is an honorable and trustworthy man. I don't know how much he's told you, but it is the truth," Deka kept a safe distance from the others. Nate stayed two steps behind him.

Taye stepped closer to protect his new ally. "Why are you back, Capt. Weiseman?"

"I'm protecting my crewman and my friends. You used to be one of them, Taye. Please don't force me to make those kinds of choices," Nate's words were calm, yet pained.

Ajani shook his head at his brother. "Deka, you're young and inexperienced. You don't understand fully what's going on here. Capt. Alexander and his crew are the reason Supreme Executor Hale no longer trusts us. I'm trying to get our lives back."

"You're the one who doesn't understand what's happening," Deka argued. "Capt. Alexander risked the lives of himself and his crew to save my life and Elize's. You need to listen to him."

Ajani stared at his younger brother in disbelief. "He's turned you. You've disgraced our family. You both need to leave. This is no longer your concern."

Deka looked at Marissa. "Let me take the place of Lt. Holden."

"What? Deka, have you lost your mind? Why does she mean anything to you?" Ajani fingered the weapon in his hand nervously.

Deka moved a couple of steps closer to his brother. "She obviously means nothing to you, or you wouldn't be threatening her life like this."

"I never threatened her life," Capt. Davu rebutted.

"Remember when I said you were the one who didn't understand what was happening? You just proved my point," Deka glanced at the others in the room. He hoped they were paying close attention.

"I never threatened her life. I threatened to stun her, that's it. I'm not a monster," Ajani defended himself.

"The Nefil came for us on Ela Prime. They planned to kill our entire crew and everyone aboard the *Evangeline* except for Capt. Alexander. His defiance rubbed Executor Hale the wrong way. He wanted the Captain and his wife brought back alive. If you make that call to the Commonwealth, they will kill her, her husband, and probably her child. He may still want Capt. Alexander alive, but he won't let you go free. He may agree to it at first, but later you'll have some sort of unexpected accident. Let her go, or she *will* die."

Sarah, Chris, and Taye glanced guiltily at Marissa. They had no desire to see the young woman dead.

Ajani shook his head. "If they choose to execute her, that isn't my problem."

Marissa shifted uncomfortably. "Capt. Davu, I won't live to see a trial. We'll be executed the second they get their hands on us. We won't get a trial, no re-education, no prison, no due process, just an execution."

Sarah stared at Marissa. "You don't know that for a fact."

Capt. Alexander's head was clear now. "We do know it. There's proof on the data crystals I gave you."

Capt. Smith, Capt. James, Capt. Gellert, and Capt. Roan entered in time to hear the exchange. Angela and Alec were quick to support Capt. Alexander. Their own encounters with the Nefil convinced them of the Commonwealth's ill intentions.

Deka stepped closer to his brother. "Ajani, let me take the woman's place. You aren't a killer."

His proximity was making Capt. Davu nervous. He aimed his weapon at his younger brother. "Keep your distance, Deka. I will stun you if I have to."

Deka smiled ironically at his brother. "I know you will. I am ready to face whatever I must to guarantee that what's right and good happens. Turning these people over to the Commonwealth isn't the right thing to do."

David cautiously repositioned himself onto his knees. He eyed Capt. Logan to be certain he wasn't going to object. "Capt. Davu, this war isn't new. Both sides have been active for thousands of years. Our lives mean nothing to Luciano Hale. If he wiped out entire planetary populations, he's not going to think twice about one hundred forty-four soldiers. He may accept your peace offering and give you a medal, then when no one is looking he'll take you out. He's afraid that one day, everything you've heard will make sense. You'll realize what a mistake you've made. He knows you'll turn on him. The difference is, Pateras is trying to save lives, not destroy them."

Nate stepped toward Deka. "There's something else you really need to know. We were warned about Pateras taking over our minds. Here's a piece of irony for you. Supreme Executor Hale has done the very thing he warned us about."

Angela glanced at Patrick. They had seen it in action the same way Nate had.

Capt. Davu shook his head and closed ranks with his comrades, sensing something was about to transpire. "You're lying. That's not possible. You must really be desperate."

"It's true, Ajani. The Nefil used it against Capt. Weiseman," Lt. Davu hoped his brother would have more cause to believe him than the others.

Capt. Logan snidely remarked. "I suppose the proof is on the data crystal again."

David answered Capt. Logan. "Yes, but since you aren't likely to look at it, I've arranged for a live demonstration. Nate?"

Capt. Weiseman pressed a button on his bracelet and reached for his weapon. Deka and the four other Captains who sided with David and Nate drew their weapons. They hadn't had much time to prepare a plan to rescue Capt. Alexander and his two crewmen. Their plan was roughly to watch Capt. Weiseman and follow his lead.

The button on Capt. Weiseman's bracelet activated a program which sent commands out to the four aggressive Captains. Nate spoke into the speaker in his bracelet. "The Tri-EMPs are hot. They're burning your hands."

The four Captains gave each other confused looks. Chris Logan glanced at his weapon. The hand holding his weapon shook, and in a second, he dropped it onto the floor. "Ah! I can't hold it! It's hot! What did you do to it?"

Capt. Davu tried to wrap his hand more tightly around the grip and mentally force the pain away. His hand shook violently until he was forced to drop his weapon. He cried out in pain and grasped his wrist. He looked at his shaking hand. The skin was red and blisters were forming.

Sarah dropped hers nearly as quickly as Capt. Logan. Taye held his weapon as long as he could. He swapped hands and tried to aim at Capt. Weiseman. He surmised Nate was the cause of his pain. His non-dominant hand was unable to control the weapon through his pain. He finally released the weapon. "Errr" He growled through gritted teeth.

Capt. Talaith Bowen and Capt. Bryan Wallace were uncertain who to support in the current conflict. They stared in horror. Their eyes landed on their confiscated weapons laying on the front row seats. It was clear they wanted access to them, but now they were afraid to touch them.

Nate wasn't done with his demonstration. He casually whispered into his bracelet again. "Go watch the fish."

Deka was the only one close enough to hear his command audibly. It earned Nate a hasty annoyed glance from his navigator. Chris, Ajani, Sarah, and Taye walked to the observation window and stared out it.

Nate nodded to the Captains who were supporting him. "Go free them."

Alec freed Capt. Alexander while Tas Gellert freed Jake. Angela released Marissa's binders and checked to be certain she was alright. Marissa assured Capt. Smith she was fine. Jake and Tas helped Marissa to her feet.

David paused long enough to speak to the couple. "Retrieve your weapons and get back to the ship. Marissa, no more heroics. If you stay, you'll only interfere with my job. Thank you for what you tried to do, but I can't work if I'm worried about you."

Marissa bowed her head slightly. "Yes Captain, I'm sorry, sir."

Jake hastily escorted his wife from the room. He wasn't keen on her coming in the first place. The events served only to confirm his belief that her idea was a bad one. David heard them arguing before the door to the corridor closed. He shook his head. Their arguments rarely ended quickly.

David faced the two undecided Captains. "If you promise not to use them against me, you're free to retrieve your weapons."

Talaith and Bryan glanced at each other nervously. Talaith eyed the weapons. She felt vulnerable without it. David assured her they were safe to touch. He retrieved the two weapons and returned them to their owners.

Tas and Angela collected the discarded "hot" weapons. Tas approached David carefully. "These aren't hot at all. What exactly happened?"

David held up his finger asking Capt. Gellert to wait a moment. "We'll show you. Capt.s Davu, Silvain, Logan, and Clements, please come have a seat."

The four stayed where they were, staring into the ocean in front of them. David turned to Capt. Weiseman. "Nate, if you would be kind enough to help me out here?"

Nate whispered into his bracelet again. The four turned away from the seascape and moved into the seating area. Their eyes were glazed and unfocused. As soon as they were settled into their seats, David nodded for Nate to release them from their controlled state. Nate shut down the program. As their minds regained control and their memories of what happened replayed, tension appeared on their faces.

Sarah was frightened. "What did you do to us?"

Capt. Davu gripped the wrist of his shaking, blister-covered hand. "You see. They are controlling our minds."

David kept his weapon visible in his hand. He was taking care not to point it at anyone. He stepped closer to Ajani. "Yes, we are controlling your minds… using Commonwealth technology. Do you remember those nanites Adm. Deacons brought you? The ones to aid in language translation? You remember those, right?"

Ajani looked stricken as the possibilities ran through his head. "Y-yes. What about them?"

Nate joined David. "The Nefil use them to interface with their equipment and communicate with each other. They used them to try to get me to kill David. It nearly worked. The Commonwealth is trying to control your minds. I just borrowed the technology long enough to help my friends and get your attention."

Ajani questioned his brother, "Deka, is this true?"

Deka nodded. "I'm afraid so. If they ever get close enough, they can program your nanites so that you either kill each other, walk yourselves out the nearest airlock, or activate the self-destruct sequence on your ship. As soon as we knew how they were being used, Capt. Weiseman ordered us to get them removed."

Capt. Logan sat frozen in place. He looked down at his body. "Why do I suddenly feel like a ticking time bomb?"

David slipped his Tri-EMP into its holster. "We were all ticking time bombs, the second we signed up for this mission. Pateras knew it and placed a warning out there, but Executor Hale did everything in his power to hide that warning from us. Whether you work for Pateras or not is entirely up to you. I called this meeting to warn you about Luciano Hale, the Nefil, and what the Commonwealth has become. You can pick up the fuel we mined for you anytime you want and whether you stay or go is your choice. The only thing I'm asking of you is that you stay clear of the Commonwealth. Don't give us up, don't try to make any deals with them, and don't give them any information."

Taye scowled. "What about these… these things in our bodies? What can we do about them?"

"We can help you with that, too. It will require a little bit of trust from both of us. Can we reach our first agreement? This mining colony will be considered neutral ground. Do you agree?" David eyed each Captain, including the four antagonists. Each one agreed, some more willingly than others.

Capt. Davu sat down dejectedly. "What else do you want? What's the cost of freeing us from these nanites?"

"We'll give you everything you need to deactivate the nanites and remove them. No charge. I would love it if we all agreed to follow Pateras, but I'm not holding my breath for that one."

"Get to the point!" yelled an angry Capt. Silvain.

"I'm looking specifically for allies to expose Executor Hale's crimes and to stop him from destroying more innocent lives. I follow Pateras. My crew follows him, and we will continue to do so. We're not demanding that you follow him. Just work with him, and us, to stop Executor Hale. I don't want to see you, or your crews get hurt," David explained. He was repeating himself, but this time, they were listening.

Sarah Clements was staring at the floor in front of her. She raised her head slowly. "So, you're saying lead, follow, or get out of the way."

David nodded. "Pretty much. Everything you need to know and more is on those data crystals. If you want in on this, join us tomorrow evening. If you want no part of it, take your fuel and leave quietly. The nanite protocols will be transmitted to your bracelets before you leave."

Capt. Davu scowled. "How do we know you aren't transmitting a virus or tracking program?"

David returned Ajani's scowl. "You remember that trust thing I mentioned? How do I know you won't walk out of here, remove your nanites, then bring a Pacification ship to our front door?"

Ajani stared at David. Neither flinched nor blinked. David kept his eyes on Ajani while he spoke to the man's brother. "Lt. Davu, are you a follower of Pateras?"

"Yes, Capt. Alexander, I'm a follower of Pateras. I would give my life for him if that's what he asks of me," Deka answered honestly.

"There is one more thing each of you should know. Executor Hale won't hesitate to use your families to get to you. They're probably being watched. If you go near them, you'll get yourselves caught or your families arrested," Capt. Alexander's point was to make sure Ajani knew the civilians in his family were already at risk. If Ajani tried to report them, Deka and his other family members would be in danger.

"Capt. Davu, I'm not a fool. My crew will continue to monitor all traffic and comm signals in and out of the mining colony. If we detect any hint of the Commonwealth, we'll evacuate everyone and send them different directions. All I'm asking is for you to review the evidence and as Sarah said, lead, follow, or stay out of the way. Can you do that? If you want to fly straight to the Commonwealth and turn in all your evidence on us, then so be it. Just give us this one place as neutral ground. You might also want to let your crew know what they are risking if you try making a deal with the Commonwealth. They deserve to know before joining your suicide mission," David tried to lay things out as plainly as possible.

Ajani continued to stare at David. His doubts rolling loudly in his head like large marbles in a wooden box. The noise in his mind was deafening. The questions in everyone's minds were nearly as pronounced.

Silence settled on the room. David nodded at Nate to transmit the data for the nanites to everyone in the room.

Nate stepped forward. "I've sent you the protocols for overriding the nanite programming. I strongly urge you to remove them. It's possible they're programmed with a back door which could reactivate them. If that's the case, changing the primary access codes is pointless."

Several Captains gave wary glances at their bracelets. Chris Logan finally asked. "Are we done?"

David nodded. "For now. Unless someone betrays our agreement, I'll be here tomorrow evening to start planning our next moves. You can join me tomorrow by yourselves, with a security detail, or you can bring your entire crew if you wish. I will have some of my people here as well. It's your decision. Take your weapons and your data crystals. You're free to go."

The Captains were arranged in two distinct groupings based on which way they were leaning. The ones in support of Capt. Alexander were scattered around the room, protecting Capt. Alexander and Capt. Weiseman. Those who were opposed were in the seating area along with the ones who remained unsure. Nate pulled his impromptu security force to the front of the room, so the path out was clear.

Each one retrieved their weapons. Sarah touched hers gingerly, fearing it was still warm. She glanced at Ajani's blistered hand. "If these weapons weren't really hot, why did Ajani get blistered?"

David and Nate exchanged glances. Nate volunteered to answer. "I suspect the nanites convinced his brain that they were hot and his brain reacted as though they really were. One of the Docs or Psychs would know better than I do."

The answer made sense, but only added to their concern. The wary Captains, weapons in hand, scurried for the exit. Deka moved closer to the exit to catch his brother.

Chris and Sarah left quickly with Talaith and Bryan not far behind them. Ajani stayed inside the room in a heated discussion with Deka.

Angela, Patrick, and Tas expressed their support to Nate and David and assured the two they would present the situation to their respective crews and return the following evening. Their primary concern was whether the others would lay a trap for them even in the minutes after leaving the room.

****

Nate glanced at his bracelet. "Davie, I have a confession. I did stick a tracker in with that nanite program. The program will shut itself off in forty-eight hours, and I'm the only one with access. It shows the others took the elevator

131

to the plaza, and split up after that. Sorry, I just wanted a little more security. It does give you plausible deniability."

David pressed his lips together in frustration. "Not anymore. You just told me about it. I wanted to be sure they knew I was trustworthy, Nate. You've put that in jeopardy."

Nate shrugged his shoulders. "Sorry. If it makes things any better, I can confess it first thing tomorrow, if we survive that long."

David paced aimlessly for a moment. "Let me think about it tonight and let you know tomorrow."

Angela scowled. "David, you might not want to say anything. If they don't find it and it does shut itself down in forty-eight hours, why risk alienating them."

David shook his head. "I'll confess it myself tomorrow. I really don't want them to have any reason to doubt me."

David glanced at Deka and Ajani. Deka and Ajani were speaking in heated albeit low tones. His eyes swept the rest of the room and saw Capt. Silvain waiting patiently to speak with him. "I suppose I should come clean with those who are still here."

Nate shook his head. "Let me do it. It's my fault. Capt. Davu, Capt. Silvain could I speak to you both for a minute."

The two Captains approached cautiously. Nate confessed his subversion to the two men and promised not to use the tracking program against them. He assured them it would only be active for forty-eight hours and it wouldn't be passed on to any other computers or bracelets.

Capt. Davu was irritated by the information. Capt. Silvain wasn't disturbed by it, but *something* was on his mind.

David offered his apology to the two affected Captains and told the others if they needed to go, he would be fine. Everyone left except Capt. Silvain, Nate, and the two arguing brothers. Ajani and Deka did step into the corridor to continue their argument.

****

Capt. Silvain stayed to unload his burden. "Capt. Weiseman, Capt. Alexander, please forgive me for opposing you. I didn't know what else to do. If what you've said is true, I have no hope of having a life again."

Nate attempted to offer some cheer. "You're still Captain of a ship, and you have a crew that needs your leadership. We have a mission to complete. The only thing that's different is our list of resources has changed, we no longer get a standard pay allowance, and we work for somebody way cooler than before."

Capt. Silvain tried to swallow a lump deep in his throat. "Capt. Alexander, I wanted to blame you for my current predicament. I have nothing to offer you. My ship's gone, and most of my crew were captured, including my wife."

David and Nate exchanged sorrowful looks. "Taye, I'm so sorry. What happened?"

"We got the recall order and did what we were ordered to do. I took the shuttle and two of my crew members to visit some friends on the far side of Raesii. My wife got word to me that the crew was being arrested. She was the last one taken because she was finishing her reports from our last mission. She saw the crew get arrested right after they disembarked. She hailed me and tried to hide. I heard them find her. She was shot while her comm link was open. I can only hope she was stunned, not killed. I recalled my two remaining crewmen, and we headed for a remote travel terminal, booked passage to a larger terminal, then jumped the first ship off-world. We changed ships several times. I kept one of the data modules we stored on the shuttle to pick up any transmissions meant for the *Advocate*. Somehow I knew someone would be reaching out to us," Taye's pain etched deep lines on his face.

Nate broke the silence. "Are your other two crewmen here, or did you leave them someplace safe?"

Anger flared in Taye's eyes again. "Are you trying to trap me? You want me to reveal their location to capture them. I failed to protect my crew! I will never reveal their location to you."

Nate raised his hands and motioned for Capt. Silvain to calm down. "Taye, I don't have to know. It's fine. Take it easy. I am not your enemy."

David stepped between the two. "Capt. Silvain, Nate understands your feelings. He lost two crew members early last year. I can partly understand your pain as well. I lost Marissa on our second mission. It was only because Arni graciously restored her that I have her back. It doesn't erase that feeling of failure."

Nate looked every direction except Taye's eyes. "Davie, my situation was far worse. You didn't just lose a crewman. I condemned two of my own to die."

Taye grabbed Nate by the front of his jacket and jerked him forward. "You condemned two of your own to die, and you expect me to trust you?" Taye was several inches taller than both Nate and David. His stature and posture were clearly intimidating.

"I didn't execute them. I abandoned them for being sympathetic to Pateras on Strabothon. The Commonwealth went behind us and wiped out the entire population. I didn't know what I did was going to get them killed. I thought I was sparing their lives," Nate explained quickly.

David didn't try to separate the two physically. "Taye, he didn't know. It was early in the mission. We were all believing the lies," David waited to see if Capt. Silvain was comprehending the information.

Taye slowly released his grip on Nate's jacket. "I'm sorry. Do you think my wife and crew are still alive?"

David relaxed a little. "It's possible, but I can't say for certain. The time I spent with Executor Hale, he was all over the place with his plans. He would say one thing, then do another. He changed directions so many times, I couldn't even guess what he was going to do next."

Taye's eyes narrowed. "You worked directly with Executor Hale? Is that why you changed your loyalty?"

David laughed ironically. "Uh… no, I didn't work with him. I was his prisoner on Romajin. He took a lot of pleasure in telling me what he had planned for me and for my crew. He wanted to watch me squirm."

David could see a new barrage of questions welling up in Capt. Silvain's mind. "I might have one other piece of intel. He threatened to send us to Mara for re-education. I was also told when I picked up some prisoners for transport, they were cleaning house on Mara to prepare for an influx of Liontari conscripts for re-education."

Taye's eyes lit up thinking his wife and crew might still be accessible. Nate raised his hand to slow Taye's thought processes. "Capt. Silvain, Executor Hale knows that David has this information, which means he can potentially entrap anyone coming to rescue them or he could change the plan."

The light dimmed. David tried to offer the man some sort of hope. "Nate and I have a couple of sources. We can make some inquiries to see what we can find out. Just don't do anything rash, okay?"

"He's right, Taye. It's us against the entire galaxy. We have to do this the way Pateras wants, or we'll get more people killed," Nate wanted to be sure Taye was thinking rationally.

"Capt. Alexander, I have one more problem. Since I have no ship…" Taye looked at the ground. "I have no way to remove these nanites."

Nate and David looked at each other. If Taye were trying to entrap them, this was the way to do it. Nate decided his friend was already putting himself at high enough risk. "Capt. Silvain, my ship is docked here under a false I.D. I can take you to it. Stephanie got them out of the rest of my crew. She can take care of those nanites for you, if you're willing to trust me."

Taye searched Nate's eyes. There were no evident signs of deception. Taye's eyes revealed he had nothing left. "My two crewmen are in the plaza. We can pick them up on the way. I think I'm tired of running. If this is a trap, then I surrender to it."

Nate offered the man his hand. "My crew and I are followers of Pateras. You have my word, this is no trap of our making. You'll be safe with us."

Taye accepted the man's assurance. The men headed for the plaza. Reaching the arboretum, Taye reunited with his crewmen and followed Nate to the *Emissary*. David returned to his ship alone.

INTERNAL TURBULENCE

The next morning, Capt. Alexander briefed his staff on the ups and downs of the meeting with the other Captains. He listened carefully to their concerns and expectations. Lexi and Jake often suffered a great deal of frustration as the Captain made decisions without appearing to consider their concerns. This time he listened and heeded their warnings. Jake was adamantly opposed to taking the entire crew to this second meeting. Lexi agreed, but she believed they needed to make a strong showing.

Capt. Alexander glanced at his wife and First Officer. "Commander, what are your thoughts?"

Brynna was unusually quiet this morning. She pondered for another moment.

When her thoughts reached their conclusion, she leaned forward on the table in front of her. "Captain, I agree with Lexi and Jake about keeping our people split. We showed the Captains last night we were all committed to this. I think we need to keep a minimal amount of people visible. This situation with the Malos still has me concerned. I'm not sure it's been resolved. I suggest you keep Thane, Marissa, Aulani, Braxton, Lazaro, Jason, and Laura on the ship. I want Jake, Lexi, and Cheyenne to accompany us to the meeting. I really see Jason and Laura as being the only ones who are… uh… negotiable."

Jason looked concerned. "Do you mean negotiable or expendable?"

Brynna's eyes snapped. She slapped her hands firmly on the table in front of her. As she spoke, her posture tensed and her tone became more emphatic.

"*No one* is expendable. If this goes south, the ship needs an expert pilot capable of aquatic and aerial maneuvering, and a navigator. The ground team doesn't need a member who's nine months pregnant. The ship needs a qualified commander, engineer, and comms officer. A case could be made for putting Laura on comms and bringing Aulani, but that's what I meant by negotiable. I would strongly prefer to keep you on board the ship, but if we need a stronger showing, you and Laura are the only ones I would be willing to pull away from your stations, and I'm barely willing to do that."

Jason sat stunned by the Commander's blunt attack on his question. "I'm sorry, Commander. I didn't mean to question your judgment."

David was taken aback by her reaction as well. He tried not to draw attention to it, but if there were concerns about anyone's importance, they needed to be addressed. He looked around the room making eye contact with everyone, starting with Lexi and Jake and finishing with Jason, Laura, and lastly Brynna.

"No one, I repeat, no one is expendable. This is not my mission. This mission belongs to Pateras. I'm just a ship's Captain. Brynna, I think you were mistaken about one thing. I don't believe Jason and Laura are negotiable. If Marissa goes into labor, she'll need Jason, and Braxton will need Laura on the bridge. If she doesn't go into labor in the next twenty-four hours, we still have guests on board that need to be monitored. We're going with the Commander's recommendation. I want full weapons complements for the ground team and standard weapons issue for those staying aboard. We'll monitor scanners from the ship. Anything else I need to consider?"

No one had any other questions. Brynna's irate tone reverberated in David's mind. He couldn't shake it. "Here's the duty roster for today. We'll need to keep somebody on scanners and comms at all times. I've got command this morning, Cmdr. Alexander will have it this afternoon, and Lt. Cmdr. Flint will have it this evening. Do NOT let yourselves get overly tired.

This thing could reach crisis mode in a heartbeat. I want everyone on top of their game. Marissa, feel free to bow out at any time. Cmdr. Alexander, Lt. Holden, I need to see you both in my office as soon as we're done here. Dismissed."

Capt. Alexander grabbed his coffee cup and made a hasty egress. For half a second, Brynna thought he was calling her out on her earlier tirade. When he called for Lt. Holden to join them, she decided he was calling the young lieutenant out on her failure to obey orders the previous night. Brynna picked up her cup of coffee and followed her husband to his office. She arrived before Marissa.

****

Capt. Alexander hoped Brynna would arrive first. He set the tone immediately. "Commander, before the lieutenant gets here, I need to ask you a question. Did you know she was coming back to the conference room?"

"No, she said she needed to catch her breath a minute in the Plaza. I had no idea what she had in mind. Why would you think I did?" Brynna wondered if he was about to make an accusation.

"I just wanted to be sure before I reprimanded her. If she had your blessing, I was going to reprimand both of you. It would be embarrassing if I jumped down her throat first then found out later you were responsible. I want to make sure we're in sync. I need to support your decisions as much as you support mine."

Before Brynna could respond, the door chimed letting them know Marissa had arrived. David called out to open the door for her. He remained seated at his desk with his hands clasped on top of it. Marissa marched to the desk and reported as officially as she could, considering her current physical condition. David stared at her holding her salute. He finally gave the counter-gesture. The look on his face revealed his obvious frustration with her. She had never broken a single regulation or challenged him in any way until last night. The Captain invited her to have a seat. He was not happy with the situation, and if her husband were the one in trouble, Jake would not have been offered a chair. "Lt. Holden, I gave you my word, did I not, that I would protect you and your baby?"

Marissa knew he was upset with her. She struggled to get comfortable in her chair. "Yes, Captain. I'm sorry I disobeyed your orders last night. I just thought—"

"I haven't asked you for an explanation, Lieutenant. When I agreed to protect you, I didn't expect you to make my job harder. I've come to expect this type of behavior from Jake, not from you. If I give an order, I expect it to be obeyed. I can *not* do my job if you're going to put yourself at risk. You've never been even remotely insubordinate. Why now?"

Marissa tried hard to swallow the lump in her throat. She had never cried so much in her life as she had in the last eight months. She struggled to speak without crying. Tears slowly escaped despite her best efforts. "I'm sorry, Captain. I didn't mean to make your job harder. I thought I could help. I thought if the others knew what Pateras did for me… they would trust him."

David took a slow, deep breath. "Lieutenant, if they believe you were telling the truth, then yes, the information could improve their trust. They don't know that your story is any more truthful than mine. Yours is just more… colorful. Marissa, in order to keep you and your baby safe, I need to know where you are and what your situation is. You can't hide contractions from me, and you can't second guess my strategies. I gave you my word, and I intend to keep it. It's my job to strategize. It's why I get paid the big credits."

Marissa looked at the floor. She couldn't bring herself to look him in the eye. He had risked his life to protect her and her baby. Marissa felt she had betrayed his trust. "Are you putting me on report, sir?"

David scowled. His tone got softer. "No, Marissa, there's no one to report you to. We are way past breaking regs. I want you to follow my orders and understand the difficulties that occur when you don't. I have a ship to run. I can't do that without a crew. I know what you were trying to do, and I appreciate it, but please don't do it again. Do I have your word?"

Marissa wiped the tears from her cheeks again. She awkwardly pulled herself from her chair. Her eyes fixated on the Captain's desk and not his face. "Yes Captain, you have my word. May I go now?"

David moved from behind his desk. "No, not yet. You're still crying. Why are you crying? Was I that hard on you?"

"I didn't m-mean t-to disappoint you, sir. I was trying to help," Marissa's tears turned to sobs, "I hate crying!" she trembled.

David rubbed his face with his hand and glanced helplessly at Brynna. Brynna shrugged at him. David wrapped an arm around Marissa to offer her some comfort. He spoke softly. "I didn't mean to make you cry. I wanted to keep you safe like I promised I would. You didn't disappoint me. I was caught off-guard, and it wasn't the worst idea. I just wasn't willing to risk your safety."

Marissa's crying finally settled. David relaxed his hug, and Marissa pulled away from him. An odd look crossed her face. She wiped her tears away again. She finally managed to look the Captain in the eye. "You aren't mad at me?"

"No, I'm not mad at you. I'm a little freaked out by your pregnancy hormones, but you've never given me cause to be angry," David answered candidly.

"I—I'm kinda freaked out too. I'm not used to this either. I hate being this… unstable," Marissa confided.

Brynna leaned forward. "You aren't sorry about having the baby, are you?"

"No, that's not what I'm saying at all. I didn't expect to be an emotional basket case. I'm not sure what I really expected. When I first found out I would never be able to have children, I distanced myself from other women. I never knew what pregnant women go through. I'm glad I chose to keep this baby," Marissa lovingly caressed her belly.

David motioned for her to sit back down. "This brings me to another question. Lieutenant, are you and the Chief still committed to staying aboard the *Evangeline*?"

Marissa's face changed drastically. She went through a gamut of emotion in the few minutes she was in the Captain's office. Fear was the next one in line. The young mother-to-be was suddenly terrified the Captain was going to change his mind about allowing them to stay aboard the ship. Had her actions caused him to re-think his decision?

"W—Why are you asking?"

Seeing her reaction, Capt. Alexander explained his question in more detail. "Lieutenant, I'm not asking you to leave or throwing you off my ship, if that's what you're worried about. I just wanted to know if you and Jake rethought your situation over the last few months. If you wanted to get away from this, now would be the time. You could return to Drea with Aulani's family if you wanted."

David watched her fear give way to apprehension. He continued with his explanation. "When we meet with the crews of the other ships, there may be others who want completely out. We may be forced to reorganize all twelve ships and crews. We could end up with fewer than twelve ships. I just want to know what the two of you are thinking before I go into this."

The Lieutenant's face relaxed. "Captain, I can't run away and hide. I know this mission puts me, Jake, and our baby at risk. I want our son to know what's happening and what's at stake from the very beginning. He needs to know who Pateras is and what this fight is about. I don't want to hide away in some obsolete corner of the galaxy and hope it all works out. This is worth fighting for and worth dying for."

David wanted to be certain she thought everything completely through. "I understand your willingness to die for what you believe in, but are you willing to raise your son without a father? Would you be willing to sacrifice your son's life?"

Marissa's heart pounded as she weighed the answer to his questions. Her hormones tried to respond first. She forced them to yield to her more stoic nature. She shuddered briefly and raised her eyes to face him. She calmly asked. "Can you assure me that Luciano Hale's attention will never land on Drea? Do you know we will be safe there?"

David scowled. "You know I can't tell you that. The more people we send there, the greater the risk to Drea. Another ten to twenty years and he'll have no reason at all to spare them. I'm hoping he won't be in power at that point, but I have no idea what the future holds."

Marissa knew the answers to her questions. Her questions were more to make sure he understood her point. "Captain, I will discuss it with Jake one more time, but I doubt we'll change our minds. If you're having second thoughts about allowing me to stay, then tell me now."

Capt. Alexander leaned back in his chair. "Cmdr. Alexander mentioned when this decision first came up, that it's against the regs for a reason. It's disruptive to the ship's routines and a distraction for the crew, myself included. We weren't trained or prepared for dealing with this sort of situation."

Lt. Holden steeled herself for what he might say next.

Capt. Alexander saw her brace for the mental impact as he leaned forward and took her hand. With his peripheral vision, he saw a concerned look form on Brynna's face behind Marissa. He spoke as gently as he could. "We've run into a lot of things on this mission we weren't prepared for. It's caused some really rough patches. You know that personally."

David took a deep breath. "So far we've handled everything that's been thrown at us with Arni's help. Things are only going to get more complicated from this point on. After you have the baby, you're going to have to arrange for someone to watch him while you return to active duty. Your attention can't be divided while you're on duty. You understand that, right?"

Marissa nodded. She wasn't sure where he was going with this. Was he throwing her off his ship, or not?

"Captain, please make your point," She asked tersely.

Sensing her mood was about to change again, David tried to make his point quickly.

"I'm not asking you to leave. I just want you to understand what staying means. When you are on the bridge, navigating this ship, all lives will depend on you being focused on where this ship is going. That includes your son's life. If we were fired on, you have to continue focusing on my orders and maneuvering this ship… not wondering if your son was injured by the impact. I want you to know, going in, what the risks are.

I'm willing to give it a try, but if it proves too problematic, we may re-evaluate it later. I want you to talk to Jake and Arni. If you can still do your job, then by all means, stay."

David felt Marissa's hand relax. Her hand became ice cold when her fear of being put off the ship spiked. It only took seconds for them to warm up again. As he released her hand, he saw Brynna's face reflecting similar relief. The Captain moved his chair out of the way and stepped behind his desk.

Sensing they were done, Marissa stood slowly. "Will that be all, sir?"

"Yes, that's all. Let me know if you and Jake change your minds. For now, I am going to assume everything is status quo unless you tell me otherwise. Don't bother with the salute this time. You are free to go," David smiled at her. Since finding out about Marissa's pregnancy, David took on the role of protector and even something akin to an older brother to her. He wasn't around his sister during her pregnancy and wondered if this was what it was like. He really had no clue how to be an uncle.

Before Marissa turned to go, she added, "Captain, Commander, I appreciate your help through all of this. I know a lot could happen in the next few days, but no matter what, I'm really grateful for your support."

Brynna smiled weakly at her. She wasn't sure what could happen in the next few days either. Any member of the twelve crews could notify the Commonwealth of their location, getting them captured or killed.

Brynna was strangely envious of Marissa. She and David had spoken on numerous occasions about having children. The method of birth control used by the Commonwealth on them prior to their departure on this mission would prevent that possibility for a minimum of another year. The doctor could reverse the procedure easily enough, but this didn't really feel like a good time to be starting a family with the entire galaxy breathing down their necks. The Commander knew her husband had a lot on his mind, so she didn't want to burden him with a personal desire. Maybe if they survived another week, they could discuss the reversal procedure.

David noticed the hesitation in Brynna's smile. He bolstered his own to make up the difference. "Lt. Holden, you are a valued member of this crew, and you are family to both of us. We could not, and *would* not, have done anything any differently."

Brynna's smile brightened. "He's right. You are family. I'm looking forward to meeting my new nephew."

David's eyes sparkled when he heard Brynna use the same relational terms he thought moments earlier. It made him feel that much closer to his wife.

Marissa left to find her husband and have the long, hard discussion she knew they needed to have.

****

Brynna started to follow her out of the office when David called her name and asked her to stay. The Commander wasn't sure what level of conversation they were about to have. Despite their treason, she was trained to treat him as her commanding officer as well as her husband. David relieved a bit of her angst by moving to the table to sit. His conversation with Lt. Holden was mostly business, as demonstrated by positioning themselves at the desk. Moving to the table could be viewed as a more equal placement for an open table discussion.

David sat for a moment pondering which approach to take with the pending discussion. He decided to keep it light and shallow unless he saw a need to go deeper. His discussion with Lexi on a similar matter earlier in the week indicated these were clearly symptoms of a bigger problem. "You know, I'm not sure if I am asking this as your Captain or your husband."

"What is it, David? I promise to respect you, no matter who's asking," Now Brynna was really confused. If this were about her earlier tirade, she was sure it was the Captain who would address her.

"I had a discussion earlier this week with Lt. Flint. Our mission parameters have clearly changed. Along with those changes, our roles have also changed. Lexi was feeling lost, and she thought I was giving her mercy assignments. Jason's comment about being expendable is another symptom of the

145

problem. I can only imagine the others among the diplomatic team having similar issues. I don't want anybody thinking they no longer have a purpose aboard this ship. This mission isn't about me or simply manning the ship's stations. How do I address this?"

Brynna stared at him as she considered his question. "Is this about my tantrum with Jason?" She finally asked.

David's eyebrows knit themselves together. He had hoped to slip his point past her without drawing attention to her ill response to the Doctor. It was one of the things he was taught when taking on this mission. His instructors educated the Captains on the importance of not making enemies of their First Officers. He was pulled aside and given specific instructions since his First Officer was also his wife. "Well, indirectly, perhaps. It's a symptom of a larger problem."

Brynna grimaced. "I'm sorry if I came off sounding hateful. I can go apologize to him if you want me to."

"Brynna, this isn't about a simple apology, although it might be in order. I need every member of this crew to know they are valued and needed on this ship. We've all got jobs to do," David was troubled. Brynna was not assigning his statement to herself, but to Jason and Lexi.

He finally leaned back in his chair and put things more bluntly. "Commander, I need you to address the Explorer Fleet crews tonight."

Brynna scowled. "Okay, I'm with Lexi. Is this a mercy assignment?"

"No, it isn't. I need to be free to do my job, which is to protect the crew, and support you. You're the diplomat, not me. I think I've moved in and taken over where I shouldn't. We need to handle this the way we handled the mission on Drea."

As Brynna tried to bring his point into focus, David saw her injured psyche manifest itself. "David, my feelings haven't been hurt. I'm your First Officer. I thought I was doing my job. Was I wrong?"

David leaned forward, propping on his knees as he looked at the floor. He rubbed the palms of his hands together as he prepared his answer. When he decided how to respond appropriately, he reached across and gently took her hand.

"You… are… an excellent First Officer. That is not your primary position though. You are the diplomatic team leader. I have… usurped your position, title, role, however you want to say it, and I apologize for that. I've taken on this new mission as though I'm the only one responsible for it. I keep trying to leave this in Arni's hands, but every time I turn around, I've pulled it back into my own. I'm not Pateras. I can't take on the galaxy. Brynna, I need your help," The Captain's words grew softer and more strained as he spoke. His tone indicating the heavy weight of the burden he carried.

Brynna's eyes softened. Her husband had shown no signs of the things he was expressing to her. Her throat ached as she spoke. "What is it you want me to do? I'm not Pateras either," Her eyes darted back and forth, searching for the answers David needed.

"This mission should be led by you and carried out by all of us. Every time you see me move in and take over, stop me," His face entreated her to help him. His demeanor was calm, but his heart was regretful of placing such a burden on her.

"I don't understand. You spoke to Pateras. He asked you to lead this mission. Why are you deferring to me?" Brynna was confused. David was the Captain. This was his job.

"It's my job to plan where we go, how we get there, and to protect the crew. I am not the lone spokesperson of Pateras. I get us where we need to go. All of us need to teach those we come in contact with. I can only reach so many by myself. Pateras asked me to introduce him to the people of the Commonwealth. He knows I can't do it by myself. He gave me resources to accomplish our mission, but I keep neglecting to use what he's given me. Those ten other crews may come in blaming me and me alone for their predicament. They don't need to see me as being the one in charge. I'm not trying to put any wrath off on you, well, not exactly. Strategically speaking, putting someone other than me in front of them divides their attention and any aggression. I can focus on protecting you, the rest of the crew, and myself if you're the one they're targeting with their aggression."

Brynna squinted at him. "Uh—huh."

David sat back in his seat again. "I'm not sure I said that quite right."

Brynna knew he didn't want any hard feelings focused specifically on her. She knew he couldn't work on the other aspects of his job if he were focused on controlling the crowd's perceptions of the situation. She did enjoy making him squirm sometimes. They were so busy with work, there was little time to enjoy each other's company. "You want any aggressive actions aimed at me, so you can escape. Right. Got it."

The Captain's face reflected his mortification over her description of his plan. "No... NO! That's not what I meant at all."

Brynna grinned slowly. "I know. I couldn't help but tease you a little. I know exactly what you meant. I'll handle both assignments."

David gave her a confused blink. "Both?"

His loving wife smiled. "I'll address the assembly tonight, and I'll reign the Captain in as necessary."

David grinned sheepishly. "I'm sorry."

"Sorry for what?"

"Sorry for giving you such difficult assignments," David confessed.

Brynna grinned mysteriously. "Only one of those assignments is difficult. The other one is going to be a breeze."

"You're addressing approximately a hundred confused, but well-trained military personnel. If you have doubts about it, please let me know. I will give you whatever support or back-up you think you need. Maybe I *should* be the one to address them," David began rethinking his decision.

Brynna nodded her understanding then shook her head at his ridiculous behavior, "You just proved my point."

"Proved your point? How so?"

"Addressing the assembly was the one I considered a breeze. Keeping the Captain in check, that's the difficult assignment," Brynna chided.

David bolted from his chair, mentally kicking himself for jumping right back into the thing he was trying to get away from. He paced two tight loops in the small office then stopped to face her. "Again, I'm sorry. It's your baby… do what you need to. I am in charge of security."

Brynna laughed softly. "You know I love you, right?"

David shook his head. "Yes, but I have no idea why."

"It's probably because I'm drawn to hard-luck cases," Brynna teased. She stepped in front of him and wrapped her arms around him.

David instinctively returned the gesture, although mentally he was kicking himself.

Brynna put her face directly in front of his. "Hey, you're a man, a normal human, not one of those superior alien beings. You can't do what they can. Cut yourself some slack."

"I don't know why he asked me to do this. I'm afraid I'm going to get everyone killed. Bringing all twelve crews together in one place is asking for trouble. I don't know why I ever did this," David lamented.

"You did it because I asked you to," A familiar voice spoke from behind him.

David and Brynna released their holds on each other and turned to face the voice. Their anxiety and tensions drained away.

"Arni! You're back! We've missed you," Brynna rushed to hug him.

As soon as she released him, David hugged the man with the same fervor as he hugged his uncle the day he graduated from the CIF Academy.

Arni reciprocated warmly. He smiled broadly at the two. "You do know I never left you, right?"

David nodded abashedly. "I know. It's just easier to talk to you when I can see you. Sometimes I feel like I'm talking to myself, especially when you don't answer right away."

"My answers will always come when they are needed," Arni assured him. "The delays only serve to build your trust in me."

Brynna jumped in quickly. "How long can you stay this time?"

Arni smiled again. He knew she wanted to keep him there physically as long as she could. He also knew his answer would not please her.

"I cannot stay as long as you would like. I have work to do at my Father's side. I won't leave you alone though. My Father is sending you a gift, an infusion of power. This power is a non-corporeal manifestation of the Father capable of revealing truths to you, enhancing your memories of everything I have taught you and he will always be with you. He is known as the Neumatos. My Father sent me to you to bring you back to him. I came to free you from the prison Luciano Hale placed you in, and I am not referring to Romajin. I am doing what my Father sent me to do here. When I am done, I have to return to him. That day is coming soon, and you will see me no more."

David and Brynna were alarmed. His absence from the ship was difficult enough. To learn Arni was going to leave and return to his Father's plane of existence gave them cause to be alarmed. Brynna's face paled. "Arni, we can't take on an entire galaxy without you. It's surprising we haven't already been caught and killed. How are we going to survive if you leave?"

Arni put a reassuring hand on her shoulder. "I told you I wouldn't leave you alone. I know this concept is difficult to understand, but I reside in my Father even now, and he resides within me. When I leave for the last time, he will send the Neumatos to reside within you. He will tell you what you need to know. You will have power after he comes to you and you will be able to face everything ahead of you. The galaxy and even the Kingdom of Luciano Hale will not be able to stop you."

"Does he control us, our actions?" David asked. It was the one thing they were told to be the greatest threat of the Liontari forces.

"No, your right to say no and refuse to do as he asks or as I ask will always remain intact. Remember that whatever we ask of you is what's best and obedience to what we ask is in your best interest. I haven't lied to you. He is a part of my Father just as I am."

Arni's words were confusing, yet strangely reassuring. David knew he needed to spend as much time with Arni as possible if he was about to leave permanently. He would have preferred to spend the next few hours alone with Arni gleaning as much as he could from the man with unending power and knowledge at his disposal. With every passing moment, the young Captain felt more inept. Arni's words were meant to offer encouragement. David knew that was his intent, but he was feeling fearful and abandoned.

Arni moved their conversation to the Dining Hall where the entire crew could join them. Word spread quickly and soon the room was full. Mr. Bennett and the Malos joined the crew. The Malos came mostly from curiosity. Mr. Bennett was enthralled at being in the presence of the "Intercessor."

After a couple of hours, Brynna decided she regrettably needed to step away to prepare her address for the meeting later in the evening. As she stood to leave, her eyes locked on Arni's. His voice spoke to her mind. "You don't need to prepare. I will give you the words when it is time."

Remembering their time on Ela Prime, Brynna knew she should listen to him. She had not listened and nearly lost her life that day. Brynna refilled her coffee cup and sat back down. David gave her a puzzled look but let her stay.

ARNI

The Captain and crew were reluctant to leave Arni's side to attend the meeting. Capt. Alexander fully staffed the bridge, just in case. As David stepped foot into the amphitheater-style meeting room, he glanced at Brynna. "Are you ready for this?"

A case of nerves overtook her. "I hope so."

"Where's your data pad with your notes?" He asked.

"I didn't bring it because I… don't have any notes," she confessed anxiously.

David whipped around. "What?! Why not?"

Brynna chewed on her lower lip. "Arni told me not to."

David slapped his forehead and rubbed his face. "Oh boy," he looked at her and shrugged. "Okay, this is his show."

Brynna heard him mumble to himself as he walked away. She couldn't make out exactly what he was saying, but she fully understood his sentiment. She felt the same way he sounded.

Capt. Weiseman and his crew arrived next, along with Capt. Silvain and his remaining two crewmen. The crew of the *Evangeline* was quick to welcome the crew of the *Emissary* and continue catching up on their adventures since leaving Ela Prime.

Nate looked around the room. "Where's the rest of your crew? I thought you would bring all of them in again tonight."

"I wanted to. I would like to show everyone that the entire crew is committed to this, but there are more lives at stake tonight. I brought as many as I dared. They're watching the skies for trouble."

David continued, "With Lt. Holden getting close to delivery, I had to keep Laura and the Doc close to her. Laura's also my backup navigator."

Nate scowled. "Are you really going to let her and that baby stay aboard your ship? I really think it's a bad idea. Stephanie wasn't happy seeing her here last night. By the way, you didn't authorize her little stunt last night, did you?"

David shook his head emphatically. "Oh, NO! I definitely didn't. We had a *discussion* about it this morning. That will not happen again, or she'll find herself sidelined."

"Oh good, I was worried about that. I was hoping you hadn't lost it. It's lucky for you that Stephanie didn't find out about it," Nate left a few details out when he updated the rest of his crew.

"Find out about what?" Stephanie's voice came from behind Nate.

Capt. Weiseman's face froze. He didn't have an answer that he wanted to share with her.

David came to his friend's rescue. "He didn't want you to find out what an unreasonable lout I am. I had to lecture one of my crew for failure to obey an order last night."

"Why is it a problem for me to find out?" Stephanie was still highly suspicious.

"It was Lt. Holden," David confessed.

"You put a pregnant woman on report? What could she have done to warrant that?" Stephanie asked.

"I didn't put her on report, and I handled it as gently as I could, but she recklessly endangered herself and her baby by not following orders last night," David hoped he wouldn't have to go into detail. If it went any further, Nate's omission would come to light. He wasn't trying to lie for his friend, but he preferred not to get his friend into trouble with his wife and Chief Medical Officer.

"Somehow, I think there's more to this, but if you two want to keep secrets like little boys, I suppose I'll let it go... this time," Stephanie eyed the two suspiciously as she walked away.

Nate shook his head. "Oh man, now she's going to wait until we're alone to try and drag the information out of me."

"Oh, come on, Nate, just tell her. It's old news now, and the situation has been rectified. What's it going to hurt for her to know?" David wasn't good at hiding things from Brynna either and had mostly given up trying.

"Yeah, but then she'll spend the next hour ranting about how you shouldn't have allowed that to happen, and how could you be so careless," Nate explained.

"If you think it will help, I can explain it myself later," David offered.

"That's okay. I'll deal with it. It's kind of fun trying to distract her and derail her rants," Nate grinned.

Capt. Alexander threw his hands up. "I'm not going there. I need to check in with Brynna before we get started."

David, Stephanie, and Nate were friends since their first days at the CIF Academy. David viewed Stephanie like a sister, Nate had not. It was hard to think of Stephanie from a romantic perspective.

The other ships' crews slowly filled the room. In a few minutes, everyone was accounted for. Capt. Weiseman agreed to open the meeting and deal with obvious security threats. He approached the podium and took control of the meeting. "If everyone would please take their seats, we'll get started."

The room was oddly quiet as the twelve crews settled in. Soft whispers were the only voices heard.

"The first order of business for tonight is this: Captains, did you remove the nanites from your crews?" Nate made eye contact with each Captain. Some gave him grateful nods, while others grudgingly gave him affirmation. Capt. Davu avoided eye contact. "Capt. Davu, did you remove the nanites from yourself and your crew?"

Ajani cast an angry glare at Capt. Weiseman. "Yes, they're gone."

Nate moved on. "If anyone has attempted to turn us in, I suggest you speak up now. We won't harm you, but you need to know, *none* of us will live to see tomorrow if you've betrayed us. That includes any potential betrayer. Executor Hale will not spare your life for turning us in. Anyone care to volunteer that information?"

There were wary looks and blank stares. Nothing indicated anyone had turned them in, but Nate seriously doubted anyone would confess. "Capt. Alexander's people are watching for approaching ships, and comms in this room are being actively jammed to prevent signals from leaving this assembly."

"Why are we here and exactly what's going on? Why are there super soldiers trying to kill us?" One voice abruptly demanded.

Capt. Weiseman was done with his portion of the opening, but the question begged for a personal response from him. "You're here because we are trying to save your lives and put a plan in motion to protect all of us and our families. Executor Hale lied to us. He said Pateras would force our cooperation in his service. The truth is, Pateras will never force our cooperation. He asks for it, but he doesn't force it. Executor Hale knows that if we've seen the truth, we are a danger to his power base. He doesn't want the truth getting out. We are witnesses against him, and he doesn't want us sharing what we know."

Another voice called out, "Exactly what is it we're supposed to know?"

Nate plugged a data crystal into the podium. He opened a video file of his crew working on Strabothon. The images were of peaceful families enjoying their simplistic lives. He let the images play for a moment. He turned the volume down, eliminating the sounds of children playing, dogs barking, and men and women working and talking.

"This was our first stop on our mission. This was a Level III planet. We discovered the majority of the people worshiped a single deity despite the presence of numerous temples or houses of worship. Two of my people spent an inordinate amount of time studying this deity worship and determined the deity in question was Pateras. They claimed the teachings were in contradiction to what we learned in our mission briefings. They insisted Pateras was not the danger we were told he was. I ordered the two crew members to be abandoned on the planet. CIF Headquarters replaced our two crew members with two 'specialists' to keep an eye on the rest of us. Capt. Alexander came to me a couple of months ago and told me the planet was destroyed by the Pacification Fleet."

Nate paused a moment to let his words sink in. He stopped the recording as the image of a smiling child eager to investigate the strangers appeared on the screen. Nate closed the file and opened a second one. The file was recorded after the devastation occurred. The town was littered with decaying bodies, including men, women, and children.

Capt. Weiseman continued his dissertation. "We returned to Strabothon a few weeks ago to investigate what happened there. The crew scanned the area for highly refined metals and located our two marooned crew members. The two procured housing in one of the temples of Pateras. They were still wearing their Commonwealth uniforms when we found them."

The images of the two decaying crew members in their Commonwealth uniforms appeared on the screen. "For those of you who knew them, this is—was Elijah and Aneska Perdy."

Capt. Weiseman heard a few random soft gasps and a couple of sniffles among the crowd. The images were hard for even Nate to look at. He rightfully blamed himself for their deaths. Clearing his throat, he went on to explain. "We scanned the area and traced the energy signature back to the Pacification Fleet. Everything was exactly like Capt. Alexander told us it would be. My crew and I stand with Pateras."

Soft whispers and disgruntled murmurs traveled through the assembly.

Capt. Weiseman waited for the room to settle, "Cmdr. Alexander, the floor is yours."

Brynna approached the podium slowly. She wished she had some idea what she was going to say. She wondered why Arni didn't want her to prepare. Mentally she called out to him—*Arni, help me. I don't know what you want me to say to them.*

A voice spoke calmly—*Start at the beginning. Tell them what they need to know about my Father and about me.*

Brynna took a deep breath as she traversed the final two steps to the podium. "Good evening, ladies and gentlemen. I am Cmdr. Brynna Alexander of the SS *Evangeline*. I know all of you are concerned about your current situations. I'm concerned about my situation as well. I do not know what the future holds or how we're going to escape this. What I do know is this; Pateras El Liontari *does* know what the future holds. He is timeless as we were told. Luciano Hale has lied to us about many things, but he wove those lies amid several truths. We researched a document which is thousands of years old. It was transcribed by Pateras to various human beings. The document includes certain predictions about the future. A lot of them are vague and unclear, but some are *very* clear."

"Do you expect us to listen to this ridiculous propaganda?" A voice butted in.

Brynna linked the podium computer terminal to the ship's data files. She uploaded a visual record of the Ancient Texts, displaying a specific selection of the prophetic texts. "Our linguistics expert translated the texts for us. I'm going to read one small portion. Please let me know if anything sounds familiar to you.

Twelve messengers will come forward, even twelve times twelve, who will serve the Master of Darkness. Pateras will call to the messengers and one by one they will answer his call. One by one they will leave the darkness and enter the light, though not every one of them. A few will cling to the darkness and take up their swords against those in the light. The Master of Darkness will seek out his lost ones to destroy them. The Master of Darkness shall reach out his hand across the stars to smite all the sons and daughters of Pateras. The evil one will destroy the world of his one promised Son, but his Son will not die by the hand of the Evil One. The Promised One will give up his life to defend the defender of the twelve and even the twelve twelves. The Promised One will return from death on the third day to offer new life to all.

One who will betray the messengers of Pateras will also betray the Dark Lord.

The angry voice who challenged Brynna earlier belted out again. "Oh, yeah let's do like all these enlightened low-tech worlds and seek the light and truth and whatever crazy daydreams you think will improve your life."

Brynna wanted to rebut him, but something held her back. "There were twelve teams of twelve crewmen who started out carrying Commonwealth messages. I believe all twelve teams have had some sort of encounter with Pateras. Our ship found the homeworld of Arni Sotaeras Liontari, the son of Pateras on Galat III. It was our very first stop. It was destroyed just like Strabothon and some other worlds. Supreme Executor Hale is the Dark Lord referred to in the text."

Brynna's heckler shifted in his seat and started to launch another attack. The Commander didn't know his name but caught sight of his rank and put him in his place before he could speak. "Ensign! If you expect me to believe you are a loyal Commonwealth Officer, then act like one. Wait until after the briefing before you poke holes in what I've said. I will gladly address any worthwhile comments when I am finished."

The man closed his mouth, set his posture defiantly, and glared at her. The Commander couldn't help but notice a few amused faces looking discreetly away from the disagreeable Ensign.

"One by one, we are turning away from the Commonwealth and joining Pateras. The crews of the *Evangeline* and the *Emissary* have chosen to change sides, or commit treason if you prefer that terminology. We have no delusions about what we've done. Executor Hale is doing everything in his power to destroy those who side with Pateras."

Another voice jumped in. "Of course, he's going to destroy the bases where enemy troops are. That's why it's called war!"

Brynna was ready for such an objection. She flipped to another file which displayed images taken from Galat III after its destruction. The images of the infant twins in their cradle hugging each other, the mother huddled in the basement with her son and daughter, a farmer plowing his field and several other clearly benign individuals flashed across the screen.

As the last image faded away, her words came back with a grave tone. "Yes, these were truly dangerous people. They were a level II on the tech scale. Another few thousand years and the Commonwealth would've had a real fight on its hands."

The room fell silent. Someone finally broke the silence. "Why would Executor Hale send us out to find them if they weren't dangerous?"

Brynna nodded. "That's a great question. It's the same reason he would execute patients in a mental hospital. They are a threat to *him*, not the Commonwealth. He tried to destroy the worlds we identified, then when the twelve crews were affected, he sent out the Nefil to try to destroy us. It takes eighteen months for the Nefil to reach maturity. Supreme Executor Hale knew before we ever launched on this mission that it would fail. Those soldiers were already waiting for us to fail because of the Ancient Texts. Pateras put this warning in print thousands of years ago. Arni asked us to join him and gave us a choice. We were told in our briefings our minds would be taken over. I suppose in some ways that's true, but it's my choice. I've been consumed by a desire to learn as much as I can about Pateras and to do whatever I can to serve him."

Brynna clipped a portable voice projection relay to her uniform and moved back and forth at the front of the room as she spoke. She quoted a portion of the prophecy again.

The Promised One will give up his life to defend the defender of the

twelve and even the twelve twelves. The Promised One will return from death on the third day to offer new life to all.

"The crew of the *Evangeline* witnessed this on our third mission. Our crew was arrested, tried and convicted for conspiracy to commit genocide for what happened on Galat III. Capt. Alexander negotiated a plea agreement with the local government. He confessed to the crimes and took full responsibility for what happened. In exchange for his confession, the crew was to go free. Arni Liontari, being the son of Pateras, has immeasurable power. Capt. Alexander was seconds from being executed. They placed a hood over his head. Before he was hit with the first blast, Arni took his place."

"He—He," Brynna's eyes teared up. Her memory of that day brought mixed emotions. The pain of losing her husband, the relief of finding he hadn't died as expected, and the debt she owed Arni for saving all their lives flooded her mind. She paused a moment to push away the deluge assaulting her psyche. Swallowing the lump in her throat, she took a deep breath and continued. "Arni is the Promised One. He died defending us."

"What about the part about the third day? How was that supposed to work? Did it happen?" A sympathetic voice asked.

"Don't be ridiculous. No one can come back from the dead after that long. He was probably just in stasis," another more skeptical voice rebutted.

Brynna stepped forward to regain control. "Arni died. I saw his body. The sun and the stars went... dark, the day it happened."

The soft whispers emanating from the group faded away. Everyone remembered the day the stars went out. The SS *Ambassador* was traveling in space when it happened. The ship's scanners lost guidance and dropped the ship automatically to sub-light speeds. They spent three hours dead in space until the stars reappeared.

It was the middle of the night for the SS *Malachi*. The locals discovered it and thought their gods were angry with them. They attempted to attack the *Malachi* with crude instruments which would have done little more than make a few scuff marks on its hull if they had gotten that far. The ship's sensors alerted the nighttime duty officer in plenty of time to raise the shields.

"Arni's father restored him to life early in the morning on the third day. I have data files of these events if you want to see them. Pateras conveyed these events to men who wrote them down thousands of years ago because he is not bound by time. I personally witnessed events predicted on another planet several thousand years ago. I saw Arni take my husband's place and die. I saw him come back to life in time to save our lives a second time. I have never seen Arni harm another soul, but Luciano Hale has destroyed millions, perhaps billions. His next target is us. I'm not about to turn myself over to him willingly. I'm not going to try to hide and wait for this to blow over. I'm not going to sit back and let him get away with this. The *Evangeline* stands with Pateras. My question to you is, 'What are you going to do?'"

Capt. Roan stood to address her question. "What can we do? We are a pittance compared to the twenty-four-quintillion people in this galaxy. One Pacification ship could take all of us out."

Jake couldn't resist stepping forward despite the potential backlash. "Arni got us and our ship off Romajin despite the presence of ten thousand armed ground troops, two Admiral's Flagships, and Supreme Executor Hale's ship."

Capt. Davu was the fastest to hit Jake with the accusation that was on everyone's mind. "We know how that went. You activated the self-destruct sequence for the military base and destroyed it. I imagine that's how you orchestrated your escape. You used the ensuing chaos to get away."

Jake swallowed hard and glanced at Capt. Alexander. David whispered something into his comm unit and nodded to Jake to continue his explanation. "Our ship got out of the system clean. We caused no casualties whatsoever. Supreme Executor Hale destroyed that base and framed me for it. We didn't know until several days later what happened. Only a couple of the crew were in any shape to fly the ship, let alone destroy a military base. I sent most of them to the infirmary. The Captain barely had the strength to walk. I got our ship and a second ship out by flying them in tandem with our best people doing little more than babysitting. Arni laid in the course, and I commanded the ships. I never sent any self-destruct codes, and I never fired a single shot. We have proof that I was framed if you aren't afraid to look at it."

Another round of unsettled murmurs swept through the room. Brynna moved to the podium and selected another video file to play. This one was of the Supreme Executor's address to the Commonwealth regarding the Nefil Forces and his intentions to send them to destroy the original Explorer Fleet. As the file finished, Brynna gave the group another second to process the information before speaking again.

"Whether you believe us about Pateras is your choice. Please believe this one thing—there is no getting back into Executor Hale's good graces. He has termination orders out on all of you, and he's not going to think twice about it. You and your families are in danger. We have a plan to protect all of us, but we need your help."

"What do you need from us? I no longer have a ship or a crew. My wife and most of my crew were already captured," Capt. Silvain made himself vulnerable by airing his pain.

"It's time to decide who you'll stand with. If you already know where you stand, your choices are simple. Those who want to join us stay here in this room. Those who want no part of us may leave. I do recommend that you abandon your ships and keep to the colonies or settlements with minimal CIF presence. Do not attempt to contact your families, as it will only get them arrested. They'll use them to get to you, then they'll be re-educated if they're lucky or executed with you if they aren't."

Brynna took a deep breath before continuing. The Captains were not going to appreciate her next suggestion, "If you need to decide or discuss it, Captains, there are small meeting rooms adjacent to the hallway outside this room. Each individual is free to make their own choices. If you want to join us, return to this room. If you want us to send you someplace safe, remain in the smaller meeting rooms, and we will make those arrangements. If you prefer to make your own way, you are free to leave. We can reshuffle crew assignments if needed. Remember one thing, we have agreed this place is neutral ground, and no one is to report us until the conference is concluded."

"Are you suggesting I give my crew the *option* of committing mutiny?" Capt. Davu spat.

"Your people are already wanted criminals, Captain. They deserve to choose for themselves how they handle it. You can't protect them alone," Brynna gently chided.

"What about the proof you said you had?" the heckler demanded.

"Your Captains were given the proof yesterday, and the files will be available in the adjoining rooms," Brynna answered without any hint of malice toward the antagonistic ensign.

****

Six of the Captains and crews left the room while the other six remained. Capt. Silvain approached Nate and Brynna. "Capt. Weiseman, Cmdr. Alexander, may I speak with you?"

Capt. Weiseman took the lead in the conversation. "Of course, Taye. What is it?"

"I assume you know my situation, Commander?"

"Yes, Captain, I was briefed on the situation this morning," Brynna was sorry for his loss, but wasn't sure how to help him.

Taye's aggression from the previous night was spent. He was ready to listen and learn. "I have no ship and no crew. What can I do to help? I am not sure about who or what this Pateras is, but I want to save my people."

Capt. Gellert overheard the conversation and stepped forward. "Pardon the interruption. Taye, I may have an option for you. My ship was destroyed. My brother owns a repair shop, and he sometimes gets ahold of small spare ships. They are mostly small transport or cargo ships. He provided us with a ship. It has enough space for you and your other two crew members. You're welcome to join us."

Taye nodded his thanks. "I would be honored."

Capt. Weiseman placed a reassuring hand on Taye's shoulder. "Davie has an idea about getting your crew back. The one thing you need to be careful about though is, if your crew's been subjected to re-education, they may no longer be trustworthy."

"If we must, we will withdraw from the field of battle. Drop us off on a low-tech world, and we will stay there and out of trouble," the sorrowful man relented.

The group milled around talking softly and asking as many questions as they dared of the crews of the *Evangeline* and the *Emissary*. Over the next hour, four of the six crews returned to the room. The last two crews remained in their private meeting rooms.

****

Jake made laps in the hall and kept his eyes on external monitors and scanners. Muffled voices resounded in the hallway. The meetings finally broke up. A few of the crew members left their Captains and made skittish entries into the larger meeting room. Jake moved toward the entrance of the large assembly room. He turned to face those reluctant to take up their cause. "I really hope you will honor this place as neutral ground. You may not want any part of us, but I wouldn't want Pateras as my enemy."

Capt. Logan and Capt. Davu, along with several of their crew, were the final holdouts. Capt. Logan stepped forward. "Are you threatening us?"

Jake left the doorway and stepped closer to the reluctant few. "No sir. I've seen what he can do, and I know on a general scale what he intends to do. I also know the treachery Luciano Hale is capable of. I know whose side is the best choice. I'm never going back. The possibilities are… frightening."

Jake started to walk away again, but stopped. He turned to add one last thought. "I don't scare easily. I'm from Demarius II."

Demarius had a start far rockier than Drea. It had no loyalty to Pateras as Drea had, but it was warlike, and the factions were divided between the privileged and the underprivileged. Jake was one of the latter. His parents went their separate ways when he was young. He was raised by his mother and grandmother. The Commonwealth came in and discovered a particularly rich supply of tetratachium, the fuel source for their engines. The rich tried to get richer by exploiting the workers and doing whatever they could to mine and sell the mineral. The workers rebelled. Bitter skirmishes broke out. The supply was too rich for the Commonwealth to abandon the planet.

Jake's mother was badly injured in the riots when Jake was a preteen. His mother begged him to leave Demarius and make a better life for himself. His mother made a full recovery, but Jake stuck to his promise. A recruiter for the CIF youth academy came to his school and Jake jumped on board as quickly as he could. He earned himself a full scholarship to the academy, escaping the constant violence erupting around him. His violent beginnings turned him into a fearless, determined individual. It also cemented his loyalty to the Commonwealth, making him the last to turn among the crew of the *Evangeline*. Jake knew his reputation and the reputation of his home planet would say the things he couldn't adequately communicate with words.

The reluctant group stared at him angrily. They wanted someone to blame for their current situation, and Jake was the convenient one. Their angry stares did little to appease them.

****

The last few holdouts stepped back into one of the conference rooms to discuss their situation. The group wanted their lives back. They were a mixture of crewmen from several ships.

Brynna's heckling Ensign was quick to speak up again.

"Capt. Davu, Capt. Logan, I don't think they were telling the truth when they said we couldn't get our lives back. If we break this truce and report them, I think Executor Hale would reward us handsomely for it. I think they were lying just to protect themselves."

Capt. Davu squinted at the man. He glanced at his psych officer who nodded her agreement. "Executor Hale has proven himself to be a peaceful man, time after time. Capt. Alexander is the one whose mind has been corrupted."

Capt. Davu spoke to Capt. Logan. "Capt. Alexander did say he preferred to be handed over to the Supreme Executor as a corpse. Is there some way to shut off the life support to that room? We could take the entire group out in one swift move."

Capt. Davu's computer tech sat down at the nearest terminal and began to research the systems in the room as the Captains discussed their situation. In a moment he had an option. "Those glass windows are docking ports. They can be retracted. I can lockout the emergency shielding and override the doorlock."

Capt. Logan frowned, "Ajani, your brother is in there, and so is my wife."

"Chris, they've been turned. Do you really want to put them through the embarrassment of a public trial, the pain of re-education or prison? This would be a merciful ending to their enslavement to Pateras. We can report what we've done after it's over."

"What if Capt. Alexander is right about Pateras?"

"Then he and the others will join him in whatever reality they belong in, and they will no longer be a threat to the Commonwealth. It's what Capt. Alexander desires anyway."

Ajani searched Chris' eyes for dissent.

Chris looked away, "Do it, quickly, before I change my mind."

Ajani nodded at his technician to commence.

****

Jake headed into the assembly. Stepping inside the door, he nodded to Cmdr. Alexander to suggest this was the best she was going to get. Fifteen crewmen of the one hundred thirty-five chose not to join them. Capt. Alexander watched the exchange between Jake and Brynna. He was disappointed. He had truly hoped they would all join him. He did take a small amount of pleasure in the thought that the two Captains refusing to join wouldn't have sufficient crew members to cause any significant problems.

Brynna moved to the podium and encouraged everyone to return to their seats. She outlined the basic plans and who Pateras truly was.

167

"Ladies and gentlemen, I'm going to give you the basics of what needs to happen. Supreme Executor Hale's crimes need to be revealed to the general public and to the Commonwealth Advisory Council. Revealing it to the general public is what will protect your families. He won't move against them because he'll be under close scrutiny. Public opinion will put pressure on the Advisory Council to investigate the matter. The remaining Captains of the Explorer Fleet will get together tomorrow to discuss the particulars and get everyone moving."

Brynna glanced at the giant window to the seascape outside their assembly. The sun had set, but exterior lighting kept the immediate view visible. It was a peaceful scene of reefs and sea life. She opened her mouth to continue when she saw Jake abruptly pull his arm up and speak softly into his bracelet. She saw her husband freeze for a second. He leaned over the computer to run a search for information. A familiar voice redirected her thoughts. "Introduce them to my father."

Brynna moved away from the podium again. She spoke candidly about the lies they were told since childhood and gave them the true background of Pateras and his nemesis, Luciano Hale.

Capt. Weiseman noticed her attention was divided and discreetly stepped to David's side. The two whispered for a moment, prompting Nate to hail his Security Chief and First Officer to join them. The two quickly and quietly evacuated the seating area. Jake kept his comm line open to hear their conversation from the back of the room.

Just as Brynna finished explaining exactly who Pateras was, an alarm sounded. Emergency lights flashed above them.

Security Chief Holden, standing near the entrance, heard the sickening familiar sound of a door locking, or rather an airlock being secured. Jake jabbed the mechanism to open the door. He was greeted with the sound of rejection. He quickly informed the Captain.

The computer blared an audio warning, "Containment failure imminent. Warning. Leave the area immediately. Flooding in progress," the warning repeated in a continuous loop.

In the pause between warnings, the frightened audience clearly heard Brynna call out, "Arni?"

Several bolted for the door. Being trained military personnel, no one panicked, yet they moved with haste and purpose. Jake wisely got out of their way. He knew the door was a dead end, but he also knew they wouldn't listen to him. They would have to figure it out for themselves, and he would only get hurt if he got in their way. The crowd amassed at the door. Some remained near their seats knowing something out of their control was about to happen.

New lights flashed. Yellow lights framing the window keeping the sea from rushing into the room blinked frantically. It's last act of warning was to turn a solid color of red. As soon as Brynna saw the new lights begin flashing, she pressed her comm link and called out to her husband. "David, the seascape window is about to open," Brynna turned to move away from the wall.

Capt. Alexander didn't answer. Brynna saw him whip around to see for himself. At that second, the window began to lower, and seawater rushed in. The corralled crewmen watched in horror. Several scrambled away from rushing water climbing to the back of the room.

The highly pressurized water shot through the narrow opening knocking Brynna off her feet. David stopped what he was doing and raced to pull her from the floor. The water hitting the upper seating areas flowed down the sloped floor toward the lowest point in the room. Brynna struggled to get to her feet as she fought two distinct currents. David dove straight through the increasingly larger blast of water. The force of his dive pushed him closer to the window and behind the waterfall. He grabbed onto Brynna's hand as he slid past, pulling her with him. Helping her to her feet, the couple waded into the corner farthest from the door.

David stared at the horrifying scene in front of him. He knew Arni could save them, but where was he? Surely, he knew what was happening. If he didn't intervene, everyone in the room would be dead in minutes. David looked at Brynna. There was only one thing they could do. The two lowered themselves to one knee on the floor now flooding with water.

The crew of the *Evangeline* and the *Emissary* stopped trying to rescue themselves. They each knew help would have to come from outside or from Pateras. They followed David and Brynna's example as the wall continued to lower itself and the volume of water increased. Some froze in morbid curiosity or shock. Others searched for ways to escape the locked room. Most stayed near the door because it was the highest point of the room. They knew they would last longer there.

David's head was bowed and his eyes shut. There was no panic on his face, only a look of concentration as though he could will the water away. Brynna knelt next to him, equally calm and focused. The water was already reaching their chests in their kneeling position.

As the deluge obscured him from sight, a calm settled on the room. The shouting ceased. The manual override for the door failed. Couples reached for their spouses fearing this would be their last moments together. Most moved to the back-right corner of the room. It would be the last place to fill up and the closest to the open window. They thought perhaps they could swim out once the room filled up. Even Jake, who had fought Pateras the hardest, declined to send a farewell message to his wife aboard the *Evangeline*. He simply knelt on one knee and waited for Pateras to reveal himself. As he waited, he thought the water should've at least hit his knee by now. He opened his eyes and looked toward the front-left corner of the room. It was the corner where his Captain and Commander had disappeared behind the deluge.

Those who were watching saw Jake's face change. He was pleased about something. Their attention turned the direction the young man faced. The window was completely open and out of sight, and the water still churned, but the inward flow was diminishing. A man, who was clearly not a CIF soldier, had entered the room unobserved by anyone. The water stopped flowing in through the massive opening. The facility was equipped with a pumping system to remove excess water in the event of an emergency. The pumps were automatically evacuating the water through grated intakes at the lowest points in the floor. A wall of water, outside the fully open window, remained at bay.

The startled gasps of those watching the laws of gravity bend and break got the attention of those frantically trying to open the door. As the crew of the *Evangeline* and the *Emissary* spotted the man, they trudged through the receding waters. Shouts of excitement were heard from those who recognized the stranger. The stranger had the attention of the entire room. By the time he reached the lowest point of the room, every eye was riveted on him. The last of the water drained away leaving several small fish flopping helplessly on the floor and one rather large beautiful exotic fish. It flipped and flopped in its panic on the dry floor.

Jake had mercy on the smaller helpless fish and tossed them through the large opening and back into the sea. Several people gasped and yelled at him to stop, fearing the water would again come rushing into the room.

The last fish, despite its fantastic beauty, was quite poisonous to the touch. Jake stopped short of touching it. He wanted to rescue it as well but knew the danger.

The strange man joined Jake and bent to retrieve the frightened creature. Jake started to warn him about the dangerous nature of the fish.

The man smiled knowing Jake's intention. He appreciated the concern, but it was too easy for the crew to forget who he was.

The man cradled the creature gently in his hands. In the sea, it was magnificent to look at. Without the water, it was a crumpled mess. Stepping to the wall of water, he slipped the majestic beauty back into its natural environment. The fish's fins twitched and flipped until the creature faced him. It expanded its aquatic plumage to its fullest expansion and held it there for a moment expressing gratitude. Seconds later, it zipped away.

With the immediate panic over, the group moved closer. The alarms silenced, and the flashing lights stopped. The man invited everyone to join him. The group eyed the wall of water suspiciously. Jake clearly recognized their hesitation. He approached the wall. The window was completely opened. The room should be full by this point. Jake stuck his hand and arm through the opening. He pulled it back inside without any ill effects. Seeing Jake's confidence, the others returned to their seats. Their fear gave way to trust in the calming presence of the stranger who was clearly capable of manipulating matter.

Brynna introduced those present to the stranger. Seeing his power for themselves, they were ready to listen to him. "Ladies and gentlemen, may I please introduce you to Arni Sotaeras Liontari."

A voice called out, "Did—Did you just stop the water?"

Arni nodded. "Yes, I did."

One of the more scientific minds asked. "How?"

"Is it more important to know how I did this or why?" Arni answered.

Jake stepped forward. "I don't need to know how you did it. I'm just glad you did. Thank you."

Several voices joined in to thank the mysterious stranger. Others were grateful, but they were still leery of the situation. Arni waved Jake forward to ask him a question.

****

In the next room, Capt. Logan and Capt. Davu watched the scene until David and Brynna were nearly overcome by the water. Capt. Davu's computer technician completed the infiltration and wreaked the havoc in the next room. He looked at his Captain, "Can we shut down the audiovisual feed? It'll be over in no more than ten minutes."

He was personally uncomfortable watching people die, especially when he was responsible for their deaths.

The *Pioneer's* psychologist seconded his request. "Captains, there's no need for either of you to watch this. Capt. Davu, you shouldn't watch your wife and brother die. Capt. Logan, you shouldn't watch this happen to your wife either."

Capt. Logan was torn. It was his duty to see that the job was finished. A piece of him also wanted to punish himself for killing his own wife.

Capt. Davu took one last look at his brother. He was calmly holding his wife's hand. There was no sign of panic on his face. "Turn off the sound and take it off the main screen," Ajani ordered. The picture was reduced to smaller screens at work stations in the room. The sound of rushing water and panicked shouts disappeared. A heavy silence filled the room as they waited.

The lieutenant who hacked the computer systems focused on the clock. Three minutes later he glanced at the screen, partially from morbid curiosity and partially because he was anxious for the dastardly act to be at an end. His eyes widened as he looked at the screen. His mind couldn't reconcile what should be happening with what his eyes were seeing. He frantically reviewed the readouts. Yes, the seascape window was fully retracted. No, the shields were not activated.

Capt. Logan noticed his sudden flurry of activity contrasting the heaviness in the room. "Lieutenant, what's wrong?"

He shakily informed the two Captains, "The—The seascape window is fully retracted, and the shields are offline. That room should be completely flooded. Everyone in that room should be dead!"

Capt. Logan scowled. Everyone's attention focused on the lieutenant. They sensed something was wrong. His emotional response did not support his message. Was he trying to express regret or was something else happening? Capt. Logan was forming an appropriate question when the lieutenant punched a control and displayed the audio-video feeds from the amphitheater on the main screens in the room. He doubted he could adequately explain what he was seeing. The picture defied human words and concepts.

The stubbornly loyal Commonwealth officers stared at the screen in disbelief. They saw the last of the sea water disappear into the emergency water evacuation drain. The group watched Jake gingerly rescue the floundering fish yet stop short of helping the last pitiful creature. The reason for his obvious consternation was apparent as the group realized the fish was deadly to the touch.

The crews of the *Evangeline* and the *Emissary* along with several others were thronging around a man the group had never seen before. The man, knowing Jake's frustration extricated himself from the crowd and gently rescued the fish. They continued to watch in awe as the fish seemed to thank the stranger for his rescue. The man turned to speak to Jake. Before he spoke, he looked directly into the surveillance camera.

Capt. Davu needlessly issued a hasty order. "Turn the sound up. I want to hear what he's about to say!"

The lieutenant was already making the adjustments before Capt. Davu could get the words out.

Through the feed, they heard the stranger ask Chief Holden, "Jake, do you trust me?"

"Of course, I do, Arni."

Capt. Davu stepped forward when he saw what was happening. "Th- That's Arni Liontari, son of Pateras. He's here. He's protecting them."

The Lieutenant looked incredulously at the two Captains and reiterated. "Sirs, the display shows that wall as open. That room should be full of water. There's no energy shield in place. There's NOTHING to keep the water out. This isn't possible."

The room grew silent in time to hear Arni respond to Jake. "If you have even the tiniest amount of faith and trust in me, you can do far greater things than touching a deadly fish."

Arni glanced at the cameras again. His look pierced the communications network and their souls.

Ajani looked at the astonished faces of his co-conspirators. "My brother talked to me at length last night about that man. He tried to convince me I should change my loyalty. We exchanged some rather harsh words before I left. I accused him of being weak. His views of me were even less flattering. I think I owe him an apology. Lieutenant, open that door. I need to get in there."

Most were in agreement; they had underestimated the stakes in this conflict. Capt. Logan wanted to beg his wife's forgiveness. A few were not convinced, but they *were* curious. The Lieutenant got the door open. When he tried to put the wall back up, his access was denied, "Captain, I'm locked out. I can't reinstate that wall."

Ajani glanced at the young man. "Apparently we don't need it," his analysis was simple yet accurate.

****

The group rushed into the room. Some hung back near the door, skittish about the unrestrained wall of water on the opposite side of the room.

Arni looked up when they entered and waved them forward. Capt. Logan looked back and forth between his wife and Arni. His wife hadn't come to the full realization that her husband had just tried to kill her. Her focus was on the man in front of her who saved her life. She smiled weakly at Chris and invited him to join her.

Deka saw Ajani enter the room. For a second, anger flooded his soul as the water tried to do moments ago. The desire to wrap his hands around his brother's neck rose up in him as his eyes darted back and forth. His gaze landed on Silas and Claire. Silas had attempted to execute his own wife months ago for following Pateras. The two had a rocky but complete reconciliation. Deka's anger subsided. He moved to greet and forgive his brother. Ajani offered the desired apology and begged to make amends. As soon as he spoke, his eyes landed on Arni. The pain and heaviness from what he had done left him as Arni released him from his sorrow. Arni greeted each newcomer personally. It took some time, but Arni finally got everyone to settle in to listen to him.

The door at the back of the room opened. Several maintenance workers, a couple of trusted security guards, and Neal Rune rushed in. They stopped in amazement as they looked at the wall of water. Neal, along with his two Drean security guards immediately recognized the Intercessor from their homeworld. Few had seen him in person. They were in awe of his presence and distracted from their task of rescuing those trapped by the flood of water.

Arni invited Neal and his companions to join the assembly. Neal accepted the invitation conditionally. He preferred to re-establish the barrier between the room and the ocean. He hastily worked with one of his technicians to raise the window and reactivate the shield. Silence enveloped the room as the wall worked its way back into position. The crowd's emotions drained as quickly as the water from the room.

Arni addressed the entire assembly rather than greeting individuals. "Soldiers of the Commonwealth, you are fighting a war you cannot win. Follow me, and you will fight a war you cannot lose. I came to bring you the only life that will satisfy. Luciano Hale has demanded your lives, and now he demands your deaths. My Father sent me to give up my life in payment of the debt you owe. I gave my life to save yours. The crew of the *Evangeline* can bear witness to my death. It was slow and painful. Pateras restored my life on the third day so that you could also be restored to life. Any who choose to believe this truth gains the light of my life to guide yours."

Capt. Davu stepped forward. He didn't exactly disagree with the man, but he needed to understand. "What is it you think is wrong with our lives? I mean, I am a CIF Captain. Aside from the fact the CIF wants me dead, I believe I have done well for myself."

A few others nodded in agreement. Arni wasn't even slightly offended by the question. "Do you believe Luciano Hale has been successful and done well for himself?"

Several nodded in agreement.

"Luciano's path is one of destruction. He is powerful, yes, but he betrayed my Father's trust and his love. He was exiled, and now he seeks to bring his fate upon each of you. You may be successful by Commonwealth standards. As far as my Father is concerned, you are on a path headed for destruction. The Commonwealth has taught you that this life is all there is, and you should make the best of it. I am telling you that this is only the beginning of life. Your bodies will die, but your souls live on forever. Your souls are immortal. When you die, you will face The Reckoning, where all debts will be settled. You each owe my Father your lives and your deaths for the crimes you have committed against him."

One reluctant voice cried out, "What crimes? Until a year ago, we'd never even heard of you. How can we be guilty of crimes against you?"

"You are not held accountable for things my Father hasn't revealed to you. I didn't come to pronounce judgment against you. I came to warn you of what lies ahead and to show you the right path to take. My Father created you. He created all of mankind. He loved you and gave you great gifts. Your ancestors rejected him and chose to follow the Evil One. The greatest crime you can commit is to take this knowledge and walk away from him. All Pateras desires is for you to love him as much as he loves you. Luciano Hale has managed to separate you from everything and everyone except the Commonwealth and him. You are alone. Your marriages are fleeting and transient. You have been separated from parents, siblings, and even your children. Friends are only temporary. Who can and will stay with you through everything? It isn't Luciano. Accept me into your lives, and I will never abandon you. Whether you trust me or believe me is up to you. I can rescue you from the path of destruction. Please, put your trust in me."

Ajani was one of the most ardent opponents of this new movement. Now, he said nothing. He stared at Arni and waited for him to continue. He was nearing the point of being persuaded.

"Ajani, I don't care who holds the office of Supreme Executor of the Commonwealth. I'm not here to tear down a government. I'm here to mend the rift between Pateras and man, between my Father and you. I'm here to heal the deepest pains of all mankind and introduce you to a life you never expected. My Father could have written you off. He could have destroyed you himself. He chose to find a way to preserve your lives and remake them into something far greater. He chose to help you. You have to *choose* to accept his offer and my sacrifice. What do you choose, Ajani?"

Ajani looked at the wall of seawater outside the window. The awesome power of the sea was no match for the man in front of him. He turned his gaze back to Arni. "I choose to accept… your offer."

Ajani closed the gap between himself and the stranger. Arni offered Ajani his hand and welcomed him warmly.

Capt. Logan found himself strangely drawn to Arni as well. He walked to the front of the assembly and waited for Arni to finish greeting Capt. Davu. Ajani moved aside for Chris. Chris looked into Arni's eyes. "You can see straight into my soul, can't you?"

Arni smiled and nodded. "I thought the Commonwealth didn't believe in souls."

Chris looked around nervously. "I guess I'm not part of the Commonwealth anymore. Sir, I'm not sure what exactly you want from me, but I'm willing to listen," he lowered his voice in shame. "I just tried to kill every single person in this room. Can you trust me after this? Will they?" He asked glancing at the crowd.

"I do trust you, and if they are truly a part of me, they will as well."

Arni welcomed the crowd collectively into his household. "I have spent time with the crews of the *Evangeline* and the *Emissary*. I will take turns traveling on each ship as you begin your journeys. You are not simply soldiers in my army. You are family. I will not abandon you. The day is coming when I will have to leave, but Pateras will send another to always remain with you."

An hour later Arni stepped aside and turned the meeting over to Capt. Alexander. Capt. Alexander confirmed Arni's claims and encouraged anyone with questions to feel free to ask his crew anything they wished. The meeting ended but numerous other conversations commenced.

****

Neal Rune pulled Brynna aside. "What happened here, and how am I supposed to explain this to my superiors?"

Brynna took a deep breath. She gave him the short version of what happened, "I don't really know what you should tell your superiors. Are there force-fields in place to stop the water in an emergency?"

"Yes, but your hacker deactivated them," Neal was in shock.

"You can tell them someone attempted to hack the system, but a force-field kept the water at bay," Brynna offered.

Neal shook his head. "I told you, the fields were rendered inoperable."

"*Your* force-fields were, but Arni's weren't. The biggest problem is going to be these maintenance workers and security officers. Keeping them from raising alarms is going to be the hard part. Introducing them to Pateras might keep them quiet about this. Watch them closely. Worry about the quiet ones who just sit back and watch," Brynna advised.

Brynna had one more question for the man, "Mr. Rune, why do those windows even have the option of opening underwater?"

"Those are designed to be both decorative and functional. We have some ships that come in and dock here during our busy season. Normally if those windows are down, that opening is sealed by a docking hatch."

Brynna nodded. "That makes sense. I couldn't imagine why you would have an opening to the ocean here."

The crew of the *Emissary* and the few present crew members of the *Evangeline* shared at great length everything they knew about Pateras. Cheyenne was prepared with files to share. She distributed files on the Ancient Texts and numerous files about their interactions with Arni. The security officers and maintenance workers were invited to join in.

Capt. Alexander had planned to wait until the morning to discuss their next moves. The excitement of the moment caused everyone to crave knowledge of Pateras, particularly his plans for the immediate future. He convened a meeting of the Captains in an adjoining conference room, the same room Chris and Ajani had used to orchestrate their demise.

****

Word reached Neal's superiors sooner than he expected. They came to see the "damage" for themselves. Neal decided to tell them exactly what he knew, then offered a plausible alternative. "We discovered someone hacked the wall and the shield. They weren't very good at it, and the program was glitched enough that we had trouble bringing the wall back up."

One of his superiors wasn't happy with the answers yet. "So why isn't this room full of water and dead bodies?"

"Well, it appears there was some sort of shielding over the opening. My best guess is the hacker didn't account for something in his programming and the shield generated from another nearby source. I suggest we chalk it up to a fluke and leave it at that. I really would rather not have Commonwealth experts in here trying to figure it out. We don't need that kind of attention here."

Neal knew his superiors did a lot of under-the-table dealings, and they didn't want extra attention either. The men left puzzled but satisfied that everything was under control. Neal called his staff together and gave them a casual warning not to do anything to upset the "Big Bosses" before dismissing them to return to their regular duties. He decided if he made a "big deal" of the situation, it would get more attention than he wanted it to receive. He answered questions with as little information as possible and left them wondering for themselves what happened.

It was late when the Captains' meeting let out. Brynna took the liberty of releasing the crews to go back to their ships. No one left quickly. As the hour got later, many decided it would be prudent to head back and get some rest.

BIRTH OF A REVOLUTION

David found Brynna alone on the bridge when he returned to the ship. She was sitting in the command chair monitoring the scanners when he stepped wearily onto the bridge. She scooted forward to relinquish his chair. David waved her back and sat down at her station. The bewildered look on his face was difficult to discern.

Brynna rotated her chair to see him straight on. "David? Are you okay?"

He blinked heavily. "I'm not sure."

His face wasn't troubled, so Brynna shoved her immediate worries away from the forefront of her mind. "Would you like to talk about it?"

"I'm not sure I know how to explain it. This whole night was amazing, to say the least. I think I'm comfortable with everything that happened tonight except one thing," David was looking befuddled.

Brynna's eyebrows knit themselves together. They were nearly executed by flood waters. Arni saved their lives, again. Was that the part her husband was having trouble with? She didn't know if she should wait for his explanation or ask bluntly. When he didn't volunteer the information, she gently prodded. "We did experience some unbelievable things this evening. Which one are you having trouble with?"

David laughed weakly, "Not the ones you would expect."

David leaned back in his seat, stretched his arms and legs out restlessly. He rubbed his tired face and brought his gaze back to face his beautiful wife and trusted First Officer.

"Do you remember Supreme Executor Hale offering me the rank of commodore while we were on Romajin?"

"Sort of, yes," Brynna answered. Executor Hale told her he granted David the rank and tried to convince her he had abandoned her for another woman and his freedom. She tried hard not to believe the Supreme Executor, but the evidence gave her some doubts.

"He offered me the chance to become the youngest Admiral on record if I changed sides. I don't think I mentioned that to you."

"No, I don't think you did. Why does it matter now?"

"Well, guess what the Captain's board just did," David shook his head in disbelief.

"What, David? Get to the point," Brynna was about to lose patience.

"I argued against it. I really did. I'm having a hard time accepting this," David stared off into space.

"Against what? What did they do?" Brynna persisted.

David shook his head in disbelief again. "They voted on establishing a new chain of command including only the Explorer fleet. They insisted it had to be done to maintain support and accountability."

Brynna was beginning to connect the dots and surmised what he was saying. "You're saying, they gave you the rank of commodore , a field promotion of sorts?"

David shook his head. "No, it's worse than that. They gave me a field promotion to the rank and position of Lead Admiral."

Brynna pondered this new train of thought. She never doubted he would continue to advance in rank, although committing treason had quashed the thought. She did expect him to be a great leader in spite of their treason. Something dawned in on her. "You said 'worse.' David, how is this worse?"

"I'm the second youngest Captain in the Explorer Fleet. There are nine other Captains out there with more experience than I've got," David argued.

Brynna gave him a look of consternation. "Please tell me which one of those has more experience with Pateras than you."

David jumped up and paced. "I do NOT have a monopoly on Pateras. Yes, I suppose I may have known him longer than the others, but we're talking months difference, not years."

Brynna chuckled softly. "You're whining."

"I'm not whining. Why would you say I'm whining? I don't have any reason to…" David stopped talking and pacing. "I *am* whining."

Brynna smiled and laughed again.

Perplexed, David asked. "What's funny now?"

"Supreme Executor Luciano Hale offered to make you the youngest Admiral on record. You would have been famous for that fact alone. Arni gave you, not just the rank of Admiral, but you're the LEAD Admiral, and you're definitely known throughout the galaxy."

David smiled at her. "I love the way you look at things. Thank you."

"Thanks for what?" She thought she knew what he was thanking her for, but she wanted a little clarification.

"This whole Admiral thing had me scared to death on several levels. You have a way of putting things into perspective and keeping me from getting hung up on the things that aren't important. Do you suppose Pateras arranged for us to be together?" David asked.

"Of course, he did. He knew you wouldn't have survived without me," Brynna grinned impishly.

David scowled, "Thanks for that vote of confidence."

"You're welcome, Admiral," Brynna grinned. She stood and saluted him.

David drew closer and countered her salute. He appreciated the respect and admiration she demonstrated by offering a purely elective affirmation of his new rank and position. He embraced her and kissed her passionately. He enjoyed their intimacy for no longer than a moment. There was more on his mind.

"What else is bothering you, David?"

"How am I supposed to lead eleven ships against the entire Commonwealth?" he asked and immediately felt like he was whining again.

"The first thing you need to do is talk to Arni. Find out what Pateras wants, then lead them the same way you were going to lead the twelve of us. You lead eleven ships instead of eleven crewmen. The next thing you need to do is get some sleep."

"Yeah, I know. How long are you staying on duty?" His mind jumped into business mode.

"I'm staying on for three hours. Jason and Laura will pick up the next two hours at 0200, then Lazaro and Cheyenne will take two hours from 0400 to 0600. Thane and Aulani have 0600 to 0800. That's as far as I went with the duty roster. What does tomorrow look like?" Brynna stopped counseling her husband and sought information from her commanding officer.

"We have one last assembly at 0900 hours. I have advised each Captain to keep a skeleton crew aboard their ships and link in remotely. We need everyone there either in person or linked in via comms. Our ship is the only one that will be vacant," Capt. Alexander was torn by the decision. He wanted to keep minimal personnel safely aboard the ship, but his crew needed to be there tomorrow. The longer they lingered here, the greater the chances were of being discovered. "Can Thane and Aulani keep the watch for one more hour? We can have Braxton take the watch at 0900 by remote."

Brynna nodded. "Sure, I'll leave an entry in the ship's log for them. Anything else I need to know?"

David thought for a minute. "Yes, there is one more thing. Leave a message for Lexi. I want her to stay in a position to watch the crowd. If anybody seems disgruntled, I need to know about it."

Brynna nodded again and waited. The Captains had met for a rather long meeting. Surely there was more accomplished than what little he had already revealed. "Anything else?"

"There is more to discuss, but I would rather do it after the meeting tomorrow. I'm tired, and I need to get a hot shower," David griped. His exhaustion was probably a contributing factor to his earlier propensity for whining.

He moved to the back of the bridge. "Have I told you how much I love you recently?"

Brynna grinned. "Yes, but I would love to hear it again."

David smiled his best, tired smile. "I love you more than I can adequately express. Goodnight, my love."

Brynna hastily asked one more question. "David, can I ask you one more thing?"

"What is it?"

"Whose idea was it to put you up for Lead Admiral?"

David sighed. "Taye."

"Capt. Silvain? Why would he do that after the trouble he caused you last night?" Brynna was shocked. Was this a ruse or distraction? Could Taye be trusted?

"I think because I was sympathetic to his situation and provided for him and what's left of his crew. He saw the truth of the situation. He knew I wasn't being controlled by a strange alien being, and I genuinely cared about what happened to him and his crew."

Capt. Alexander also considered that the man's actions might be a ploy to distract him. Taye could have made the suggestion to convince David he was an ardent supporter. He could also be hoping the idea of being an Admiral would go to David's head and cause their tiny revolution to fall apart before it even got started. David shook his head. He was in denial of these most recent events. He understood the logic, but this was not what he expected at all.

The Captain gave his wife a proper good night and headed to bed. As he lay down alone, he smiled to himself. He had chosen the right woman to marry. She knew he needed rest, and this was the only way he would get it. She knew going to bed alone was what he would need long before he returned to the ship. If she had come to bed with him, they would have talked late into the night.

****

David woke early the next morning. Finding Brynna asleep beside him, he reached out to touch her. Realizing she was still several hours short of a full night's sleep, he denied himself the pleasure of her company and slipped out of bed. He dressed and headed to the dining hall for breakfast. He perused the redundant options of prepackaged foods for a moment. Tired of the ship's stores, he decided to head to the Plaza for some *real* food. Neal Rune provided them with some restaurant vouchers, which David had neglected to use. He hailed the bridge and told Aulani where he was headed. "Ensign, inform the crew that the assembly begins at 0900. Have them travel in civilian attire but bring their dress uniforms. There will be rooms set aside to change clothes in before the meeting. Keep the uniforms covered until they reach the meeting area. Your family and Mr. Bennett are welcome to attend as well."

"Sir? You want us to bring dress uniforms, and you're willing to let my family off the ship? What's going on?" Aulani didn't mean to question his orders, but they struck her as odd.

Capt. Alexander headed out the airlock with his dress uniform carefully stowed in a small bag. "You'll find out when we get to the assembly, Ensign."

Aulani cast a concerned glance at Thane, who was only hearing her half of the conversation. "Captain, forgive me for asking, but are you sure my family will be safe if they go out in public?"

"Ensign, if someone has turned us in, the assembly hall and the ship will be in equal danger. Make sure they keep their heads down and don't stop anywhere along the way," Capt. Alexander was in an unusually good mood for some reason. He closed his communication with the Ensign.

****

David found a quiet corner to eat his breakfast in the Plaza. As David finished eating, his mood changed. He looked around the area, feeling uneasy. He had chosen a place where he could keep an eye on his surroundings yet stay out of sight. He decided it was time to go. He settled his bill quickly and took a circuitous route to the assembly. Despite his abrupt departure and surveillance counter-measures, he couldn't shake the feeling that he was being followed or watched.

Stepping off the elevator outside their conference area, Capt. Alexander was immediately greeted by his suspicious security officer. "Is everything okay, sir?"

David frowned. "I'm not sure. Maybe I'm being paranoid, but I got the feeling I was being watched."

"Is that why you're running late and coming from the wrong direction?" Jake saw the elevator come from below them instead of from the Plaza above them.

"Yes. I'll feel much better after this last meeting is over. We need to get these ships out of here. We've been sitting still for far too long. Maybe I'm getting a little jumpy," the young Captain glanced at the elevators as the doors opened to reveal more new arrivals.

"You aren't the only one. I'm ready to get moving again too. We're sitting ducks down here."

David stepped into one of the conference rooms and changed to his dress uniform. He couldn't shake the feeling of being watched. After he had his uniform on and in pristine condition, he moved to the main conference room. He stood in front of the window, looking into the sea. Mentally, he reached out to Arni. He silently unloaded his extensive list of concerns before being interrupted by another Captain asking questions about the meeting agenda.

****

David assigned Capt. Silvain to open the meeting. The entire idea of having a promotion ceremony was ludicrous to Capt. Alexander. The entire galaxy was hunting them down to destroy them, and the other Captains wanted to trifle with something that might not matter in the slightest days from now.

Each Captain was seated on the small stage. Capt. Silvain approached the podium. The room was filled with a sharp sea of dress uniforms with the exception of Capt. Silvain's crew, Marissa, and the four visitors. At exactly 0900, hours the room was called to order. Capt. Silvain solemnly addressed the assembly. "Ladies and gentlemen, we are embarking on a journey I never expected to go on. Our worlds have been turned upside-down. I am one who fought the hardest to deny this path. I was wrong to fight it. I now embrace this new journey. It may cost me everything, but I am willing to pay this price. If you are not prepared to do this, I advise you to leave. I excuse you from this assembly. If you can't fight this fight, go now!"

Taye waited. No one moved. He offered one last admonition. "No one will think less of you for leaving. We *will* think less of you for faltering because you follow a cause you don't truly believe in. This is the final moment of decision. Who do you stand with, Pateras, or the Commonwealth?"

David advised the other Captains to keep their seats and wait for their crews to declare their loyalties without any pressure. Henry and Luna Oliver, two of Capt. Weiseman's crew, stood together and loudly proclaimed, "We stand with Pateras."

They had spent the last several years hiding their loyalty. It was exhilarating to admit it openly.

Jake was sitting at one of the computer terminals next to Braxton. He stopped watching the scanners, stood sharply, and faced the assembly. "I stand with Pateras!"

One by one the declarations were heard throughout the room until everyone was standing. Lastly, the remaining eleven Captains stood and proclaimed their loyalty. It was more patriotic and inspiring than Capt. Alexander expected.

Taye smiled, which was surprising to most. He was not the *smiling* type. "Capt. Alexander has proven to be a source of knowledge, leadership, and inspiration to myself and many others. As we are starting down this long, difficult course, the Captain's board voted, against Capt. Alexander's objections, to a restructuring of the command chain. He believed this was a waste of our time and energy. Most of us know nothing about Pateras except the lies told us by the Commonwealth. It was clear to everyone but him. We needed new leadership."

Taye grinned mischievously, another unnerving action, and twisted to look at Capt. Alexander. David resisted the urge to shift in his seat, which would reveal his discomfort to everyone present. "I personally found great comfort in establishing him as the new commander of our tiny army. It keeps the Commonwealth target off my back and on his."

Several were shocked by the statement and stared at the brazen Captain.

Knowing what he did about Capt. Silvain, David decided it was time to react. He readjusted his position in his chair, finally revealing his discomfort over the topic, then loudly responded, "Thanks, I appreciate that!" His face revealed a slight smirk.

Taye continued to grin. "Capt. Alexander is not only the foremost authority on Pateras. He has managed to bring all of us here together safely and provide for our needs. I have no ship and virtually no crew left. Capt. Alexander and Capt. Weiseman provided us with a place to go and a way to remove the nanites from our systems. Capt. Alexander is not the enemy we were told he was. I do not believe his people destroyed the military base on Romajin. He may be young and inexperienced, but Pateras guides his steps and protects him.

"In establishing a new chain of command, we have decided to approve several field promotions. We will begin with the lowest ranking promotions. When I call your names, report to your Captains."

The affected Captains knew who they were and moved into place on the floor in front of the platform. The Captains of the *Evangeline*, *Messenger*, *Concord*, and *Emissary* lined up across the front. Each ship's First Officer was called forward. Brynna quickly figured out what information her husband neglected to tell her when they talked the previous night. She knew he was holding back. Now she knew why he disappeared for breakfast. He wasn't good at keeping things from her.

The *Explorer* was not going to promote its First Officer, as Capt. Silvain would replace Capt. Gellert.

Brynna reported formally to her husband, keeping her full military bearing. Each Commander was promoted to the rank of Captain. With supplies being scarce, the Captains removed their rank insignia and pinned them on their Commanders. Some of the crews were in shock over the recent developments and gave a less than enthusiastic round of applause with their leaders' promotions. Those who were more used to the situation were generous with their displays of approval. As Brynna gave her final salute to David before returning to her seat, he was sure he saw a brief glint in her eye reflecting her perturbed mood.

Capt. Silvain indicated further promotions aboard each ship could still occur as the reshuffling of the command tier settled into place. "As I mentioned before, the Captain's board has voted Capt. David Alexander in as our commander. Capt. David Alexander, please join me at the podium."

David took a deep breath. He really didn't want to do this. He moved to stand facing Taye. He stood at attention. Taye turned to face him. "Capt. David Alexander, the newly formed Liontari Fleet has elected to promote you to the rank and position of Lead Admiral. Do you solemnly swear to execute the duties and responsibilities commensurate with this rank and leadership station to the best of your abilities?"

David raised his hand to take the oath. "With the leadership and guidance of Pateras, I so swear it."

"I hereby convey on you the rank of Admiral and the role of Lead Admiral," Taye's stoic nature made him ideal for solemn situations.

Capt. Silvain took the liberty of using his last remaining credits and had new rank insignia for Admirals and Commodores fashioned by a shop in the Plaza. They weren't the same high-quality metal normally used, but he decided it would do. Capt. Silvain surprised David when he pinned the new Admiral ranks on his uniform. Taye stepped back and saluted his new Admiral. The Captain's board stood and saluted him as well. David countered the salute to Taye. Next, he turned to face the Captain's board and saluted them. Taye called the entire room to attention. Everyone stood as ordered. He called again, "Present arms!"

The assembly raised their salute. Aulani's family was unaccustomed to the military displays. They stood to show their respect and support. Mr. Bennett was used to such displays. He stood at attention and offered the Drean form of a salute.

David saluted the audience. Capt. Silvain released the audience and allowed them to be seated. Before anyone sat down, a rousing cheer and round of applause erupted from the audience. His own crew and Capt. Weiseman's were the most enthusiastic.

Taye stepped aside to offer David a chance to address the audience. David declined to speak as yet. The two whispered back and forth. David stepped away from the podium and stood off to the side. Taye turned his attention back to the audience.

"Adm. Alexander would prefer to speak after the promotions are complete. The following promotions were voted on and approved by the Captain's board. Report to Adm. Alexander as you are called. Capt. Tas Gellert. Capt. Gellert is being promoted to the rank of commodore ."

David and Tas exchanged the appropriate salutes and congratulatory handshakes. The Captain's board and audience saluted as before.

Taye announced the promotion of Capt. Patrick James to the rank of commodore . Capt.s Angela Smith and Nate Weiseman were promoted to the rank of Admiral and the position of Vice-Admiral answering to David. Each one received the appropriate laud and honor due them. Once the promotions were complete, Taye turned the meeting over to his new commander, Adm. David Alexander.

David took a quick sip of water and began his address. "I am honored by the obvious confidence you have in me. I hope your confidence isn't misplaced. I will do my best to lead you wherever Pateras wants us to go. I admonish you to learn who Pateras is and speak to him personally. Get to know who he is and how he works, because it's not normal. Nothing he does is ordinary. If you get odd orders from me, assume they are his orders. I'm not that imaginative. I need you to promise me something of paramount importance."

David grinned as he anticipated his words. "I need you to promise me to wait at least a week, a full week, before getting yourselves caught or killed. It would really look bad if, as a new Admiral, I got my entire fleet wiped out in the first week. You have to stay alive and free for at least that long. Deal?"

Soft snickers could be heard through the audience. Nate leaned forward and hollered, "Deal! I'm not about to give up my Admiral's pay!"

This time outright giggles could be heard. Everyone knew their pay was suspended as soon as the Commonwealth recall order went out. None of them were getting paid.

David used the levity to worm his way out of a lengthy acceptance speech and moved to more serious business. "On a more serious note, the following ships, with the exception of the flagships, will report to Commodore James; the *Advocate*, the *Ambassador*, the *Deliverance,* and the *Herald*. Commodore James will report to Adm. Smith. The following ships will report to Commodore Gellert; the *Pioneer*, the *Malachi*, and the *Bounty*. Commodore Gellert will report to Adm. Weiseman."

David paused for a moment. His next words were going to be a little harsh, but he needed to say them.

"Capt. Silvain was right earlier when he invited anyone not committed to leave. I would ask each of you, if you aren't committed to this, leave now. Don't betray us or your crew, just walk away, please. We've got the entire galaxy looking for us. Don't turn in your own shipmates. That is betrayal of the worst kind. I can accept a straightforward disagreement. I'm not nearly as tolerant of deceit. I am capable of forgiving deceit, but my forgiveness won't come easily. I've been betrayed once already. I would prefer you tell me outright that you're going to turn me in. If you need to leave quietly, then slip out today and leave your Captain a note in the ship's log. Leave honorably."

The new Admiral spoke a few minutes longer giving them a general idea what his plans were and his version of a rallying battle cry. He finally dismissed the assembly in favor of yet another meeting of the new ship's Captains and his command staff. They took an hour in between the two meetings to socialize and offer congratulations. It wasn't David's favorite pastime, but he knew it was a necessary evil. It was necessary to maintain troop morale.

As first act as Captain of the *Evangeline*, Brynna ordered the crew to get changed into civilian attire and head back to the ship in small groups taking varying routes. Jake and Marissa were the last to leave. They stayed to watch scanners from the assembly hall until Braxton checked in aboard ship to take over the watch.

****

The first questions on the new command staff's minds were; where are we going and what are we doing? David discussed their goals, methods of communication, and things to watch out for.

"I am not going to mince words here. There are a lot of things that need to happen. We can't do them all. We need to stop the destruction of innocent civilians at the hands of Luciano Hale. We need to get our proof of these atrocities to the press, the Commonwealth Advisory Council, and the Judiciary Board. We need to free Capt. Silvain's crew and destroy the Nefil Development Center. Our *primary* goal is to spread the information about Pateras. Putting Luciano Hale in an unfavorable light will help protect your families. The more favorable attention we get, the better. I have reason to believe we have potential allies among the advanced worlds."

Capt. Clements raised her hand to question her new Admiral's supposition. "Admiral, what gave you the idea anyone in the Commonwealth still knows and supports such a being as Pateras? We were trained to discount such… ideas," Sarah couldn't come up with the right words to describe the recent events. She was taught they were fantasy and the result of someone with a weak-minded imagination. Seeing the incredible power of Pateras for herself, she now believed in his reality. She struggled with changing her vernacular.

David smiled, "That's an excellent question. While I was on Romajin, before being captured, I ran across a display in a museum designed to ensnare anyone showing interest in Pateras. If knowledge of him were totally stamped out, why lay such a trap? I can only guess there are others out there, staying hidden. If we get Pateras' name in the press, any others may gain the courage to join us in our fight."

The new Adm. Smith was skeptical. "Surely you aren't basing that on one little display in a tiny unknown museum."

"No, I'm not. First of all, that display was under a high level of surveillance by a Commonwealth security officer posing as a librarian. I managed to set off all kinds of alarms before getting out of there," David shook his head

193

remembering his clumsiness. "The second reason I know we have allies yet to be discovered is during our mission, we discovered a world that was rejected by the Commonwealth. After further digging, we learned that leading scientists were abducted, imprisoned, and forced to choose between serving Pateras and serving the Commonwealth. A lot of them died in prison, but some didn't."

David was choosing his words carefully. He didn't want to reveal his background if he could avoid it.

Capt. Silvain scowled, "These people would be traitors to Pateras, would they not? We couldn't trust them."

"They would be no more suspicious than any of us. Some of you have seen the truth and embraced it. Unfortunately, it's possible some of you have joined us simply because you feel you have no other choice. Does that make you any more or less trustworthy than them?"

Capt. Davu and Capt. Logan exchanged guilty looks. They were probably in the latter category. They were attempting to embrace these new ideas, but they weren't quite there yet.

Capt. Clements wasn't completely sold out either. "Admiral, I applaud your desire to get us some help and allies, but this sounds really thin."

David glanced at Brynna and Nate. Brynna returned a slight shrug. Nate gave him a distinct scowl.

Sarah saw the exchange and knew there was a lot more information to be gleaned from the reluctant new Admiral. "Adm. Alexander, you've asked us to trust you and to trust Pateras. Don't hold out on us now. I don't need to know all your secrets, but I think we need something to hold onto."

No one visibly joined her in her request, but several were thinking the same things. Seeing the doubt in their eyes, David knew he needed to go further. "I have a list of known conscripts who were forced to work for the Commonwealth. The thing I don't know is; were they bribed or were they blackmailed. The list is from one world alone. I have taken a personal interest in this… because two of the conscripts… were my grandparents, Saul and Tyra Paulson," David was careful to use their Drean names. If he used their

Commonwealth names, they could be tied to his uncle, Adm. Robert Deacons. Most didn't know David's tie to the Admiral, nor the Admiral's true loyalty.

David hastily moved on to prevent more personal questions. "Before anyone asks, no, I didn't leave the Commonwealth because of my family's history. That was one small piece of the puzzle. My point is, if they did this to one world, they may have done it to others. We need to find and recruit those who still carry that bitter taste in their mouths."

Nate jumped in to move the conversation along. "Alright, we seek out allies and reveal the atrocities of the Supreme Executor to the appropriate Commonwealth authorities and the press. What else?"

David knew his next words were going to evoke a negative reaction. He took a deep breath. "We need to destroy the Nefil development facility on Ahnak III."

Commodore James bolted upright in his seat. "You want us to hunt *them* down? Are you insane? Those soldiers are bigger, stronger, and more heavily armed than we are. We'll get slaughtered!"

David leaned over and put his hands flat on the table. "Which is exactly why we need to shut that facility down. We don't need Executor Hale cranking out an entire army of those monsters. We have to limit him to those he already has. They aren't impossible to stop. I saw several Level II natives take out an entire crew. They were armed with swords, spears, bows, and arrows."

"My other goal is to get Capt. Silvain's crew out of the prison on Mara. Commodore Gellert, if we get them out, do you have room for them on your ship?"

Tas shook his head. "Not comfortably. I have two empty crew quarters which will now be occupied by Capt. Silvain and his two crew members. That's all the space I have unless we find a way to convert the cargo hold to crew quarters. I could transport them somewhere, but I can't keep them."

David stood upright. "We can work that out later. The thing we need to worry about is where they are in their reprogramming. Will they be the same people they were when they were arrested?"

The new Admiral moved on. He handed each one a data crystal with their specific assignments. "I've discussed numerous possible missions so that you know what the ultimate goals are. As a group you don't know which missions I have chosen to start with. You each know our primary goals are to discredit Supreme Executor Luciano Hale without getting into what we truly know about his background, educate and inform the general population about Pateras, and gain new allies or places of refuge. I've put your specific assignments on these data crystals. Do not discuss them with anyone else. This information is 'need to know.' Share among your staff only what they need to know to do their jobs. If anyone is captured, they will only be able to reveal their assignment. No one except myself and the appropriate command staff will know where you're headed. Take whatever circuitous route you deem necessary to get you to your goals.

"If you're in danger of getting caught, program your computers to wipe its memory and program a data module to send a time delayed message to let us know what happened. Watch for those hidden carrier waves that could disable your ships. Change all your access codes. There's a computer program on this data crystal, which I'm sure your people could create, but it monitors file access and usage. If somebody copies a file, deletes a file, or alters a log entry, the program sends a notification to whoever you deem necessary. It could warn you if you have someone on board that's not entirely trustworthy."

Capt. Logan held up his crystal. "I take it you put this program into effect after you were captured on Romajin?"

David was not completely blameless in their capture on Romajin and his face revealed a hint of complicity. "No, this is a complicated issue, but this was in effect before we were captured. We knew we had been betrayed. We didn't have a lot of details, but the evidence was there. Arni told me what was coming and asked me to let it happen. I trusted him, and it worked out for the best. It didn't feel like the best at the time, but it was."

David glanced at the expectant faces. Capt. Clements, one of the more reluctant participants, wasn't sure she was ready to face what was ahead. "Adm. Alexander, what will they do to us if they capture us?"

The former Captain didn't hold back. "If you had asked me that last week, I would have said there won't be any 'capturing.' They would have shot your ship down and killed you as quickly and quietly as possible. If you ask again next month, the answer will be different. If this plan works, it will put us in the public eye making it difficult for Executor Hale to take liberties with our treatment. He will expect we have information on each other's locations and targets. I anticipate he will do to any of us what he did to me and my crew on Romajin. We were tortured. He started the re-education process on us, and to me personally, he tried to use my family against me. My plan should offer our families some protection and what happens to us also depends on Pateras. His plans can obviously break the Laws of Physics. Learn to listen to him and hear his voice. He may ask some hard things, but he knows what's best. Trust him."

Sarah set her jaw firmly. Holding up her data crystal she responded. "I hope this assignment gives me some time to learn those things. You're asking a lot."

David smiled warmly. "You will have some time. I want to start each mission simultaneously. I've planned out the time for each attack in a way that they won't know where to send their defensive forces. We will be launching our offensives in numerous locations across the entire galaxy simultaneously. I'm trying not to ask anything of you except, listen to Pateras. If he changes your assignment, then so be it. I *am* trying to protect the fleet. Your departure times are in with your instructions. We'll start sending ships out this afternoon one or two at a time. I don't want a mass exodus to get unnecessary attention, or we won't be able to use this location again. Continue to keep a low profile here on the colony. Get your people aboard your ships and slip out quietly. Any questions?"

The room remained quiet. David studied his new allies. "Pateras has granted you power. He will lead you and tell you what to do. I'm a normal human being with a small amount of knowledge and experience. I can't take you very far. He can, and he will. Those of you with early departures, hail me in the next hour if you have questions about your assignment."

David looked out the smaller window in the room revealing the majestic seascape. "Arni, keep them safe and grant them long lives in your service. You're dismissed."

Most agreed it was odd to speak out loud to someone who wasn't in the room. They assumed it would become more natural… later.

The new Commodore Gellert stood first. "Well, here we go. Win or lose, we're in it now."

A meager course of agreement filtered through the newly established Liontari command staff.

David stepped forward. Fire flashing in his eyes. "Pateras may or may not require us to give our lives, but we are not leaving here with the intention of dying. I've been dead. It's a great place to be, but it's not time for us to go there yet. We've got an enemy to defeat."

Ajani Davu stared at David in disbelief. "You aren't dead. What are you talking about?"

Adm. Weiseman leaned forward and propped on the conference table. "You need to review the data files he gave you yesterday. The information was in them. Adm. Deacons attempted to execute him on Tudoren, but a local shaman beat him to it."

Ajani looked back and forth skeptically. "Is this true?"

David glanced at Nate, knowing what information he had concealed. "Adm. Deacons knew about my treason. He attempted to test my commitment to Pateras and tried to convince me to come back to the Commonwealth. A local tried to protect me. I got in the way and was hit in the chest with an arrow aimed at the Admiral. I died from the wound. Arni restored my life a day later. One of my officers died on our second mission, remember the young woman on my crew who's pregnant? Arni healed her, but he neglected to inform her that the Commonwealth birth control no longer worked. Death is nothing to fear if you serve Pateras and his son. It is something to fear if you don't."

"So, a religious zealot with a primitive weapon gets a lucky shot, and now you don't fear death?" Chris Logan was having trouble coming to terms with this new line of thinking.

Brynna was having trouble being patient with this discussion. "It wasn't a lucky shot."

David glanced quickly at his wife. He didn't want the others to know about his relationship with the Admiral. He gave her a hard stare. If he verbally tried to shut her down, the others would recognize his actions and interpret it as a cover-up.

Brynna continued, "David knew the Admiral would face The Reckoning if he died. He doesn't want to see that happen to his worst enemy. David, being a servant of Pateras, was safe from The Reckoning. He jumped in front of the Admiral and took the hit for him. He saved the Admiral's life by giving up his own."

All eyes turned to David.

Chris Logan stood, "We were taught as leaders and officers the right and wrong ways to inspire loyalty among our subordinates. Soldiers are more likely to follow someone who is willing to get into the trenches with them and get their own hands dirty. You are that kind of man. You have my complete loyalty."

David offered Chris his hand, "Thank you. Give your greatest loyalty to Pateras though, not me. I'm a fallible human. I can choose unwisely, too. Just ask my crew. I appreciate all of you for your support. Remember to be cautious where your crews are concerned. Every man has the right to change his mind. Don't go on any witch hunts, but watch your backs."

Chris shook the man's hand and the meeting ended as intended. The officers gave each other farewell greetings and filtered out to change from their dress uniforms and return to their ships. Brynna gave David a quick message indicating she would see him aboard the ship. She knew he would need to answer any last-minute questions or address issues that may pop-up. She would have her turn with him later. It took nearly a full hour to get everyone on their way.

CH 11 - BIRTH OF A REVOLUTION

M.I.A. — AGAIN

Now alone in the conference room except for Nate, David confided in his closest friend. "Nate, I shouldn't be in this position. I'm only marginally ready to be a ship's Captain. This is way beyond what I'm prepared for."

Nate shook his head, "Davie, my friend, who would you care to recommend?"

"Tas or Angie have more command experience than I do. To be honest, my first choice would be to get my uncle out of CIF HQ and put him in charge," David confessed.

"Your uncle is more useful to us where he is," Nate knew his friend needed to get past this point of doubt.

"My uncle didn't want me in the command track at all," David informed his friend, "He told me just before we shipped out."

"What? Why would he tell you that just before you took command? Was he trying to sabotage you? Destroy your confidence?"

"I think at that point he was worried about me and wanted to push me a little harder," David surmised his uncle's intent, but it still haunted him.

Nate pushed back in his chair and made himself comfortable. "Considering your family's past, are you sure he wasn't just trying to protect you?"

"What do you mean?" David stared out the window at the colorful underwater reef.

"Your uncle has known Pateras since he was a boy. He knew what happened to him and his family. He knew what sort of treachery the Commonwealth was capable of. Maybe he was trying to keep you away from all of that, keep you safe. He might've been worried about what would happen to you if you succeeded."

David faced Nate. "I suppose it's possible. It's not exactly something I could ask him about."

"Let me ask you a question. Looking back on this last year, is there anything you would've done differently?" Nate placed his hands behind his head and laced his fingers together. He swiveled casually in his seat.

"Do you mean given the information I have now or knowing what I did at the time?"

"Both," Nate continued to swivel nonchalantly.

"Knowing what I did at the time, no, I can't really think of anything I would change. Knowing what I do now, yes, there's a couple of things I would do differently," David folded his arms across his chest. "What's your point?"

"What decisions would you change?" Nate persisted.

"I wouldn't have reported Galat III. I wouldn't have sent Lt. Holden out into that storm. I wouldn't have fought Arni so hard. I would have sent my crew away on Romajin and turned myself in rather than let them get caught."

David sat down dejectedly. The rehashing of things he counted as mistakes was making him ill.

"Maybe you shouldn't lead us, because those are all bad decisions, except maybe the one about not fighting Arni," Nate argued.

"Just how do you figure that?" Adm. Alexander looked like he was about to come out of his chair.

"If you hadn't reported Galat, what would have happened on Drea? Better yet, what *wouldn't* have happened on Drea?" Nate knew David would get his point fairly quickly, but he pushed on anyway. "If you hadn't reported Galat, Arni wouldn't have died and saved your life or your crew's lives. If Marissa hadn't died in that storm, she wouldn't be pregnant right now. If your crew hadn't gone to Romajin, they wouldn't have learned to trust Arni the way they do. You did the right things. Yes, bad things happened, but they were ultimately for the best. You do see that, don't you? This wasn't your plan, it was Pateras' plan. If you changed those things, you would have screwed it up."

"Alright, you made your point. I'm just saying I feel incredibly inadequate to serve as the leader of a—a revolution."

"Listen to Pateras and follow the instincts he gave you. Luciano Hale wants you to doubt yourself. There's a section in the Ancient Texts that talks about fear and doubt being the weapons of the Dark Lord. Sounds like you've been hit. I'm really hoping it's just a flesh wound," Nate teased his friend hoping to shake his mood. "Arni told us he would give us the weapons we needed for this fight."

"I just keep thinking about the blood on my hands. He should use someone with a cleaner past than mine," David argued.

"Would you mind telling me which one of the fleet Captains has a cleaner past? Maybe he wants and needs someone who's seen the ugliness up close and personal," Nate countered, "Answer this one question for me. Would you do anything Arni asked of you, or have you put limits on what he can ask?"

"No, I haven't put limits on him. I owe him my life. I'll do whatever he asks," David answered honestly. He did leave an obvious "but" hanging in the air.

"You just think his judgment is impaired," Nate harshly responded.

A heavy silence filled the room as David weighed Nate's accusation. "No, I don't think Arni's judgment is impaired. I think mine is."

David visually searched the room for the invisible being, "Arni, I'm sorry. I didn't mean to doubt you. I'll do whatever you need me to. Forgive me."

A feeling of warmth and forgiveness entered the empty room. Neither one heard a word physically or mentally.

David stood up. "We should get back to our ships. We've got work to do."

Nate smiled, "Glad to hear you say that."

Before David could respond, his comm link beeped at him. He tapped his comm unit and responded as confidently as he could. "This is… Adm. Alexander, go ahead."

Brynna responded with an equally awkward pause at the newness of the ranks, "Admiral, Lt. Holden and Chief Holden haven't made it back to the ship. I hailed the Chief, and he indicated the Lieutenant was having trouble with the walk back. They are in the Plaza's main level. Could you see what you can do?"

"Sure, Nate and I are on our way out. Have the Doc on standby. I'll hail you when I locate them."

Neither David nor Nate had changed out of their dress uniforms. David didn't want to take the time to change but didn't want to attract attention either. He pulled his dress tunic off, and stuffed it into his bag. The shirt underneath was more colorful than the black tunic, but it was plain in style. There were no rank insignia or other distinguishing marks. If anyone looked closely enough, they could tell that he was wearing dress pants and a casual long-sleeve shirt. Nate quickly did the same only he pulled a casual jacket on over his shirt. Two men, wearing identical clothing not corresponding to security or maintenance uniforms, were equally as likely to get unwanted attention. The two rode the elevator up to the Plaza. Nate volunteered to go up one more level to get a better view.

Before the two went their separate ways, Nate gave David one more piece of advice. "Davie, you need to forgive yourself. If Arni can forgive you, you should forgive yourself. Everyone's made bad choices. Some far worse than yours. You're no worse than anybody else."

The new Admiral eyed his friend closely, "As my new Vice-Admiral and adviser, I would be remiss if I didn't listen to your wise counsel. I'll do my best. You have my word."

"I suppose that's the best I can expect. I know you can't let go of something like this overnight."

Adm. Alexander stepped off the elevator and nodded his appreciation to his friend. He watched the doors close before turning his attention to the task at hand.

****

David hailed Jake, "Chief Holden, what's your location?"

"Captain… uh… sorry sir, Admiral, we're at the edge of the food district near elevator number eight," Jake replied.

David glanced at the elevators nearest him to see which way the numbers were going. Getting his bearings in the large Plaza, he hastened toward Jake and Marissa. David hailed Nate with Jake's location.

The Admiral located the two sitting on a bench near the indicated elevator at the edge of the Plaza. Nate made it to a spot on the mezzanine above them more quickly. There were fewer pedestrians, trashcans, or even potted plants to slow him down. David had to zigzag around the winding pathways and obstacles to reach his destination. He couldn't see over the heads of pedestrians, around signs, or plants like Nate could. He kept glancing up at Nate for clarification of his destination.

David knelt in front of the two while signaling Nate to stay put. "Marissa, what's going on?"

Marissa glanced nervously at him, "I'm tired. I can't go very far without getting winded. We stopped to get a bite to eat before going back to the ship. I think I let myself get dehydrated again. Between the meal and the dehydration, the contractions started again," Before she could say anything else she winced.

Jake was paying close attention to every nuance of her behavior. "What? What was that?"

"I'm trying to drink more, and now I need to go to the restroom again. I'm getting frustrated."

Marissa wasn't due for another week. She wasn't sure she was going to have the patience to wait that long, "Jake, help me up, please."

Jake and David gently eased Marissa to her feet. She had already visually located the nearest restroom and wasted no time getting there. Seeing her have no difficulty walking David surmised she could make it to the ship without help. He signaled Nate to let him know they wouldn't need him any longer. Nate headed past them toward another elevator to take him to his ship's berth.

David and Jake talked as they waited for Marissa.

"You know, Captain… sorry, Admiral. It's going to take some time to get used to that," Jake's frustration with Marissa was spilling over to other topics.

"Tell me about it," David lamented.

"Sir, I'm sorry we haven't made it back to the ship. We've stopped for water. She had to catch her breath and she needed to find a restroom. This is the fourth restroom!"

Jake glanced at the bench where they had been sitting. Since the dehydration incident on the bridge, Marissa kept a small water canteen with her. Jake grabbed the canteen and shook it. It was nearly empty.

"Maybe I better refill this… again."

"Jake, only one more week. Things will be better when we get back into space. I'm taking her off active duty as soon as we leave this star system."

Jake looked at the canteen. He could relate to its perpetual state of emptiness. He was woefully unprepared for dealing with this pregnancy. "Thanks, sir. I'll be right back."

Jake headed back up the winding walkway to the last place he saw a water dispenser.

Marissa emerged as soon as Jake disappeared. Seeing her, David hailed Jake to tell him they were heading to the seventh elevator. Jake acknowledged and finished getting the water before heading their direction.

The two reached a similar bench behind the seventh elevator and Marissa sat down to wait for Jake.

The feeling David had at breakfast returned. Someone was watching him. He looked at the people passing by. No one was paying them any attention. He wondered if he was imagining things. A sense of urgency descended on him.

"What's going on, sir?" Marissa could see he was unsettled.

"I don't know. I keep thinking someone's watching me. Let's get moving. Jake can catch up," David urged.

David grabbed her right hand in his and wrapped his left arm around her waist to help her up. He escorted her to the elevator. The doors opened and two men stepped off leaving two others inside the car. Something about them made alarm bells go off in his head. David held Marissa back.

"Sorry, wrong elevator," He gruffly addressed the two occupants.

David swiveled away from the elevator keeping Marissa tightly in tow. He ran straight into the two men who had just exited. The two had weapons drawn. They motioned for David and Marissa to get into the elevator. The men who remained on the elevator pulled weapons as well. They grabbed David and Marissa's bracelets and tossed them into the nearest potted plant, just before the door to the elevator closed.

The men searched their prisoners. Their captors quickly relieved them of their bags and weapons. The leader of the group stood directly in David's face. "You cooperate and your girlfriend… and her baby, might get out of this alive. You don't, and she'll be the first one to go. Got it?"

David showed no fear, "I got it. There is something *you* need to understand, she's in labor. I was trying to get her to the Infirmary. You need to let her off the elevator. She'll only slow you down."

Marissa looked nervously at her commanding officer. "You knew? I didn't want to mention it. I was afraid Jake would freak out."

The man in David's face glanced at Marissa. He was certain they were trying to play him. David added one more piece of information. "Something else you should know. Jake is her husband and he was only a couple of hundred yards behind us. Let her out, and he'll be distracted getting her to safety. He won't come after us until it's too late. You have my word, I won't cause problems."

"I'm sure you won't. The lady stays with us," The man was so close David felt his hot breath.

The elevator went to the lowest levels. These were inactive mining levels.

****

An alarm sounded aboard the *Evangeline* the second David and Marissa's bracelets were removed. It was a safety feature the Captain had programmed into the bracelets. Cheyenne looked immediately at Braxton and Brynna, "Ma'am, sir, I think the Captain, I mean Admiral, and Lt. Holden are in trouble. Their bracelets have been improperly disengaged! I show this to be their last known coordinates."

Cheyenne put up a display of the colony with two bright red dots where their bracelets were abandoned.

"What's the Chief's location?" Brynna snapped.

Cheyenne added a green dot to the display which was moving toward the two red dots.

"Hail him! Commander, access the audiovisual footage in that area and start looking for them," she ordered.

Braxton jumped into the chair at the First Officer's station to access the feeds for the time frame before the alarm was triggered.

"Chief Holden, do you have a visual on Adm. Alexander and Lt. Holden?" Brynna demanded.

Jake stopped moving, as did the green dot on the screen. "Not currently, what's wrong?"

"Their bracelet alarms have been triggered. I'm showing they're near elevator number seven. We're checking surveillance videos. See what you can learn on your end and we'll let you know what we find."

Brynna glanced at Braxton, "Anything yet, Lt. Cmdr.?"

"Nothing yet, Captain," Braxton answered without taking his eyes off his display.

Brynna turned to Cheyenne, "Ensign, hail Mr. Rune!"

Seconds later, Neal's face appeared on the main screen.

"Yes Commander, what can I do for you?"

Mr. Rune wasn't present for the promotion ceremony. His vernacular reflected the previous ranks. Rather than confuse matters, Brynna kept her terminology in line with his. "Mr. Rune, the Captain and one of my officers are in some kind of trouble. The reports I have indicate they were somewhere in the neighborhood of elevator seven, Plaza level when their comms went offline. We're currently searching surveillance footage. Can you assist?"

"Of course, I'll get my people right on it. Who's the officer? They need to know who they're looking for."

Brynna braced herself for the words. "Lt. Marissa Holden, our Security Chief's wife."

Neal scowled, "The one who's pregnant?"

"Yes sir, she's the one. My Security Chief was out there near them. He's already investigating."

Before Brynna could say anything else, Cheyenne interrupted. "I've got the Chief again."

"Standby, Mr. Rune. Go ahead, Chief."

"I've found their bracelets in a planter outside elevator seven. There's no sign of them or indications of a struggle. Do you know which way I need to go?"

"Not yet Chief, standby. Mr. Rune did you catch that?" The new Captain was handling the situation calmly and efficiently despite her underlying concerns.

Before Neal could answer, Braxton interrupted. "Commander, I show them on the elevator headed for the lower levels. The elevator stopped on three of the lowest levels. Not sure which one they got off on because the feed scrambled as it reached the mining levels."

Neal jumped in, "The minerals in those mines interfere with the surveillance feeds. It's what I warned you about when you arrived. None of those levels are in use and those tunnels are extensive. It will take time to search all three levels. There's ten or more miles of tunnels on each of those levels."

"Captain, I can get Nate to send a team to one level if Mr. Rune can take a second and we can take a third," Jake hastily interjected.

Brynna issued orders without hesitation.

"Mr. Rune take the first level the elevator stopped on and search it. Jake send Nate's team to the bottom level. Lt. Cmdr. Flint take Jason and Ensign Ryder and rendezvous with Chief Holden to search the second level. All teams remember to link your comms in through the mining substations and report back to me when you have something. Chief, wait for your backup or so help me I will have your hide thrown out the first airlock I can find. Are we clear?"

"Yes ma'am," Jake answered tensely.

Knowing Jake's patience was about to be tested to the furthest limit, Braxton jumped out of his seat and hailed his two other crew members ordering them to report to the weapons locker on the double. He ordered the Doc to bring his emergency med kit.

Jason grabbed his kit and met Braxton and Aulani at the air lock. Braxton set the pace at a trot until he could bring the others up-to-speed on what the situation was. As soon as they understood, the three accelerated their pace to an all-out run.

****

Every fiber of Jake's being pushed him to jump onto the elevator and head to his assigned level. His assignment to contact Nate was the only thing slowing him down. "Adm. Weiseman, this is Chief Holden. Come in please."

The Admiral's voice came back quickly, "This is Adm. Weiseman. What's wrong, Chief?" Hearing the stress in the Chief's voice, Nate made a quick turn-around and hastened his pace back toward the place he had last seen the Chief.

Jake filled the man in on their missing crewmen and what help they were requesting. Nate's voice came through Jake's earpiece. "I'm almost back to you. I'll meet you at the seventh elevator, Plaza level."

Nate broke into a run. He knew Jake was probably chomping at the bit to head into the mining levels. Adding the information that he was close enough to rendezvous with him would hopefully placate him. He assumed Brynna had crewmen in route too and that Jake would have orders to stay put until reinforcements arrived.

Nate hailed his crew and requested Milo, Stephanie, and Henry to join him fully armed. He updated Silas on the situation and requested that he link in with Brynna to coordinate their search efforts. Nate finished with Silas in time to step onto the elevator from the mezzanine level and take it down to the Plaza where Jake was ready to rip the elevator doors off with his bare hands. Before Nate could step off the elevator, Jake jumped on with him and sent the compartment to the second possible level of access.

Nate started to object but knew he would have to physically restrain the Chief if he attempted to stop him. The new Admiral showed restraint of his own and told his team and Brynna's that he and Jake were going to begin their search together on the second possible stopping point. He requested they reshuffle the search teams appropriately.

Brynna acknowledged him. She ordered Jason and Aulani to join Jake and Nate. She sent Milo, Stephanie and Henry to join Braxton and proceed to the third level.

****

Brynna called Lexi to the bridge to help review the surveillance footage. Lexi saw the four men force David and Marissa onto the elevator. She watched the footage in reverse. The men came from two levels above the plaza. She switched to a different camera to see if she could determine where they came from.

Brynna watched for any other elevators stopping on the three lowest levels of the mine. The computer program recording elevator activity detected a second elevator stopping at each corresponding level about thirty seconds after the previous elevator. She loaded the surveillance feed and backed it up to a point before the elevator dropped into the blackout zone. A man with a dark hooded jacket was riding down in the elevator. Brynna ran her own footage backward to see where the man entered. She was hoping to get a view of the man's face as he stepped aboard the car. The video was moving at an accelerated rate backward. Brynna caught a rough glimpse of the man's face and saw him make an odd movement before he turned to face the elevator doors. She stopped her feed and ran it forward at half the normal speed. The man stepped onto the elevator, looked directly at the camera, and gave a curt salute.

The man's behavior was so suspect, it startled her. Brynna reviewed the sequence twice more. She froze the picture and enlarged it to see the man's face more clearly. He appeared to be in his fifties, and something was familiar about him. The salute was troubling. It was a proper sharp salute. The man probably had a military background.

Brynna was about to ask Lexi to take a look at her footage when she heard her mumble, "Oh no."

Brynna looked up, "What is it, Lieutenant?"

Lexi put her footage on the main screen. "Those men were watching and following the Admiral. They were watching him from the moment he and Adm. Weiseman got off the elevator. I've looked at a couple of different angles. I isolated their faces and sent the pictures to Cheyenne. She's running facial recognition on them. Captain, they were stalking the Admiral. L-Lt. Holden was not targeted at all. I think they only took her because she was with the Admiral."

Brynna watched the footage from morbid curiosity for a moment. Tearing her eyes off the screen she placed her images on the main screen. After playing the short clip, she froze the image on the mysterious man's face.

Lexi squinted at the image. She studied him for a minute. "He's not one of these four, but I feel like I've seen him somewhere."

Brynna nodded, "Interesting. I thought he looked familiar too."

Lexi turned to face Brynna, "It's possible we've been here long enough to see the same faces in passing and they're starting to register in our memories."

Brynna shook her head, "No, I don't think that's it. Send his picture and the other four pictures out to the search teams and Mr. Rune. Make sure they know the last one may or may not be related to the other four."

Lexi sent them out as ordered. A couple of minutes later Jake reported in. "Capt. Alexander, I recognize this last man."

Brynna agreed with the Chief that the man looked familiar to both her and Lexi. Jake came back with a definitive, "No Captain, he doesn't just look familiar. I saw this man the first day of the conference. He came to the conference center. He appeared to be drunk and had two women with him. They were looking for some party. Braxton saw him, and so did Adm. Weiseman and Lt. Cmdr. Weiseman."

Lexi gave Brynna a concerned look.

Brynna scowled, "Chief, the other four were clearly stalking the Admiral and this other man could well have been watching him too. Keep your eyes open for all of them. Detain all five men."

There was a long silence before Jake answered. "Acknowledged Captain. Holden out," his comm link shut off.

****

Lexi's face continued to display concern. This time it was over a different matter. "Captain, if they've caused any harm to Marissa or her baby, I don't know if we can trust Jake to simply detain those men."

Brynna's expression remained neutral, "He's not alone."

Lexi didn't know if Brynna was referring to Pateras, herself, or the rest of the search team. The three waited in silence for what seemed to be an eternity.

Cheyenne finally interrupted the silence. "Captain, I have a report on the first four men. They're miners. They've been here for about eight years. They have small time criminal records, some drunk and disorderly conduct, brawling, resisting arrest, illegal gambling, nothing major."

Lexi looked puzzled. "What would cause them to jump from that to kidnapping?"

Each of the women knew several reasons, none of them good. The men could have been paid, forced, or perhaps there was something personal. Were they paid or coerced by the mysterious fifth man? Was the fifth man a CIF soldier? If they were hired hands, they wouldn't risk their lives just for a payout. That was best case scenario. Worst case was if this was personal.

Brynna shook herself out of her sea of thoughts and worries. "What about the fifth man? Have you identified him yet?"

"No ma'am. There's no record of him entering the colony and no record showing he was born here. He's a ghost."

Cheyenne tried to stare the report into a submissive recant. It refused to change its empty answer.

Lexi replayed the image of the stranger saluting the camera. "He knows who we are and that we're watching him."

Brynna looked up suddenly, "What do you mean?"

Lexi forced her eyes away from the screen and turned to face Brynna. "His salute is a CIF salute. Local security uses a different salute. He knows we're watching and he's either taunting us or..."

"Or what?" Brynna persisted.

"The look on his face doesn't really look like a taunt. It looks more like a promise or an admission," Lexi explained.

"What kind of promise? Admission of what?" Brynna wasn't finding a lot of reason to put her fears to rest yet.

"I don't know, but it's definitely resolve to do something, and he wants us to know about it," Lexi finished.

"You aren't helping," Brynna replied wryly.

"Sorry Captain, I'm still working on it," Lexi lamented.

Brynna's pictured the face again. She continued to wonder who this man was and what he was resolved to do. Mentally, she called out to Arni for help. She closed her eyes to shut out the external stimulus and focused on listening for Arni's voice. She smiled as she heard the familiar voice softly speak to her mind, "I got this."

Lexi and Cheyenne saw Brynna smile. In turn, they both relaxed a little. There were still a lot of unanswered questions, somehow, they were less unnerving.

SINS REVISITED

The four captors stopped their elevator three times on closed levels to throw off anyone attempting to follow them. They took their two prisoners off on the bottom floor and forced them into the long tunnel. Fifty yards in, Marissa had a contraction. She stopped walking, grabbed onto the nearest wall with one hand and massaged her abdomen with the other. She took a slow deep breath when one of the ruffians behind her shoved her roughly. Marissa stumbled forward a couple steps and landed on her hands and knees with a loud grunt.

David was being led by the arm by a second man wielding a Tri-EMP. When he heard Marissa fall, he shoved the man holding his arm off balance. He leaped toward the one who shoved Marissa and belted him soundly across the face. Turning his attention to the fallen lieutenant, he ignored the four weapons their captors trained on him and the angry men yelling at him.

"Marissa, are you okay?"

Marissa stayed in place breathing slowly and deeply, waiting for the contraction to pass. She nodded her answer to him.

The men continued to shout at them and each other. The noise of their shouts obscured the sound of the elevator door opening and closing again. When the men realized their prisoners weren't attempting to escape, they settled down. The one in charge stepped forward.

"Mr. Alexander let's get moving. You've got an overdue appointment with destiny. It's time to pay your debts."

David stood slowly. Stalling for time was one of his higher priorities. "You seem to know who I am, but I don't know who you are or what you believe I owe you. What's this about?"

"I'll explain when we get to our destination. Let's go," the man replied coldly.

David helped Marissa to her feet, "Are you good?"

Marissa was sweating. She took off her scarf and wiped her face with it. "Yeah, I'm okay."

David took her left hand in his and wrapped his right arm around her waist. He looked at the man who was wiping the blood from his nose. "You touch her again, I'll give you more than a nosebleed next time."

The man glared at David. Their leader glanced toward the elevator. "Chuck, go pull that transport pod up!"

The man trotted back and started the pod. The vehicle was designed to transport ore. It held four passengers. They sat David and Marissa in the back seat. The leader reached into David's bag. He located a set of binders and bound his arms around a safety bar on the pod. Their leader sat in the front seat with Chuck. The other two men climbed into the ore hopper and positioned themselves to watch David and Marissa.

David reviewed his tactical position. The engine of the pod wasn't loud, but it was enough to obscure his voice as he spoke softly to Marissa. "This isn't going to slow them down any," The pod moved at a speed equal to a slow jog.

"I'm sorry, sir. I lost my balance and the contractions are getting stronger."

David gave her one admonition, "If the opportunity presents itself, get yourself out of here as fast as you can and don't look back, no matter what."

"Yes sir," She replied weakly. She didn't want to agree to leaving him behind, but she knew it was the wisest course of action. The Captain, now turned Admiral, could work better if he didn't have to worry about her. He made that point quite clear when he lectured her for disobeying orders.

David saw the leader of the group staring at him. This one man was older than the other three. These men obviously weren't thieves. Thieves would've taken their bags and been gone by now. They weren't looking to collect a reward for turning them into the Commonwealth. To want this much privacy, they either wanted information they were willing to go to extreme lengths to get, or it was somehow a personal vendetta. Were these guys friends to the five men they sent off-world after the rescue of Aulani's family? If that were the case, why come after him and not the security officers? They would have needed inside information to know he had anything to do with that. If they saw the entire incident, they might have seen him participate, but the colony's security troops placed the men under arrest. Was this something older than that?

An image nearly a dozen years old flashed through his mind. David tried to shake the image out of his brain. The more he tried to erase the image the more vivid it became. A voice whispered in his mind, "Listen to me."

David adjusted his mindset. He did his best to clear and focus his mind, "What do you want me to do?"

"Take responsibility for your actions, and don't fight them. Show them Pateras. I've got this."

****

The voice stopped speaking, but the images repeated with an amazing clarity in his mind. It was eleven years ago— David had been an Ensign in the CIF. A new world, Ardara III, was being transitioned into the Commonwealth. As an Ensign, he was assigned to a police action to put down a group of insurgents who opposed the Commonwealth. David killed three men during his time there. The first two were actively shooting at him and his fellow soldiers. The third saw his circumstances and was in the process of surrendering. David shot the third man despite his obvious attempt to turn himself in. He received an award for his actions, but he had always regretted killing the third man.

Pateras reiterated his guilt in the crime. He forgave him for it, along with so many other crimes. David had tucked the incident into the deepest darkest regions of his mind. Any time it tried to resurface, he would shove it down again. His heart pounded loudly in his ears. Pateras wanted him to take responsibility for his actions. These men had to be co-

217

conspirators or family members looking for revenge. What was he supposed to say to them? Nothing would fix this. Were his words supposed to stop them or maybe slow them down? The voice whispered to him, "I will tell you what to say when it's time to speak. Rest in my words."

David took a deep breath and exhaled slowly, forcing himself to relax. He glanced at Marissa who was watching him. Her gaze asked an unspoken question. He smiled with more confidence than he felt. "Pateras says he's got this."

Marissa smiled weakly at him.

****

The ride to the other end of the tunnel took nearly thirty minutes. Marissa had several contractions during the trip and was in the middle of another when they stopped. The group waited impatiently for her to relax enough to walk again.

David turned to the leader and begged one more time.

"Please let her go back and get the medical attention she needs. I know what this is about, and she has nothing to do with it. I'm her commanding officer, and I'm responsible for her."

The leader's name was Quinn Donahue. He was in his early fifties and had a cooler head than his friends. He looked at Marissa. Her pain was clearly not a ploy to escape. Quinn was the father of the third man David killed. He understood the love of a father for his child. He doubted that this was the Commander's child but he was obviously passionate about the situation. Although, he didn't understand what the situation was, he chose to act honorably.

"When this is done, I'll turn her loose. You have my word. We'll take the pod back and leave her to walk out on her own. That will give us time to get away. It's the best I can do for you."

The younger hothead was fast losing patience, "Why are you doing anything for him? You know what he did," He ran his hand through his curly red hair in frustration.

Quinn grabbed the young man by the shirt and jerked him forward. "He's the one guilty of taking innocent lives. I'm not going to be guilty of killing the innocent. Nobody touches her or her baby. Got IT?"

Russ looked genuinely worried, "Alright, I got it!"

Russ Braden was in his late twenties, slim build and had a similar temperament to Jake, though less disciplined. Russ's older brother was one of the men killed in the police action on Ardara. Russ was only sixteen at the time when his twenty-year-old brother died. Russ had dabbled in the resistance movement until his brother was killed.

The other two men were in their late thirties. The older of the two was Danny Corrigan. Danny was not involved in the resistance and had discouraged his brother, Riley, from getting involved. They had a huge fight the night before. Danny tried to remind his brother about the danger to himself and his family. Riley was married and had two small children to care for. Riley's wife and children simply disappeared after Riley died.

Chuck Egan hadn't lost any relatives in the incident, but the three who died were his friends. He lost other friends in similar situations. He was looking to get some payback as well.

****

Quinn led the group to a closed hatch. He opened the hatch to reveal a stairwell down to another tunnel. David's hands were bound in front of him. He stayed close to Marissa and helped her down the steps.

The lower chamber was much cruder than the one above. David familiarized himself with the new setting. The room was small with one narrow passageway running back the direction of the tunnel above. Large pipelines ran through the tunnel. The pipelines disappeared into the wall. The only other things present were the generator and pipeline control panel.

Quinn nodded to one of his companions, "Chuck, shut the flow off to the bottom pipeline and open the hatch."

The man did as he was told.

David looked at the menacing opening. It was dark and wet, soon to be wetter. He waited on the words promised to him. Nothing was coming to mind, so he kept his mouth shut.

Quinn placed himself in front of his prisoner, "I suppose you're wondering what this is about."

"I already know. I was hoping you would send her out of here. I'd rather she didn't hear this," David pleaded.

Quinn squinted at his prisoner. How could he possibly know?

"This is about Ardara III, eleven years ago, right? I haven't forgotten it, as much as I would like to," David added.

Danny moved in closer, "How does he know what this is about? Are they testing us?"

"I'd love to be able to tell you, 'Yes, I'm testing you and the authorities are on their way to arrest you,' but that isn't the truth. My people are looking for me, but they aren't Commonwealth authorities. They may have requested assistance from the local security force."

David was doing his best to follow the instructions he was given.

"How *did* you know this was about Ardara III? What is your current rank and position with the Commonwealth, Mr. Alexander?" Quinn asked gruffly.

"My Commonwealth assigned rank and position is… was Captain. I have… an inside source who told me you were here because of Ardara. Can you please send the Lieutenant out of here now? Don't make her watch this."

David watched Marissa breathe through yet another contraction.

Quinn noticed David's peculiar wording and explanation of his rank and position. He looked at David oddly. "I'll make you a deal… Captain. You tell her what you did, and I'll let her walk out of here, unharmed."

Russ and Danny both objected, "You can't turn her loose. She'll have the authorities on us in nothing flat."

David flexed helplessly against his binders, "It took almost thirty minutes to get here in the pod. As strong and as fast as those contractions are coming. She'll be lucky to make it out of this tunnel without help. It'll take her at least ninety minutes to get back to the elevator.

"Captain, please don't make me leave. You've been there for all of us. I should be here for you. You shouldn't have to face this alone," Marissa took a slow deep breath. Sweat poured down her face. The contractions were coming harder and faster. She wondered if the stress of the situation was exacerbating her labor.

David smiled, "I appreciate your support, Lieutenant, but I won't be alone. You aren't alone either. Arni said we would never be alone.

Danny, who kept hold of Marissa's arm to control her, gave the others a confused look. "No way, nobody followed us. There's no one else here."

David smiled even bigger, "Our companion isn't visible to the human eye. He isn't a human being."

Chuck was disgusted, "He's trying to fake insanity to save his neck. He's too much of a coward to take responsibility for his actions."

Quinn grabbed Marissa's arm and pulled her forward. "I'm not buying it, Captain. Let's get on with this. I'm sure there are people looking for them. She needs to know what kind of commander she serves and why you're about to die."

Marissa looked at Quinn defiantly, "I know what kind of man I work for. I know he's made some bad choices and more people than you know have paid the price for it. I also know he's learned from his mistakes. He's taken full responsibility for his actions and offered his life to save others. He's a good man no matter what he did in his past."

Quinn's face matched her defiance with a determination of his own. He was going to shake her confidence and destroy her trust in her commanding officer.

"Explain it to her."

David looked at the ground for a moment. Marissa probably didn't have a lot of time left before her baby was born. He took a deep breath and recounted a low point in his life.

"My first assignment after leaving the Academy was a police action on Ardara III. Ardara was in the process of being admitted to the Commonwealth. There were three insurgents shooting at our troops from a rooftop. I was sent to an adjacent building to stop them. My orders were to 'take them out.' I got into position and took the first one out. The second one spotted me when the first one fell. He opened fire on my position. I returned fire and dropped him. I shot the third man a few seconds later."

Russ could wait no longer. He bolted to the Captain and belted him across the face. "You killed my brother!"

David wiped a speck of blood from his lip. He looked at the blood on his hand. Under other circumstances, he would have reflected on the irony of yet another split lip. This time his thoughts were about the amount of blood on his hands.

"Supreme Executor Hale and the Commonwealth killed your brother. I was the weapon they used to do it. I'm no longer a part of the Commonwealth because I refuse to kill for them anymore."

Marissa watched her Captain. She understood the pain reflected on his face.

Quinn pulled on her elbow tightly to make his point. "You see what kind of man you work for. He's a cold-blooded killer."

David's conscience pricked him. He had left out an important detail, "Colder than you think," he looked Quinn in the eye, "Mr. Donahue, there's something else you should know."

"How do you know who I am? You didn't know what any of this was about earlier," Quinn eyed his prisoner suspiciously. The two had never crossed paths. Why would the young soldier have any reason to know him?

"This might be hard to believe, but a Supreme Alien Being known as Pateras told me. You're Quinn Donahue, the father of Kevin Donahue," David faced each man as he identified them.

"You're Russell Braden, Brian's younger brother. You're Riley Corrigan's younger brother, Danny, and your name is Chuck Egan. You are a friend and associate of the men I killed. You were arrested shortly afterward along with several family members. They sent you to a re-education facility, then relocated you off-world. You were forbidden to return to Ardara."

"You kept up with our whereabouts?" Danny asked nervously.

David shook his head, "No, I memorized only the names of the men who died by my hand. I never knew your names. I tried hard to forget the past. It hasn't gone away, no matter how badly I wanted it to. I remember it as well today as I did eleven years ago. Pateras wanted me to know what crimes I was guilty of, so I would understand how much he was forgiving me for," his voice grew softer as he spoke. The heaviness of the memory weighed his voice down.

"Is that what you wanted me to know? That your conscience is bothering you? It should! There's no forgiveness for you!" Quinn responded hatefully.

David glanced at Marissa. This was the part he really didn't want her to hear. He stared off into the distance as he explained the one thing he didn't want to face.

"I am so sorry, Mr. Donahue, but your son Kevin shouldn't have died. I murdered him outright. My orders were to take out all three men. When his two companions died, he took one look at me and the laser sight on his chest. He dropped his weapon and raised his hands in surrender. There were other troops closing in. I followed my orders. I… shot him after he surrendered. I'm sorry."

The one who had remained calm through their vendetta, lost it. Quinn grabbed his prey. Slamming him against the wall of pipelines, he pummeled David with a series of blows to the abdomen.

Marissa cried out and tried to go to her Captain's aid. Danny held her back. Despite her compromised condition, it proved to be a difficult task.

It took several blows before the Captain's knees buckled and he slid to the cavern floor. Quinn stopped his onslaught. He looked at his shaking hands, horrified by his fit of anger as David rolled painfully on the cavern floor.

David wheezed as his lungs attempted to draw the much-coveted breaths. When he finally drew in enough air to speak again, his words were broken and punctuated with attempts to breathe. "M-Marissa, I'm s-sorry. It's t-time for you t-to go."

Quinn was a man of his word. He turned to his companions. "Chuck, take her back up, and shut down the terminals on the entire level. Let her walk out of here. Disable the pod so she can't take it, but make sure we can."

"Quinn, she knows our names. We can't let her go," Russ objected, "We'd have to leave Zulimar. They'll come after us for killing a Commonwealth officer. There wouldn't be anyplace safe for us in the entire galaxy."

David worked his way onto his knees. Sitting on his heels he rocked back and forth trying to catch his breath.

"If you get… off-world… no one will come looking for you," David forced his muscles to relax and drew one long slow forced breath.

"We committed treason. The Commonwealth wants us dead. I wouldn't suggest you try to take credit for it though," David drew another full breath, "Executor Hale promised to kill anyone I spoke to. He doesn't want anyone to know about Pateras."

Quinn stared at David. He wasn't sure how to interpret his words. They weren't making sense. He turned to his companions. "We're going to have to leave Zulimar anyway. By the time they know what's happened we'll be long gone. I know a guy who can get us some new I.D.'s."

Russ opened his mouth to object again. Before he could speak, Quinn shut him down. "I'm not stooping to his level. I'm not murdering an innocent woman or baby. Get her out of here! Don't touch her. Lock her out of the terminals so she can't call out for help and get back down here. Let's get this over with so we can get off the planet."

Danny grudgingly followed his instructions and started to escort Marissa up the stairs. Marissa jerked her arm away from him. "Wait! Captain, you need to know something. Jake and I decided on the baby's name."

David smiled, "Tell me later."

"But…" She objected.

"Tell me after he's born," David insisted. His face was calm and peaceful. She followed his lead and allowed Danny to escort her upstairs.

****

Chuck went to the computer terminal on the upper level. He was done programming it as ordered by the time Danny escorted Marissa up. The tunnel lighting was motion sensor activated. Danny motioned toward the dark tunnel behind the pod. "Go on, unless you want to give birth alone here in a mine tunnel."

Chuck trotted over to the pod and disabled it, keeping one eye on Marissa. He wasn't convinced she wouldn't attempt to fight back and try to save her Captain's life. Her loyalty to the man despite his confession was bizarre.

Marissa kept an equally close eye on the two men as she shuffled down the tunnel. She wasn't sure she trusted these men to truly allow her to walk away. A calm settled over her. She moved to a nearby wall to lean against it as another contraction overtook her. This one was particularly virulent. She bent over and groaned as she tried to force her body to stop fighting her.

The two men took one more look at Marissa before heading down the steps to the maintenance corridor below the mining tunnel. They decided she was no threat to them, but they closed the hatch behind them.

Marissa caught her breath as the contraction passed. She walked through the tunnel as quickly as she could. She knew she wasn't going to be able to travel far between contractions. She reached the last hopper at the rear of the pod and stopped. There was no way for her to get help in time to save the Captain. He would have to depend on Pateras or himself. She winced at the thought. She wanted more than anything to help him. Her secondary training as a security officer was of little use to her now. The one thing it did do was to tell her that the Captain was on his own and she needed to do whatever she could to help herself. The thought was cold. If she climbed into the last hopper and hid, they hopefully wouldn't find her until they were back to the elevator. If she tried to walk out, the pod would inevitably pass her on its trip back. It wouldn't take them long to dispose of her Captain and head back. Slow tears ran down her face as she put her foot onto the coupling to climb into the hopper. Just as she lifted herself up, she heard a noise and someone grabbed her from behind.

Brynna and Neal Rune continued to trade information. The three levels possibly accessed were closed for various reasons. One level was the Drean mine shaft, another was closed for maintenance. Brynna tried to trace energy usage in the three tunnels. Having search teams in the tunnels caused the lights to come on in all three tunnels. She tried to pinpoint where the lights were on and where they weren't while coordinating with the three search teams. The tunnels were arranged in a wheel pattern. There were varying numbers of spokes to the wheels. Tracing the energy usage quickly became impossible.

Braxton and his team reached the lowest level. When he surveyed the layout, he hailed Brynna from the closest terminal.

"Captain, can you ask Mr. Rune to reprogram the lighting so that the lights stay on after we leave the area? It'll help maintain the efficacy of our search pattern."

Brynna acknowledged his request and referred it to Mr. Rune.

Neal sent additional troops to add to the second and third level search teams. He kept Constable Hinson in the loop. The Constable researched the four men. Thirty minutes into the search, he realized, he would have to reallocate some of his resources. "Neal, there's a problem with these four guys. They're maintenance crew, not miners. They have access to everything, including the ventilation tunnels and service hatches. We've got to add another dimension to our search."

Neal sighed, "Those two are in Pateras' hands. It's already been long enough that we may never see them again."

He didn't want to do it, but he had to inform Brynna of this new development.

Marissa tried to scream and fight off her attacker. A voice whispered into her ear.

"Don't scream! I'm here to help your Captain. Can you trust me long enough to listen?"

Marissa stopped fighting. The hand over her mouth relaxed. The stranger turned her around but held onto her arms. "Listen, I need to get down there, but I need your help. Can you help me?"

"What do you need me to do?" Marissa asked softly.

The man escorted her to the hatch and explained his plan to her.

****

Chuck and Danny rejoined their friends. David was still kneeling in front of Quinn. He searched their faces to be sure Marissa was safely away. Their faces showed annoyance, not guilt. Quinn knew his thoughts. "Is she okay?"

Danny shrugged, "Yeah, I guess. She was walking down the tunnel. She seemed kinda skittish like she was afraid we weren't going to do what you told us to. I think she was having another contraction though. Can we get this over with and get out of here?"

Quinn glanced at David, "Satisfied?"

David nodded. If they had harmed Marissa, he was sure they would want to rub his nose in it before they killed him. "So how were you planning on doing this? Are you going to shoot me outright or would you prefer to prolong my pain and add to your personal satisfaction by killing me with your bare hands?"

The four looked at each other. They'd spent eleven years fantasizing about how to hurt the man who caused them so much pain. Now, they weren't sure how to proceed. Time was short, and they hadn't planned this out.

Russ, the youngest most impetuous of the four grabbed a large wrench. "I say we do it the slow painful way."

Danny and Chuck looked at each other. Eleven years ago, they were part of the resistance movement and fought the Commonwealth. They participated in their fair share of brawls and riots. If they had actually killed anyone, they hadn't been close enough to know it. They realized at this point, their pain had dulled enough to want justice, not bloody vengeance. Time was the other issue to consider.

Quinn saw their hesitation and pulled his Tri-EMP out. "Let's each fire a level two at him simultaneously. Four level twos are enough to kill him, and they can't pin it on any one of us. It's close enough to look like an accident."

David glanced at the open hatch on the water pipeline. "You accidentally shoot me and shove me into a pipeline? I'm not sure that's believable."

Danny was liking the idea. "We panicked and tried to get rid of the body."

David shook his head. "It's not going to make that big of a difference. No one's going to chase you down once you get off Zulimar. I told you the Commonwealth wants me dead or at least under arrest. If anybody comes after you, it will be to do the same to you."

Quinn powered his Tri-EMP. "The Commonwealth doesn't execute people anymore. There's been something like one execution in the last thirty years."

David got to his feet. "That's where you're wrong. Followers of Pateras get death sentences. Supreme Executor Hale has ordered the execution of the entire population of several lower level worlds for the sole crime of serving a being known as Pateras. Your world is new to the Commonwealth. Did you have people who practiced what was considered primitive deity worship?"

The four men exchanged confused looks. They weren't sure if they should give any credence to David's suggestion.

"Quinn, stop listening to him. He owes us. Can we just do this?" Russ was getting impatient. He was afraid his friend was going to go soft on them. He had already let the woman go. Would he go through with exacting the revenge they desperately wanted?

Quinn nodded. Each man readied his weapon. Quinn shoved the Captain against the pipeline nearest the open hatch. He shoved him onto his knees with his back facing them.

David spoke loudly over his shoulder, "Your accident story won't hold water if I've been shot in the back. I'm afraid you're going to have to look me in the eye to shoot me."

The four were silent.

David added more fuel to the fire. "I looked Kevin in the eye when I killed him. Are you afraid to look me in the eye when I die?"

Quinn hated to admit it, but his prisoner was right. He jerked David up and turned him to face them. This time he left him standing. Quinn positioned himself directly in front of David. His anger seethed within him, "Any last words, Captain? Make them short."

"I can do that. First, I'm sorry for the harm I did to you and your families. I hope someday you can forgive me. Second, search out Pateras and get to know him, but don't let the Commonwealth find you. Third, you might want to fire multiple times, to add to your accident idea and lastly, I forgive you," David's demeanor remained calm which served only to infuriate and unnerve his captors.

"Quinn, why is he so calm? He's not going to pay for this if he doesn't feel pain. We've lived with pain for the last eleven years. He acts like nothing's wrong at all," Danny groused.

Chuck surmised, "He's trying to unnerve us, so we can't go through with this. Can we hurry and finish it?"

For once the young Russell was perplexed and hesitant, "What does he mean about forgiving us? This is justice. We deserve this."

Quinn saw their plans on the verge of falling apart. "Let's do this."

He raised his weapon and pointed it at David. The others slowly joined him. "Fire multiple shots on the count of three."

The four heard a creaking at the top of the stairs. The hatch opened slowly. They heard Marissa's shaky voice.

"Please help me. My—My water broke and there's blood everywhere. I—I don't feel…" Her voice stopped, and they heard the sound of someone hitting the ground.

David stepped forward. His face reflected genuine concern. He had told her to leave and not turn back. This couldn't be a rescue attempt.

"Marissa?!"

Quinn looked at David's face. His calm was gone. He nodded at Danny and Chuck, "Go check that out."

****

The two trotted to the bottom of the stairs. They could see nothing more than one of Marissa's hands lying in the opening with fresh blood stains on it. They stopped at the bottom of the steps. Seeing the blood, they darted up the steps two at a time when the lights in the lower cavern went dark.

David wasn't sure what to make of this turn of events. He didn't take any chances. He threw himself away from the stairway, tucked into a ball and rolled in a tight somersault further into the darkness.

Quinn and Russ reacted firing wildly—their pellets hitting nothing of consequence. They heard the sounds of Chuck and Danny falling down the stairs. In a few short seconds the lights came back on. Quinn found himself staring down the barrel of a Tri-EMP and Russ was struggling with Capt. Alexander. David, despite the binders on his wrists, quickly got his adversary under control. The four men were disarmed and placed on their knees in front of David and his mysterious rescuer.

David finally got a look at the man who came to his rescue. His mind instantly filled with more questions than he had time to ask. Keeping a careful eye on his prisoners, he started with the most obvious questions.

"What are you doing here and how did you find me?"

The man kept a close eye on the four prisoners. "What? Not even a 'thanks for saving my hide?' I'll give you all the answers you want shortly. We have more important things to deal with right now. You have a crew member near delivery and we have to do something with these guys. Why don't you get the young woman some medical help and I'll deal with these four?"

"What exactly do you intend to do with them?" David queried.

"I'll take care of them… permanently. They can't be allowed to report you. If word gets back to Supreme Executor

Hale, he'll send everything he's got out this way to find you," the man explained.

The men looked nervously at each other.

"No, I've harmed these men enough. The local police owe me a favor. They can sit on them until I get clear of this place," David argued.

"You don't owe them any favors. They just tried to kill you," the man argued back.

"Yes, I do. I killed their family years ago. They only wanted justice. Let's get them to the authorities," David said with a degree of finality.

The man started to argue again, "Are you sure about this, Davie?"

David gave the man a pleading look, "I'm sure."

"Okay, we'll do this your way… for now. Don't make me regret this."

The stranger had a set of binders and David had carried the set which they used against him. Marissa was caught without any security gear, save her personal weapon and a knife her captors had relieved her of. The man put two of the men in binders and tied the third man's wrists with Marissa's scarf. Chuck was escorted untied.

David ushered Chuck to the computer console in the upper cavern.

"Mr. Egan, if you wouldn't mind, please release the lock out on this computer console."

Chuck cussed at him and refused to cooperate.

"Mr. Egan, my lieutenant needs emergency medical attention. Whether you release that console, or not, isn't going to hurt me. It could cause harm to the young woman and her baby. I won't ask you again. I'll just turn you over to my… friend. He's not as forgiving as I am," David gave Mr. Egan a long hard stare.

The man glared at the Captain. Sensing his adversary wasn't bluffing, he pushed the correct combination to release the consoles for the entire level. Marissa sat in the front seat of the pod while the Captain's new friend escorted their prisoners into the hopper. Once they were seated on the floor, the stranger went to the back of the hopper and uncoupled the three extra cars.

David pressed the controls on the console and hailed the *Evangeline* through the internal comm channels. He chose his words carefully when the channel connected.

"*Evangeline*, this is…Capt. Alexander. I'm on the bottom level mine shaft. I have a medical emergency and an unexpected guest along with four prisoners for local authorities. What's your status?"

Brynna gave the other two women a quizzical look.

"Captain, there are search teams on the lower three levels of the mine. Lt. Cmdr. Flint is leading the team on your level. Dr. Weiseman is with him. Dr. Adams and Chief Holden are one level up from your location. What is the nature of your medical emergency and what assistance do you need?"

"Lt. Holden is in heavy labor. We have a mining pod and we're heading toward the elevator. Have the other teams rendezvous with us at the elevator on this level. Our ETA is twenty to twenty-five minutes," David rattled off quickly.

"Acknowledged Captain, I'll get everyone moving," Brynna could hear the tension in his voice and handled his request promptly and efficiently.

No sooner than he closed out his communication with the ship, Marissa grunted painfully again.

David raced to her side. "Lieutenant, you *cannot* have this baby without Jake being present. Are we clear?"

Marissa nodded as she tried to relax and breathe slowly through the contraction.

"Are you really bleeding?" David asked nervously. He covered delivering babies in his field medic course but had never actually delivered one. He really didn't want to put his knowledge to the test.

His new ally quickly volunteered, "Unless something new has developed, that blood's mine. I thought it would be more convincing."

"Are—Are you injured?" David asked nervously again.

"No, I gave myself a little nick just to sell the story. I'm fine. Can we go before one of us has to deliver that baby?"

The stranger was as unnerved as the Captain. He took off his jacket and put it across Marissa's shoulders. "You're drenched in sweat, young lady. This trip back is going to give you a chill when that breeze hits you."

The two men climbed aboard the pod brusquely. Before they could start it, Marissa turned to the man in the back seat . "Wait, I need to thank you for saving the Captain's life. I'm Lt. Marissa Holden."

David looked guiltily at the new friend. "I'm sorry, Marissa. This is…uh…Capt. Tristan…Alexander, my father."

234

FATHERS AND SONS

Capt. David Alexander pushed the mining pod as hard and as fast as he could to the mine entrance. Without the weight of the extra hoppers, its speed was better than the trip out to the far end of the mine.

There was a juncture where four tunnels came together at the halfway point. David spotted the search team as he approached the juncture. He slowed to find Braxton, Stephanie, Milo, and Henry waiting on him. He brought the pod to a stop.

"I thought I ordered you to meet me at the far end of the tunnel" David snapped.

Braxton didn't flinch, "Lt. Cmdr. Weiseman wanted to get a scan of Lt. Holden before she was moved any farther than necessary. We were nearly to the midway point when we got the orders. I thought it more prudent to wait here, unless you wanted to deliver her baby yourself."

Braxton never changed his face or intonation, but David was sure some part of the brazen Lt. Cmdr. was poking fun at him. David gave him a brief hard stare which told him this wouldn't be the end of this jovial little war. He finally managed to answer. "I suppose that was a good call. Steph?"

Stephanie hadn't waited for permission to proceed. She ran a scan over Marissa. "Aw, Davie, I think you need a refresher medic course. She's hours away from delivery."

"I didn't have the benefit of a scanner," David groused.

He quickly derailed what could have become an uncomfortable conversation.

"Uncouple the hopper from this pod and the hoppers from your own. We only had two sets of binders. Get binders on the other two prisoners. We'll proceed with Stephanie to the elevator and get Marissa back. Hook your pod to this hopper and take the prisoners to Constable Hinson."

Braxton nodded and curtly responded, "Yes sir. Sir, can I have a word with you privately? It's important."

Tristan recognized Braxton, and he knew Braxton remembered meeting him once before. "Davie, this is about me. I ran into your Lt. Cmdr. a couple of days ago. I thought I saw you in the Plaza, and I followed you to the conference center. I pretended to be drunk to see what I could find out. Sorry, yes, I was stalking you. You're in a lot of trouble. I was trying to be cautious."

Braxton continued to eye the man suspiciously, "That's exactly what this is about. Do you know him, sir? Can we trust him?"

David wanted to get things settled down and under control. He was beginning to be annoyed on several levels. "Yes, I know him. Can we trust him? That I have no idea about."

Tristan gave his son a wry, "Ouch, that hurt. I just saved your life."

David twisted in his seat to face his father. He could hear Marissa combating another contraction. Emotionally it was pressing him to get her back to the ship. "I really don't have time for this. Yes, you saved my life, and I appreciate it, but was it for my sake, your sake, or Executor Hale's?"

The man looked genuinely wounded, "Davie, how can you ask me that? You're my son!"

Braxton blinked. He was shocked by the revelation.

David winced. He wasn't sure he was ready to introduce his absentee father to his crew. "Lt. Cmdr. Braxton Flint meet Capt. Tristan Alexander. We'll discuss this more later. We need to get the Lieutenant someplace more comfortable, and we need to get her reunited with Jake. I'm sure he's ready to tear a hole in something by now."

While the two were talking, the others released the pod coupling and took over guarding the prisoners. David powered up the pod and took off for the elevator. He pushed the thing to full speed as fast as he safely could. The engine whined in complaint the rest of the trip.

Braxton hastily uncoupled the cars on his pod and hooked onto the Captain's discarded hopper carrying the four prisoners. He didn't want to leave his Captain unprotected. Several concerns ran through the Lt. Cmdr.'s mind. His Captain could be blinded by his close relationship. No one likes to consider their parent might betray them. It was a possibility. Admiral Deacons was certainly in no position to offer any obvious support. The Captain's father had a Commonwealth rank. Exactly where did his loyalties lie? Did he come out here thinking he could get his son re-educated thereby saving his life? There was every chance his father couldn't be trusted. He sincerely hoped the Captain knew that. He didn't want to be the one to point it out. He suddenly realized he was thinking like Jake. Braxton smiled. Jake wouldn't have any bones about pointing this out to the Captain. Maybe he could pawn it off on Jake? He frowned again. Jake was about to be distracted by the birth of his son. He wouldn't be much help. Braxton pushed his pod as fast as he could, trying to catch up to the Captain.

****

Braxton arrived in time to see Jake and Jason helping Marissa out of the pod. They offered her a stretcher. She refused to use it. She insisted it might take a few minutes to get there, but she could walk to the ship. Jake and Jason tried to insist. They attempted to recruit Stephanie to their cause. Stephanie wasn't easily swayed. She quickly informed the men that her scans revealed she was still several hours away from delivery, and she could in fact walk if she wanted to. Jason and Jake reluctantly allowed her to walk and boarded the elevator along with Aulani and Stephanie.

Nate's search team was waiting on them before heading back to the *Emissary*. Nate wanted to be certain his friend was safe before leaving.

Jake was focused on his wife. Before the elevator doors closed, he finally surveyed the situation around him. He saw the man leaving the pod behind his new Admiral. Jake threw his arm out to stop the doors from closing. He gave his wife an

237

apologetic, "Go on without me. I'll be right behind you. I promise." He jumped off the elevator and let the doors close behind him. He heard several voices call his name as the doors closed.

Jake drew his weapon and moved in a direct path to the stranger. Tristan abruptly found Jake's weapon in his face, "Whoa! What's this about?"

Tristan took his focus off the weapon and onto the face of the man holding it. He recognized Jake as the one who turned him away at the conference center. "Davie, would you care to call off your watchdog?"

"Jake, you are officially off-duty. Stand down, Mr. Holden."

There was a tense pause as Jake stared at the man who was now doubly familiar.

"Captain, he's a security risk. I've seen him before," Jake objected.

"I know. Braxton told me. Mr. Holden, if he proves to be a viable security threat, you have my permission to shoot him. I would prefer you merely stun him."

Tristan glanced sharply at his son. David showed no signs of bluffing. Tristan had to admire the young man. He knew how to do his job.

Jake lowered his weapon and backed away cautiously. He conspicuously adjusted the setting. "Yes sir," was all he said.

His actions left Tristan unsettled.

Constable Hinson ushered his prisoners onto the secondary elevator with his security officers. He approached Capt. Alexander tenuously. He decided it was best to cover his tracks. "Capt. Doherty, do you have another prisoner for me to take into custody?"

David glanced at his father. There was every chance he was a security risk. This could be a trap to get them caught again. He didn't know that for certain. Arni told him the situation was under control before they escaped their captivity. Was his father sent by Arni or by Executor Hale? He finally decided on his answer. "No, not at this time. I'll let you know if the situation changes."

Tristan was becoming visibly annoyed. "Davie, do I need to leave? Would you feel safer putting binders on me? When I saw you in the Plaza the other day, I wanted to find out what happened to you. I'm starting to think I should have let you go and forget I ever saw you. Do you want me to go?"

David stared at his father. He wasn't sure how to answer. A part of him wanted to spend some time with him, but he had eleven ships and accompanying crews sitting in the surrounding docks. If this was a trap, it was a bad time to get caught in it.

Tristan heard David's silence loudly and clearly. "Fine, I'll be on my way."

He turned on his heels and circumnavigated the awkwardly silent group. He pressed the elevator call button.

"If you change your mind, I'm staying in H227," he added in an annoyed tone.

Nate met David's father years ago. He finally remembered who the stranger was. He stepped forward. "Isn't that your—"

"Yeah," David didn't let him finish his sentence.

"Davie, you can't let him leave like this. They could use him against you. You have to at least warn him."

David's face remained troubled. He finally called out as one of the elevators returned. "Wait! We need to talk."

Tristan stood in the doorway to the elevator. He was uncertain whether to stay or go. His face showed the pain of rejection.

"Wait… please," David had only revealed the stranger's identity to Braxton and Marissa. Nate remembered meeting the man years before. Jake and Constable Hinson both gave the Captain confused looks. David indicated this man was a security risk, but he clearly had deep ties to him. Exactly what sort of situation were they in?

"Are you sure? I could wait in the Plaza on neutral ground if you'd rather," Tristan offered.

"No, give me a minute to tie up some loose ends. Chief, take the elevator and catch up to your wife. Constable Hinson, I appreciate your help and your discretion. I think we'll be okay. Nate, I need to talk to you privately for a moment."

David's words set the world in motion again. Jake and Constable Hinson boarded the waiting elevator and departed. Braxton approached David's father and distracted him with idle introductory chatter.

Henry and Milo stood halfway between the Captains, aka admirals, and chatted about nothing in particular.

David pulled Nate further into the tunnel. "Nate, I need you to push the departure timetable up and get our people out of here as fast as possible."

Nate glanced at David's father. "Just so I know we're on the same page, tell me exactly what you're worried about."

David pressed his lips together, "I can't say for certain. It's a really big coincidence that he showed up here and now. Is he being followed by someone trying to get to us? Did Arni arrange it so that the last of my family could be moved away to safety? Was he the one tracking Ensign Ryder's family? Did Executor Hale send him to find me and bring me in? There's a lot of questions that need to be answered. I'm not even sure how to get answers to any of them without risking everything we've put together this week."

Nate nodded, "I'll take my people back to my ship. I'm not leaving until I know everything's secure. I'll notify Angela and Tas about the altered departure schedule. I'm the last ship to leave before you, so Stephanie can stay as long as she's needed. Davie, keep in mind, even if they did send your dad to trap us., he's your dad. They can still hurt him to get to you."

"I know. I'll figure something out to keep us all safe. I don't know what that is yet, but I'll figure it out," the young Admiral looked like he was somewhere between being nauseated and ready to slug something.

Nate tried to lift his friend's spirits. "Don't let Steph see you looking like this. She'll accuse you of looking like a lost puppy or something."

David returned a wry grin. "Thanks for the warning."

Nate smiled. His friend was on his way back up. "Besides if your dad is up to something, it'll be easier to catch him if he thinks your guard is down."

"True," David agreed solemnly.

"Have you introduced him to Brynna yet?"

"No, I need to do that. No matter what, I need to do that. Let's get moving," David gave his friend a hearty handshake. "No matter what happens, thanks for being my friend."

"You're welcome. It's not an easy job, but somebody's got to do it," Nate grinned.

The two headed to the elevator. "Thanks."

David raised his voice to speak to the remaining crewmen. "Let's make this official. Gentlemen, I would like you to meet my father, Capt. Tristan Alexander. Dad, you remember Nate Weiseman?"

Nate offered Tristan his hand. Tristan shook it firmly, but tentatively.

This is Nate's Security Chief, Milo Griffin and his ship's psychologist, Henry Oliver.

Tristan cocked his head, "Psychologist? What sort of mission were you on before the bottom fell out?"

David sidelined the question. "I'll give you the gist of it later. I need to introduce you to someone else. Dad, I got married a little over a year ago."

Tristan smiled, "Really? Is she pretty? Never mind, I'm sure you chose a good woman. I'd love to meet her, if you trust me that far."

David called for one of the elevators to return, then turned to respond to his father.

"Just for the record, since I'm on the Commonwealth's *Most Wanted* list, I have a lot at stake. I can't afford to trust you. Keep that in mind. Lt. Cmdr. Flint scan him for tracking devices and any power sources."

Tristan smiled, "You've been well trained. Good job, son."

The man spread his arms and legs out voluntarily and waited patiently for Braxton to run the scanner slowly over every inch of his body.

In a minute Braxton put the scanner away and shook his head. "I got nothing. He's clean."

"Okay, let's go. If he touches anything on the way to the ship, I need to know it," David snapped.

"You seem disappointed that you didn't find anything on me. I'm trying really hard not to take this stuff personally. You aren't making this easy," Tristan complained.

David didn't want to put his personal life on display for the others. He chose not to respond any more than necessary.

"If I found something to indicate you were here to trap me, I would at least know for certain what I'm dealing with. Just because I didn't find anything doesn't mean there's nothing there to find."

The elevator door opened once again. Nate and his crew moved into the compartment quickly. David stepped in behind them. Braxton followed him in.

David held the door open and waited. "Are you coming?"

The man was hesitant, "Do you *want* me to come?"

David realized if this situation wasn't a Commonwealth setup, he was being awfully hard on his dad, the same man who had just saved his life. "Yes, I want you to come."

Tristan stepped in with the others. The elevator stopped to allow Nate and his crew off. It stopped a second time to allow David and the others off.

****

Jake caught up to Marissa and the medical team just before they reached the ship. Jason and Stephanie got Marissa settled into a bed in the infirmary aboard the *Evangeline*. They did a more extensive scan on her to be sure all was going well. Once she was settled, Jake begged her indulgence a moment longer.

"Jake where are you going? Our baby's coming!" Marissa protested.

"The Docs say it will be awhile yet. I need to report off to the Commander and I'll be right back. I promise," Jake squeezed her hand warmly, brushed a stray hair out of her face, and kissed her gently on the forehead. "Five minutes, I promise."

She nodded but struggled to release her grip on his hand. This was a frightening occurrence. She knew the basics of childbirth, but somehow when it was actually happening to her, all the knowledge in the universe meant nothing.

Jake hollered at the two doctors and Laura. "I have to report to the Commander… uh… Captain, whoever. I'll be back in five minutes. I swear!"

Stephanie went with him. She fully intended to make sure he kept his promise to hurry. The moment they were alone in the corridor, she gave him a word of advice. "Chief, I suggest you let David introduce his father to Brynna."

"His father? That was his father?" Jake squawked.

"Oh, you didn't know?" Stephanie had recognized him this time but didn't realize Jake only saw him as the belligerent drunk in the corridor.

Jake was so stunned he stopped walking. "That explains why he was willing to let me stun him."

Stephanie took a couple more steps forward to encourage Jake to keep walking. When he remained in place she gently prodded, "Four minutes and thirty seconds, Chief."

"Huh? Oh yeah. Is he going to see his father as a security risk? I know I do," Jake started moving again. The two reached the ship's elevator and rode it to the Bridge level.

Stephanie shook her head. Jake was definitely distracted. She calmly laid it out for him.

"Jake, he gave you permission to shoot his father. I think he knows the risks. It also put his father on notice. He knows David is looking at him suspiciously. He won't double-cross him without thinking twice about it."

Jake's mind was running too many directions. Stephanie knew she needed to refocus him. She stopped him before they entered the bridge. "Jake, your job is to report off to your commanding officer, and help your wife get through this. Having a baby is a scary time in one's life. David knows what he's doing, and his command staff will have his back. You stay focused on your wife and baby. Okay?"

Stephanie watched the wheels turn in his head as he processed her message.

He finally nodded. "Yes ma'am."

Stephanie smiled and nudged him through the door. "You're down to three minutes," she didn't really know how long they had been gone, but she wanted to keep him on task.

Jake stepped onto the bridge. "Commander, I mean Captain, the four men who took Marissa and the… Admiral are in Constable Hinson's custody. Marissa is in the infirmary and doing fine. There were no injuries or losses. The C—uh—Admiral has officially put me on leave. The others should be returning shortly. They had one other issue to deal with, but it wasn't an emergency."

"What other issue, Chief?" Brynna queried.

"It pertained to his unexpected guest, and it's something you better ask *him* about. Is it alright if I get back to the infirmary? I promised Marissa I'd only be gone five minutes. I think I'm down to two."

"Of course, Chief. If you have anything to add, send it to me via comms, or I can come to you. Don't leave your wife unless lives are in imminent danger. Got it?" Brynna sternly admonished.

"Yes, ma'am," he turned and hastily exited. He raced to the elevator and impatiently rode it to the bottom floor. The doors were only half open when he bolted through and ran down the corridor to the infirmary.

Marissa gladly welcomed him back. She touched a computer screen at her bedside. "You made it with almost a minute to spare."

The computer screen had a timer programmed. She had set it the second he left. Jake's eyes widened as he realized she was holding him to his word.

Jake scowled, "Marissa, why did Jason move you to this bed? I thought you hated this bed."

Marissa squeezed Jake's hand tightly, "I do. I need to put this to rest," Marissa glanced at Jason who was across the room talking to Laura. "I think Jason needs to know I'm not afraid of him, and that I've forgiven him for what he tried to do to me and our baby."

Jake trusted the Doc, but a piece of him held onto some anger. Marissa saw the anger subtly slip across his face. She whispered again, "Jake, I need you to let this go too. It was the

Commonwealth, not the Doc, that deserves the blame. The Doc saved our son when Luciano attacked me, remember?”

A contraction overtook her. Marissa took some slow deep breaths, but they were becoming insufficient. She groaned with the pain. Laura offered assistance. After the contraction passed, she reluctantly offered a suggestion.

“Marissa, Jason is afraid to offer this. He can use a neural inhibitor on your lower back to block the pain receptors. It’s what he used on you before, but since you chose to move to this bed, he was afraid it would open some old wounds.”

Marissa declined the option. Laura understood her situation. She offered the alternative of changing positions, a warm shower, or a massage. Marissa chose to stand and lean over the edge of the bed while Jake massaged her back.

****

David escorted his guest to the Infirmary aboard the ship. The two waited by the door for Jason. When Jason approached them, David asked, “How’s Marissa?”

“She’s doing fine. Baby’s doing fine too. Did you need something?” Jason was listening to the two men but was clearly distracted by Marissa.

“Yeah, I’d like you to do a thorough scan of our guest before I allow him access to my ship. If you wouldn’t mind submitting to another scan?” David asked politely.

“Davie, this is getting old,” the man argued.

“Last time, I promise. Scans are becoming SOP for anyone coming on board,” David explained.

“Your other man scanned me already. I’m not carrying anything that would be considered contraband. What else do you expect to find?”

“We’re also looking for nanites.”

“Nanites? What sort of nanites?”

“Adm. Deacons brought some to us before we went rogue. They had some rather unorthodox applications. Let’s just say they are extremely dangerous.”

Tristan grudgingly gave in, “Alright. Fine. Where do you want me, Doc?”

245

Jason pointed at the closest bed, "This one's fine."

The man hopped agilely onto the bed and got comfortable. Jason routinely instructed, "State your name for the medical record."

"Tristan Alexander," came the reply.

"Alexander?" Jason gave the new Admiral a puzzled look.

"Dr. Jason Adams meet my father, Capt. Tristan Alexander," David was incredibly uncomfortable. He wasn't sure why. The crew had met his mother, sister, half-brother and step-father. Why was meeting his father such a problem?

"Uh, nice to meet you?" Jason offered. He sensed the situation was tense. The two shook hands and Tristan offered a response with equal voracity. Finishing with the pleasantries, he laid down to let the doctor do his job.

While David watched the scan, he slipped behind Jason and quietly asked, "Why is Marissa on that bed? I thought she hated that one."

Jason shrugged, "I don't know if she's trying to prove something, get over her fear, or getting some closure. I certainly didn't have anything to do with it."

Tristan was close enough to hear the conversation and asked, "Did somebody die in that bed or something?"

Jason winced, "No, not quite. That baby almost died there."

Jason turned and walked away. The conversation brought back painful memories for him. He came as close to hating himself for the incident as the crew did.

Tristan knew there was more to the story, but he refrained from pursuing it. In a minute Jason pronounced the man to be free of tracking devices, nanites, or any other implanted devices. He sat up and offered, "Did you want to implant a tracking device of your own? I'll submit to it if it will make you feel safer."

David shook his head, "I don't need to feel safer. It would lull me into a false sense of security. I know you know how to defeat such a device. If I think I'm protected by a tracking device, I'll let my guard down."

"If you believe I'm such a big security risk, why let me on board?" Tristan was ready to leave again.

"I'll tell you why after I introduce you to my wife," David escorted his father into the corridor and headed for the bridge. They passed Stephanie on her way into the infirmary. She and Tristan exchanged brief pleasantries and moved on.

Before stepping onto the bridge, David stopped his father. "Listen, Dad, I don't like putting my private life on display for my crew. This is a small ship, and I'm trying to keep it from being any smaller. You and I have some issues to work out, and I'm doing my best to keep them to myself. I'm glad to see you again, really, I am. I'm just concerned about the threat you represent. If this were a Commonwealth mission and I accidentally bumped into you, I'd be thrilled. It's not. Are we clear on this one point?"

"Yes, thank you for being straight with me."

David started to lead his father onto the bridge. This time Tristan stopped David, "Just for the record, considering the situation in your infirmary, do I have any grandchildren I should be aware of?"

David shook his head, "No, Brynna and I don't have any children. Although… when was the last time you talked to Abby?"

"Abby has a baby?" Tristan smiled, "I'm a grandpa?"

"His name is Joshua Aiden Williams. You really should have called her more often," David chided his father.

"I'll call her the next chance I get," He promised.

"I'm sorry, Dad. She went into hiding because of me. You can't reach her anymore. Let's go introduce you to Brynna," David escorted his father onto the Bridge.

****
●●●●●●●●

Brynna stood when he entered. David was relieved to see she was still wearing her civilian attire. He didn't want his father knowing a new chain of command existed or his role in that chain.

"Dad, this is my wife, Cmdr. Brynna Alexander. Brynna, sorry to spring this on you, but this is my dad, Capt. Tristan Alexander."

Brynna cast a concerned and surprised glance at Lexi. Lexi stood from her station with equal amounts of surprise and concern. The Commander pulled herself together and offered him her hand. "This is certainly a surprise. It's a pleasure to meet you," she smiled warmly.

Tristan shook her hand and smiled at her in return. "I was right. You chose well, Davie. She lies better than you do."

Brynna gave David a confused look, "Excuse me?"

David just looked annoyed.

Tristan explained himself, "I actually believed you when you said it was a pleasure to meet me. Davie insisted he was glad to see me too. I'm no fool. I know what dangers I represent to him and your crew."

"I see," Brynna responded cautiously, "not to sound impertinent, Capt. Alexander, but what brings you here?"

Tristan smiled again. "I like her, son. She gets right to the point. Commander, please call me Tristan, or even Dad if you like."

"We'll start with Tristan. It's uncomfortable to refer to a total stranger as 'Dad.' We'll work up to that one. Please call me Brynna."

Brynna was trying her best to be polite without being overly friendly. She wasn't sure if this man was friend or foe.

David turned slightly and motioned for Lexi to approach. "Dad, this is our ship's psychologist, Lt. Lexi Flint. Lieutenant, this is my father Capt. Tristan Alexander."

Tristan continued to pleasantly greet David's crew. Cheyenne was on the Bridge watching and listening eagerly. She was genuinely excited to meet the Captain's father. Her youthful appearance, bubbly personality, and petite stature made her seem younger than she actually was. Tristan casually joked about the recruits getting younger every year.

David's eyes twinkled as he responded, "She may be chronologically one of the youngest on board, but I think she's wiser and more mature than all of us."

Cheyenne giggled. She had managed to call the Captain out, on more than one occasion, when his temper had gotten the best of him.

David finally made a move to isolate himself and his Dad from the rest of the crew. "Let's grab some coffee, and we can talk. Commander, get with the mining facilitator and get our cargo taken care of as soon as possible. I'll let you know if I make any other changes to the manifest. Our departure schedule has been moved up. Check with Nate to get the updates. When you get everything squared away, you can join us in our cabin at your leisure. We've got lots to talk about."

As soon as the two left the Bridge, Brynna got to work.

****

David and his father stopped in the dining hall for coffee on the way to David's quarters. The two sat in the living area to talk. "So, who's going to start?" David asked.

Tristan's brow knit together, "Maybe you better start. You seem to have more on your mind than I do. I just know you're in some serious trouble."

David took a sip of his coffee and stared at the hot liquid. He softly asked, "Pateras, guide me."

He looked up at his Dad, "It's hard to know where to begin. I've got a million questions and concerns."

"Just start firing questions. The ones bugging you the worst will come out first," Tristan was willing to do whatever it took to get his son talking.

David scowled, "They may not be the questions that matter the most."

"Where do you propose we begin then?"

"Let's lead up to it a little. Would you really have killed those four men in the mine?" This seemed like the safest place to start. It would give him a small amount of insight into his father's mindset.

"Yes, I would have. It wasn't what I went down there to do, but if they were intent on killing you, I assumed it was important enough to return the favor," Tristan coldly answered.

"What if it was merely a robbery gone wrong or mistaken identity?" David wasn't amused with his father's response.

249

"That's why I didn't shoot first and ask questions later. I knew you wouldn't let me mishandle the situation," Tristan explained.

"Were you testing me?" David grimaced as he asked the question. He was doing exactly that with his father right now.

Tristan hesitated, "Maybe a little. I didn't know what you had gotten into, but I know Supreme Executor Hale wants to get his hands on you badly. If those guys reported your presence, I knew you wouldn't get far. I wondered if you would let me kill them. Why didn't you? Another few seconds and they would have killed you."

"I told you in the mine. I've caused them more than enough pain already. It's my fault they wanted me dead to begin with."

"If it were me, I would have shot them and tossed them into that pipeline they had waiting for you," Tristan was genuinely annoyed at his son's weakness.

"Why are you here on Zulimar?" David decided it was time to move on.

"I was doing reconnaissance. I'm undercover. My unit got reports of tetrabradium and tetratachium getting smuggled out of this colony under the table. There were discrepancies in the tax reports and the mining input and output reports. The mine should be producing fifteen to twenty percent more than they were reporting on their tax documents," Tristan explained.

"Tax evasion? Seriously?" David's skepticism was riddled with sarcasm.

"Laugh if you want, but this colony could supply half the Pacification Fleet for a year. The amount of ore going out of here unaccounted for is significant. It's not the taxes my superiors are worried about. The question is, 'Who are they supplying?' It would supply the Explorer Class Fleet for the next three years. Based on what little I know of your situation, this wasn't caused by you or your co-conspirators. This started before you went rogue. I have a ship that's supposed to meet me here in a couple of weeks and pick up a load to deliver, under the table. In the meantime, I'm supposed to get a job on the mining crew to work my way in," Tristan watched David's eyes to see if he was willing to accept his story.

"You know my situation, and you expect me to believe running into you was purely a coincidence? Let's get to the crux of the matter. Who sent you to find me, and how did you manage to track me down?" David asked bluntly.

"Are you sure we don't need to have this discussion in a detention center of some kind?" His father challenged.

"What good would that do? You're a trained soldier, like I am. I was just hoping you would do me the courtesy of answering honestly," David countered.

"What makes you think I'm lying to you?" Tristan asked, "I'm your father."

"No, not really. Steven and Uncle Rob have been more of a father to me than you have," David retorted.

Tristan smiled, "Now, we're getting somewhere. You're ticked off at me for abandoning you, your sister, and your mother. Your mother had things under control and my job changed. I couldn't go to Raesii and your mother refused to stay. I met Steven. He's a good man and he's taking good care of your mother and sister. How's their kid, Stevie?"

David set his coffee cup down and began to pace. He knew he needed to sell his abandonment issues, to gain his father's trust. "Are you saying you didn't abandon mom? She abandoned you?"

"No, that's not what I'm saying. You were headed to the Academy and she was freaking out about it. Your Uncle Rob and I both thought it would be good for you. I really don't know why she reacted so badly. Maybe it was all she could do to put up with my job as a soldier and when you headed that way, it was too much."

Tristan watched David as he paced. He wanted to see every nuance of emotion.

David wisely turned away frequently as he paced.

"Where was mom born?"

"What?" David's question seemed to be totally misplaced in the conversation. Tristan didn't know why he would ask such a remote question.

"Do you know where mom was born?" David repeated.

"Ju–ran-ta. Why would you ask me that?" Tristan responded hesitantly. Somehow this felt like a trick question.

"How long have you been doing undercover work for the Infantry?" David asked.

"Most of my career since I graduated from the Infantry Academy. I transferred to the Governmental Fiscal Oversight Department for a few years, but I transferred back to Covert Ops after your mother and I split up. You know this stuff. Why are you asking me this?" Tristan was concerned. These questions were unsettling.

"Was mom an undercover assignment?" David asked tersely.

"Was mom a *what*? What are you suggesting?" Tristan's voice was strained, "No, forget I asked that. I loved your mother. I love you and your sister. I think I need to go," Tristan's face flushed. He roughly slammed his cup on the table sloshing coffee over the brim and moved toward the door.

David intended to rattle his father, but it would be pointless if he actually left. "Wait, don't go. I really need some answers."

"Not to those questions, you don't. What happened to you? You had a stellar career, no pun intended, and you've thrown it all away. Why? What did you run into out there? Do all of these ships have a psych monitor on board? Is there something out there messing with people's heads?" Tristan's frustration kept his face a steady shade of red.

A silence fell on the two as they gave each other frustrated stares. Tristan was the first to speak again.

"I let your mom leave because you were headed down a good path and Robert was there to keep an eye on you. I could have requested a transfer, but your mom and I had… a lot of arguments and they were all about you. Don't misunderstand me. I'm not saying you caused us to go our separate ways. Your mom objected to you going into the Academy, but she could never give me a good reason why. I always wondered why she was so against it. Did she ever say anything to you about it?"

"No, I know she cried a lot and Steven was the first person to make her smile again," David's eyes reflected the emotions dredged up from the past.

"Davie, what have you done to yourself? Why did you ruin your career?" Tristan asked.

David decided it was time to explain Pateras to him. He returned to his seat and picked up his cup again.

Seeing David sit down, Tristan decided the answer must be lengthy. He moved back to his seat and retrieved his cup of coffee wiping the spilled droplets from the cup and the table.

"Our Commonwealth mission was to search out the strongholds of a superior alien being known as Pateras and report their location. Part of our mission was to establish the Commonwealth on the technologically undeveloped worlds, so they would warn us if Pateras contacted them," David watched his father for reactions. The man seemed to be focused on listening. His personal opinions weren't manifesting themselves on his face. David was not the best at hiding his thoughts. He wondered if his father had mastered the skill or if he really wasn't ready to form an opinion.

"I remember seeing Supreme Executor Hale's address about declaring war on the Liontari forces. You've thrown in with our enemy? Why?" Tristan questioned.

David pressed his lips together in an attempt to hide his emotions. He was right. His father was sent by the Commonwealth. He debated whether to explain himself or challenge his father. He set his coffee cup down and rubbed his face with his hands. He stood to pace again. He explained slowly about the crimes Luciano Hale committed. He told his father about the undeveloped worlds the Pacification Fleet laid waste to. The next thing he covered was the good he had seen Arni do. When he reached the point of explaining about the dead returning to life, his father was caught between laughing or calling his son a liar.

"Dad, I saw this with my own eyes and experienced some of it personally. Uncle Rob can even corroborate a little of it. Dad... I died. I was completely dead. I took an arrow to the chest. I died in Uncle Rob's arms. Lt. Holden died. I saw her body myself. Her neck was broken among numerous other injuries. She was dead for nearly twenty-four hours. Arni healed her. She wasn't able to have children before he healed her and now she's down the hall about to give birth," David argued passionately.

"You chose to follow an advanced civilized race because of their healing technologies? Why didn't you just quit the CIF and apply to their medical school or something?" Tristan countered.

"There's no technology involved. I've seen him heal people with a look or a touch. It's not physical healing that's the issue. Have you seen the death rates for assisted suicides for psychological impairment? They are at an all-time high. We weren't meant to live like this or die like this. Luciano Hale doesn't care about human life. He's the one who destroyed the base on Romajin, not us. If I have to choose between superior alien beings, I'm choosing Pateras not Luciano Hale," David said with finality.

"Wait, what are you saying?" Tristan looked at David like he had lost his mind.

"Luciano Hale wants me out of the way because I am a threat to him. The knowledge I have about him is dangerous and he thinks I'm the one destined to destroy him," David knew he sounded insane. He went to his computer and pulled up a file of the Ancient Texts. He displayed the passages about the twelve twelves and the destruction of the Dark Lord by one of the Messengers.

David read the passage to his father:

Twelve messengers will come forward, even twelve times twelve who will serve the Master of Darkness. Pateras will call to the messengers and one by one they will answer his call. One by one they will leave the darkness and enter the light, though not every one of them. A few will cling to the darkness and take up their swords against those in the light. The Master of Darkness will seek out his lost ones in order to destroy them. The Master of Darkness shall reach out his hand across the stars to smite all the sons and daughters of Pateras. The evil one will destroy the world of his one promised Son, but his Son will not die by the hand of the Evil One. The Promised One will give up his life to defend the defender of the twelve and even the twelve twelves. The Promised One will return from death on the third day to offer new life to all.

One who will betray the messengers of Pateras, will betray also the Dark Lord.

Tristan shook his head, "What are you saying?"

"Pateras is a—*the* Supreme Being. He created all life, including another superior alien being known as Luciano Hale. Luciano Hale tried to overthrow Pateras and got exiled for his actions. Oh, don't look at me like that. He wouldn't have sent people out to kill me if I were simply mentally unbalanced."

David changed gears to deal with the changing look on his father's face, "Do you really believe he would be all that concerned with one man who's lost his marbles, even one who has possession of one small Commonwealth ship?"

Tristan had to admit something was off about the situation. He had to offer some small concession or the two would have to go their separate ways. Tristan had his orders and if he didn't see this through, his son would pay the price.

Tristan moved around the room in quiet contemplation. "Okay, maybe, just maybe, there's something to this. Why can't we go through proper channels to work this out?"

"I would not live to see a trial for one. For another, the courts would give me the same look you just did," David moved closer to his Dad.

"Dad, the reason I really wanted us to go through with this conversation is to warn you. Your life is in danger. If you told me the truth, and I'm not saying I believe you, your life is in danger. If they find you, they'll use you to get to me. They'll accuse you of treason and put you on public display to get my attention then they'll offer to let you go, if I come in and face the charges myself. I'll be found mentally incompetent or I'll be found dead in my cell of an apparent suicide. You know the drill."

Tristan frowned, "You think *I'm* in danger?"

"I know you are. Executor Hale threatened Abby's baby. He paraded the entire family in to see me when I was in prison, broken, bruised, and bleeding. Dad, you can't go back out there. Let me move you someplace safe."

Tristan didn't commit to needing a place to go just yet. The two men continued their lively discussion for nearly two hours without interruption.

Brynna took her time joining them. She discerned that they had a lot to discuss. She wisely chose to give them as much time to talk as she could. When she could delay no longer, she entered cautiously. The two got quiet when she came in. "I hope I'm not interrupting. Captain, the mining facilitator has made arrangements for our cargo. I thought you might want to oversee the transfer."

David glanced at his father. "Would you mind if Brynna kept you company for a little while?"

Tristan smiled. "I'd love to spend some time getting to know my daughter-in-law. Is there anything you *don't* want me to ask her?"

David grinned knowingly. "Ask what you like, she's smart enough to know what to answer and what *not* to answer."

****

David joined Aulani's family. "Mr. Malo, Mrs. Malo, Kina, it's been a pleasure meeting you. I'm sorry it was under such difficult circumstances. Mr. Bennett will get you to safety. I don't know how long we can keep your location secret, but we'll do the best we can. Pateras is really the only one who can protect you. Do you have any questions or concerns before you leave?"

"I have one," Inoke stated.

"What is it? I'll answer it if I can," David promised.

"Is this journey worth your life?" Inoke's face was unreadable.

David never hesitated, "Absolutely."

"Very well then, I am content to allow my daughter to remain with you. I know you will do whatever is necessary to protect her," Inoke's glassy eyes reflected his sense of loss and admiration simultaneously.

"Thank you for trusting her to my care. You would do well to put her under Pateras' care. He asked me some time ago to put my entire crew in his hands. I shudder to think what might have happened if I hadn't done that. I'm just a man. It's hard to put one's responsibilities into the hands of another," David did his best to point the man in the right direction.

"I will learn who this Pateras is. I wish I had known him when my son grew ill," Mr. Malo lamented.

"Your son is safe with Pateras. If you continue on this path, you may see him again someday." David wasn't sure what life was like with Pateras and where those who died actually go. There was a lot to learn from the Ancient Texts.

Constable Hinson arrived to escort the family to meet the pod. The Drean section of the mine had one cavern carved out and a tachyon landing pad built to guide the pod to its precise landing area.

****

David went to the Bridge to monitor their progress. Thane, Aulani, and Lazaro accompanied the Constable and his team. Lazaro linked in through the computer station, so the

Captain could continue to monitor the situation. The pod materialized as expected and a messenger exited. She gave Lazaro a data crystal. The messenger was Robin Alberto. She gave Lazaro a hasty explanation then climbed back aboard behind the Malos. David couldn't hear what she said from the computer input. He knew Lazaro would update him later, but his curiosity was piqued.

Adm. Alexander watched the pod light up and disappear. A small piece of him wished he could go with it. He had lived without his family for several years now. Somehow, the events of the last few months gave him a desire to reconnect with them.

Lexi was still on the Bridge. She saw the faraway look in his eyes and asked, "Would you like to talk about it, sir?"

David refocused his eyes on her, "Do we always have to want the things we can't have?"

"No sir. We do want the things we took for granted, when they are no longer within our grasp. It's more a matter of losing what you had than wanting what you don't. We've all suffered the same thing, sir. Just so you know, you aren't alone in this."

Lexi was right on target. Her family was also relocated to Drea. She never had the chance to talk to them before they were evacuated. David got to tell his family goodbye and now, Aulani had as well. The crew and their families exchanged recorded messages periodically, but it wasn't the same as a proper goodbye.

David was suddenly thankful for what he had been given and ashamed for taking it for granted. "Lexi, I'm sorry you never got a chance to tell your family goodbye."

"Thank you, sir. I wish I could've explained what was happening to them in person, but sir, I'm just glad they're safe. Don't feel bad for my loss of opportunity," Lexi smiled gratefully at him.

"Thanks for your help, Lieutenant."

David left orders for Thane and Aulani to clean the guest quarters in anticipation of his dad needing them. He sent out a message to every crew member and labeled it high priority. He instructed the crew to address him and Brynna with their previous ranks. Finishing up his business, he headed back to his quarters.

JAKE JUNIOR

Marissa reached the final stages of labor without medical interference, but her progression stalled. Her pain was so intense her body couldn't relax enough to allow her labor to progress.

Jake's nerves were getting frayed from trying to ease her pain and give her whatever she needed. Nothing he did helped. While Marissa rested in between contractions, Jake stepped outside the privacy screens to talk to Jason. "Doc isn't there anything you can do to help her?"

Jason was equally as frustrated, "She won't let me help her. She's willing to let me deliver her baby, but at this rate we're headed for a surgical delivery."

"Doc... Dr. Weiseman... somebody, please do something. I can't stand to see her like this," Jake pleaded.

A contraction roused Marissa from her brief nap. She cried out for Jake, who quickly rushed back to her side.

Jason and Stephanie discussed the situation without reaching a definitive solution. Jason finally excused himself for a moment and headed to the Bridge.

****

When Jason arrived on the bridge, he sat down with Lexi and discussed the situation.

Lexi's brow furrowed, "Jason, I can get somebody else to take my shift if you need me to, but she's in no shape for a therapy session. What I would suggest is a straightforward confrontation of her fears. Is she afraid of you, the treatment, of being a mom, or the end of a pregnancy she never expected to have? Find out and challenge it outright. I also suggest you not allow anyone else to interfere. Force her to do what needs to be done."

Jason scowled, "I can't force treatment on her."

"I'm not suggesting that," Lexi argued, "I'm suggesting you tell her outright what her choices are leading to, find out what she's afraid of, and make her deal with it."

Jason nodded, "Thanks, Lieutenant."

As soon as he left the room Lexi smiled to herself. A few days ago, she thought her job was becoming irrelevant and obsolete. In the few days since, she had offered counsel to a large number of people. The Captain was right to berate her for her ill behavior. Why was he right on so many things?

****

Jason returned to the infirmary. Each step more confident and purposeful than the last. When he entered the room, he sent Laura and Stephanie out. He pulled Jake out of the screened in area, "Jake, I need to talk to Marissa, and I need you to stay completely out of it. I'm not about to harm her in any way, but I need to push her a little. Can you let me do this? If you can't I would prefer you wait in the corridor."

Jason saw Jake's professional mask cover his emotions. He nodded his approval and followed the Doc back into the tiny cubicle.

Marissa was lying on her side. Jason stepped behind her and gently moved her bed linens and gown aside. "Marissa, I'm going to apply a small amount of pressure to your lower back for a moment."

What he didn't say was with that pressure, he was placing the neural inhibitor across her vertebrae. The small amount of pressure he applied gave her a tiny amount of relief from her discomfort. With the patch in place, Jason picked up a small data pad and walked around the bed. He slid a nearby chair forward and sat in front of her speaking candidly, "Marissa, I need you to listen to me."

Marissa opened her weary eyes. "What's wrong? Is something wrong with my baby?"

"No, but if you don't let me help you, you're going to need surgery to get this baby out. Do you want that?"

Marissa's eyes welled up with tears, "No, please don't do that. Jake, please don't let him do that."

Jake stepped forward, but one harsh look from Jason kept him from coming any closer.

"Marissa, I'm proud of you for overcoming your fear of this bed, but there's something else you are afraid of. Is it me, or is it the neural inhibitor?"

A contraction began to build, and Marissa squirmed painfully in the bed. Jake took another step forward. Jason waved him back.

Jason did the one thing, that could be considered medical assault. He pressed a button on the data pad, activating the neural inhibitor. The thing caused a slight burning sensation in Marissa's lower back. She gasped in surprise, more due to the release from the painful contraction than the burning sensation. "Don't! Take it off! Jake help me!"

When Jake didn't move Marissa reached to pull the device off her back.

Jason grabbed her arm. Holding it in place he put the data pad in her hand. "You have every right as a patient to refuse treatment. It is my advice as your physician that you utilize this neural inhibitor to aid your labor. This is the control mechanism for the inhibitor, if you wish to refuse the treatment, turn it off yourself."

Marissa gave Jake a frightened look. Jason turned to leave the room. He stopped next to Jake. "The longer she keeps that thing turned on, the more she'll relax, and her muscles will do the job they need to be doing. Try to get her to leave it on."

Jason stopped at the cubicle entry, "Marissa, I gave you my word, I wouldn't hurt you or the baby. I technically, and legally, just broke that promise. I'm sorry. If you must, report me to the Admiral in the morning. Dr. Weiseman can deliver your baby if you would be more comfortable with that."

Marissa froze in place. She was terrified of the neural inhibitor, but now that it was giving her some much-needed relief, she was hesitant to remove it. Her mind flashed back to several months ago when the doctor used this same device to forcibly attempt to end her pregnancy. Tears flowed down her face. She looked at Jake crying. "I can't do this. Don't make me do this. I can't…"

Jake sat beside her, whispering calm reassurances, he stroked her hair. Her words weren't making a lot of sense. In a few minutes, she drifted off to sleep. Once she nodded off, Jake removed the data pad and placed it on a nearby counter. He didn't want her to move in her sleep and accidentally disengage the device.

Jason came in to check on them a little while later. He thanked Jake for moving the pad from under Marissa's hand. He also thanked him for not interfering.

Seeing his wife resting, Jake slipped out to get a quick bite to eat and a cup of coffee.

****

He ran into Lexi coming off-duty. The two talked as Jake wolfed down his food. Jake took a minute to thank her for everything she had done for him, and more recently for the situation with the Doc and Marissa. Lexi smiled at Jake as he left and thanked him in return. "Jake, thanks for showing your appreciation. I've felt out of place recently. It's nice to know I'm needed and appreciated."

Jake flashed a quick grin at her and headed back to the infirmary.

****

The neural inhibitor was set on its maximum setting, taking away even the slightest sensations. As her body stopped tensing with every contraction, the contractions became more effective. Two hours later, Jason decided it was time for her to wake up and deliver her baby. He lowered the strength of the inhibitor which slowly increased what she could feel. Marissa stirred as her discomfort returned. When she was fully roused she found herself surrounded by Jake, Jason, Laura, and Stephanie.

Jason asked point blank, "Who do you want to deliver your baby, me or Dr. Weiseman? Normally, you wouldn't have an option, but today you do."

Marissa took a slow deep breath as a wave of pain washed over her. It was not a heavy pain at the moment, but it was clear discomfort. As the pain passed again, a single tear rolled down her cheek, "Jason, it wasn't you. It was the neural inhibitor. I forgave you a long time ago. I'm sorry, I didn't mean for you to think… I'm sorry…"

More tears escaped her eyes. Jason placed his hand on her head, "It's okay. Would you like for me to help you get this baby delivered now?"

Marissa nodded.

****

Laura, with Jake and Marissa's permission, kept the crew updated on Marissa's labor. She was both glad and relieved to be able to post a favorable update.

As the word spread about her labor, the crew's anxious anticipation climbed. The later it got, the more they congregated in the common areas of the ship. Ultimately the majority came together in the Dining Hall to wait for news of the baby's delivery.

David and Brynna escorted Tristan to the Dining Hall to introduce him to the others. The three sat down to eat.

"Son, I mean no disrespect, but why are you allowing a baby on your ship? Aside from being against regulations you are no longer bound to abide by, it's a bad idea."

Finishing the last bite of his food, David leaned back to answer the question. He smiled as he reflected on the discussion he'd had with Jake and Marissa. "Well, it is a multifaceted situation. First of all, they wanted to stay. I offered to move them someplace safe."

Brynna smiled as she remembered the situation as well, "The Chief actually wanted to do that. He didn't want Marissa to stay."

"Jake thought I would put them off because it was against the regs. Since we were committing treason, I didn't have to follow the regs. I gave them the option of staying on board because one, I needed them. We're running a skeleton crew already. Two, if the Commonwealth finds them on the run somewhere, they aren't any safer. Lastly, that baby is a symbol of hope for this crew. He's being born out of his mother's death," David explained casually. He wasn't worried about his father using the baby against them if he truly were a spy.

"I understand all of that, but what kind of life is that child going to have? There are no other children to play with, no grandparents. Living life on the run, he could even lose his parents. At least I waited until you and your sister were older before I went back to doing undercover assignments. I didn't want you two wondering if I was never coming home," Tristan defended his position as a good father.

"I can't guarantee any playmates for a couple years, but hopefully this will be over before that's an issue," David replied lightly.

"You are *not* taking your situation seriously," Tristan was done playing games.

Brynna twisted uncomfortably in her seat. She knew her husband was taking the situation *quite* seriously. She wanted to jump in and defend his position. Stepping between a father and son was not someplace she needed to go.

David glanced at Brynna. Seeing her discomfort and subsequent restraint, he smiled and patted her hand, "Dad, I chose this knowing the consequences. If you had seen and experienced the things we had, you wouldn't say that."

Thane raced into the room with a data pad in his hands. He rushed to one of the groups of crewmen, talking excitedly to them.

His actions caught David's eye and momentarily stalled his response to his father. He forced his attention back to the conversation at his table, "What is it you think I should do?" He asked, turning the question back on his father.

"Let me bring you in. I could get in touch with Robert to get you brought in safely. We could hire the best legal team available," Tristan offered.

"I'm not in a position to trust Uncle Rob to do that considering what he's already done to me. Besides, I'm guilty of capital crimes. I can die in the service of Pateras, I can die in an unfortunate accident as I attempt to surrender, or I can die after being found guilty. I'd rather take my chances out here."

Thane's excitement was infecting the entire room. David's curiosity got the best of him. Whatever Thane was involved in looked like more fun than rehashing the current conversation. "Mr. Ryder, may I ask what you're doing?"

"Sure Captain, I started a baby pool. You want in?" The energetic young pilot offered.

David grinned at Brynna and Tristan, "Sure, I think it's a boy."

Thane glared playfully at his Captain, "It's a weight pool. We already know it's a boy."

"Isn't there usually some sort of wager with these things?"

"Yes sir, it's five credits," Thane grinned. He knew the Captain would take issue with the wager.

"Just how do you propose collecting that? You do remember we're no longer getting paid, right?" David eyed the young man suspiciously.

"We know, sir, but one day this will be over, and we'll get paid again. It just might take a long time to collect if you win," Thane grinned, "It also means we have to stay alive long enough to settle our debts."

David shook his head and rolled his eyes, "Okay, put me down for five credits. I think he will be six pounds and twelve ounces."

"Yes sir. Commander, you want in?" Thane offered.

Brynna grinned, "Six pounds, *thirteen* ounces."

"What's that about?" David was vexed at her choice.

"That is the only bet I would take against you, Captain. I'm no fool," Brynna smiled playfully as she went to refill her coffee cup.

Thane turned to David's father, "I know you aren't familiar with us, sir, but you did help Marissa and her baby earlier today. Do you want in?"

"Sure, I'll give it a go. I'm guessing seven pounds three ounces. And I *can* pay *my* debts," Tristan twisted the metaphorical knife.

Thane grinned, "You better hope you don't win. It'll be awhile before we can pay up."

"I might have to stay with you to be sure you don't skip out on paying if I win," Tristan joined the tomfoolery.

Thane grinned and moved on. David leaned in as soon as he was gone, "Dad, listen. I'm really concerned about you. If you just started this new assignment, someone is going to know where to find you. Word will come down the chain of command, and you'll be picked up. My guess is, it will happen sooner rather than later."

"Davie, I haven't done anything wrong. They've got no reason to pick me up," Tristan argued.

"You're my father. That's reason enough!" David was genuinely concerned for the man's well-being. "Executor Hale can and will destroy anyone who doesn't have the protection of Pateras. That would be you."

"So why hasn't he harmed your uncle? Does he have the protection of Pateras?" Tristan challenged.

"That would get the attention of too many people and Adm. Deacons has shown himself to be quite loyal. If he gets desperate, I wouldn't put it past him to try though," David slammed his fist on the table, "I wouldn't put it past Uncle Rob to agree to let Executor Hale arrest him and charge him with treason just to get to me."

"You're pretty sure of yourself, a little too sure. Why?" Tristan watched David carefully. There had to be some telltale sign of weakness, or a secret… something.

David stepped away. He stopped with his back to the table. He wanted to explain everything to his father, but he was too close to the situation.

Brynna watched him for a moment, "Tristan, Adm. Deacons conspired with… with one of the crew to get us arrested. He's responsible for our arrest and torture. David was tortured horribly, worse than the rest of us. He escorted David's entire family in to see him. Jessica had to see him beaten, bruised, bleeding and in a great deal of pain. His grandmother saw it. His sister, his little brother Stevie and even baby Aiden. How anyone could do that is beyond me."

David looked at the floor. He knew his next words were going to be difficult and risky. "That's not all," his voice was soft and low.

He returned to his chair. "Mom didn't come from Juranta. She came from a planet called Drea. Grampa and Gramma were taken along with their three children, Abigail, Robert, and Jessica. The Commonwealth wanted Grandpa and Gramma to work on a project for them. They refused. I don't know the whole story, but they refused until they were pushed too far. They killed mom's oldest sister, Abigail. Do you really think they would hesitate to kill you?"

Tristan stared at David for what felt like forever. "What do you want me to do? Do you really expect me to drop everything and walk away from my life?"

"Yes, please," David beseeched.

"I thought you were mad at me for walking out on you and your mom. Why do you care what happens to me now?" he argued again.

"I've always cared. Yes, I'm ticked off about the way you handled your life, but that doesn't mean I stopped caring about you. If they take you, I *will* turn myself in to stop them from hurting you. I won't turn my crew in. If you are here as a spy, then you have the information you came for. You and my crew are my weakness. I will not turn on Pateras. As long as I'm alive, I will be loyal to Pateras," David's sullen appearance gave way to a look of determination.

"Where would you hide me?" Tristan leaned forward and rubbed his brow.

Brynna glanced nervously at David. She wasn't sure if Tristan was trying to get information out of them or if he was genuinely ready to accept the situation.

David shook his head, "I don't know. You can't stay here though."

"What about your mom and sister? Where did you take them? Did you take them to, where did you say, Drea?" Tristan asked.

He thought better of his question, "Forget it. Don't answer that. I don't need to know."

"We couldn't go back to Drea. It would've been the first place they'd look for us. We met up with another ship on Galat and it took them to safety. Drea was invited to join the Commonwealth fifty years ago. They couldn't bring themselves to meet Commonwealth standards, so the Commonwealth put four satellites in orbit around the planet, and left. The satellites eradicated their space program until we gave them the override codes. Now they've got a chance to start over. I really don't want to try getting back in there. It would put the Dreans at risk. I won't be responsible for another world's destruction."

"Tomorrow, let me pick up a few things from my room. I don't want to empty it in case anyone is watching. I also don't want to close out the lease or check out. If you don't mind, I'll ride this out with you for a while, until I can find a safe place to go. Do you mind letting me sleep on your couch? I could even pull some shifts as a pilot, if you need the help," Tristan offered.

"Sure, I'd be glad to have you on board. We'll have to scan your belongings for trackers. We have a guest cabin available. You are welcome to live there for the time being. Do you want to get your stuff tonight? I'm not sure anybody is getting any sleep until this baby is born."

"Tonight's fine. Am I going alone, or do you want to send a security detail?"

"Brynna and I can go with you. Let me hand command off to Lt. Cmdr. Flint. Brynna, grab some weapons from the locker please."

David pulled Braxton aside and gave him some explicit instructions. He was used to Jake questioning him, but this time Braxton objected.

"Sir, I should go. It isn't safe for you and the Commander to both be gone."

"Lt. Cmdr. Flint, I understand the risks, really I do. If he were going to try something, this would be his best chance. That's why I am giving him the option. I want to know before I let him stay on this ship, what he's willing to risk. Brynna and I are also the only ones I'm willing to take a chance with. If we aren't back in an hour, you have your orders. Carry them out," David ordered.

"Yes sir!" Braxton still wasn't happy about it.

****

Twenty minutes later, the three were in Tristan's rented quarters gathering half his clothes and a few personal items. It only took him about five minutes to gather his things and place them in a small bag. Before they left, he pulled a small medallion from the lapel of his jacket and casually tossed it on his bed.

David scowled, "What's that?"

"I was supposed to wear that, so my contact could identify me. I probably don't want him to identify me anymore," Tristan's explanation was credible.

"I suppose you're right. Now would not be a good time to be identified by anyone. I hope it didn't get noticed on the way over here," David mused.

Brynna added, "It's late enough we really didn't cross paths with anyone. I doubt it's an issue."

The three made their way uneventfully back to the ship. They slipped into the infirmary and ran their scans as quickly and quietly as possible. David escorted his father to the guest quarters and showed him around.

"Dad, I know it's getting late. We're going to head to the Dining Hall and wait for the baby."

David knew he had pushed his Dad quite a bit. He thought perhaps he might want a little time alone to think about what he had done. He hadn't exactly committed treason, but he *had* abandoned his commission, at least David hoped he had. The other alternative was that, he hadn't abandoned it, and capturing the crew of the *Evangeline* was his current assignment.

"Are you kidding? I'm going with you. I've got money riding on this baby. I'm not going to sit this one out. You're all a bunch of criminals. You'd probably conspire to say the baby weighed something different just to get my five credits," Tristan teased.

David gave his father a funny look. "For five credits? Yeah, we could buy a whole meal in a modestly priced restaurant for that. Well, come on, I wouldn't want you to lose your credits to a bunch of thieves."

****

When they walked into the Dining Hall, the crew was playing a game on the computer. David, Brynna, and Tristan joined in the frivolity. It was a great stress reliever. They desperately needed the relief.

An hour later, Stephanie stepped into the Dining Hall. As the crew became aware of her presence, their jocularity ground to a halt.

Cheyenne could stand the wait no longer. "Well, do we have a baby?"

Stephanie smiled, "Yes, we do. Jake and Marissa want to see you all briefly tonight and introduce you to their little one. They would like to see David and Brynna first."

Thane popped up, "Wait, what did he weigh? We have a baby pool going."

Stephanie thought perhaps Jake should be the one to announce it. She realized neither Jake nor Marissa had even asked how much the baby weighed. "Seven pounds, three ounces."

Tristan raised his arms in victory, "Yes! I win!"

Several moans and groans erupted from the crew. Stephanie approached Tristan, "Capt. Alexander… Senior, Jake and Marissa wanted you to come in with David and Brynna."

"Me? Why?" Tristan knew he had helped the young woman, but she barely knew him.

"She didn't say. I'm just the messenger," Stephanie yawned. She was ready to get some sleep.

David and Brynna escorted Tristan and Stephanie to the infirmary. The group found Marissa in bed holding her newborn baby. Jake was stretched out with her. His arm wrapped around her, touching his son's face in amazement. When he saw the Captain walk in, he hopped off the bed and took the baby from Marissa. "Captain, Marissa and I wanted you to be the first one to hold our son."

David reached nervously for the baby. He hadn't been near a baby since his mother gave birth to his half-brother Stevie. He forced himself to relax as Jake placed the baby in his arms. "I am honored. I'm also glad I wasn't the one to deliver him."

Tristan looked over David's shoulder at the tiny baby, "That goes for me too."

David looked at Marissa. He smiled, "Now you can tell me."

Jake gave his wife a confused look. Marissa took her husband's hand, "I tried to tell the Captain what we were going to name our son when we were in the mine tunnels. He refused to let me."

"Captain, Commander, you've both done so much to protect our son and Marissa. You've meant so much to us. We wanted to thank both of you the only way we knew how. Capt. Alexander, Cmdr. Alexander, we'd like you to meet, Jacob Alexander Holden." Jake was proud of his son and the couple who had protected his son's life repeatedly.

David's eyes were glued to the tiny face in front of him until Jake told him the baby's name. As the words came out of his mouth, David looked up sharply at Jake and Marissa.

Marissa smiled at his reaction, "We're going to call him, Jax."

Brynna peered over David's other shoulder at the baby. "Oh, Marissa, he's beautiful, and we are honored that you would name him after us."

Seeing Brynna's interest, David handed the little one off to her. "He's going to be a fine crewman. Is his hair going to be red like Jake's?"

David watched Brynna gazing at the precious bundle of joy. He saw the sparkle in her eyes and her face glowing. They were so preoccupied with work and staying alive, he hadn't seen that sparkle lately.

Marissa finally addressed Tristan, "Capt. Alexander, Senior, Jake, and I wanted to thank you for helping us in the mine and for saving our Captain's life. We owe you a great debt."

"Oh, you don't owe me anything, besides I just won forty credits because of this little guy," Tristan grinned playfully.

Jake and Marissa exchanged curious glances. David quickly explained, "Thane was running a baby pool. Dad won."

David moved from the foot of Marissa's bed to stand beside her. "Lieutenant, you did a good job out there today. I hope what you learned doesn't destroy your faith in me. I'm not the same man I was back then."

"I have a confession of my own to make. The day I died, Pateras showed me that day in your past. I had already seen it for myself. He told me everyone's done wrong, and I shouldn't be afraid when the day came for this to come to light. I've known who and what you are for months. I trusted you with my life a year ago, and I lost that life. I trusted you with my life yesterday, and my baby and I are alive and well. You aren't the same man you were a year ago. I trust this man more than the one from a year ago," Marissa gave him a smile that came from the deepest part of her heart. She sat up off the inclined mattress, "May I?"

David nodded and leaned closer to her.

Marissa wrapped her arms around his neck and hugged him. The fear of losing her baby from several months ago finally dissolved into tears and flowed down her face. Marissa's teetering hormones, exhaustion from the work of giving birth, and their recent trauma caused her military bearing to melt into an emotional blob. She grasped the Captain's neck tightly and sobbed openly.

David returned the hug, but after a moment of leaning awkwardly over the bed, he shifted to sit beside her. As she finally got her emotions under control, she whispered softly to him, "Thank you. Thank you so much."

Her grip on his neck loosened. As David started to pull away, Marissa's grip suddenly tightened again. She kissed his cheek before totally releasing him. David had gotten more comfortable over the last year with hugs, but the kiss was pushing him again. "Uh, what was that for?"

Marissa wasn't sure she could explain the profoundness of her gratitude adequately, so she pawned the explanation off in a simpler way. "I figured this was my only chance to ever kiss an Admiral," she grinned sheepishly.

David looked at Brynna. He debated putting her off playfully to explain away the misspoken rank, ignoring it altogether or explaining it outright to his father and potential spy. David pulled back and smiled. "I'll forgive you… this time. Listen, I know the others are… eager, and that's putting it mildly, to get in here. If we can manage to get Jax out of Brynna's arms, we'll go so the others get a chance to come in. Congratulations Marissa. Congratulations Jake. He's a beautiful baby. You both did great."

Brynna instinctively handed Jax off to Tristan who was startled by the sudden bundle in his arms. The baby wiggled and stretched. He whimpered slightly before settling back down to sleep.

Brynna hugged both Jake and Marissa. She offered her congratulations and praises of their new bundle of joy. Her intention was to slow David down. She knew why he was suddenly ready to leave.

David moved away from the bed, "Brynna, we need to go. It's late and everyone is tired."

Tristan was looking at the precious baby in his arms. Hearing David's admonishment, he tore his eyes away from the baby. "I'm right behind you, just give me a moment to return this precious cargo to his mom and dad."

David hollered back, "We'll be in the corridor."

****

As soon as the door closed behind them, David planted the soft side of his fist against the nearest bulkhead. He searched his mind for an appropriate expletive. Nothing came to mind. He was frustrated, but reality told him, this was Pateras' plan and it couldn't be thwarted.

Brynna hastily affirmed. "David, Pateras knows what he's doing. We've been betrayed before, and Pateras protected us. I think this is a good thing. We don't have to divulge our plans, but he needs to know exactly what he's dealing with."

The infirmary door opened, and Tristan stepped cautiously into the corridor, "I hope I'm not interrupting anything."

"No, just thinking out loud. Let's let the others know they can go in. I need some sleep. I'm getting dangerously close to being up for twenty-four hours," David encouraged them to move toward the Dining Hall.

Brynna stepped in front of them, "I'll do that. Why don't both of you return to the guest quarters. I think there's something you need to deal with."

David gave her a tired nod, "You're probably right. I'll meet you back in our cabin shortly."

****

David and Tristan entered the guest quarters. David remained by the door. Tristan moved into the seating area. "Would you like to have a seat… Admiral? I assume that's what you needed to talk about."

"I'm tired, like I said earlier. The short answer is this, yes, the other Captains gave me a field promotion to Admiral. They believe a chain of command is going to be important to holding us together. Since I'm the leading authority on Pateras, they chose me to lead this… revolution. So, yes, I am an Admiral… of sorts. I'm not taking any pleasure in that title, if that's what you're thinking." David made his point as quickly and bluntly as he dared without exposing his cranky disposition.

"Revolution? Ten, tiny, infinitesimal ships can't start a revolution," Tristan shook his head at the situation. He was too tired and cranky or he might've laughed outright.

"Dad, here's the point. I'm going to do my best to keep you alive and well. You are welcome to stay with us or you can leave. If you stay, then for tonight, I'm going to confine you to quarters and basically put you under house arrest. We're leaving the colony tomorrow. You can think things over and leave in the morning, if that's what you want. I can talk more tomorrow. I'm done talking tonight. What's it going to be?" David stood patiently awaiting his father's decision.

Tristan looked equally as tired. "You're right. Neither one of us are capable of anymore civil conversation tonight. I'll stay tonight and give you my decision in the morning. Good night, son. It's good to see you again."

A strange sense of relief washed over him, "Goodnight, Dad."

David headed into the corridor and pressed a button on his bracelet. "Computer, secure door to guest quarters. No access by anyone other than the command staff. Secure guest quarters computer access to local usage only."

Local usage would enable David's father to adjust atmospheric controls, alarm clocks, music, entertainment, and inbound communications. It prevented his access to ship's files, communications, or control of anything else aboard ship.

****

David returned to his cabin. He sat down at the computer and stared at the blank screen. After a moment he started pressing controls. The computer came to life. Brynna came into the room. Seeing his sudden flurry of activity, she cocked her head and asked, "Did I miss a memo? I thought we were getting some sleep."

David looked up, "I'm coming. I want to put some security protocols in place, just in case."

"What sort of protocols?" Brynna looked at him skeptically.

"I'm setting the computer to scan for any type of signals coming from the guest quarters and monitoring all computer accesses," David kept his eyes glued on his screen.

"David, are you kidding? Why are you so paranoid?" Brynna was quickly getting frustrated with him.

"He was sent here to find us," David stopped what he was doing.

"How do you know?" He wouldn't have said it if he didn't know something definitive. Brynna trusted his judgment, most of the time.

"Two things: the first one was when I used the words 'superior alien being' he never questioned it. The only people who know about them were those on the Supreme Executor's staff, the Admiral's Board, and those in the immediate chain of command above the Explorer Fleet. The second thing is he said we were just ten ships up against the entire Commonwealth. He should not have that information. He was briefed," David stared at her stricken face.

"What are you going to do with him?" Brynna knew he was right. No one except the twelve Captains and CIF brass knew there were only ten ships left. Taye's ship was sequestered and most of her crew arrested. Tas Gellert's ship was reported as destroyed, but the CIF didn't know he had acquired a new vessel. Nate's ship was supposedly destroyed a couple of months ago. Tristan, having seen Nate, knew his ship had somehow survived.

"I'll make that call tomorrow. He…" David sighed, "He may have been pushed to do this. It's possible we can get him to see our side of things. I'm going to challenge him in the morning."

Brynna smiled.

"What? You're smiling. I'm on the verge of lethargy and you're smiling," David scowled at her.

"You wanted him to see our side of things. I've already been working on that. Do you remember when I handed Jax off to him?" Brynna continued to smile as she remembered the look on her father-in-law's face.

"Not really, I was distracted."

"Your dad was startled, but he held Jax comfortably and looked at him. He looked long and hard into the face of that baby. If he turns on us, I wanted him to see exactly whose lives he was destroying. Now he knows," Brynna folded her arms resolutely across her chest.

David smiled, "You are as brilliant as you are beautiful. Computer run program."

He stood and wrapped his arms around her.

She laid her arms on top of his. "There's no guarantee he'll even think twice about hurting that baby, but I thought it was worth a shot."

Brynna's brow wrinkled, "David, do you think you should be the one to challenge him tomorrow? You're really close to this situation."

David thought about it briefly, "I don't know. If I don't feel confident, I'll hand it off to you. I would like either you or Braxton and Lexi there when I talk to him. You need to feel free to jump in and take over if I'm not handling it well."

Brynna nodded, "We need to get to bed. Morning is coming too fast."

David and Brynna crawled into bed. Brynna curled up in her husband's arms and settled in rather quickly. David forced himself to lie still to avoid disturbing his wife, but his thoughts would not allow him to sleep. His tired mind finally called out to Arni.

Arni whispered quietly to him, "Why did you wait so long to ask for my help? I'm here all the time, not just when you get desperate."

David shifted in the bed more from the psychological discomfort rather than a physical discomfort. He pressed his lips together reacting to Arni's chastisement. "I'm sorry. I'll try not to wait so long next time. I need to know this is going to be okay. I don't want to be betrayed again, especially not by my own father. Please tell me he isn't going to betray us."

Arni's voice came slowly and quietly, "No, you need to put this under my control and let me handle it, then you need to get some sleep. Whether he betrays you or not isn't the problem. Trusting or not trusting me is. Am I in charge, or are you?"

David sighed quietly. This time he spoke audibly, yet softly. "It's yours. You're in charge, not me."

Brynna rolled over and opened her eyes to look at him. His face was silhouetted by a clock on the computer screen. "Finally. I *knew* you weren't resting. Arni's got this—always."

"I know. He's got it now, because I just gave it to him. I have a hard time letting go of things. I'm sorry to you too," David added.

Brynna smiled, "You can thank me by getting some rest. Good night, Dear."

"Good night, Brynna."

GETTING SITUATED

Brynna was up early the next morning for her shift as the duty commander. She met Cheyenne who was also headed to the bridge for her duty shift. Braxton had the night shift alone. With Jason, Laura, Jake, and Marissa out on account of having her baby, the number of personnel available for duty was drastically reduced. The *Evangeline* was scheduled to launch late that morning, which would require a full ship's crew. David and Brynna arranged the schedule to keep the launch crew off-duty the last few hours prior to launch.

Brynna reviewed the ship's log with Braxton. The night after the birth of Jacob Alexander Holden was uneventful. After getting report from Braxton and relieving him of his duty shift. Brynna headed to the Dining Hall. She grabbed two breakfast trays and took them to her quarters.

David had just gotten out of the shower when she arrived in their quarters. Stepping out of the bathroom, he headed to their bedroom to get dressed when he heard Brynna call out to him.

"David, I brought us some breakfast."

David stopped towel drying his hair and stepped toward her. Looking at her curiously he replied, "Sounds great. Let me get some clothes on and I'll be right back."

Brynna frowned playfully, "I kinda liked what you're wearing now."

David looked at the towel wrapped around his waist. He smiled back at her appreciatively. "You're on duty… Captain."

Brynna continued to admire her husband's handsome physique. "On duty or not, I can still admire the scenery—Admiral."

David winked at his equally attractive wife. "I'll be right back."

He disappeared into their bedroom and reappeared two minutes later wearing his pants and the teal form-fitting inner uniform shirt. He hadn't taken the time to put his socks or shoes on. Sitting down at the table, David got to the point. "So, what did I do to deserve this?"

Picking up his fork, he opened his mouth to take the first bite when Brynna responded, "Nothing, I just thought we should talk."

His first bite was nearly in his mouth. Her words stopped him cold. He put his fork down slowly. "So, I did do something, or you think I'm *about* to do something."

"You aren't in trouble, if that's what you're thinking," Brynna laid her napkin in her lap. She picked up her fork and took a bite. Her goal was to bring down the defensive barrier he erected.

David resumed eating. He waited for the hammer to fall, as he ate. Several bites later, he could handle the suspense no longer. He put his fork down and asked, "What do we need to talk about?"

"Were you having bad dreams again last night?" Brynna's face was serious, yet unworried.

David was taken aback by the question, "Uh… no, not that I recall. Why? Did I kick you in my sleep or something?"

Brynna smiled, "Not more than three or four times, you know, the usual. You just weren't sleeping well. You tossed and turned a lot. You were mumbling. I couldn't make out anything, but you were disturbed by something."

By the time she finished speaking, her smile had faded into a look of concern.

David's brow furrowed, "I don't know what to tell you. I feel fine and I don't remember dreaming about anything last night."

"I can think of several things that could be bothering you: becoming lead Admiral in the new Commonwealth revolution, having a baby on board, our own choices about having children, your father's potential betrayal, and probably the most promising suspect, not telling your wife beforehand you were promoting her to the rank of Captain. I still owe you for that one."

Brynna gave him her most menacing face. It wasn't particularly effective as David was able to take another small bite of food while grinning at her. "Good luck getting me back for that one."

"Seriously, David, is it your dad or the whole campaign?" This time Brynna stopped eating, "I need to know."

"If you're this worried, should you have pulled Lexi in here?" David stopped eating again.

"Do I need to?" She countered.

"No, I'm fine, really," David raised his fork cautiously sensing their conversation was far from over.

Brynna decided to change tactics, "What are you going to do about your dad?"

"If he's working for the Commonwealth, I can't let him stay on board," David answered resolutely.

"You know what will happen to him if you put him off the ship," Brynna carefully watched her tone to avoid sounding argumentative. Her voice ended with a pleading timbre.

David put his fork down again. This meal was not progressing quickly. His gut reaction was to demand that she supply him with options in an Admiral to Captain capacity. He caught himself in time to switch gears.

"What other options do I have? If he's working for the Commonwealth, taking him to Drea could push the military to focus their attention there. I could drop him on an uninhabited or low-level planet and hope they don't find him. I can't keep him locked up in the guest quarters for the next however long this takes. My last option is to toss him out an airlock. I really don't care for that possibility."

"That's good to know," Brynna was genuinely relieved, "David, I'm going to give you my recommendation, but it's not a tactical solution."

"Not a tactical solution? What sort of solution is it then?"

"Gut reaction I guess. I think you need to take whatever precautions you feel are necessary, but he needs to stay with us."

"Do you understand what you're asking? We're facing impossible odds, and you want me to keep a spy on the ship. I can't do that. There are too many lives at stake. You know it's not just the fleet, but entire worlds. If he stops us, billions more could die."

David knew they both understood the repercussions of his situation. He was already building the emotional wall to protect himself from the pain of rejecting his father.

Before Brynna could respond any further, the door chimed announcing a visitor. Brynna was slightly grateful for the interruption. Her response to her husband would've been less than calm. She went to the door to answer it as opposed to simply ordering the computer to open it for her. She was thrilled to see the visitor was Stephanie.

Being a physician, Stephanie noticed the signs of stress on Brynna's face right away. "Am I interrupting something?"

Brynna forced a smile and answered, "No, come on in. Are you getting ready to head back to the *Emissary*?"

David conveniently focused on his breakfast rather than answer Stephanie's question. Realizing his rudeness, he stood to greet her and echoed Brynna's answer that she wasn't interrupting anything more important than breakfast.

Stephanie frowned, "You know, Davie, Brynna's a better liar than you are. How did you ever achieve the rank of Captain?"

David's mouth fell open, "Uh… excuse me?"

Stephanie wasn't sure if she should pry into the matter or do what she came to and get out of their way. "I came in here to say my farewells, and I have obviously come at a bad time. Please, forgive me. Nate and Milo are on their way to escort me back to the ship. I can wait in the dining hall and let you know when they arrive."

Brynna made a hasty decision, "Have you had breakfast?"

"No, I was going to wait until I got back to the *Emissary* to eat."

"Why don't you eat with us? I'll grab you something and be right back." Before Stephanie could react, Brynna flew out the door to get her a tray.

Stephanie sighed. She was trying to stay out of whatever was going on, but sensed her presence and input was being unofficially requested. She took a seat at the small table, trying to wait for David to volunteer whatever information was needed.

"Sorry Steph, we were discussing the upcoming difficult task of dealing with my father. I don't think we were in complete agreement about our options," David explained as broadly as possible.

"The translation being, you've come to a decision about him and Brynna disagrees," Stephanie restated his information.

"How did you get that from what I said?" David was quickly feeling outnumbered.

"Do you really want a detailed explanation about human nature and communication intricacies, or do you want to get to the point? Besides you're a lousy liar with your friends," Stephanie wasn't going to waste the few minutes they had alone.

David pulled the napkin from his lap and tossed it on the table. He got up and paced, "I can't let him stay on board the ship. He lied to me twice last night. The Commonwealth sent him in here."

"I saw the look on your face last night when Marissa called you 'Admiral.' He knows how important you are to this mission. As soon as that information gets back to the Commonwealth, they will be all over you. They'll use everything they can to bring you and this ship down. You can't let him go, knowing that information," Stephanie watched her friend pace restlessly. From his behavior, she was reasonably certain he hadn't considered this particular piece of information.

David's first instinct was to accuse her of collaborating with Brynna. Since it was obviously a coincidence, it was a waste of time. "What do you suggest I do with him? Put him in stasis? Should I take Claire's approach and inject him with nanites programmed to incapacitate him if he attempts to access comm channels?"

"Davie, that's your decision. I'm just thinking I would rather keep him close to me. At least if he's close to you, you can keep an eye on him and the enemy can't use him against you," Stephanie explained calmly.

"He IS the enemy!" David objected.

Brynna walked in with the third tray and sat it in front of Stephanie. "I wasn't sure what you preferred so I got a little bit of everything."

Stephanie politely thanked Brynna then responded to David, "Yes, he may be the enemy, but he's a tool they're using against *you*. Use him against them instead. If he's going to betray you, make him work for it. You never know, he could turn on them. You did."

Brynna wisely kept silent. She didn't want David to feel picked on. She sat down and tried to finish her breakfast.

David sat down to finish his cold food. "You know I thought I had this all figured out. Now I don't know what to do."

Brynna smiled softly, "David, I don't want you to do something you'll regret later. He's your father, no matter which side he's on. I love you and I'll respect whatever decision you make. I'm worried about you, not him."

"Thanks, I appreciate that," his smile reflected the genuineness of his words.

Stephanie grinned between bites of food, "Now, that's an honest response."

As the three finished eating, David asked one last question of both women, "What do you both think I should do with him? Give me your best recommendations."

The two women exchanged glances, trying to decide which one should speak first. Brynna went first, "Ask him about the things he lied about and what his intentions are."

"I agree. Give him a chance to explain himself," Stephanie seconded.

Cheyenne interrupted via comms before they could continue any further. "Capt. Alexander, Adm. Weiseman is requesting either the presence of his wife or permission to come aboard."

Brynna glanced at David to see what his preference was. David grinned, "Don't look at me. You're the Captain."

Brynna shook her head at him, "Permission to come aboard. Advise him to meet us in the Captain's quarters."

David started to help Brynna clear the dishes. Brynna stopped him. "David, why don't you finish getting dressed. When you face your dad, you should present a picture of professionalism. Don't give him any doubts about your position—whatever you decide that position is."

David grabbed Brynna's hand. He raised it to his lips and kissed it softly. "You are an amazing wife and an outstanding officer. I'll be right back."

As he disappeared into the bedroom, Brynna turned to Stephanie, "I have a strange question for you before the men get in here."

"Sure, what is it?"

"You, David, and Nate were inseparable in your younger days. Just out of curiosity, how did you and Nate connect instead of you and David? Things like that could go either direction, why did you choose Nate?"

Stephanie smiled. She knew Brynna wasn't jealous, "We're either different enough or similar enough to get on each others' nerves. If we had gotten together, we would've probably killed each other before even a one-year marriage contract expired. Davie is just as bullheaded as I am."

Brynna's face contorted, "I was thinking I can be pretty stubborn too. Why does it work for us and not for you two?"

Stephanie laughed outright, "Stubbornness is either a weapon or a tool. When you use it, and I've seen this in you, it's a tool. When I use it, it's a weapon."

Brynna laughed with her, "Okay, I can see that. I'm glad you and David remained friends."

The door chimed. Brynna continued cleaning up the dishes while Stephanie admitted her husband and their Security Chief into the cabin. The group exchanged greetings and talked small talk until David returned to the room. He was wearing his casual uniform, now adorned with his Admiral's insignia.

Nate grinned, "Should I be calling the room to attention?"

David put his fists on his hips defiantly, "In my own quarters? Are you looking to get thrown out?"

"Careful Nate, he's anxious to throw *somebody* off the ship today. I'm not sure he cares who. I think he just wants to exercise his new rank," Brynna teased.

"What's the matter Davie? Not sleep well?" Nate quipped.

"Am I that transparent, or have you been comparing notes in my brief absence?" David bantered.

The room got deathly quiet as the group looked at each other.

David searched each one's face briefly. His eyes landed on Milo. "Milo, which is it?"

Feeling cornered and picked on, Milo glanced nervously at his commanding officer. Nate grinned and waved at him to answer.

"You're slightly transparent... sir," Milo answered honestly.

The room erupted with laughter. David nodded then shook his head in response to his conflicting emotions, "Remind me never to play poker with you guys."

Milo stepped forward, "Actually, sir, you could pull off a bluff in a poker game, just not personal issues. I've seen you cover your feelings to get a job done. Your feelings were visible, but you did what you needed. You wouldn't be emotionally invested in a poker game."

Nate clapped his hands and laughed. "Nice save, Chief. Good job."

"I'm glad I've got one friend in the bunch," David announced. He looked at Milo, "I'm still not playing poker with you though."

The talk changed gears as Nate reported the last ship was safely away and only the two of them were left. "We're ready to launch as soon as the three of us get back to the ship. How much longer until you're ready to go?"

David looked at Brynna. The answer to that question hinged on how his conversation went with his father.

Nate picked up on the glitch immediately. "I'm sorry, Admiral, I didn't mean to question you. Would it be possible for us to get a peek at your newest crewman before we leave?"

David turned his gaze to Stephanie. "As far as I'm concerned you can, but you should check with the docs first."

Stephanie nodded, "Jason is about to release them from the infirmary. I can go see if Marissa is presentable."

Brynna grabbed the stack of dishes. "I'll go with you. We can drop these on the way."

Nate watched her leave. "I'll give her a few minutes before I follow you."

The second the door closed behind the two women leaving the three men alone Nate whipped around. "What was that about?"

"I told Brynna my dad is a Commonwealth spy, and I'm going to throw him off my ship. She disagrees with my plan, and so does Stephanie," David explained.

Nate pondered the situation, "What did they suggest?

"Brynna thinks he should stay on board. They want me to confront his lies and give him a chance to explain himself."

Milo kept quiet but listened closely.

Nate was as frustrated by the situation as David. "He's a security risk either way. I'm guessing you aren't afraid to let him know you're in charge now?"

"The information came out last night accidentally, so he already knows. I just planned on capitalizing on it this morning. Stephanie thinks we should keep him close to us. She's concerned about the information getting out about my part in this new mission making us an even larger target. How can I possibly keep him on board? If he finds out the missions I gave the rest of the fleet, we'll all be in danger. I can maroon him on a low-level planet, but if they find him, we're back to them using him against me."

Milo stepped forward, "Admiral, you can't be captured. They would do whatever it takes to get the mission information out of you. If they captured him, you can't turn yourself in to save him. Could you really let him die if they get to him?"

David paced aimlessly as he considered the question. In actuality, he wasn't considering his answer as much as he was trying to talk himself into a *particular* answer. He finally turned to face his friends and fellow soldiers, "Why do I feel like I am being remade into something new?"

Before either one could answer, a voice from within answered, "I make all things new. You have a new life and a new purpose now."

David stepped closer to the two men. "I don't suppose… you heard him answer that question, did you?"

Nate and Milo both nodded. Nate put his hand on David's shoulder. "Let's go question a Commonwealth spy. There's no reason why you should go alone. Milo, let the ladies know, we're going to be delayed."

"Yes sir," Milo promptly headed for the infirmary.

****

David and Nate went to the guest quarters. They rang the bell to politely request admittance. When Tristan responded verbally, David unlocked the door. He walked in first with Nate close behind him. Tristan was putting his shoes on. He greeted the two cheerfully.

"Good morning, I was hoping you wouldn't forget about me. I'm getting hungry. To what do I owe the pleasure of meeting with both of you?"

Neither one responded immediately. Tristan put his second shoe on as he studied their serious faces. "This doesn't look promising. What's wrong?"

David folded his arms across his chest, "You've got one chance to tell me the truth this time. How did you find us?"

Tristan studied their faces for a moment. He knew he better lay some cards on the table or he would lose his son forever.

"Adm. Garcia and Adm. Deacons sent me to bring you in, alive. They pulled me off my last undercover assignment, told me what happened and asked me to bring you back safely. They told me you were under the influence of some alien entity or something. They said if I couldn't bring you in, they would have to destroy you and your entire crew. I'm sorry I lied to you, but I had to see the situation for myself. I didn't want them to destroy you either. I know I haven't been around much recently, but you're still my son and I care about you."

Nate jumped in with an equally gruff tone. "What are your intentions, now that you've seen the situation?"

"I'm not sure I've seen the situation to my satisfaction yet. Where is this alien entity? I haven't seen any evidence of him… her… it," Tristan countered.

David jumped in again. "What are you going to do if you don't like what you see?"

"I'm not sure, yet," Tristan answered blandly.

Nate fired another question rapidly, "You didn't answer the Admiral's first question. How did you find us?"

"Ensign Ryder's sister, Iokina Malo had a tracker implanted in her. They gave me the tracker so I could follow her until she hopefully led me to you. I hired some locals to put her family in danger, hoping you would come to their rescue. I wanted to watch you from a distance in case whatever has infected you is contagious or something. And before you ask, I had nothing to do with that thing in the mine."

Tristan slumped into the corner of the sofa. He knew this was the point where David would either believe him or he wouldn't. There was nothing he could do to convince him. He looked up suddenly, "By the way, that was a nice touch putting the tracker in one of my men. I was confused, but only for about an hour."

David's eyes narrowed, "Give me one good reason why I shouldn't shove you out an airlock."

Tristan knew not to play the "but I'm your father" card.

"Son, I'm not trying to be your enemy. I'm trying to understand what's happening and to save your life. That's it. That's all I have. If I hadn't cooperated, their intentions were to lock me up and charge me with treason. I know I hadn't committed treason, and I didn't understand why you would've either. I agreed to do this, not because of their threats, but because I needed to understand this and see it for myself."

"Did you even consider what sort of options I would be faced with if you found me?" David wanted his father to understand the seriousness of his situation.

"I know I'm a security risk to whatever you're doing. I hope the airlock isn't a real option. I hope you won't do that just for the sake of your mother and sister, if not for yourself."

Tristan toyed with revealing another important piece of information. Disclosing the information would add to his appearance of being genuine. The problem with this particular piece of information was it would prove he had lied one more time and this information was older than David. It was far more deep-seated and even treacherous in nature. If he didn't present it properly, he was certain it would earn him a trip out the airlock.

"Given the information you now have about me, I can't let you leave and pass it on to the Commonwealth. I know you don't know much, but it's enough to cause us problems. If I turn you loose, there's every chance they *will* attempt to execute you, to get to me," David wanted his father to see exactly what he was dealing with.

"This may seem like weakness to you, but I can't let that happen. I was going to. I was prepared to throw you off my ship this morning and let you face whatever they decided to do to you," David continued.

"What stopped you?" Tristan asked. His face was devoid of emotion.

"Arni did. He reminded me that I am not in the Commonwealth Interstellar Force anymore, and the rules are different in his Force."

"What *have* you decided to do with me?" Tristan asked. His tone lacking emotion.

"My options are throw you off my ship, put you in stasis, allow you to stay aboard but somewhat restricted, or maroon you on a low-level planet. I've ruled out spacing and sending you to where I sent mom. I'm leaning toward the stasis option if you must know," David folded his arms across his chest. He stared hard at his father.

Tristan looked at Nate, "What is your role in this discussion? Are you here for moral support or muscle?"

"I'm here for whatever he needs, muscle and moral support included. If you were wanting to know my vote, I voted for spacing," Nate's face revealed a slightly sadistic glee at making sure his point was clear.

Tristan turned his attention back to David. "Son, I didn't come here to cause you problems. I came here to try and understand what's going on. I'll do whatever you want me to do. If you want me to leave and disappear, I can do that. I have credit stashes hidden on various worlds. I can stay hidden for a long time. I'm not a young man anymore. I was getting close to looking at retirement, or at least retiring from the field. I suppose I'll willingly submit to going into stasis, if that's what you really want."

"What I want? This doesn't have anything to do with what I want! Do you think this is easy for me? There are a lot of lives depending on me and the decisions I make. One mistake and we're all dead! I'm trying to do what's best for everyone, not what's easiest for me," David paced, waving his arms about emphatically.

Tristan jumped to his feet. "Do you think this was an easy choice for me? I could let them arrest and charge me with treason and hope my son, the little boy whose backside I used to dust when he acted out, would come swooping in to rescue me. My other option was to hunt down my only son like a criminal and bring him to justice. What would you have done?"

David and his father cast angry glares at each other. Tristan finally broke the awkward silence. "I did what they wanted me to do. I hunted you down. What happens next is up to you. I'm no longer part of the equation."

David blinked. It wasn't an emotional display, but it did reveal a side of things he hadn't considered. He glanced at Nate then back at his father. "You are a big part of the equation. I'll let you know presently what I decide," he nodded at Nate and the two moved to the door.

Just before David stepped outside he added, "For the record, spacing is not on the list of possibilities, even if you betray me."

The two stopped in the corridor to discuss the situation. Nate was the first to speak, "You know he's playing you, right?"

David nodded, "Yeah, that much was pretty clear. He gave me just enough to be believable."

"Are you gonna stick him in stasis?" Nate asked.

"Not yet. I'm going to give him a chance to try and see things our way. If he proves to be too much of a risk, then I'll definitely do that," David relented.

"Are you going to feed him some breakfast?" Nate grinned as he asked.

Seeing Nate was trying to lighten the mood, David scowled, "I decided not to shove him out an airlock and gave him a place to stay. Now, you want me to feed him too? Just how far am I supposed to go here?"

Nate shrugged, "Do you really want him to get cranky from a lack of food?"

"He's not going to bother me if he gets cranky. He's locked in his cabin…actually, he's not. Computer, secure the door to the guest quarters. Door is to be opened by ship's crew only."

The computer beeped its acknowledgment.

David and Nate headed into the Dining Hall. They found Lexi dining with Thane and Aulani. David pulled Lexi aside. "Lt. Flint, I need a favor. When you're done eating, can you take a tray to my father in the guest quarters? Let him know I'm allowing him to stay on board for now, but he is confined to quarters until further notice. He was trying to play me earlier, and I need you to do some observations of him. Let me know what your professional opinion is. He was sent here as a spy."

David heard Lexi take a deep breath as she prepared to launch into a litany of questions. He raised his hand quickly to stop her. "Uh-uh, we've already beaten this topic to death. I will make an appointment to discuss it further this afternoon if you like, but not now. I have work to do."

Lexi wanted to object, but her gut told her to stifle the objection. "Yes, Captain. I'll take care of it and I'll put you on my schedule for this afternoon."

David scowled in return, "Thanks. By the way, he found out I'm an Admiral last night. It's time to adjust the rank titles."

Lexi squinted slightly. Was this his way of warning her to tread lightly, or was the timing coincidental?

"Yes Admiral," her tone clearly indicated they had a lot to discuss.

David and Nate moved into the hall toward the infirmary. Nate chuckled as soon as they were clear of the dining hall. "That one's certainly a live wire. I'm sure keeping her at bay isn't easy."

David shrugged, "She is tenacious about doing her job, but she's learned when to back off."

Nate shook his head, "Henry's not tenacious, he's just sneaky. He gets in your head before you even know he's in the room."

David shook his head, "I think I prefer my psych to yours. I don't like sneaky."

"I'm not so sure. There is something to be said for his subtlety. He gets my head fixed before anyone even knows there's anything wrong with it," Nate responded.

David stopped walking for a second. "Maybe he could give Lexi some sneaky pointers. The whole ship knows when I have a problem even before I know it."

Nate laughed again, "I'll suggest it to him."

****

David and Nate walked into the infirmary and greeted Jake and Marissa. Marissa introduced Nate to Jacob Alexander Holden.

Nate shook his head. "You guys are never going to be able to live with Davie now. He's gotten a promotion and a kid named after him all in one day. His head's going to be so swollen, he'll never fit through the doorways."

Jake grinned at the thought, "His head can't get too big, Adm. Weiseman. We named Jax after both him and our new Captain. He has to share the honor with his wife."

Nate and Stephanie took one last turn at holding the precious baby boy while David checked on Marissa.

"Lt. Holden, are you doing alright? Is there anything you or Jake need?"

"No sir, we're both fine. We're tired, but…"

"But what Lieutenant?"

"This is all so surreal. I never expected to have a baby. I was afraid those men were going to kill you. I was afraid I was going to deliver Jax alone in that mine tunnel. I thought Jake was going to miss the birth of his son. I'm so relieved and so grateful," Marissa teared up.

"Pateras is watching out for us, even before we knew it. When you died, I couldn't bring myself to ask him to send you back to us, as much as I wanted to. Looking back, I'm glad he didn't wait for me to ask."

"Captain, did I mess up last night when I called you Admiral? I just got my messages this morning," Marissa asked.

"It's fine. I handled it," David assured her, "we're going back to the newer ranks."

"Is your father still on board?"

"Yes, he's confined to the guest quarters until we're safely underway."

"Confined? Why?"

"The Commonwealth sent him to find us. He's here to get us arrested."

"But he helped us in the mine. Why would he help us if he's here to arrest us?" Marissa was startled by the revelation.

"He says he wanted to understand what was going on for himself. I suppose it would be easier to understand if we were alive and well," David explained.

"And you don't believe him?"

"Only partially. I am allowing him to stay, but only because the risks of letting him leave are greater than letting him stay." David didn't want to go into detail. He knew she wouldn't ask too many questions.

Marissa asked one last question, "Is it alright if I go in and thank him for his help?"

David mulled over the situation. Was his father a hardened soldier who might be capable of harming a woman and baby? If it was information he wanted, he would get little from such a confrontation. Was he desperate enough to attack Marissa? He doubted it, but he wasn't about to risk her life or Jax's life based on a maybe.

"After we've engaged the tachyon drive, you can go in. Take someone with you. I doubt he would harm you, but I'm not willing to take that chance."

"Yes sir. Thank you, sir."

Marissa retrieved her baby. She and Jake excused themselves and headed to their quarters. David and Brynna escorted Nate, Stephanie and Milo to the airlock. They exchanged fond farewells and best wishes before going their separate ways.

David and Brynna moved to David's office to discuss several matters. When they reached a specific point in their discussion, David hailed Jake and Marissa's cabin.

"This is Chief Holden," came a tired reply.

"Chief, I'm sorry to bother you. I need to have a staff meeting and fairly soon. I need you and Marissa to attend this one meeting. What time would be good for the three of you?"

"Is—uh four hours from now too late?" Jake asked.

"No, four hours is acceptable. Get some rest, Chief. Sorry to disturb you," David hated doing that, but this was important.

****

Four hours later, the staff meeting convened in the gymnasium. David walked in last. Braxton noticed his absence and watched for him to arrive. He called the room to attention the second David stepped in.

David made his way to the front of the room before releasing the crew. Marissa did the best she could to come to attention while cradling a sleeping infant. Seeing her attempt, David smiled slightly. She was a good officer. The crew took their seats and David started into the heart of the meeting.

"Crew of the *Evangeline*, you have conducted yourselves expertly over the last few days and I am quite proud of each of you. We have several changes coming in the near future. First, we are going on the offensive. Second, this is now an Admiral's flagship which is going to mean some changes. Third, we have a dangerous situation on board. Because of these three situations, our mission is going to be 'need to know' only. The command staff may tell the navigator to plot a course to a specific location, and it might be only one leg of the journey. Our mission details are only to be discussed behind closed doors, not in any common areas.

297

"As most of you know, my father is aboard. He is a Commonwealth Infantry soldier. He is a spy. I've allowed him to stay on board because I believe Arni has plans for him. I don't plan on giving him any mission information until I know he can be trusted. I will put him in stasis if necessary. Right now, he is confined to quarters, but I will release him after we are underway. This is why our mission parameters are not to be discussed unless necessary and only in private. He is aware of my newly established rank of Admiral, so that is no longer a guarded secret. The rank of officers aboard the *Evangeline* is not privileged information but the rank of the others is. I trust we are clear on this matter? On a related note, just a reminder Adm. Deacons is our enemy. My Uncle Rob is to be considered loyal to the Commonwealth and we are not in touch with him."

David did a quick visual sweep of the room. He was met with serious stares.

"Now to a lighter matter. As I mentioned there will be several changes. A new chain of command was established among the Captains of the Explorer Fleet and new officers were commissioned as admirals, commodores, and Captains. The crews below the rank of commander were not advanced. I advised the Commander of each ship to promote officers from within as they deemed appropriate. Capt. Alexander and I have agreed to two promotions and advancements in position. Captain, if you would join me."

Brynna stood beside him as requested.

David ordered, "Lt. Cmdr. Flint, please report to your Captain."

Braxton reported as ordered. Brynna ordered him to do an "about face," Braxton complied. His face never showing any hint of emotion.

David reported, "Lt. Cmdr. Braxton Flint, you are hereby promoted to the rank of commander and moved to the position of First Officer of the *Evangeline*, the flagship of the Liontari Revolution. Lt. Flint, would you care to assist in the pinning on of the new rank insignia?"

Lexi came forward and pinned the new ranks on her husband. Under normal circumstances, she would have been thrilled and excited. Today, she wasn't sure if this was real or a treasonous game.

Braxton turned about again, saluted Brynna and was dismissed. As tradition, the crew applauded the promotion. They wondered who the second promotion was for.

David quickly answered that question for them.

"The next promotion is for one who is responsible not only to the ship's Captain but is also responsible to the Lead Admiral of our newly formed fleet. As Lead Admiral I am responsible for eleven ships and their crews. The entire crew of this ship now bear part of that responsibility. The entire crew may deserve a promotion, but this individual's responsibilities have increased exponentially. Chief Jacob Holden, report to the Captain."

Jake followed the same procedure as Braxton. David continued once Jake faced the crew.

"Chief Holden, your position as Security Chief is advanced to the position of Fleet Chief of Security and your rank is advanced as exponentially as your responsibilities. You are hereby advanced to the rank of Ensign. Lieutenant Holden, if you can find a volunteer to hold Jax…"

Several were quick to volunteer. Aulani was the closest and got the pleasure. Marissa eagerly came forward and tried to hold back more tears as she placed the new rank on her husband's uniform. She wondered when these stupid hormonal tears would stop. She had cried more in the last year than in her entire life. It was getting old.

Following a robust round of applause, Jake was released to return to his seat. The thing that pleased David the most was the hearty sound of approval among the crew. After Jake's betrayal of them on Romajin, it took time for the crew to forgive him. He was glad to know they had. Now Jake should know beyond the shadow of a doubt he was forgiven. Trust was a hard thing to earn and even harder to earn back.

"Last couple of things, as I mentioned earlier, my father, Capt. Tristan Alexander is being kept aboard to prevent what he already knows from falling into enemy hands and to prevent them from using him against me.

"One of my goals is to introduce him to Pateras in the hopes that he will join us. The other is to keep him from advertising our missions and getting us captured.

"Please feel free to discuss past missions with him. You can even discuss Drea, but not in relation to our families. We have not been back to Drea. We did not take our families to Drea. We sent our families into hiding or took them someplace safe. We don't need to mention Drea in the present tense. He doesn't need to know we have an ongoing relationship with them. If you have doubts about discussing something, then don't discuss it.

"Starting tomorrow morning, I will release him from the guest quarters. He will be allowed access to public areas only, such as the gym, infirmary, and dining facilities. Engineering, the shuttle bay and the bridge are strictly off-limits. If you have questions or concerns, see me in my office later today.

"Lt. Holden and Ensign Holden are on leave. This is going to mean an increase in duty shifts and when the Lieutenant returns to duty, it may mean some odd shifts until Jax is older. With his addition to our crew, I will expect Lt. Holden to need help caring for Jax when she returns to duty. I'm not making this an order, but whoever can volunteer to watch him, please let her know. It should not be just one person. We need to share so that everyone has sufficient rest and relaxation.

"The last thing on the agenda is we are launching in two hours. Lt. Cmdr. Adams, I want you at the helm. Lt. Ryder do a practice simulation of underwater maneuvers with him prior to launch and be on the bridge during departure. Lt. Adams, you are on navigation. Capt. Alexander, you will take us out and Cmdr. Flint, please be present on the bridge as well. Lt. Flint join Lt. Cmdr. Dominick in engineering. We're going to be quite vulnerable during departure, so I want a full crew complement available for launch."

Jake raised his hand. "Admiral, do I need to be on weapons during departure?"

David admired his conscientiousness. "No Ensign, I will be covering your station. Any other questions?"

The room was quiet.

"In that case, everyone who can, stow the chairs and prepare for launch. Dismissed."

The crew took a moment to congratulate Braxton and Jake on their promotions before removing their chairs as ordered. David shook Jake's hand firmly. He expressed his observation about the crew's support and forgiveness, in case Jake hadn't picked up on it. He had, but he thanked the Admiral for pointing it out.

David turned to offer his congratulations to Braxton, but his new Commander beat him to it.

"Admiral, thank you for the vote of confidence and the promotion."

David smiled and shook his hand. "You deserved it, Commander. You've done an outstanding job over the last few months. Were you interested in the command path?"

"I wasn't initially, but I've been rethinking it recently. I think I am, sir. My skills as a structural engineer aren't going to be as useful in our current situation."

David smiled, "Depending on how this campaign goes, you may get that chance."

David's eyes landed on Lexi who was standing quietly at his side, "Lt. Flint, we talked about setting up a meeting this afternoon. Would you be available shortly after we reach tachyon speeds?"

"Yes sir. On another matter, I took your father some lunch about an hour ago. Would you like me to see to his dinner this evening as well?"

"No, I want to talk to him again and tell him what to expect. You are welcome to go with me if you wish to evaluate his interactions with me… or mine with him."

David knew Lexi struggled with feelings of uncertainty about her role among the ship's crew. He wanted to be certain she knew she was needed as a psychologist, not just as a relief engineer. He needed her in both capacities.

CH 16 - GETTING SITUATED

FAREWELL TO ZULIMAR

Two hours later, the ship was getting ready to depart. Brynna took her place in the command chair. She glanced anxiously at David. The weapons console was angled toward the command chair. To avoid any mental confusion, the helm and navigation faced forward but the other stations angled inward, so orders could be heard clearly and acted on hastily. David smiled and gave her a subtle wink. Brynna was trained to handle the situation, but it was like her field medic training. You know what you're supposed to do, but you aren't necessarily practiced at doing it.

Braxton placed himself at the commander's usual station. He was in the same predicament as Brynna, only Lexi wasn't there to give him a reassuring smile.

As everyone settled into their positions, Brynna called out, "Ensign Ryder, hail the dock master."

The dock master answered, and Brynna addressed him, "This is the SS *Talon*, requesting permission to launch."

The reply came back, "Standby *Talon*, we have three ships ahead of you for departure."

Brynna responded casually, "*Talon* standing by."

Brynna waited quietly for a solid minute. Something was off. She glanced at David, "Anything on long-range scans?"

"Nothing for now," David replied. His gaze stayed focused on the scanners.

"Three ships departing right now seems rather odd. This colony isn't that busy. Cmdr. Flint, get us into the colony's computer database. I want to know what's happening internally. Ensign Ryder, hail Mr. Rune," Brynna was getting concerned.

Another minute passed, Braxton scowled, "Captain! I can no longer access the colony's database or security feeds."

"We've been found out. Navigation plot our course off the planet and out of the system. Don't forget, after an underwater docking maneuver, we have to toast the hull. Prepare to release docking clamps manually. Admiral get scans of local traffic to the helm."

Aulani jumped in, "Captain, I've got Mr. Rune!

"Put him through!" Brynna ordered.

"Capt. Doherty, your ship has been flagged for investigation. You are to stand down and prepare to be boarded. You and your crew will be detained until cleared by CIF officials. Two ships are currently in route here to investigate your situation," Neal was hastily pressing buttons and trying to look as official as possible, "any attempt to leave this facility will result in punitive action."

Brynna's eyes narrowed, "Mr. Rune, I understand your situation, really I do. I feel I must inform you though that we are leaving—*now*. I suggest you secure your side of that airlock within the next thirty seconds, or your colony is going to spring a leak. Are we clear?"

Neal finally punched the appropriate control. His face displaying an ample amount of frustration. "Alright! The airlock is closing now."

"Release the docking clamps, Mr. Rune, or our lasers will have to start punching holes until we cut through the struts."

Neal pressed the controls. The sounds of the clamps releasing could be heard through the frame of the ship.

Brynna gave Neal a syrupy smile, "We appreciate your facility's hospitality, Mr. Rune. We'll be sure to send out a glowing recommendation to all our friends. Don't send any ships after us. They could get hurt."

Brynna cut the communication. She glanced at Aulani, who was busy pressing buttons of her own.

Brynna turned to Aulani again, "Ensign Ryder, report!"

"I have a secondary message from Mr. Rune. He says the Commonwealth sent them a message to hold us here. He gave the coordinates of two ships headed this way."

"Show me!" Brynna barked.

A three-dimensional hologram of their current location appeared and shifted outward to show the entire planetary system. Two flashing symbols could be seen on course for the colony's location from the outer edges of the system. The colony was abuzz with traffic, some were official vehicles, some were civilian craft. It was difficult to know whether the vehicles were capable of air, surface, underwater maneuvers or some combination of the three.

"Helm, fire maneuvering thrusters. Move us away from the colony and into deeper water. Navigation, show me a display of the deep-sea trenches in the area," Brynna ordered.

Laura pulled up the display of the underwater landscape. Brynna tied her console into the projection, "Plot our course through here."

The path Brynna indicated lit up on the display, "As soon as we clear that last mountain range submerge to a depth of 2400 ft."

The land mass fell away as the ship headed out to sea.

David detected three vehicles giving chase. He wasted no time in updating Brynna. "We've got three vehicles converging on our location. Right now, they're on the surface. Scanning to see if they have submersion capabilities."

Before he could conduct the scan, the vehicles submerged. He continued to scan the vehicles for any information he could find out before they were surprised by something. "The vehicles are submersible, still scanning."

A laser blast shot past the bow of the ship. David scowled. His scanner suddenly posted a warning: "Laser Cannon Capabilities." Why was the information coming through seconds too late? He didn't waste a lot of time pondering one of the unfortunate mysteries of the universe. "Captain, they do have laser cannons, and they aren't afraid to use them. Still scanning."

Brynna's face remained neutral yet focused. "How much longer until we make it to those trenches?"

Laura promptly answered, "Three minutes and forty seconds."

Brynna punched a button on her console and hailed Lazaro. "Engineering, get ready to activate the camouflage net to mimic the terrain on my command. Keep the comm channel open. Keep us close to the bottom as the terrain changes but leave me a little wiggle room."

Aulani interjected, "Captain, they're hailing us. They're ordering us to come to the surface, surrender our ship, and prepare to be boarded."

About that time a second laser blast crossed their bow. Brynna gripped the arms of her chair. "Helm, increase speed to maximum."

Jason wanted to request that Thane take over the helm. He was accustomed to being a relief pilot. Thane was the expert. Jason was too involved in manning the controls to take his eyes off them.

David finally got information from his scans *before* he needed it. "Captain, they have sonic blasters and they're preparing to use them."

Brynna grinned, "Oh, they better not wake the baby. How much further until we reach the deeper channels?"

"Two minutes forty-five seconds," Laura updated.

"Jason, take evasive action. Engineering, raise shields," Brynna ordered.

"Those ships will be in firing range in thirty seconds," David announced.

Brynna tapped her ship-wide comm control. "All hands prepare for possible impact!"

****

Hearing the warning, Cheyenne thought the Admiral's father, being unfamiliar with the ship, might not know where to secure himself. She raced to his quarters. The ship aggressively altered its course to avoid being hit by one of the sonic blasts. The inertial dampeners reduced the effect of their movements, but the aggressiveness was impossible to completely counter. Cheyenne couldn't get to Tristan's cabin as quickly and as efficiently as she hoped.

Every major room had seats mounted on the walls with restraints to keep them from being thrown out of the seat.

Jake and Marissa put young Jax into his crib, which was specifically designed for space travel. When activated, the crib placed the infant in stasis and covered him with a protective shield. The crib generated a magnetic field to hold itself in place on the deck. Marissa and Jake jumped into their seats and fastened in. Marissa's eyes locked onto the sleeping baby in the crib.

As the ship rocked dangerously, Thane stayed at Jason's side giving him support and advice until the first of the three ships reached firing range.

Brynna realized Thane hadn't secured himself. "Lt. Ryder! Move to the auxiliary station and get strapped in!"

Thane's chair was a spare carried onto the bridge and wasn't even secured to the deck plates. Thane paused to offer one more quick suggestion before moving as ordered. Seeing him hesitate, Brynna wasted no time in getting his attention.

"Thane! Move! Now!"

Thane stood as Jason jerked the controls to turn tightly around a rock formation. The movement knocked him to the floor. He righted himself and moved toward the assigned station. One of the approaching ships got a lock on the ship with its sonic cannon. It fired. Jason swung the ship enough to miss most of the blast. A vibration resonated through the ship as it hit the outer wing. Thane grabbed onto the nearest pieces of furniture as he worked his way toward the auxiliary station. Another ship fired. The shields protected the ship from damage. It did push the ship downward so that the inertial dampeners were unable to compensate quickly enough. Thane was thrown backward and hit the edge of the engineering station. He collapsed unconscious onto the deck.

Thane's wife was directly across from him and cried out when he fell. Ensign Ryder clawed at her restraints to go to her husband's side.

Brynna quickly and firmly ordered, "Ensign Ryder keep your seat or more people will get hurt!"

****

Tristan was quite familiar with safety equipment and procedures aboard space faring vessels. He secured himself to the seat closest to the cabin entrance. When Cheyenne came through the door, the ship lurched. Tristan reached his hand out and grabbed Cheyenne's arm. His grasp prevented her petite frame from flying across the room. He guided her to the seat on the other side of him. Cheyenne turned to climb into the seat when the sonic blast hit the ship. The jolt threw her into the air, hitting her head on the way back down. The blow caused her to lose consciousness. Tristan pulled her small frame into the seat and fastened her in.

****

As soon as Brynna was sure the Ensign was going to follow her orders, she issued another for Aulani.

"Check in with all personnel for injuries."

Jason's attention was divided between Thane and trying to evade the pursuing crafts. He kept glancing toward Thane. Brynna knew she needed to make a change and make it fast. "All stop, fire reverse thrusters. Admiral, fire lasers at their engines when they pass us. Jason, on my command, get out of your seat and tend to Lt. Ryder. Cmdr. Flint, you have the bridge."

Braxton was startled. He didn't have objections to being in command, but with two superior officers on the bridge, he wasn't sure what sort of game they were playing. Knowing the gravity of the situation, he didn't pause to question it. As the three ships overshot the *Evangeline*, there was a moment of calm as David fired the lasers at the three ships giving them reason to pause before returning too quickly.

During the brief lull, Brynna took the helm and Braxton moved to the Captain's chair. Jason always carried a portable scanner with him. He scanned Thane quickly. His face went from concerned to gravely apprehensive. He glanced at Braxton. "I need some equipment from the infirmary before he can be moved."

David glanced at Braxton, "They're coming back around, twenty seconds to firing range."

Braxton didn't like the command he had to issue, but he issued it with conviction. "Doc, strap into the auxiliary station. Thane will have to wait thirty more seconds."

Aulani's eyes were glued on her injured husband. She understood why they weren't tending to his injuries, but it was no less painful for her to watch.

Jason clenched his jaw and did as he was told. Braxton leaned forward preparing his next moves.

"All ahead full."

Braxton put the engineering displays on the control panel. "Laz, I'm going to cut power to certain systems. Do NOT restore power to those systems. Navigation show me the upcoming landscape."

Laura put up the display as ordered. Braxton saw something that got his attention. "Show depth markers."

The requested data appeared on the display. Braxton looked relieved. Fifteen seconds later, the bottom dropped out from under the ship. Five seconds after that, the three ships came directly at them firing their sonic cannons. All three ships hit the ship squarely. Braxton reduced the shield strength manually. The ships fired again. He ordered Brynna to kill the forward thrusters one side at a time. He gave her one last unusual order, "Make them flicker then go out."

The sonic blasts were having only a minimal effect on the ship. The biggest concern with the blasts was that it could slow the ship down enough for their adversaries to take out their propulsion with the lasers. In the water, the lasers had to be short range use. Knowing most people didn't know the capabilities of this ship, Braxton decided he could fake a damaged ship fairly well.

Understanding what Braxton was trying to do Brynna kept the thrusters firing in an erratic manner. In actuality, she was maneuvering the ship into a particular position. With the help of the sonic blasts, the ship was pushed downward. It sank at an awkward angle. The ships stopped following the *Evangeline* at eighteen hundred feet and circled cautiously overhead, never venturing any deeper.

The ship continued to drift downward, the thrusters firing in their random pattern. Braxton dropped the shields. He ordered Brynna to extend the landing props. At twenty-three hundred feet the ship settled onto an underwater plateau. A cloud of sand and debris scattered upward as the thrusters fired again. Braxton initiated the camouflage net causing the ship to disappear into the cloud of debris. As the debris settled, the three ships scanned nothing more than a ledge giving way to a deep-sea channel. As soon as they were momentarily safe, Braxton looked at Jason. "Go get what you need, quickly."

Jason nodded, "I'll need help getting him to the infirmary."

"You'll have it as soon as you get back," Braxton assured him. He didn't like seeing Thane lying so motionless. He hated ordering Jason away from rendering aid to their fallen comrade.

Jason disappeared and headed to the infirmary. Braxton turned his attention to the bridge crew. "Admiral transfer firing controls to communications. Help Jason get Thane to the infirmary. Laura watch the scanners. I need to know if they find us."

A heavy silence settled on the bridge as everyone waited for Jason to return. Braxton realized Brynna had asked for a report from the other crew members. He glanced at Aulani who was trying her hardest to stay focused.

"Ensign Ryder, any reports of injuries?"

Aulani was staring helplessly at Thane.

"Ensign Ryder! Report! Has everyone reported in?"

Aulani forced her eyes off Thane and onto Braxton.

"Jake and Marissa reported with no injuries. Cheyenne hasn't reported in, and the Captain's father doesn't have access to comms. Engineering reports no injuries."

The Doc bounded onto the bridge. He glanced at Laura, expecting her assistance. Instead, David came and knelt beside the two. Sensing the Doc was rattled about Thane's injuries, David asked before taking initiative. "Doc, what do you want me to do?"

Jason was focused on placing a device around Thane's neck to stabilize it. He held off answering until his patient's neck was secure.

"Get that stretcher ready to go. Be ready to activate the stasis field on my order."

Aulani was suddenly more alarmed than before. "Stasis field? Doctor, how bad is it? Is he… Is Thane…" Tears formed in her eyes.

Jason mercifully answered, "He's alive, but I have to stabilize him for transport. The tissue is swelling around his injury. If it continues to swell, it could cause irreparable damage to his spinal cord. If we're knocked around anymore, it could cause more damage. I'm putting him in stasis for his own good."

Aulani stared at the Doctor blankly. The words weren't making it through the haze. "I don't understand."

Jason approached her station. He took her hand and softly explained again, "Aulani, Thane is alive, but I have to put him in stasis to protect him."

David helped Jason get Thane onto the stretcher. They activated the stasis field and carried him off the bridge.

****

The two entered the infirmary to find Tristan standing next to an unconscious Cheyenne lying on a bed. Tristan was glad to see the doctor, but one look at Thane gave him pause. Thane's condition was far worse than Cheyenne's.

David said nothing to his father while he and Jason secured Thane in a bed with the stasis field activated and a restraining field in place. Jason didn't want another jolt to throw Thane out of the bed. Jason programmed the computer to do a thorough scan of the young lieutenant.

While the computer was conducting its scan, the two turned their attention to Tristan and Cheyenne. Her vital signs were already displayed on the screen behind her bed. Jason took note of them on the way into the room long enough to see that she was stable and kept going with Thane. With Thane secured, he approached Tristan and asked, "What happened?"

"She came in as the first jolt hit. I caught her and pulled her toward the seat to strap in. The second blast hit before she was in the seat. She hit her head. I secured her in until everything calmed down, then I carried her in here."

Cheyenne moved and moaned. Her eyes opened slowly. Jason ran a scan on her. Scowling he held his hand in front of her. "Cheyenne, how many fingers am I holding up?"

Cheyenne forced her eyes to open and focus on his hand. "Two," Jason looked relieved until Cheyenne spoke again, "but I'm seeing four of them."

Now the Doc was frowning again. "Remind me to be careful how I word that next time. Cheyenne do you remember what happened to you?"

"Can I close my eyes to talk to you?"

"Sure, why?"

"Because I don't know which one of you to look at and it makes my head hurt worse."

Jason patted her arm. "That's fine. Close your eyes, but I need you to stay awake and tell me what happened."

"I went to the guest quarters to check on the Admiral's father, and the ship got hit as I walked in the door. Mr. Alexander caught me and kept me from falling. While he was helping me get to my seat, we got hit again and I flew backward. I hit… something, the wall maybe? That's the last thing I remember."

David pulled his father aside while the Doc worked on Cheyenne. "How did you get out of your cabin?"

"I pressed her hand against the access panel."

David scowled.

Tristan mistook his scowl for disapproval. "That young woman needed medical attention, Davie. What was I supposed to do? I don't have any computer access to call for help. She was unconscious, so voice access wasn't an option. I did the only thing I could."

"You did the right thing. I wasn't accusing you of anything," David defended himself.

"That's not what your face was saying," Tristan retorted.

"Don't pretend to know what I'm thinking. You don't know who or what I am anymore. I'm not that wide-eyed kid you left behind."

David was getting distracted too easily and he knew it, "I'm sorry. I shouldn't have snapped at you. You did exactly what I would have done. I was just curious. I also realized we have a security weakness."

"A security weakness? Davie, what is my status here? Am I a prisoner, a guest, a refugee? What am I?"

"This isn't a discussion I'm prepared to have right now. I need to notify the bridge of the Ensign's status… and yours," David headed out the door.

Tristan followed him into the corridor, "You need to notify the bridge? What kind of Admiral are you? I don't know how you ever made Captain," Tristan was not over his imagined slight.

David stopped and turned to face his father. Stepping uncomfortably close to him, he answered the man's accusation. "I made Captain because I trained my people to do their jobs and do them well. I can't expect them to do their jobs if I'm going to withhold the information they were told to gather. I'm going to be the same type of Admiral. I'm not going to set my people up for failure."

Tristan glared at his son, "So, what am I, a guest or a prisoner?"

"I don't have time for this. There are lives at stake. If we survive the next few hours, we can discuss it then," David snapped, "Don't make me lock you up again."

"You think you can take your old man?" Tristan challenged.

David's demeanor changed, "Don't make me try, please."

Tristan was confused by David's change in temperament. "Do you want me to go back to my quarters?"

David stepped back to give his father some space. "See if the Doc needs any help. I've got his nurse tied up on navigation."

Tristan's face contorted, "I'll do whatever you think is best, but I'm better at navigation than… nursing."

David searched his father's eyes. Tristan appeared sincere. Maybe it was time to give him a little trust. Something told him to wait a little bit longer. "I'll give your request some thought. See if the Doc needs help until then."

There was a hint of fight in his father's eyes, but the man being a lifelong soldier, responded appropriately.

"Yes Admiral," Tristan turned on his heel and headed into the infirmary.

****

David raced to the Bridge and his station. He reported to Braxton, "Commander, Lt. Ryder is safely tucked into a stasis chamber until the Doc can study his situation more thoroughly. Ensign Dominick is also in the infirmary with a concussion and is being treated. Capt. Alexander is assisting the Doc… for now. He did offer his services as a Navigator if the Doc needs Laura."

Cmdr. Flint gave the admiral a stern look. Surely, he wasn't seriously considering giving his father access to the Bridge. Braxton touched his comm unit. "Lt. Cmdr. Adams, how long until you have Ensign Dominick patched up?"

There was a brief pause while Jason glanced at the equipment displays. "Her treatment will be completed in approximately ten to fifteen minutes, but I want to keep her here and resting for a few more hours to be certain she's fine."

"Understood. Doc, get her treated and get everyone secured. We're going to leave this position and get into space as soon as we can. We can't be here when those two ships arrive."

"Yes Commander, I'll notify you as soon as we're secure down here. Let Ensign Ryder know her husband is safely in the stasis chamber, but I can't proceed with treatment until the ship is out of danger." Jason spoke with far more confidence than he felt. He glanced nervously at Tristan as he closed the comm link. He muttered under his breath, "If I can treat him at all."

Tristan, looking equally concerned, asked, "Not that I know that much about medicine, but what's his situation and how bad is it?"

Jason moved out of Cheyenne's range of hearing to answer him.

"It's bad. The bones in his neck are broken and because we weren't able to stabilize him immediately, the added trauma of rolling around on the deck and the delayed treatment allowed swelling to begin. There are bone fragments pressing into his spinal cord. I'm not entirely sure I have the equipment necessary to work on him here. If I tried to do this while we're being fired on, I could kill him. Pateras may be the only one who can help him."

Tristan was only vaguely familiar with the crew and had no emotional attachments to any of them except for David and Brynna. His attachment to Brynna was only because of her importance to David. David was almost a stranger to him. He looked at the young man lying on the treatment bed with the stasis field shrouding his visage. Something in his heart ached for the young man's predicament. "Can you contact this… Pateras?"

"I've been talking to him since it happened."

"Wait. What? How?" Tristan hadn't seen him using comms or conversing with anyone.

"I've been talking to him… uh, mentally I guess you could say. He hears our thoughts. He… uh… He's always listening. So far, he's told me to wait and trust him. He says that a lot," Jason scowled as he looked down at Thane.

Looking back at Tristan he added, "Sometimes it's hard to set aside my faith in the sciences in favor of trusting someone who can break the laws of science and physics."

Tristan struggled to understand what Jason was saying.

"You can't break the laws of science and physics," Tristan argued.

Jason gave Tristan a sideways smile. "No, I can't. Pateras wrote those laws. He can break them anytime he wants to."

Tristan gave Jason an unbelieving stare.

Despite his desire to laugh at the comical expression on Tristan's face, Jason maintained his professionalism. "Arni has appeared and disappeared at will, in and out of closed rooms. I've seen him bring the dead to life. The fact that Arni, the Admiral, and Marissa are alive is unbelievable. For that matter, Supreme Executor Hale has tried to kill all of us at various times and situations. It's amazing any of us have made it this far. What he did that night in the meeting was… indescribable. He held back a wall of water with nothing more than a thought."

Jason looked at Thane's motionless form. He smiled, "Okay, you win."

"Win what?" Tristan was suddenly lost in the conversation.

"He's asking me to wait and trust him. He used you to remind me exactly what he's capable of. Thanks, Mr. Alexander," Jason left Thane's bedside to check on Cheyenne.

Tristan muttered a confused, "You're… welcome?"

Tristan helped Jason get Cheyenne's treatment completed. The two secured her in the bed, and themselves in chairs at the two computer stations in the room. Jason offered Tristan the opportunity to ride out the next part of their trip lying comfortably in a bed. Tristan preferred to stay upright in a chair especially if his life could end at any moment. Against his better judgment, Jason linked in to the bridge surveillance.

****

Braxton was glad to give Jason time to treat Cheyenne. The submerged vessels above, lost them under the water and were widening their search pattern. When it was time to move again, the *Evangeline* would have more room to escape detection. While he waited for word from Jason, additional ships joined the search. One ship remained in the vicinity of where the *Evangeline* disappeared searching in tight circles for any sign of them. The others spread out in case their prey was escaping beneath them. None of the ships ever strayed below eighteen hundred feet.

Laura disrupted the suspenseful silence on the bridge. "Commander, there is a new ship encroaching on our position. It doesn't match the configuration of the others. Scans indicate it may have deep sea capabilities. At present speeds, it will reach our coordinates in seventeen minutes."

Braxton routinely responded, "Run it through the database. I want that ship and its specifications, now."

"Yes sir," Laura responded. Seconds later the computer displayed the ominous vessel and its technical specs. "Commander, that's a Guardian Class Vessel. It's capable of reaching depths beyond our own. It's armed with sonic cannons, lasers, torpedoes, shields, deflectors and tractor beams. Sir, that thing can destroy us or disable us and drag us back to the colony and our executions. According to this readout, they can even detect us when camouflaged."

Braxton frowned, "How close does it have to be to find us?"

"Their underwater scanning range is about three thousand feet. Our scanners are the only advantage we have. That ship is superior to us in every other way... well, it can't fly or travel in space, but in the water, she's better than we are."

Braxton tapped his comm link. "Doc, finished or not, you have ten minutes to get everyone locked down."

Jason's voice came back through the speaker, "I'll be done in three."

"Hail me as soon as you're ready," He ordered before closing the link.

Braxton moved to David's station, "Admiral, would you care to take command?"

David turned his back to the rest of the bridge crew and spoke softly. "Do you have a plan to get us out of here?"

"Nothing particularly concrete, sir," Braxton admitted.

"Then I suggest you solidify a plan... and quickly," David advised.

"Why me, sir? There are two superior officers on the bridge. One of you should be in command," Braxton argued.

"Are you incapable of getting us into space and away from those approaching ships?" David queried keeping his voice low.

"No sir, I don't think so," Braxton knew what needed to happen, but he also knew what could go wrong.

"If you believe you are incapable of handling this situation, then I'll take command, but if you can do this... then do it," David ordered.

Braxton wanted to know why. He determined the Admiral was not likely to answer that question. He finally gave David a less than enthusiastic, "Yes sir."

Cmdr. Flint started to return to his station. David caught his arm, "I've got your back if you get into trouble."

Braxton looked relieved, "Thank you, sir."

He returned to his seat and studied the tactical display. He did what his commanding officer ordered and cemented his plan. Presently Jason hailed the bridge to report their status.

Braxton took a deep breath and muttered, "Here we go."

He took a more authoritative voice and posture. Sitting upright in his seat, he leaned forward slightly. "Bring the thrusters online and push us just enough to get over the edge of the ledge. Keep the camouflage netting in place until we reach twenty-five hundred feet. At twenty-five hundred feet, transition the camouflage over to the shields. Let us continue to drop to thirty-two hundred feet before engaging the forward thrusters."

Laura glanced nervously at Brynna. Brynna returned a calm reassuring smile. Laura was not comforted by the gesture. She turned to Braxton. "Commander, are you certain about those depths? The ship can't-"

Braxton gave Laura a stern look. "I know what I'm doing, Lieutenant. Follow my orders."

The crew was relieved to know Braxton had a plan, but Laura's question gave them additional cause for concern. The fact that David and Brynna weren't questioning the orders offered them some reassurance.

Brynna fired the thrusters gently. The ship raised slowly and edged forward. The second they were clear of the ledge, she cut the thrusters off. The ship drifted downward. Laura and Brynna watched the scans of the ocean topography carefully. Brynna tapped the thrusters gently to avoid bumping into outcroppings of rock. The ship moaned and groaned as the pressure increased. The crew were used to the silence of space. The sounds were unnerving. David brought the shields up when the ship passed twenty-four hundred feet as ordered and continued to drift downward. Brynna finally announced "Approaching thirty-two hundred feet."

"Level us out and initiate forward thrust. Take us out to deeper waters but follow the currents," Braxton ordered.

The crew was quiet as they kept their focus on the task at hand. Laura broke the silence five minutes later. "That

Guardian Class submarine just picked up speed. She's headed on an intercept course."

Braxton scowled. He wanted to know how the ship found them. The "how" wasn't nearly as important as the fact that the heavy-duty vessel out-classed them in the water. They had to make their getaway into the atmosphere—now.

"Full thrusters now! Dump the ballast tanks, get us out of the water."

Lazaro's voice came through the speaker from engineering, "Commander, I recommend dropping the shields as soon as we're above twenty-five hundred feet. The shields are slowing us down. Use the deflectors if you need to against those sonic cannons."

David looked at Braxton awaiting his order. Braxton saw no angst on his Commander's face. He nodded and abruptly added, "Do it."

David watched their trajectory and the position of the submersible closest to them. It was inevitable their paths would cross close enough to be potentially problematic. The deflector was basically a shield that could be directed away from the ship and shaped either convexly or concavely depending on what the desired effect was. David chose a narrow concave configuration to catch the sonic blast, concentrate the sound waves into a narrower wavelength and reflect it back to its point of origin. The blast from the sonic cannon would be deflected to the sending vessel although the impact would be less damaging to the sender. The *Evangeline* would get a solid shake from the blast but avoid getting damaged.

The *Evangeline* barreled toward the surface of the water. As she reached the eighteen hundred foot depth that stopped the smaller vessels, the submersible vessel closest to them fired their sonic cannon repeatedly. The *Evangeline* was knocked off its trajectory but kept climbing. The deflector caught the blasts and promptly returned them. The ship rocked precariously when served with the very thing it was dishing out to the *Evangeline*. The vessel tipped downward and slipped below the eighteen hundred feet limit they had strictly adhered to until now.

David watched the scans. The enemy vessel was clearly taking on water. He turned to Braxton, "Commander, that vessel is badly damaged. She's sinking."

Braxton's eyes locked onto David's. An unspoken conversation ensued. Braxton clenched his jaw. This was already a close encounter. Stopping to rescue their enemies from certain destruction would make their escape even riskier. Braxton knew he couldn't leave the crew of the vessel to die. "Helm, change our course. Put us under that vessel. Admiral use the deflector to push them to the surface ahead of us."

Aulani and Laura were both concerned. The only reason they didn't object were their beliefs that the Admiral or Captain would have intervened if Braxton were making a mistake.

****

In the infirmary, Jason and Tristan were staring wide-eyed at the displays. Tristan glanced at Jason, "Your Commander's got guts."

Jason shook his head, "I'm kind of glad I'm not at the helm."

****

The *Evangeline* pushed the enemy vessel to the surface and held it there until the other vessels converged on their location. Once the other ships were nearing the point of attacking, Braxton ordered the release of the deflector and Brynna to get the *Evangeline* into the air. The damaged vessel began to sink again forcing the other vessels to choose between rescuing their colleagues or chasing the *Evangeline*. Fortunately, they chose to aid their colleagues. The *Evangeline* skimmed the top of the water until she was ready to gain altitude. She spewed the remaining seawater from her ballast tanks, showering the sea with a salty rain shower. The ship climbed through the outer atmosphere, into space, and dipped back into the atmosphere. It climbed again, rolled over and dipped into the atmosphere one last time, toasting both sides of the ship. With the ship cleansed of seawater and any possible invasive sea creatures, she was ready for space.

BACK IN SPACE

The *Evangeline* gained speed as it raced away from Zulimar. There were two Pacification Fleet ships heading toward them. The two ships were coming at ninety-degree angles from each other and heading directly for Zulimar. Braxton chose to head toward the sun. The ships had the *Evangeline* in their sights. Braxton was hoping they would lose sight of them near the sun. The net filled with bradyon particles increasing their speed. The two approaching ships altered their course to intercept. Braxton used the sun's gravitational pull to increase speed. The *Evangeline* whipped around behind the sun and back toward Zulimar. Braxton changed their direction to dip beneath the planetary plane. He ordered Lazaro to replace the bradyon particles with tachyons.

As the ship accelerated, two new ships emerged from behind the gaseous giants halfway through the star system. The new ships' nets were already fully loaded with tachyons. The two ships were Nefil vessels. They were smaller, but faster than the Pacification ships. They were slightly larger than the *Evangeline*, yet faster and more aggressive. The *Evangeline's* weapons were only for defensive purposes.

The Nefil ships were advancing quickly. They knew if the ships fired on them now, they could explode in a ball of fire which would hastily die out as the oxygen was lost into space. Braxton could feel the Admiral's eyes on him. He knew David wanted him to do this. He didn't know why, but he had better make sure it got done and quickly.

"Laura, plot a course out of here on a straight line. Make sure we're clear of obstacles for ten light years. I don't care what direction. Admiral, change the shield configuration to match the specs I'm sending you. Make sure they match exactly. Engineering, prepare to use the energy from the shields to power the ship like we did when we left the Pillan system."

David changed the configuration as ordered. He looked at Braxton. His look asked, "Do you know what you're doing?"

Braxton was afraid to meet the gaze of his Commander. Brynna glanced nervously at David. She wondered if he was ready to step in and take over or if he was waiting for her to make that call. David shook his head subtly at her. Her eyes widened at Braxton's next order.

"Turn us about and point us straight at those two ships. Navigation have that new course laid in and be ready to initiate it the second they fire on us. Don't change course until I give you the order."

Brynna swallowed hard and did as she was told. She remembered Arni's repetitive words, "I've got this."

Mentally she called out to him. *Arni, you said you wanted me to ask for your help sooner rather than later. I hope this is soon enough.* She wasn't certain, but she got the distinct impression Arni was laughing at her for thinking he was limited by time.

David glanced at Braxton. This maneuver had worked before, but there was no guarantee all the variables were in the right places. Braxton was feeling a little uncertain about it himself. These two ships would undoubtedly destroy them given the right opportunity. The ships were faster and *would* catch them. The only option was to go some place the Nefil couldn't find them.

As Brynna brought the ship around to face the Nefil, Braxton verbally requested a boon, "Pateras, protect us."

The *Evangeline* flew straight at the two menacing ships.

****

The two Nefil Captains conferred. They determined the Captain of the oncoming vessel knew his days were at an end. They decided the plan was an attempt to take out at least one of the Nefil ships. Their options were simple, disable the ship or destroy it. Their scanners clearly showed a tachyon saturated net. Disabling was highly unlikely. The two Captains chose to protect their ships. They needed to destroy the Explorer ship before it got too close.

****

Braxton watched the engineering energy displays. He reiterated his last order. "Wait for my order to change course and activate the tachyon drive."

The *Evangeline* crew had grown anxious during the underwater escape. Seeing Braxton's success and David and Brynna's confidence in him, their tensions eased. A peace even their Commanders couldn't inspire settled on the crew.

****

Jake and Marissa were sitting in their quarters watching the feed from the Bridge. Marissa looked at her sleeping baby. She smiled and reached out for Jake's hand. Jake took her hand and squeezed it lovingly.

Jason was sitting stiffly in his seat, pressed against his protective restraints. He relaxed and sat back in his seat.

Tristan glanced at Cheyenne. She was watching a monitor closer to her. She was as unconcerned as the others. To Tristan's eyes, the crew was resolved to a fate of death. He was not so inclined. "What's going on? Why is he giving up? Do you people want to die?"

Jason realized what Tristan was perceiving, "No, we're not preparing to die. He's not giving up. We're winning this one."

"This ship can't defeat those two ships. I've seen the specs on them. We're outclassed. He certainly doesn't look like he's preparing to surrender," Tristan argued.

"Pateras is going to get us out of this one safely," Jason said calmly.

Tristan wasn't ready to die, "Let me talk to my son. Activate the comms."

Jason shook his head, "He's got work to do. I'd never hear the end of it if I interrupted him right now. We'll be fine. Watch Pateras work."

Tristan slumped in his seat. His blocked access meant he couldn't do anything more than jump into an escape pod. At this range, the escape pod might not get far enough away to be clear of the blast when the ship exploded. He continued to toy with the idea of bolting for one of the pods. He might get out of this alive if he did. A part of him didn't want to leave his son to die. Maybe he could force the doctor or the ensign in the bed to take him to the bridge.

Jason glanced at Tristan. He was obviously weighing his options. Knowing the potential problems he could cause, Jason pressed a control on the computer console. The control locked the restraints on Tristan's chair. His movement came just in time.

Tristan reached for the control on his seat to release the restraints. He punched it twice. Pulling at the locking mechanism he demanded, "Doc, what did you do? Release me. You may not care whether or not you die, but I don't want to die. Let me go."

"I locked you in to keep you safe. I don't want you, or anyone else, to get hurt," Jason explained.

"Tell that to the Lieutenant lying under that stasis field over there," Tristan argued.

"I don't know why that happened, but it'll work out," Jason assured him.

Tristan jerked at the restraint one more time to no avail. He finally resigned himself to the same fate as the crew.

****

The *Evangeline* reached firing range. Braxton ordered David to fire lasers at their adversaries. The two ships raised their shields, and returned fire. Braxton watched his displays. When the levels maximized, he barked his next orders in rapid sequence, "Break away now. Activate the tachyon drive!"

The Nefil continued to fire, but with less accuracy and less voracity. The two ships adjusted their course to give chase. Another blast hit as the ship activated its tachyon drive. The ship disappeared in an explosive blast of light.

The lights inside the ship blinked several times, but stayed on. Braxton leaned forward anxiously, "What's our present location and the location of those other ships?"

When the *Evangeline* left the Pillan system, she was flying through space without power or scanners for a period of time. Braxton and Lazaro had made changes to the power configuration allowing the flow to remain uninterrupted. Hopefully, it was enough.

David looked up from his scans. "No ships within scanning distance."

Laura reviewed her star charts and compared them to the coordinates she had input minutes earlier. She happily gave Braxton their current location. She followed her report with an incredulous, "We're right on the course I laid out for us."

Braxton wasn't as happy as he was relieved, "We need to change course. Admiral, do you have a preference?"

"Head along the outer rim in a nondescript pattern. I'll give you our destination a little later," David said simply.

Capt. Brynna Alexander turned away from the helm for a moment. "Wait, why didn't we lose power? We lost power the last time."

Braxton was slightly pleased with himself but tried to conceal it, "Lt. Cmdr. Dominick, Lt. Flint, and I worked out the bugs while we were on Zulimar. We got a report back from Mrs. Deacons about how this occurred the first time. She made some suggestions about avoiding the overload on the power couplings. It worked."

After three more course adjustments, they decided they were safe for now.

Braxton dismissed Aulani from the bridge and issued an all-clear signal to the rest of the crew, so they could release themselves from their restraints.

Aulani wasted no time in heading to the infirmary. Jason was waiting for her. He went over Thane's condition in detail. Her husband would need to be carefully evaluated before he could be treated. For now, he would have to remain in stasis.

Braxton, Brynna, and David stayed on the bridge to discuss staffing and duty shifts. Laura remained at her station to program their course for the next twenty-four hours. David summoned Lazaro to the bridge and asked Lexi to continue covering engineering for a while. He made a quick inquiry to check on Thane and Cheyenne's status. As soon as Laura finished, David excused her from the bridge and blocked all surveillance feeds. David left Brynna at the helm and watching scanners.

David started, "With Thane out of the picture, the Doc's time split, Marissa and Jake on leave, we're severely handicapped. We don't have sufficient manpower to keep three people on duty anymore."

"Admiral, are you pulling me out of my engineering duties?" Braxton asked.

"Capt. Alexander, what is your preference in this situation?" David deferred to her.

"We're going to have to double up on duties and shifts until everyone gets back on their feet. Ensign Ryder and Ensign Dominick will need to be manning scanners and helm or navigation. The computer is capable of most of this on its own. I want someone on duty at all times capable of handling piloting, command, and engineering. That can be one, two, or three people. I'm leaning toward two for now. Aulani is going to need some time to process Thane's injury." Brynna was definitely concerned about their current circumstances.

Neither one had answered Braxton's question. David redirected the conversation to answer his inquiry. "Cmdr. Flint, as to your question, are you comfortable moving more into the command path? We talked about it earlier, and I know you haven't had time to give it much thought. I still need you to be strong in engineering, but I also need you in command."

"Is that what this little command escape exercise was about? Were you trying to see if I had it in me?" Braxton was annoyed that they were testing him.

Brynna grinned and shook her head, "I'm not sure he's there yet, Admiral."

David grinned back at her as he watched Braxton put the pieces together.

Braxton squinted at the two then looked at Lazaro who was being exceptionally quiet. Suddenly everything fell into place for him. "No, you knew I could handle it. You offered the job of First Officer to Lazaro and he turned you down, didn't he? You let me command our departure so the crew would trust me."

David clapped his hands and rubbed them together briskly, "Now he's there. Let's get down to business. Commander, the Captain and I knew you could handle this, although that last maneuver was a bit of a surprise. We didn't exactly plan to put you in that position, but we did decide we were safe in your hands. Now the entire crew knows they're safe. They trust you and they know *we* trust you."

Braxton looked at Lazaro, "Laz, you've got a lot more experience than I do. Why didn't you accept the position?"

Lazaro smiled, "I'm a follower, not a leader. I'm an engineer, and it's what I'm good at. I can't inspire the crew to do their jobs when things get hard, but I can do my job. You can. You did, for that matter. I watched it on the surveillance feed. That's you. It's not me."

Braxton didn't want his friend to feel slighted. Lazaro was a little older and had been a Lt. Cmdr. for longer. He deserved a promotion sooner. Braxton was promoted to Lt. Cmdr. just prior to the start of this mission. Lazaro's explanation helped alleviate Braxton's concerns.

The four continued to discuss options about staffing. They finally concluded that over the next twenty-four hours the four of them would take six-hour shifts along with a secondary crew member. The unfortunate part was being short on secondary crew members.

As they discussed the options, Jake stepped onto the bridge. "Admiral?"

"Yes, Ensign?" David answered purposefully.

"I just heard about Thane. By my count, we're short on duty personnel. I came to volunteer to go back on the duty schedule," Jake offered.

"I appreciate the offer, really I do, but Marissa and Jax need you right now."

"You and the crew need me too, sir, especially with Thane down. Let me at least take a few odd shifts, even if it isn't full-time," Jake pleaded.

Lazaro grinned, "You aren't tired of being a dad already, are you?"

"No sir, and I'm not running away from my wife either. When we were locked down earlier, I felt... helpless. It was like there was nothing I could do to protect my family. I need to do my part. I wouldn't mind a little sleep before I take on a duty shift, but I can't sit in my cabin when this crew needs me," Jake explained.

"Does Marissa know what you're doing?" Brynna wisely asked.

"Yes, she does. I think she does. She had a look on her face," Jake was having difficulty explaining the unspoken conversation he and his wife had minutes ago.

David glanced at Brynna, who gave a slight nod of approval. "Alright Ensign, your next duty shift starts in twenty-one hours, give or take a few minutes. Please inform your wife first, if she isn't in agreement, get back to me ASAP."

Jake gave a curt, "Yes sir."

He promptly left the bridge to update his waiting wife. Marissa was already prepared for it.

As the deliberations came to a rough ending, the new admiral offered one more option. "I have one more possibility to offer as far as staffing goes. I know I said I wouldn't do this, and I won't make it an order."

Brynna reacted. "David, you can't."

"My father is a qualified pilot and navigator. None of you know where we're going. He wouldn't be privy to any classified information, and he would have someone on duty with him at all times. I'm only offering this as a possibility. You have every right to shoot this idea down if you want. He's going to be on this ship anyway, and if he causes one ounce of trouble, I'll throw him in stasis and not think twice about it. He said he wanted to understand what was going on. My idea was if he gets a better view of what we're doing, maybe he'll learn what he wants and even join us."

The three other bridge officers sat in silence. No one knew what to say. David finally broke the silence he created, "Do I need to leave so you can discuss this?"

Brynna volunteered to address the situation, "Is it alright with you if we take this outside the chain of command?"

David nodded and covered his rank insignia, "Off the record."

"David, you know he's a spy, and he admitted he's here to get us arrested. Forgive my bluntness, but are you out of your mind?" Brynna knew the others wouldn't venture so openly.

Lazaro was leaning forward in his chair, resting his forearms on his lap. He continued to stare at the floor as he quietly addressed Brynna's concerns, "So was Jake."

Brynna scowled, "That's not quite the same thing. Jake was part of this crew. He saw the same things we all did. He had a bond with us that should've been unbreakable. We had every reason to believe he would accept Arni, and eventually he did. Tristan Alexander, although he's David's father, is a stranger to all of us, even David."

David wanted to interject his opinion but held his tongue. He did decide to add one crewman to the meeting. "Lt. Flint, report to the bridge."

The instant Lexi came through the doorway, David waved her in and covered his rank insignia again. "This discussion is off the record."

He brought her up-to-speed on the topic of conversation and the points that had been made so far. "Forgive me for not calling you sooner."

Lexi's face contorted displaying her frustration, "Has everyone offered their opinion?"

David motioned to Braxton, "Braxton, you're up. Lay it all out. Don't hold anything back."

"I'm siding with Brynna on this. If he's determined to get us arrested, let's not make it easy for him."

David looked at Lazaro, "Lazaro, did you have any other thoughts?"

"I—uh—I recognize this is a subject that's close to your heart, so to speak. Jake was indeed part of the crew and in space there is a… bond that should have been unbreakable, but he broke it. I don't really know what your relationship with your father is, but it's supposed to be unbreakable as well. Since knowing Pateras, I've come to see that no bond is permanent. At least no bond between people. Pateras won't betray or abandon us. He's allowed us to go through some rough times, particularly on account of Jake, but he didn't abandon or betray us."

Braxton was losing patience waiting on Lazaro to get to his point. He shifted his position in his seat abruptly. Lexi gave him a stern look when Lazaro paused.

Sensing his mood, Lazaro got to the point, "What I'm trying to say is, whether he's for us or against us, it's Pateras that's in control."

Lexi looked at the four participants. Having nothing else to say Lexi moved in and took over leading the conversation.

"It seems everyone's concern is with being betrayed again. There are no guarantees that any of us might betray the others if the right pressure were applied. Admiral, if your uncle were found out, what would you do to save his life?"

David began pacing, "I'd give my life to save his… obviously, but I wouldn't betray the crew. I'm not trying to get us into trouble and I'm not naïve."

Brynna jumped in again, "If he gets too close, he could jeopardize our entire fleet."

"Why is everyone so afraid of being betrayed? We were nearly blasted into oblivion an hour ago. It doesn't matter what we do. We're at risk for pain, suffering, and death. Please tell me why there's a difference," David demanded.

"Admiral," Braxton started to respond, but was cut off abruptly.

"It's David," the irate Admiral responded.

"Uh… excuse me, sir?" Braxton was caught off guard by his superior's statement.

"This is an informal meeting where we are all equals. I will abide by the wishes of the majority here. I am not acting as an Admiral and I want that clear in everyone's minds. Right here, right now, I'm David."

Brynna had no trouble with such transitions. She made them regularly. Braxton, Lazaro, and Lexi were not accustomed to making the change. Despite all they had been through the past year, David had maintained his separation from the crew. His military upbringing kept him from developing close knit relationships, particularly among those whose ranks were not equal to his. His developing relationship with Arni was slowly pulling those walls down.

"David," Braxton began again, "I understand you want to help your father, and I understand we are solely dependent on Pateras. I just think we shouldn't take what is obviously an unnecessary risk. We wouldn't take the ship into obvious military travel routes or orbit a planet with a military base on it. Why put a spy on the bridge of our ship?"

Lazaro was leaning forward. He looked up again. "Here are my questions. Who's going to be keeping an eye on him, on or off the bridge? What's he going to do if he doesn't have a job to keep him occupied? The Captain... Admiral... uh, sorry... I mean David, is right. We're short on active crewmen. We need the help."

Brynna argued, "I'm not that desperate yet."

David scowled, "You didn't want me to put him off the ship. I really don't like the idea of dropping him off somewhere remote. I would rather not stick him in stasis. He can't stay confined to quarters for an unknown length of time. What *do you* suggest?"

The room got quiet again. Lexi finally got the conversation rolling. "David, aside from the manpower deficit and the potential for getting your father to side with Pateras, what do you expect to gain from this?"

David gave Lexi a puzzled look, "What makes you think I have any other expectations?"

Lexi's eyes narrowed, "That! That does."

All eyes landed on Lexi.

"You tried to avoid answering my question by asking another question. I already suspected you had another agenda and that confirmed it, in my mind at least."

David continued to wander aimlessly about the bridge. Feeling everyone's eyes on him, he stopped and turned around,

"Yes, I have other... expectations. I expect him to betray me, like Jake did. I just want to catch him at it. I want him to think I trust him. He's given me enough information to keep me distracted. I want him to think I'm distracted enough to make mistakes."

Brynna frowned, "Are you certain you aren't making a mistake already?"

"No, I'm not certain. It's why I brought it up under these circumstances," David began pacing again.

Braxton looked concerned, "You never said anything about trapping him when you brought this up. Why?"

"It took a long time for everyone to get over being betrayed by Jake. I was afraid if you thought it was happening again, you might not handle it well. I don't want somebody trying to throw him out an airlock."

"You're not serious. Do you really think one of us would do that to your father?" Braxton was about to be offended.

"No, I don't think anyone would do that. I was just using the most extreme example. I didn't want this to be a method of dredging up the past. I have the distinct feeling, Arni put him here for a reason. I don't think this will play out the way it did with Jake. I don't really know what's going to happen, but I think there's a reason for it," David returned to his seat.

The room grew silent again. Lexi looked at each one and asked, "He's left it to you to decide. What do you want to do?"

"Should I leave the room?" David volunteered.

Brynna didn't have any reservations about speaking her mind in front of David. Lazaro wasn't sure he had much else to say. Braxton wasn't sure enough of his opinion yet, but he didn't want his commanding officer believing he was afraid of him. No one answered right away which left David believing they were in fact feeling intimidated by his presence.

David moved to leave, "I'll wait in my office."

Braxton blocked his path. "No, don't go. Give me a minute to think and I'll give you my honest opinion. How about I go grab us some coffee?"

Brynna glanced over her shoulder from watching the scanners, "I'll take some. I've got the next watch."

Lazaro shook his head, "I have the watch after her, so I need to get some sleep in a little bit. I'll pass."

David requested a cup as well.

The four said little while they waited on Braxton to return with the coffee.

****

Braxton ran into Tristan preparing his own cup of coffee in the dining room. He gave the man a polite nod and a nondescript greeting, "Mr. Alexander."

"It's Lt. Cmdr. Flint isn't it? I haven't learned names yet. Oh, wait that's a commander's rank. I thought you were a Lt. Cmdr.. My apologies."

Braxton's answers were short and cryptic, "It was. Field promotion."

"I saw you commanding our escape from Zulimar. You did an amazing job. I'm both grateful and surprised to still be alive," Tristan attempted to stir up the conversation as well as express his gratitude.

"Thanks," Braxton muttered as he continued preparing the three desired cups of coffee.

Tristan looked at the man's demeanor and listened to his tone of voice. "You don't trust me."

"No sir, I don't," Braxton admitted succinctly.

"May I ask why?" Tristan inquired casually.

Knowing what David was trying to do, Braxton answered carefully, "The Admiral says they sent you in here to bring us down. Would you really do that to your son?"

"They told me they could bring him back to the Commonwealth. They said he was under an alien influence and they could free him of it. Why would I not want to help my son?" Tristan answered feigning a certain naivete.

Braxton knew he was being manipulated instantly. He retorted quickly, "What if you are the one under an alien influence? Do you know what they did to him the last time they got their hands on him? They mistreated all of us. What we went through was nothing compared to what they did to him. They tortured him repeatedly. They filled him with drugs to enhance his pain receptors, beat him, and hit him with those EMP rods. They ran him through the infirmary to heal his wounds then started all over again. He was beaten and tortured over and over, and you want to take him in? What father in his right mind would want their son to go through that kind of pain?"

Tristan jumped to his feet. "Just what sort of monster do you take me for? No, I don't want that for my son. I could have reported him days ago if that was my intention. I want to understand what's going on. If he really is better off doing whatever it is he's doing, then I'll leave him to do it. He's my son! My firstborn!"

"So why come here? Why accept this assignment?" Braxton was no longer concerned with the coffee.

"Two reasons. First, I had to see this for myself. Hearing that my son had gone rogue was hard to fathom. Second, if I didn't take the assignment, they were going to use me as bait to draw him in anyway. This seemed to be the best option."

Tristan stopped bristling and eased back into his seat. "I don't want to see anything happen to Davie or any of you. You seem like good soldiers. I just don't understand what you're fighting for… or against. I want to understand. If I can't, then drop me off somewhere and I'll disappear. My life, as it was, is over. This is all I have left. I have the right to ask that much, don't I?"

The tension drained from Braxton. He turned to finish pouring his coffee and gathering the appropriate additives. Setting the last item on the serving tray, he turned back to Tristan. "I suppose you have the right to ask to understand. You don't have the right to betray him. He's been betrayed before. Please don't do that to him again. It would be better if you killed him outright because they'll do worse than that to him if they get their hands on him. First, they'll try to break him and when they can't, they'll execute him. Make sure that isn't left on your conscience."

Tristan grabbed his cup of coffee. "It won't be," he left the dining room and headed to the guest quarters.

Braxton watched him leave and stood reliving the conversation. He wasn't sure how much was truth and how much was intended to ensnare him. He grabbed his tray and returned to the bridge.

****

The look on Braxton's face was difficult to read by those waiting on him. It was even more suspect when he sat down without sharing the three cups of coffee he brought with him.

Lexi studied his face closely, "Brax? Is everything okay?"

He looked up, confused by her question, "Yes, I'm fine. Why?"

Trying to lighten the mood a little she teased, "Were you planning on drinking all of those by yourself?"

Braxton looked at the tray. "Sorry," he promptly offered the extra cups to Brynna and David.

Lexi waited on him to speak. When he didn't volunteer, she prompted him, "Braxton, what happened while you were gone?"

Braxton scowled at his wife, "What makes you think something happened?"

Lexi bit her lower lip trying not to laugh at her husband, "I have two reasons to think something happened. The first one is you left the room to come to a decision and you've yet to give us anything in the way of your decision or thoughts. The second is you answered my question with a question, like David did."

Braxton knew better than to argue with his psychologist wife. "Alright here's my thoughts. David, I ran into your dad a few minutes ago. He may or may not be trustworthy, but he does deserve to know the truth and working alongside us may be the only way for him to understand what we're doing and why. I do recommend you limit what he has access to. No access to external comms and somebody needs to closely evaluate every action that occurs during his duty shifts. We don't need to leave a trail of tachyons across the galaxy for somebody to follow."

"But tachyons don't…" Lazaro started to object when he realized Braxton was being sarcastic. Tachyons dissipate and degrade rapidly. It would be nearly impossible to track them across the galaxy. Braxton's specialty was architectural engineering not mechanical or astrophysical engineering, but he did know the basics. When he realized his mistake in assuming Braxton didn't know what he was talking about he shook his head and stopped talking.

Lexi decided this needed to be finished and soon. "Anyone else have any points they need to make before we come to a resolution?"

Everyone made clear eye contact with her. No one had left anything unsaid.

"Alright then, what's your final decision, Lazaro?"

Lazaro was annoyed about going first. He hoped he wasn't about to get on anyone's bad side. "I say we give him junior assignments with strict supervision."

Lexi looked to Braxton next. Braxton didn't wait for her to ask, "I'm willing to go along with Lazaro for now. If he proves to be a security risk, I'm recommending we throw him into a stasis pod and drop him on the nearest habitable planet."

Lexi saw a look on Braxton's face punctuate his last sentence. It was clear he preferred the option of throwing the potential traitor out the airlock. She wasn't sure if it was the wife or the psychologist in her who spotted the thought. She decided to provoke him a little more, "Are you sure you wouldn't prefer to space him?"

Braxton stiffened, "No, I wouldn't. The thought crossed my mind, but I have no real desire to harm him. I just don't want to go down this road again."

David swallowed hard. He was trying to keep his profile as low as possible on this matter. "You do realize if we do this, it means your life could be in his hands. You might have to trust him at some point."

The new Commander stared at nothing for a moment. The stiffness in his body relaxed, "My life is in the hands of Pateras. Your father has to go through him to get to me."

The Admiral suddenly took on the countenance of a proud father. He had put the crew into Arni's hands a couple of months ago. He continued to hope they had each put their lives in his hands.

Brynna quickly volunteered, "I am in agreement with Braxton on all points."

Lexi looked to David, "Do you still think this is a good idea, sir?"

David leaned back in his seat, "No, I never said it was a good idea. It's just the best thing I can come up with. This decision is up to you four. I'm not voting on this one. I will abide by the consensus."

Lexi was startled that he had added her to the panel of decision makers. She had assumed she was present merely as a mediator.

Seeing the shock on her face, David motioned to her. "Lexi, as ship's psychologist, what is your take on the situation? Is the Admiral using his position of power to bully his subordinates into agreeing with him? Is David Alexander blind to the risks of accepting his father as part of the crew?"

Lexi squirmed in her seat. She wished she had accepted Braxton's offer to get her a cup of coffee. She smirked slightly as she considered her answer, "In my professional opinion, the Admiral is not using his position to bully his subordinates, with the possible exception of his ship's psychologist. The simple act of presenting the request by the Admiral does weigh more heavily than if it were presented by someone of lower rank. That much cannot be avoided, and the Admiral has done an excellent job of leveling the playing field. David Alexander is not blind to the risks, but his hopes may be misplaced. Whether that is true or not remains to be seen and only Tristan Alexander can make that determination."

"What's your vote, Lexi?" David persisted.

"There are already three votes in favor. Why does my vote matter?"

"I want to know where you stand," David held his second reason for wanting to know back. He wanted the decision to be unanimous. If he told her that, it could affect her answer at this point.

"I think I want to spend more time getting to know him. I don't have a clue what he's capable of or what his limits are. Having said that, I think giving him a little slack might relax matters a bit. If he thinks we've dropped our guard, his might drop just a little too."

Lexi watched the others for a reaction. They were at peace with the situation.

"My dad asked me what his status was earlier. I'll talk to him after Brynna comes on duty. Meeting adjourned?" David wanted to be sure there was nothing else to discuss. The group dispersed with the exception of Lexi who stayed behind to aid the Admiral in his duty shift and to discuss the effect his father was having on him.

The Admiral freely admitted feeling abandoned by his father and suspicious of his recent re-emergence at such a dangerous time. He told Lexi as many details as he could remember about the most recent events and the events that occurred eleven years ago on Ardara III. He also told her the one thing he had revealed only to Brynna. Pateras had shown him the ugliness of his entire life, every wrong he had ever done had flashed through his mind and nearly suffocated him. The pain of regret and guilt was more than he could handle. The two had more than two hours to discuss the events and how he was handling it.

The conversation wound down in time for Brynna and Laura to enter the bridge and take over the duty shift.

****

David asked Lexi to accompany him a little further. He found Jason and Aulani in the infirmary at Thane's bedside.

Jason stepped across the room to talk discretely to the Admiral and Lexi. "Admiral, I've had more time to study Thane's case. He has swelling and bone fragments pushing into his spinal cord. I can try to operate but I would need to keep the stasis field intact while I do that. If that field goes down the swelling could increase. If that happens while those fragments are pressing on his spinal cord he could suffer… damage that I can't fix here. He could die or become paralyzed. His injury, and the ones Stephanie had, aren't really treatable aboard these ships."

"What are our options, Doc?" David asked.

"I can operate a little at a time, give his body time to heal and reduce the swelling, but here's the catch. Swelling won't go down while he's in stasis. I could try reprogramming those nanites to reconstruct the spine. They can work inside the stasis field. The reconstruction of the bone itself would be time consuming. I can do this, but it's going to take days and that's assuming I don't take on shifts at the helm which I think you're going to need me to do. It's possible it could take a week or more to get him out of danger and a bit longer to get him on his feet again. That's assuming you allow me to use the nanites and I can successfully program them."

Lexi asked quietly, "How much of this does Aulani know?"

"She knows his condition is serious, but there's hope. She couldn't handle the details right now. She needs to go to bed and get some rest. I know it isn't late yet, but she's had a really long day." Jason sensed her presence behind him. He stopped talking and turned to face her.

David didn't wait for her to speak, "Ensign… Aulani, the Doc tells me it's going to be a little while before Thane's on his feet again. How are you holding up?"

"I—I'm tired. I'm worried. I'm lonely. I just lost my family, and now I could lose my husband." Aulani was not one to cry much, but her face displayed the pain she felt.

Jason gently prodded, "Aulani, Thane is safe. As long as he's in the stasis chamber, he's not getting any worse. He's not dying. After I get some rest, I will work on getting him better. It's going to take time, but he will get better. You need to get some rest too. Would you like me to give you a sedative?"

"Maybe a little later? I—I think I need some time alone."

"Of course, Lexi can go with you to your quarters, and I'll come by in about an hour with that sedative," Jason offered.

"Um… Admiral, would you mind walking me to my quarters? Lexi, could we talk some time tomorrow?" Aulani asked.

Despite his belief that Lexi's counsel was needed more than his, David agreed to escort the Ensign to her cabin. It was a short walk as there were only seven cabins aboard. David walked her to the door. "What's on your mind, Aulani?"

"Is Pateras going to take my husband from me?" She asked.

David shook his head sorrowfully, "I don't know. That's a question for Pateras. You need to ask him. Talk to Arni. You aren't alone. Arni said he would never abandon us. Put Thane's future, and yours, in his hands and leave it there. Use your hour before the Doc brings you that sedative to talk to Pateras."

"You need me to stay on the active duty roster, don't you?" Aulani abruptly changed the subject.

David grimly admitted, "I am severely short-staffed. I won't lie to you. I'm keeping you off the active duty roster as long as I can, but with the Doc's attention split and Thane, Jake, and Marissa out, yes, we're hurting, badly. Jake has agreed to pick up shifts starting tomorrow to help out. You can't come back if you aren't focused. You won't be any good to us if your mind is not on your job."

"I understand. Give me a day or two, to get past this and I'll return to active duty. I can't sit around doing nothing. The worry will eat away at me if I don't stay busy," Aulani knew her own mind quite well.

"I'll put you back on the roster after I get the okay from Lexi," David insisted, "If there's anything you need, please let me know," David rubbed her arm reassuringly. He wasn't much of a hugger, but the women of the crew were breaking him of the affliction.

Aulani was one of the less emotional women of the crew. She grabbed David's hand as he rubbed her arm and squeezed it, "Thank you, sir. Good night, Admiral."

"Good night, Ensign."

****

Aulani went into her quarters. There was nothing but the eerie glow of the emergency lights in the room. She took a few halting steps, dropped to her knees, and cried out to Pateras. As she cried, she curled into a ball on the floor and poured her heart out to him. Soon she felt Arni wrap his arms around her and hold her tightly. As she calmed down and opened her eyes, she discovered she was alone in the room. A sense of calm washed over her, and a voice asked, "Do you trust me?"

"Yes, I trust you" she whispered in return.

"I've got this," the familiar voice gave her the familiar message.

"Thank you, Arni," she whispered.

Jason got to Aulani's door and offered her the sedative. She looked at the hypo-sprayer. The calm Arni gave her was wrapped around her like a warm blanket. She declined the sedative and went to bed. Jason walked away concerned. He notified Lexi, but the two decided not to disturb her for the time being.

****

David took Lexi with him to talk to his father. They found him in the gymnasium sparring with the well-worn punching bag. The two approached him cautiously. Tristan pulled his gloves off and tossed them into the storage bin. "What can I do for you two?" His tone was slightly acrid.

"I'm guessing your conversation with Braxton wasn't very pleasant?" David ventured.

"Oh, he tattled on me, did he?" Tristan groused.

Lexi jumped in before David could respond, "I think it was more like he tattled on himself.

Tristan was wiping his sweaty face with a towel. When Lexi answered him, he dropped his hands to his sides. "What exactly does that mean?"

David took this opportunity to answer for himself, "He was dead-set against giving you access to the bridge until he ran into you in the Dining Hall. He agrees it would be the best way to help you understand what we're doing. If you're up for it, I'm willing to accept you as part of the crew and put you on the duty roster. I will warn you though. None of my crew trusts you, and they are going to be watching you carefully until you've proven yourself. You won't have access to external comms or other sensitive information. You may have to deal with some bad attitudes for a while. Can you handle that?"

Tristan studied his son and Lexi for a moment as though there were some other catch. He didn't want to jump too quickly. "What sort of low-level job do I get? Babysitting Jax so his mom and dad can work? It would be kind of like being a grandfather. I've never even seen my grandbaby."

David grinned, "No, that's a high-level position. You have to earn that one. This crew is cross-trained in most positions. I need someone who can handle basic engineering, scanners, helm, navigation, and weapons. You would primarily be on helm and navigation. The others would be relief positions only."

Tristan scowled, "Are you serious? That's a lot of access and a lot of trust. What's the catch?"

"I told you the catch. You won't ever be alone or not watched. You will have to be checked out on our systems and given the proper authorizations. Are you in?" David asked again.

Tristan glanced at Lexi, "Why are *you* here?"

Lexi kept a straight face as she coldly answered, "To make sure he doesn't throw you out an airlock."

Tristan laughed. He stopped abruptly when neither one joined him. "I see."

He continued to search their faces for clues or small glimmers of information.

David interrupted his search, "Dad, you wanted to understand why I did what I did. This is the best way to understand it."

Tristan relented, "Okay, fine. I'm in, anything else?"

David smiled, "Yeah, two things. First, if you cause us any problems, you get dumped on the nearest habitable planet. If Adm. Deacons or Adm. Garcia find you, you are on your own."

Tristan frowned, "And the second thing?"

"I have pictures of your grandbaby if you would like to see him," David offered.

"I would love to, after breakfast maybe?" Tristan smiled warmly. This was not a part he was used to playing. His undercover jobs generally meant being a hard-nosed Captain or criminal of some sort. Playing nice was not the norm.

The three walked out together and went their separate ways. Each headed to their own cabins. David sat down at his desk and authorized Tristan to access intra-ship comms and set up a monitoring system to record every time he accessed a computer.

****

Tristan went to his cabin and grabbed some water. He sat down and sipped his drink contemplatively. The door chimed interrupting his thoughts. Tristan stood to greet whoever was visiting. "Come in."

Jake stepped inside, "Capt. Alexander."

"Mr. Holden, what can I do for you?"

"Marissa sent me to return your jacket. She said you gave it to her in the mine tunnel to keep her from getting a chill. She wanted me to apologize for not cleaning it before she returned it to you."

"Oh, it's fine. It wasn't that clean when I let her use it. How's she doing?" Tristan asked casually. There was a certain amount of tension in the air and he was trying to ease through it.

"She's tired. Jax is not letting her sleep much," Jake even sounded tired. "Listen, we can't thank you enough for helping her and the... Admiral. Marissa and I are grateful you protected her and Jax. If you hadn't been there, she might have delivered Jax alone in that tunnel and the Admiral would probably be dead."

"I'm just glad I didn't have to deliver Jax," Tristan joked.

Jake laughed with him briefly. "We owe you one. The entire fleet owes you for saving the Admiral's life. If it weren't for Pateras, I wouldn't have a son, and my wife and the Admiral would both be dead. For that matter, we would be dead."

"I'm afraid you're going to have to explain all of this to me. I'm a little lost," Tristan confessed. He had seen no evidence of Pateras.

"We'll have plenty of time to discuss it. I'm sure the entire crew would love to share their individual stories with you. I wouldn't want you to get bored."

"I don't plan on getting bored, but I would love to hear your stories. Swapping tall tales is what star travelers do best," Tristan smiled again.

Jake smiled in return. He knew Tristan really had no idea what kind of stories he was about to hear. "Well, I need to get some rest. Good night, sir," Jake offered the man his hand.

Tristan shook it. "Good night, Chief."

As soon as Jake headed out the door, Tristan's disarming smile faded. He took his jacket to the table. He stripped it down, pulling components from the buttons, hem and collar.

He assembled the tiny components into a device capable of sending, receiving, and storing messages. He tossed the completed device into the air and caught it again triumphantly. He smiled as he recalled David scanning every item he owned for such a device. Every item except this jacket. He hadn't carried this particular jacket aboard the ship. Marissa had.

EPILOGUE

Admiral's Personal Log—First Entry

This is Adm. David Alexander. This is the first official log entry in my role as Lead Admiral over the Explorer Fleet. The past week has been interesting, to say the least. We've organized a rebellion against the Commonwealth, and although our numbers are incredibly small compared to those inhabiting the rest of the galaxy, I don't feel overwhelmed. I should, but I don't. With Pateras leading us, even if I don't survive this endeavor, we can't lose.

I'm amazed at what we've accomplished in these last few days. We've birthed a revolution and a baby where there shouldn't have been either one. A year ago, I would've written all the things we've seen off as science we don't understand. To attribute all of this to a Supreme Alien Being is certainly not where I would ever have thought I was headed. I'm glad I'm here though. It's been an amazing year, surreal, but amazing.

I do wonder why the other Captains chose me to lead them. I'm one of the least experienced and I don't have a monopoly on Pateras. Yes, I've had some very extreme experiences with Arni and Pateras, but he's directing all of us. I hope the others understand that. I tried to make it clear to them. The only thing I can do is leave it in Arni's hands. I seem to be leaving a lot of things in his hands lately. It continues to baffle me why he chose me considering how helpless I am, and the number of faults I possess.

In my first few days as Lead Admiral, I nearly got one of my own crew killed. The ship is short-staffed because of several crewmen being on medical leave. I'm not getting off to the best start. I'm hoping things get better from here.

On another note, my father, who I've not seen in years, is now a part of this crew. Adm. Garcia sent him here to bring us down. I'm hoping he learns to trust Pateras like we have. I hate to say it, but there may be some difficult times ahead of us with him. He will not give in easily.

Mission Report #3

Admiral Garcia
Admiral Deacons

I'm trusting you got my message in the room I left behind. You will be glad to know I made it in. I'm aboard the <u>Evangeline</u>. I've earned the gratitude of some of the crew. They don't trust me yet, and my son, well… I believe I have him rattled enough to make mistakes. He believes he has my trust, for now. David's no fool though. He's invited me to become a member of his crew on a limited and conditional basis. I don't know yet where we're headed or what David's intended mission is, but I can't learn everything in one day.

I do have one interesting piece of information for you. It seems my son has organized a good portion, if not all, of the Explorer Fleet. You're going to love this next piece of information. They got together under falsified ship identification codes. I couldn't locate all the ships, but I'm fairly certain at least ten ships were represented. Here's the interesting part. They've established a new command structure and granted field promotions for their rebellion or revolution. I'm not sure what to call this movement. My son has been granted the rank of Admiral. I suspect he's the Lead Admiral. Capt. Nate Weiseman and his crew were here with him. His ship obviously survived Ela Prime. He was catering to David, so I suspect in this new order, David outranks him.

On a more personal level, David has expressed his resentment over my absence in his life, yet he has grudgingly allowed me to become a part of his crew. I have reason to believe he's desperate. The young woman, Lt. Holden, that you told me about, she's had her baby and is currently unavailable for duty. Her husband is possibly unavailable too. Lt. Thane Ryder had some sort of accident and is gravely injured. He's currently in a stasis chamber. His wife has to be emotionally unsettled as well. Her family was whisked away to some unknown location. I haven't been able to determine where they were taken. I am assuming they were taken to the same place my family was. Ensign Ryder may be unable to function due to loss and grief. The ship's doctor's time has to be divided between the infirmary and the helm.

The information you gave me about the crew is proving useful and should prove more useful as I get to know them. The more I know, the quicker I can help you bring them down. Don't worry, sirs. I'll help you end this ridiculous fiasco as quickly as I can. I don't understand why they did this, but I'll help you stop it.

I hope I have more to give you in my next report. I'll get this off to you and wait for your response.

Respectfully submitted,
Capt. Tristan Alexander
Commonwealth Interstellar Force
Infantry Division: Covert Operations Department

Continued in
QUESTIONS OF TRUST

THE MISSION
BOOK 1

The newly promoted Capt. David Alexander, takes command of his first crew and starship on a multifaceted mission of diplomacy, intelligence gathering, and dangerous first contacts. He and his crew are searching out a dangerous and subversive new enemy to the Commonwealth, the ruling power in the galaxy. After finding and eluding the enemy on the ship's first contact, David discovers the enemy is now stalking him and his crew with warnings of impending doom.

A loyal Commonwealth soldier, David resists his enemies attempts to seduce him to change sides. On his second mission, David finds himself at the mercy of a primitive group of savages intent on killing him. His only hope is his sworn enemy, but what is the price for saving his life?

David learns that his enemy, Arni Liontari has gone out of his way to protect him and his crew. Could the Commonwealth's Intel be wrong or is the enemy more dangerous than he realized? Get on board the *Evangeline*, now, before it's too late.

THE DEFENDED
BOOK 2

Captain Alexander and the crew of the *Evangeline* continue their Commonwealth mission to make allies of the non-space-faring planets in the galaxy. Drea III is a technologically advanced world shrouded by a dark and bloody history with the Commonwealth.

Drean officials politely agree to hear the crew's proposal of an alliance with the Commonwealth. A series of heinous discoveries land the crew in jail, charged with several capital crimes. Capt. Alexander finds himself torn between his Commonwealth mandates and protecting an entire planet from annihilation.

David throws himself on the mercy of the courts, defending his crew to his last breath. More unexpected revelations cause the Captain and crew to question everything they've been taught.

Come discover the 50-year cover-up!

TREASONOUS ACTS
BOOK 3

The Commonwealth groomed Capt. David Alexander from birth for this mission. Learning new and unsettling truths, David rejects his Commonwealth upbringing and joins Pateras El Liontari and his son Arni. His actions create a rift among the crew, particularly for Security Chief Jake Holden.

Jake's job is to protect the crew from Pateras and the primitive planetary locals. He can handle the locals, but Pateras proves to be too much. Capt. Alexander saves the life of Jake and Marissa's unborn baby, adding to Jake's conundrum. It's his job to execute his Captain or arrest him.

The lives of David, his crew, and the local citizens hang in the balance when David challenges a power-hungry High Priest. The crew struggles to trust Arni as the priest's followers rise up against the local chancellor. An unexpected visit from David's uncle, Adm. Deacons, puts a heavily armed Pacification Ship in orbit. If Jake reports David's treason, the Admiral will be forced to arrest or execute his traitorous nephew. Can Pateras protect them from the Admiral and the powerful ship in orbit?

IN EVIL'S GRASP
BOOK 4

Capt. David Alexander and his crew are guilty of treason against the Commonwealth. Security Chief Jake Holden openly opposes the crew's treason. Arni, the superior being who now holds David's loyalty, warns him that Jake will betray him. David knows the cost and the benefits of willingly stepping into Jake's trap.

Alone, imprisoned, beaten, and drugged, David struggles to remain loyal to Pateras and to resist the urge to surrender to Supreme Executor Hale's enticing offers. David is pushed to his limits when his crew is led to believe he betrayed them, and his wife told about a contrived relationship between him and another woman.

Tortured mercilessly, Jake offers him a way out, a syringe with a lethal sedative. The drugs forced on him by his captors wreak havoc with his thoughts. Did Pateras abandon him? Was this the only way out?

MISSION ABANDONED
BOOK 5

Capt. Alexander and the crew of the *Evangeline* are running for their lives. The Supreme Executor of the Commonwealth, Luciano Hale, has framed the treasonous crew for mass murder and terrorism, making them the most hunted individuals in space.

The crew has only one chance, get the truth out to the other eleven Explorer ships. David's best chance is his old friends from his academy days, Nate and Stephanie Weiseman. David tracks down the SS *Emissary*, hoping his friends will listen. To his disappointment, Nate attempts to place him under arrest. In an effort to get the crew to trust Jake again, Capt. Alexander puts his life in Jake's hands, the one who initially betrayed them all.

Difficult losses among both crews and the planetary natives wreak havoc as David attempts to win back his best friends' trust. Time runs out when a ship of super soldiers arrives to inflict the death penalty on the crew of the *Evangeline* and the crew of the *Emissary*.

BIRTH OF A REVOLUTION
BOOK 6

Hunted for treason and haunted by his past, Capt. David Alexander attempts to unite the Explorer Fleet against the Commonwealth. The belief that Capt. Alexander mercilessly destroyed an entire military base fuels his comrades desire to turn him in. David has evidence against Supreme Executor Luciano Hale, but it's subjective. Will it be enough to convince the other crews to join him?

The tenuous agreement reached by the Fleet is put in danger when four ruffians, hungry for revenge, kidnap Capt. Alexander and Lt. Marissa Holden who is about to give birth. The two are forced into an empty mine tunnel. The odds are not good with four against one and the young lieutenant in heavy labor.

Can Security Chief Jake Holden reach the Captain and Marissa in time? Who is the mysterious stranger stalking them? Can they get off Zulimar before their enemies arrive? Get onboard before the enemy catches you!

QUESTIONS OF TRUST
BOOK 7

The newly formed Pateran Resurrection Movement is severely outnumbered and outclassed. The potential for traitors in their ranks remains high. The *Evangeline* is plagued with a manpower shortage. Can David trust his estranged father to help? When his father confesses to being a Commonwealth spy, David is forced to make some hard choices.

What else could possibly go wrong? The newly elected Lead Admiral was already one of the youngest of the Explorer Fleet Captains. His feelings of inferiority to his peers are multiplied when two ships under his command disappear. Personal tragedy adds to the young Admiral's load.

Executor Hale reveals a secret designed to hurt one person, the new Admiral. How much more can Adm. Alexander take before he cracks under the pressure? The Admiral needs all hands on deck. Join him now, before more tragedy strikes.

REVELATIONS
BOOK 8

After the devastating loss of Capt. Talaith Bowen and the revelation of several treacherous Commonwealth secrets, Admiral David Alexander moves forward with his mission to warn the newer worlds about the dangers of allying with the Commonwealth. The ruling officials on Gadola are willing to listen despite the Commonwealth's warnings about the renegade fleet. David and his crew earn the respect of the Gadolan Premier, but not the leaders of the Guilds.

The Guilds take advantage of David's status as a Commonwealth criminal. The Guilds kidnap David's father and Ensign Cheyenne Dominick to force David's hand in destroying the troublesome colonies in the Gadolan system. Elias Soren, a pesky, young Commonwealth reporter also vanishes.

Capt. Brynna Alexander tries to present evidence against the Guild leaders but is kidnapped along with the colonial representatives. Will David be forced to choose between saving his wife or his father? Can they make it out of the system before the Guilds summon the SS *Valiant* to arrest him or shoot down his ship?